GREAT IRISH TALES OF HORROR

Also edited by Peter Haining

GREAT IRISH STORIES OF THE SUPERNATURAL
GREAT IRISH DETECTIVE STORIES
GREAT IRISH TALES OF FANTASY
GREAT IRISH HUMOROUS STORIES
GREAT IRISH STORIES OF CHILDHOOD
GREAT IRISH STORIES OF MURDER AND MYSTERY

GREAT IRISH
TALES OF HORROR

A Treasury of Fear

Edited and introduced by
Peter Haining

SOUVENIR PRESS

Copyright © 1995 by Seventh Zenith Ltd

The right of Peter Haining to be identified as author of
this work has been asserted by him in accordance with
the Copyright, Designs and Patents Act 1988.

First published 1995 by Souvenir Press Ltd,
43 Great Russell Street, London WC1B 3PA

This edition first published 1999

ISBN 0 285 63515 8

Typeset by Rowland Phototypesetting Ltd
Bury St Edmunds, Suffolk

Printed in Great Britain by
The Guernsey Press Co. Ltd, Guernsey, Channel Islands

For
BRIAN CLEEVE
A devilishly good
storyteller

CONTENTS

8

INTRODUCTION

'His heart grew colder and colder as he sat with eyes full of terror . . .' Illustration by Stephen Lawrence for Bram Stoker's story, 'The Secret of the Growing Gold'.

INTRODUCTION

If there is one place in Ireland that seems to incorporate all the elements that are needed to make a great horror story, it is the aptly named ruin, Castle Freke, which looms like a set of broken and stunted teeth over the picturesque Clonakilty Bay in County Cork. Not only is the castle now derelict and shunned by the local people—it was abandoned over 40 years ago and, it is said, will *never* be made habitable again—but it was for a time the home of one of the country's most notorious and despised noblemen.

For generations Castle Freke belonged to the Carbery family and it was here that the tenth Lord Carbery celebrated his 21st birthday in 1913 with a riotous and drunken party. Subsequently, his reputation as a hell-raiser grew with tales of continued drunkenness, attempted rape, wanton cruelty to a number of local women and indiscriminate violence to their menfolk. Soon after the end of the 1914–18 War he decided to emigrate to Kenya and turned his back on Castle Freke, never to return. Before leaving, however, he committed one final act of barbarism, gouging out the eyes of all the family portraits hanging in the castle.

Once in Kenya, the Irishman changed his name to John Carberry, assumed an American accent, and then, in the Thirties, became one of the most vocal supporters of Adolf Hitler. His notoriety was further accentuated in 1941, following the brutal murder of Lord Erroll near Nairobi—a killing which has since become famous as the 'White Mischief Murder'. Once this crime became public knowledge, and later the subject of a film, Carberry was exposed once and for all as a sadistic bully who used a rhino-whip on his daughter. Even his wife, it was said, was a drunken whore.

Today, in County Cork, there are men and women who shun Castle Freke as if it were occupied by the Devil. Some actually believe that it is haunted by the ghost of the monstrous former owner, and claim that on dark winter nights his figure can be seen pacing menacingly about the castle's broken turrets. A notice warns anyone who thinks of approaching the ruined building: 'Danger—Keep Out', but those brave souls who *have* dared the wrath of Carbery say that the walls inside are now crumbling and the only legacy of the occupant is a number of swastika signs crudely drawn in one of the rooms . . .

In the light of all this it is a wonder to me that no one has yet chosen Castle Freke as the setting for a horror story, but there are many other suitably grim and legendary sites throughout the country, and these have provided the inspiration for a whole school of writers during the last two centuries. The result has been a rich vein of stories of the weird, the chilling and the fearful.

Ireland can, of course, lay claim to being the birthplace of Bram Stoker, the theatrical manager and would-be novelist who, a century ago, in 1897, wrote arguably the most famous and influential of all horror novels, *Dracula*. But he was neither the first nor the last of the Irish masters of horror.

Take, for example, Fitz-James O'Brien from County Cork, whose short story 'What Was It?' has been called 'one of the classics of horror literature'; or Dorothy Macardle from Dundalk, whose novel *Uneasy Freehold* was later made into one of the cinema's most acclaimed horror films, *The Uninvited*. To them can be added M. P. Shiel, 'one of the masters of the horror story'; Sax Rohmer who gave literature Fu Manchu, a monster of evil worse even than Lord Carbery; and, most recently, Neil Jordan, the writer and Oscar-winning film producer whose horror movies, including *The Company of Wolves*, *High Spirits* and *Interview with the Vampire*, have been as highly praised as they have been widely successful at the box office.

Other Irish names also clamour for a place in the higher, and darker, realms of the horror story genre. From the last century come Charles Robert Maturin, Joseph Sheridan Le Fanu and Gerald Griffin. From the more recent past, Vincent O'Sullivan, Elizabeth Bowen and L. A. G. Strong—not forgetting such surprise inclusions as Lafcadio Hearn, J. M. Synge and even George Bernard Shaw. And from among today's most noted literary practitioners of terror may be listed William Trevor, Brian Moore and Jack Higgins.

Everywhere the researcher turns in Ireland there are interesting stories to be unearthed about the people, the places and the traditions that have helped to inspire the country's love for, and skill at writing, the tale of horror. James F. Kilroy, in his book *The Irish Short Story* (1984), has neatly summarised this whole development:

> Coinciding with the extension of a reading public receptive to short fiction, the late eighteenth and nineteenth centuries' interest in folktales, a taste for rural subjects, and a fascination with fear and other sublime effects, nurtured the growth of the new genre of the short story. In fact, such elements are seen in the works that various critics have proposed as the first true short stories—the tales of Sir Walter Scott, Nathaniel Hawthorne and Edgar Allan Poe. Without entering the critical controversy over which author wrote the very first short story, we can note familiar and distinguishing ingredients of the new literary form in various narratives written in Ireland during the nineteenth century. In the many stories of William Carleton may be found extended descriptions of rural scenery, reproductions of dialect, and a fascination with discord and revolution; in James Clarence Mangan's few tales, a Poe-like obsession with exotic settings and mysterious events; and in the Gothic tales of Joseph Sheridan Le Fanu and Charles Robert Maturin, even more vivid expressions of mystery and terror.

Perhaps the most intriguing, if contentious, literary connection that came to my notice during the assembling of this book was a link between Ireland, Sir Arthur Conan Doyle and his creation of Sherlock Holmes. The theory was advanced by the Celtic scholar, Peter Berresford Ellis, who is also a writer of horror fiction and a contributor to this volume.

'As most people know,' Peter wrote to me in September 1993, 'Conan Doyle made his arch-villain Moriarty bear an obviously Irish name. It's a Kerry name, in fact, O Muircheartaigh, meaning "expert navigator". But few people would realise that the Holmeses were a well-known Anglo-Irish family who produced a number of intellectuals—artists and writers—in the late eighteenth and nineteenth centuries. I would venture to suggest that it was this family that Conan Doyle had in mind.

'In the first draft of *A Study in Scarlet*, Holmes' Christian name was to be "Sherrinford" while Doctor Watson was going to be Ormond Sacker. Ormond is easy to spot from the Dukes of Ormond (the Butlers of Cork). And I would also argue that Sacker was from the Sakeld family of Dublin who went out to Afghanistan in the 1870s. Blanaid Sakeld, the writer, was born there in 1880, and it was his great-granddaughter, Beatrice, who married Brendan Behan. Conan Doyle was, therefore, a prisoner of his cultural background!'

The Irish 'fascination with fear'—as Kilroy has termed it—will, I believe, be found amply demonstrated in the pages of this book. I have divided it into three sections, each featuring the major categories of horror stories, which range from traditional tales of terror based on the various creatures of the supernatural to today's more sophisticated stories inspired by the fears of the mind. Together they form a treasury of horror that is at once uniquely Irish and, equally, universal in its appeal.

And when you have read sufficient, may I bid you goodnight. *Oiche mhaith agaibh*!

PETER HAINING,
April 1995.

1

LURKING SHADOWS

Stories of Fear

'The Unburied Legs', an engraving by Alfred Crowquill for the
classic horror tale by Gerald Griffin.

THE MORGAN SCORE

Jack Higgins

Alienation has probably been one of the most enduring themes in Irish horror fiction since the genre came into being, almost two hundred years ago, in the works of the Reverend Charles Robert Maturin and it thrives today in the worldwide bestsellers of Jack Higgins (1929–   ). This writer, whose real name is Harry Patterson, grew up in Belfast in a family with a strong political background which, as a child, gave him an insight into some of the worst aspects of the Troubles, and nowadays provides the raw material for some of his best novels which have sold more than 150 million copies and been translated into 39 languages. His pen-name is derived from his mother's family and has appeared on over 50 books since The Eagle Has Landed *made him a household name in 1975. A former clerk, circus hand and teacher, he also served in the Army in the Royal Horse Guards during the 'Cold War' of the Fifties and was for a time assigned to border patrol duties in Germany. He vividly remembers 'odd shots being fired in anger' between Allied soldiers and Russians, and though for a while he seriously considered remaining in the Army, he opted instead for civvy street. Not surprisingly, soldiers and the world of soldiering often play a central part in his books.*

Among Jack Higgins' most colourful characters are Liam Devlin, the IRA man who first appeared in The Eagle Has Landed *and its sequel,* The Eagle Has Flown *(1991)—who, he says, was based on a real person—and Sean Dillon, the reformed terrorist who 'never bombed women or children', whose exploits have been recounted in* Thunder Point *(1993) and* On Dangerous Ground *(1994). 'The Morgan Score' is also about a very resourceful army man who becomes caught between feuding factions of the IRA as he trails a terrorist through the alleyways of Belfast—and then, in the best traditions of stories of lurking fear, becomes both the hunter and the hunted . . .*

*   *   *

The Europa Hotel in Belfast stands in Great Victoria Street, rising 12 storeys above the railway station next to it. Since it had opened in 1971, more than 25 separate bombing attacks had been made on it by the IRA.

Morgan remembered that interesting statistic as he stood at the window of his room on the fourth floor and looked down to the bus station and the Protestant stronghold of Sandy Row.

A cold east wind blew in from Belfast Lough, driving rain across the mean streets of the devastated city. He was restless and frustrated. This was his second day here and nothing had happened.

He had stayed in the hotel, only left his room to go down to the dining-room or the bar, and spent most of the previous night sitting in the darkness by the window, a night punctuated by the sounds of bombs exploding or the occasional rattle of small-arms fire.

He was worried because this was Friday and in less than 48 hours, at four a.m. on Monday, the 31st July, Motorman was to go into action; the biggest operation mounted by the British Army since Suez. A planned invasion of all the so-called no-go areas dominated by the IRA in Belfast and Londonderry. Once that went into operation, O'Hagan would be certain to drop completely out of sight for a while.

In the end, he could stand it no more, pulled on his jacket and took the lift down to the foyer. He told the desk clerk that he'd be in the bar, sat himself on a high stool and ordered Irish whiskey.

Perhaps he'd expected too much from O'Hagan.

He sipped a little of his whiskey and a uniformed porter tapped him on the shoulder. 'Colonel Morgan? Your taxi's here, sir.'

The driver was an old man badly in need of a shave. Not a word was said as they drove through gathering darkness and rain.

They were somewhere on the Falls Road, with the Catholic Turf Lodge area on the left. Morgan knew that and then the old man turned into one of the mean little side streets.

There was a builder's yard at the end. They drove inside.

There was a lamp above a door which illuminated the yard. The old Ford van standing next to it had *Kilroy's Bakery* painted on the side.

There was silence, only the rain. The old man spoke for the first time. 'I think you'd better get out, mister.'

This was the most dangerous moment, Morgan knew that. The moment that would tell him whether his calculated risk had paid off or not. He opened the door and got out.

A heavily-built man in a dark anorak, the hood up, came round from behind the van holding a Kalashnikov assault rifle. Morgan waited. There were footsteps and a second figure emerged from the darkness. He was just a boy.

'If you'd be good enough to assume the position, Colonel.'

He was Belfast, his accent said as much and he knew his job, running his hands expertly over Morgan as the Colonel leaned against the side of the van, arms braced.

Finally satisfied, he opened the rear doors. 'All right, Colonel. Inside.'

He climbed in after Morgan, the other man handed him the rifle and closed the doors. A moment later, they drove away.

The journey took no more than ten minutes. The van stopped, the driver came round and opened the doors. The boy jumped out and Morgan followed him.

The small terrace houses showed little sign of life except for the odd chink of light where a curtain was badly drawn. The boy lit a cigarette and tossed the match away.

'A grand place to raise your kids, wouldn't you say, Colonel?' he said without looking at Morgan, then started across the road.

Morgan followed him. There was a small café on the corner. The boy pushed the door open and entered. It wasn't much of a place. There was a row of brown-painted booths down one side, a marble-topped bar on the other.

There didn't seem to be any customers. The only sign of life was the old, grey-haired woman in the soiled white apron who sat by the urn reading a paper. She glanced at Morgan briefly.

A quiet voice called softly from the end booth, 'Bring the Colonel down here, Seumas.'

*

Liam O'Hagan was eating egg and chips, a mug of tea at his elbow. He was in his early forties with dark curly hair.

'Hello, Asa,' he said. 'You're looking well.'

The boy went to the counter and asked for two teas. Morgan sat down. 'A bit young for it, isn't he?'

'Who, Seumas?' O'Hagan laughed. 'They didn't think so in the Falls Road, back in August, '69, when the Orange mobs swept in to burn the place to the ground, chase out every Catholic family who lived there. It was a handful of IRA men who took to the streets that night to hold them off and Seumas was one of them.'

'He must have been all of 16 at the time.'

'Eighteen, Asa,' O'Hagan said. 'Fought at my side that night. He looked after my interests ever since.'

'Looked after you?'

'With a handgun, he's the best I've ever seen.'

Seumas returned with a mug of tea which he put down at Morgan's elbow. He went back to the counter and sat on a stool.

'I'm impressed.'

O'Hagan said, 'What is it you want, Asa?'

'The winter of 1950, Liam, in Korea when you were the worst National Service second-lieutenant in the Ulster Rifles.'

'Those were the days,' O'Hagan said. 'God, but we were impressed when a big man like you turned up on attachment. A real soldier, medals, everything.'

'When the Chinese encircled us on the Imjin, when the regiment had to carve its way out, I went back for you, Liam, when you took that bullet in the foot. I brought you out. You owe me for that.'

'Paid in full,' he said. 'Bloody Friday, Asa, you were standing in Lewis Street at midnight, outside Cohan's Bar which was burning rather well at the time. The boy and I were on the roof opposite. He wanted to blow your head off. I wouldn't let him. So if you've come looking for any special favours, you've wasted your time.'

'A good day for you, that,' Morgan said bitterly. 'Around 140 dead and injured.'

'Be your age. The fire storm those RAF bombs raised in Hamburg in July, '43, killed more people in three days than the atom bomb did at Hiroshima.'

'And where does it all end, Liam, all the violence, the killing?'

'A united Ireland.'

'And then what? What do you do when it's all over?'

O'Hagan frowned. 'What in the hell are you talking about?'

'You're going to win, aren't you? You must believe that or there wouldn't be any point to it or don't you ever want it to stop? Do you want it to go on for ever, like stage six at MGM? Up the Republic! Thompson guns and trenchcoats. My life for Ireland.'

'To hell with you, Asa,' O'Hagan said.

'Remember my daughter, Megan?'

O'Hagan nodded. 'How old is she now? Fourteen or 15, I suppose?'

'You read about the Maxwell Cohen shooting last week?'

'That was the Black September, not us.'

'The man responsible had to hi-jack a car to get away with the police hard after him. Megan was cycling home from school through Paddington tunnel. He ran her down. Left her lying in the gutter, like a dog.'

'Mother of God!' O'Hagan said.

'I wouldn't let it upset you. It happened on Bloody Friday, so what's one extra more or less.'

O'Hagan's face was grim. 'All right, Asa. What do you want?'

'Full details haven't been released to the press, but it looks as if the man responsible is the one known as the Cretan.'

'The Cretan Lover? I've heard of him. Some kind of international hit man who's knocked people down from both sides of the fence.'

'That's him. He shot Cohen using a very unusual handgun. A silenced Mauser, one of a batch made for SS security men during the war. They don't often turn up now.'

'I see,' O'Hagan said. 'If you could trace the dealer who supplied it?'

'Exactly. According to Special Branch, the only recorded killing in the UK using such a gun was of an Army Intelligence sergeant in Londonderry by a Provisional gunman named Terence Murphy. He was shot dead by Commandos while making a run for it along with a man called Pat Phelan who also had one.'

'And you'd like to know where they got them from?' O'Hagan shrugged. 'There's only one problem.'

'And what would that be?'

'Terry Murphy and Phelan weren't Provos. They were to start

with, but then last September, they joined a splinter group called the Sons of Erin led by Brendan Tully.'

'Would he tell you where they got those Mausers?'

'Maybe.'

'Liam, I need to know. It's the only lead I've got.'

O'Hagan nodded slowly. 'You want this man badly. What for—justice?'

'To hell with justice, I want to see him dead.'

'That's honest, anyway. I'll see what I can do. You go back to the Europa and wait.'

'How long?'

'A couple of days—perhaps three.'

'That's no good.'

'Why not?'

Morgan was in too deep to draw back now. 'By Monday night, they'll have Belfast sewn up so tight that even a mouse couldn't slip through the net.'

'Interesting,' O'Hagan said and the door burst open.

Seumas was already on his feet and O'Hagan produced a Browning Hi Power from his pocket with some speed and held it in his lap under the table.

A great brute of a man stood swaying drunkenly just inside the door. He wore a soiled reefer coat and denim overalls and his eyes were bloodshot. He didn't appear to notice O'Hagan and Morgan and ignored Seumas, lurching across to the counter and holding on to it with both hands as if to prop himself up.

'I'm collecting,' he said to the old woman. 'Funds for the Organisation. Ten quid, ma, and we'll call it quits. Otherwise we close you down.'

She wasn't in the least afraid. Simply poured tea into a mug, spooned sugar into it and pushed it across the counter.

'Drink that, lad, then sober up and go home. You've come to the wrong shop.'

He sent the mug flying with a sweep of his hand. 'Ten quid, you old bitch, or I smash the place up.'

There was a Luger in Seumas's right hand, the barrel up under the man's chin. The boy didn't say a word. It was O'Hagan who spoke.

'The IRA, is it? Which brigade?' The big man glared at him stupidly and O'Hagan said, 'Outside with him, Seumas.'

The boy swung the man round and sent him staggering through the door. O'Hagan got to his feet and went after them and Morgan followed.

The big man stood under one of the few street lamps still working, rain soaking his head, Seumas to one side covering him with the Luger. O'Hagan walked forward, paused, then kicked him viciously in the crutch so that he cried out and went down on his knees.

'All right,' O'Hagan said. 'You know what to do.'

Seumas moved in close, the barrel of the Luger poking into the back of the man's right knee-cap, and then he simply blew it off with a single shot.

The man screamed in agony and rolled over. O'Hagan stood looking down at him.

'There's good men dead and in their graves fighting the bloody British Army and bastards like you spit on them.'

At the same moment, a couple of stripped-down Land-Rovers turned the corner at the end of the street and braked to a halt. Morgan was aware of the uniforms and a spotlight was turned on.

'Stay exactly where you are,' a voice echoed over a loudhailer in crisp, public-school English, but O'Hagan and Seumas had already ducked into the alley at the side of the café. Morgan went after them, running like hell.

There was a six-foot brick wall at the end of the street and they were scrambling over it as the first soldiers turned into the alley. They found themselves in a builder's yard and blundered across in darkness to a double wooden door. Seumas got the judas gate open and they were out and into the street as the first soldier arrived on the other side of the wall.

The boy and O'Hagan seemed to know exactly where they were going. Morgan followed at their heels, twisting and turning through a dark rabbit warren of mean streets and the sounds of pursuit grew fainter. Finally, they came out on the banks of a small canal and Seumas paused beside some bushes. He took a small torch from his pocket and as he switched it on, there was a tremendous explosion from the direction of the city centre, followed by three more in rapid succession.

O'Hagan looked at his watch. 'Right on time for once.' He grinned at Morgan.

'Now what?' Morgan asked.

'We get the hell out of here. Get it open, Seumas.'

In the light of the boy's torch, Morgan saw that he had pulled back the bushes revealing a manhole cover which he pulled back. He descended a steel ladder, Morgan hesitated, then went after him and O'Hagan followed, pulling the cover back into place.

Morgan found himself in a tunnel so small that he had to crouch. The boy took a large spot lamp from a ledge and switched it on. He started forward and Morgan went after him, aware of the sound of rushing water in the distance.

They came out on the concrete bank of a large tunnel and in the light of the spot he saw that a brown foaming stream coursed down the centre. The smell was very unpleasant.

'The main sewer,' Seumas said. 'All that Protestant shit from the Shankill. Don't worry, Colonel. We'll pass right underneath and come up amongst friends in the Ardoyne.'

'Then what?' Morgan asked.

'I think, under the circumstances, we'd do better out of town tonight,' O'Hagan said. 'You, too, Asa.'

'You'll never make it,' Morgan told him. 'Not after those bombs. They'll plug every road out of the city up tight.'

'Ah, there are ways,' O'Hagan said. 'Now let's get moving.'

They emerged some 20 minutes later in what appeared to be a factory yard behind a high brick wall. When the boy turned to the building itself Morgan saw, in the light of the spot, considerable evidence of bomb damage and that all the windows had been blocked with corrugated iron.

They paused at large double doors, locked with a padlock and chain and O'Hagan produced a key. 'This was a wholesale booze warehouse, owned by a London firm. After the third bomb, they decided they'd had enough.'

He got the doors open and Morgan and Seumas moved in. O'Hagan closed the doors and the boy fumbled in the dark. There was the click of a switch and a single bulb turned on.

'Nice of them not to cut off the electricity,' O'Hagan said.

Morgan found himself standing in a garage. In the centre there was some sort of vehicle covered with a dust sheet. O'Hagan moved across and pulled the sheet away, revealing an Army Land-

Rover. The painted board mounted at the front said: *Emergency—Bomb Disposal.*

He went round to the back of the Land-Rover, opened it and took out a camouflage jacket which he threw across. 'Everything we need is here. You'll have to drop a couple of ranks though. Best I can manage are a captain's pips. I'll be sergeant and Seumas our driver.'

'To what end?' Morgan demanded. 'Where are we going?'

'You wanted to know where those Mausers came from. All right—we'll go and ask Brendan Tully.'

It worked like a charm, all the way out of the city on the Antrim Road. They were waved through three separate roadblocks by military police without hesitation and at a fourth, where there was a queue of vehicles being checked, Seumas simply sounded his horn and overtook on the wrong side of the road.

Outside Ballymena, O'Hagan told the boy to pull up at a public telephone box. He was inside for no more than three minutes. When he returned, he was smiling.

'He's expecting us. The Glenarrif road through the Antrim mountains.'

Twenty miles along the road through the mountains, they came to a sign indicating Coley to the left. Seumas turned, following a narrow, twisting road between dry-stone walls, climbing higher and higher into the mountains.

In the first grey light of day they came over a rise on to a small plateau backed by beech trees. There was a barn, doors standing open and an old jeep. Two men stood beside it. They were both dressed like farm labourers, one in a patched corduroy jacket and cloth cap, the younger one in denim overalls and Wellington boots.

'The one in the cap is Tim Pat Keogh, Tully's right-hand man. The other's Jackie Rafferty. A bit touched in the head, that one. He usually does what Tully tells him to and likes it,' O'Hagan said.

Seumas braked to a halt and the two men came forward. 'Good day to you, Mr O'Hagan,' Keogh said. 'If you'd leave the Land-Rover in the barn, we'll take you up to the farm in the jeep.'

O'Hagan nodded to Seumas who drove the vehicle under cover. They all got out and as they emerged, Keogh and Rafferty closed the barn doors. O'Hagan had slung a Sterling submachine-gun over one shoulder and Morgan carried a Smith and Wesson .38 service revolver in a standard issue webbing holster.

Keogh said, 'A friendly visit, is it, Mr O'Hagan?'

O'Hagan said, 'Don't be bloody stupid, Tim Pat. Now let's get up to the farm. I could do with some breakfast. It's been a hard night.'

The farm was a poor sort of place, in a small hollow backed up against the side of the mountain for protection against the wind. The out-buildings were badly in need of repair and the yard was thick with mud.

Brendan Tully was a tall, handsome, lean-faced man with one side of his mouth hooked into a slight perpetual half-smile as if permanently amused by the world and its inhabitants. He greeted them at the door. He'd obviously just got out of bed and wore an old robe over pyjamas.

'Liam!' he cried. 'You're a sight for sore eyes, in spite of that bloody uniform. Come away in.'

They followed him into the kitchen where a wood fire burned on an open hearth.

Tully turned, eyeing Morgan curiously. 'And who might this be?'

'An old friend. Dai Lewis of the Free Wales Army. They helped us out with guns in the autumn of '69, remember, when things were bad.'

'Does he speak Welsh then?'

'A bloody poor sort of Welshman I'd be if I didn't,' Morgan answered in his native tongue.

Tully was delighted. 'Marvellous,' he said. 'Only I didn't understand a word of it. Now, let's start the day right, while the old bag there gets the food ready.'

He produced a whiskey jug and glasses. O'Hagan said, 'A bit early even for you.'

'A short life, eh?' Tully was obviously in high spirits. 'Anyway what brings you out this way?'

O'Hagan said, 'What Dai and his people are after are some silenced pistols. He thought I might be able to help and then I remembered those two lads of yours who died last year. Terry Murphy and young Phelan. Wasn't it silenced Mausers they were carrying?'

'That's right,' Tully said. 'And damned difficult to come by they were.'

'Can we ask where you got them?'

'The Jago brothers—two of the biggest villains in London.' Tully turned to Morgan. 'I don't know if they'll still have what you want, but watch them. They'd dig up their grandmother and sell the corpse if they thought there was money in it.'

He swallowed some of his whiskey and said to O'Hagan, 'I'm glad you've come. I'd like to talk. Something of considerable importance to the whole movement. Come in the living-room. I'll show you. We've time before breakfast.' Tully could hardly contain himself.

He turned and went through into the living-room. O'Hagan glanced at Morgan and Seumas, then followed reluctantly.

'Close the door, man,' Tully said impatiently, then opened a drawer in the old mahogany table and took out a map which he unrolled.

O'Hagan joined him and saw that the map was of the west coast of Scotland including the islands of the Outer Hebrides.

'What's all this?'

'This island here, Skerryvore,' Tully pointed. 'It's a missile training base. One of my boys, Michael Bell, was a corporal technician there. Knows the place backwards.'

'So?'

'It seems that on Thursdays once a fortnight, an officer and nine men drive up by road from Glasgow Airport to Mallaig. From there, they go to Skerryvore by boat. Let's say their truck is stopped on the way to Mallaig one Thursday and I'm waiting with nine of my men to take their place, including Michael Bell, of course.'

'But why?' O'Hagan said. 'What's the name of the game?'

'The thing they're testing on that island is called Hunter, a medium-range missile. Not atomic, but a new kind of explosive that would cause a very big bang indeed. One of those things on target could take out a square mile of London.'

'You must be crazy,' O'Hagan told him angrily. 'Rockets on London? What are you trying to do? Lose everything we've fought for?'

'But it's the only way, don't you see? Take the struggle to the enemy's own doorstep.'

'Kill thousands at one blow; totally alienate world opinion?' O'Hagan shook his head. 'Brendan, at the moment in the eyes of many people abroad, we're a gallant little handful taking on an army. That's how we'll win in the end. Not by defeating the British Army, but by making the whole thing so unpleasant that they'll withdraw of their own accord, just like they did in Aden and Cyprus and all those other places. But this . . .' He shook his head. 'This is madness. The Army Council would never approve such a scheme. It would be like shooting the Queen—counterproductive.'

'You mean you'll tell the Army Council about this?'

'Of course I will. What else do you expect me to do? I'm Chief Intelligence Officer for Ulster, aren't I?'

'All right,' Tully said defensively. 'So I was wrong. If the Council won't back me, then there's no way we can do it, that's obvious. I'll see if breakfast is ready.'

He went into the kitchen where Morgan, Seumas and Keogh sat at the table. He moved to the front door and found Rafferty leaning inside the jeep, oiling the brake pedal shaft. Rafferty straightened and turned.

Tully's face was distorted with fury. 'Dump them, Jackie. Three with one blow. No messing. You understand?'

'Yes, Mr Tully,' Rafferty said without the slightest flicker of emotion. 'One of those Russian pencil timers should do it and the plastique.'

'Get to it then.' Tully went back into the kitchen.

O'Hagan was just coming out of the living-room. He had the map under one arm and the Sterling submachine-gun ready for action in his right hand.

'I've suddenly lost my appetite.' Outside there was the sound of the jeep starting up and driving away. 'Where in the hell has he gone?'

'For milk,' Tully said. 'We don't have a cow here. Liam, let's be reasonable.'

'Just keep your distance,' O'Hagan nodded to Morgan and the boy. 'All right, you two. Seumas, watch my back.'

They moved into the yard. As they reached the gate, Tully shouted from the door, 'Liam, listen to me.'

But O'Hagan simply increased his walking speed.

'What in the hell was that all about?'

'Nothing to do with you,' O'Hagan said. 'A matter for the Army

Council.' He shook his head. 'That lunatic. How could he even have imagined I'd go for such a scheme.'

They went over the rise and down to the barn. The doors were still closed and there was no sign of the jeep.

He said to Morgan and Seumas, 'You cover me while I get the Land-Rover out, just in case they try anything funny,' and he tossed the Sterling to Morgan.

He got the barn door open, Morgan turned away, aware of him moving inside. The Land-Rover door slammed as O'Hagan got in. There was a colossal explosion, a blast of hot air and Morgan was flung forward on to his face.

He got to his knees, turned and found Seumas trying to get up, clutching his arm where a piece of metal was embedded like shrapnel.

The barn was an inferno, the wreck of the Land-Rover blazing fiercely.

Morgan was aware of the sound of an engine, dragged Seumas to his feet and shoved him into the trees, crouching down beside him. The jeep approached. It braked to a halt and Rafferty got out.

He walked forward, a hand shielding his face from the heat, going as close as he dared. Morgan stood up and emerged from the bushes.

'Rafferty?'

As Rafferty swung to face him, Morgan emptied the Sterling in three bursts, driving him back into the furnace of the barn. He threw the Sterling after him, picked up Seumas and got him to the jeep.

As he climbed behind the wheel he said, 'Do you know where we can find you a doctor? A safe doctor.'

'The Hibernian Nursing Home for the Aged. It's two miles this side of Ballymena,' Seumas told him and fainted.

Morgan removed the camouflage uniform in the washroom and stuffed it into a laundry basket. Underneath, he still wore his ordinary clothes. He checked his wallet, then washed his face and hands and returned to the small surgery.

The old doctor, Kelly, who appeared to run the place and a young nun were bending over Seumas whose arm and shoulder were bandaged. His eyes closed.

Doctor Kelly turned to Morgan. 'He'll sleep now. I've given him an injection. Good as new in a week.'

Seumas opened his eyes. 'You going, Colonel?'

'Back to London. I've things to do. You know, you never did tell me your second name.'

The boy smiled weakly. 'Keegan'.

Morgan wrote his London telephone number on the doctor's prescription pad and tore it off. 'If you think I can help any time, give me a ring.'

He moved to the door.

'Why, Colonel? Why did they do it?'

'From what I could gather, Tully had come up with some scheme or other than Liam didn't approve. He was going to inform the Army Council. This was Tully's way of stopping that.'

'I'll see him in hell first.' Seumas said and closed his eyes.

At the first public telephone box he came to, Morgan phoned Army Intelligence Headquarters at Lisburn and in as convincing an Ulster accent as he could muster, indicated where Brendan Tully and the Sons of Erin might be found.

Then he caught a train in Ballymena for Belfast and went straight to the Europa where he booked out. By three o'clock he was at Aldergrove Airport waiting for the London flight.

THE DOOMED SISTERS

Charles Robert Maturin

Almost two centuries before Jack Higgins' Belfast childhood had such an impact on him, Charles Robert Maturin (1782–1824), the son of a prosperous Dublin civil servant, grew up through the unrest of the first bloody outbreaks of Irish nationalism, and this was to have an equally profound effect upon the rest of his life. In another curious parallel between the two men, just as Jack Higgins launched a new genre with The Eagle Has Landed, *so Charles Robert Maturin's* Melmoth the Wanderer *(1820), about a man's grim pact with the Devil in return for immortality, was to prove a landmark work which is today referred to as one of 'the crowning achievements of the Gothic Romance'. Maturin was educated at Trinity College, Dublin, and although he decided to become a Protestant clergyman, quickly became notorious for his flamboyant style of dress, his eccentric manner and his undisguised admiration for pretty women. When he began to write sensational novels all about murder and unholy passions, his notoriety was complete. Among his books were* The Wild Irish Boy *(1808) and* The Milesian Chief *(1812) which had been inspired by a famous local legend concerning a band of Milesians who had once founded a colony in Ireland. Despite the fact that Maturin was a rousing preacher whose church was usually packed, and the sales of his novels were substantial, he was forever struggling against poverty and ill-health. He was just 43 when he died.*

It was not, however, until the latter part of the nineteenth century that Maturin's importance to the horror genre began to be fully appreciated—and initially only in France where his translated works have continued to be reprinted ever since. In England, Melmoth the Wanderer *has been the most read of his books where it has often been compared to another of the great works of Gothic Horror, Matthew Gregory Lewis's* The Monk *(1796).*

Tragically, much of Maturin's shorter work was destroyed by his family after his death, so scandalised had they been by his behaviour and his writings while he was alive. One tale that did survive was 'The Doomed Sisters' (also known more prosaically as 'Leixlip Castle: An Irish Family Legend') which Maturin claimed was based on fact. When first published in the Literary Souvenir *in 1825, it was prefaced with a note stating that the events had actually occurred not long before in the author's own family. 'The marriage of the parties, their sudden and mysterious separation, and their total alienation from each other until the last period of their mortal existence, are all facts,' he explained. The story of lurking fear may have come a long way from Maturin to Higgins, but in this earliest example will be found a number of the elements which later writers have been only too happy to adopt and develop further . . .*

*   *   *

The tranquillity of the Catholics of Ireland during the disturbed periods of 1715 and 1745 was most commendable, and somewhat extraordinary; to enter into an analysis of their probable motives is not at all the object of the writer of this tale, as it is pleasanter to state the fact of their honour than at this distance of time to assign dubious and unsatisfactory reasons for it. Many of them, however, showed a kind of secret disgust at the existing state of affairs, by quitting their family residences and wandering about like persons who were uncertain of their homes, or possibly expecting better from some near and fortunate contingency.

Among the rest was a Jacobite Baronet who, sick of his uncongenial situation in a Whig neighbourhood, in the north—where he heard of nothing but the heroic defence of Londonderry; the barbarities of the French generals; and the resistless exhortations of the godly Mr Walker, a Presbyterian clergyman to whom the citizens gave the title of 'Evangelist';—quitted his paternal residence, and about the year 1720 hired the Castle of Leixlip for three years (it was then the property of the Conollys, who let it to triennial tenants); and removed thither with his family, which consisted of three daughters—their mother having long been dead.

The Castle of Leixlip, at that period, possessed a character of romantic beauty and feudal grandeur, such as few buildings in Ireland can claim, and which is now, alas, totally effaced by the destruction of its noble woods; on the destroyers of which the writer would wish 'a minstrel's malison were said'. Leixlip, though about seven miles from Dublin, has all the sequestered and pictur- esque character that imagination could ascribe to a landscape a hundred miles from, not only the metropolis but an inhabited town. After driving a dull mile (an *Irish* mile) in passing from Lucan to Leixlip, the road—hedged up on one side of the high wall that bounds the demesne of the Veseys, and on the other by low enclosures, over whose rugged tops you have no view at all— at once opens on Leixlip Bridge, at almost a right angle, and displays a luxury of landscape on which the eye that has seen it even in childhood dwells with delighted recollection. Leixlip Bridge, a rude but solid structure, projects from a high bank of the Liffey, and slopes rapidly to the opposite side, which there lies remarkably low. To the right the plantations of the Veseys' demesne—no longer obscured by walls—almost mingle their dark woods in its stream, with the opposite ones of Marshfield and St Catharine's. The river is scarcely visible, overshadowed as it is by the deep, rich and bending foliage of the trees. To the left it bursts out in all the brilliancy of light, washes the garden steps of the houses of Leixlip, wanders round the low walls of its church- yard, plays with the pleasure-boat moored under the arches on which the summer-house of the Castle is raised, and then loses itself among the rich woods that once skirted those grounds to its very brink. The contrast on the other side, with the luxuriant vegetation, the lighter and more diversified arrangement of ter- raced walks, scattered shrubberies, temples seated on pinnacles, and thickets that conceal from you the sight of the river until you are on its banks, that mark the character of the grounds which are now the property of Colonel Marley, is peculiarly striking.

Visible above the highest roofs of the town, though a quarter of a mile distant from them, are the ruins of Confy Castle, a right good old predatory tower of the stirring times when blood was shed like water; and as you pass the bridge you catch a glimpse of the waterfall (or salmon-leap, as it is called) on whose noon-day lustre, or moonlight beauty, probably the rough livers of that age when Confy Castle was 'a tower of strength', never glanced an eye or cast a thought as they clattered in their harness over Leixlip Bridge, or waded through the stream before that convenience was in existence.

Whether the solitude in which he lived contributed to tranquil-
lise Sir Redmond Blaney's feelings, or whether they had begun to
rust from want of collision with those of others, it is impossible to
say, but certain it is that the good Baronet began gradually to lose
his tenacity in political matters; and except when a Jacobite friend
came to dine with him, and drink with many a significant 'nod and
beck and smile, the King over the water—or the parish priest
(good man) spoke of the hopes of better times, and the final success of the *right* cause, and the old religion—or a Jacobite servant
was heard in the solitude of the large mansion whistling 'Charlie
is my darling', to which Sir Redmond involuntarily responded in
a deep bass voice, somewhat the worse for wear, and marked with
more emphasis than good discretion—except, as I have said, on
such occasions, the Baronet's politics, like his life, seemed passing
away without notice or effort. Domestic calamities, too, pressed
sorely on the old gentleman: of his three daughters, the youngest,
Jane, had disappeared in so extraordinary a manner in her childhood, that though it is but a wild, remote family tradition, I cannot
help relating it.

The girl was of uncommon beauty and intelligence, and was
suffered to wander about the neighbourhood of the castle with the
daughter of a servant, who was also called Jane, as a *nom de
caresse*. One evening Jane Blaney and her young companion went
far and deep into the woods; their absence created no uneasiness
at the time, as these excursions were by no means unusual, till her
playfellow returned home alone and weeping, at a very late hour.
Her account was that, in passing through a lane at some distance
from the castle, an old woman, in the *Fingallian* dress (a red
petticoat and a long green jacket), suddenly started out of a
thicket, and took Jane Blaney by the arm: she had in her hand
two rushes, one of which she threw over her shoulder, and giving
the other to the child, motioned to her to do the same. Her young
companion, terrified at what she saw, was running away, when
Jane Blaney called after her—'Good-bye, good-bye, it is a long
time before you will see me again.' The girl said they then disappeared, and she found her way home as she could. An indefatigable search was immediately commenced—woods were
traversed, thickets were explored, ponds were drained—all in
vain. The pursuit and the hope were at length given up. Ten years
afterwards, the housekeeper of Sir Redmond, having remembered

that she left the key of a closet where sweetmeats were kept on the kitchen-table, returned to fetch it. As she approached the door, she heard a childish voice murmuring—'Cold—cold—cold how long it is since I have felt a fire!' She advanced, and saw, to her amazement, Jane Blaney, shrunk to half her usual size, and covered with rags, crouching over the embers of the fire. The housekeeper flew in terror from the spot, and roused the servants, but the vision had fled. The child was reported to have been seen several times afterwards, as diminutive in form as though she had not grown an inch since she was ten years of age, and always crouching over a fire, whether in the turret-room or kitchen, complaining of cold and hunger, and apparently covered with rags. Her existence is still said to be protracted under these dismal circumstances, so unlike those of Lucy Gray in Wordsworth's beautiful ballad:

> Yet some will say, that to this day
>   She is a living child—
> That they have met sweet Lucy Gray
>   Upon the lonely wild;
> O'er rough and smooth she trips along,
>   And never looks behind;
> And hums a solitary song
>   That whistles in the wind.

The fate of the eldest daughter was more melancholy, though less extraordinary; she was addressed by a gentleman of competent fortune and unexceptionable character: he was a Catholic, moreover; and Sir Redmond Blaney signed the marriage articles, in full satisfaction of the security of his daughter's soul, as well as of her jointure. The marriage was celebrated at the Castle of Leixlip; and, after the bride and bridegroom had retired, the guests still remained drinking to their future happiness when suddenly, to the great alarm of Sir Redmond and his friends, loud and piercing cries were heard to issue from the part of the castle in which the bridal chamber was situated.

Some of the more courageous hurried upstairs; it was too late— the wretched bridegroom had burst, on that fatal night, into a sudden and most horrible paroxysm of insanity. The mangled form of the unfortunate and expiring lady bore attestation to the mortal virulence with which the disease had operated on the wretched husband, and died a victim to it himself after the involuntary murder of his bride. The bodies were interred, as soon as decency would permit, and the story hushed up.

Sir Redmond's hopes of Jane's recovery were diminishing every day, though he still continued to listen to every wild tale told by the domestics; and all his care was supposed to be now directed towards his only surviving daughter. Anne, living in solitude, and partaking only of the very limited education of Irish females of that period, was left very much to the servants, among whom she increased her taste for superstitious and supernatural horrors, to a degree that had a most disastrous effect on her future life.

Among the numerous menials of the Castle there was one 'withered crone' who had been nurse to the late Lady Blaney's mother, and whose memory was a complete *Thesaurus terrorum*. The mysterious fate of Jane first encouraged her sister to listen to the wild tales of this hag, who avouched that at one time she saw the fugitive standing before the portrait of her late mother in one of the apartments of the Castle, and muttering to herself—'Woe's me, woe's me! how little my mother thought her wee Jane would ever come to be what she is!' But as Anne grew older she began more 'seriously to incline' to the hag's promises that she could show her her future bridegroom, on the performance of certain ceremonies which she at first revolted from as horrible and impious; but, finally, at the repeated instigation of the old woman, consented to act a part in. The period fixed upon for the performance of these unhallowed rites was now approaching—it was near the 31st of October, the eventful night when such ceremonies were, and still are supposed, in the North of Ireland, to be most potent in their effects. All day long the Crone took care to lower the mind of the young lady to the proper key of submissive and trembling credulity, by every horrible story she could relate; and she told them with frightful and supernatural energy. This woman was called *Collogue* by the family, a name equivalent to Gossip in England, or Cummer in Scotland (though her real name was Bridget Dease); and she verified the name by the exercise of an unwearied loquacity, an indefatigable memory, and a rage for communicating and inflicting terror that spared no victim in the household, from the groom, whom she sent shivering to his rug, to the Lady of the Castle, over whom she felt she held unbounded sway.

The 31st of October arrived—the Castle was perfectly quiet before eleven o'clock; half an hour afterwards, the Collogue and Anne Blaney were seen gliding along a passage that led to what is called King John's Tower, where it is said that monarch received the homage of the Irish princes as Lord of Ireland, and which, at all events, is the most ancient part of the structure. The Collogue opened a small door with a key which she had secreted about her, and urged the young lady to hurry on. Anne advanced to the postern, and stood there irresolute and trembling like a timid swimmer on the bank of an unknown stream. It was a dark autumnal evening; a heavy wind sighed among the woods of the Castle, and bowed the branches of the lower trees almost to the waves of the Liffey which, swelled by recent rains, struggled and roared amid the stones that obstructed its channel. The steep descent from the Castle lay before her, with its dark avenue of elms; a few lights still burned in the little village of Leixlip—but from the lateness of the hour it was probable they would soon be extinguished.

The lady lingered. 'And must I go alone?' said she, foreseeing that the terrors of her fearful journey could be aggravated by her more fearful purpose.

'Ye must, or all will be spoiled,' said the hag, shading the miserable light, that did not extend its influence above six inches on the path of the victim. 'Ye must go alone—and I will watch for you here, dear, till you come back, and then see what will come to you at twelve o'clock.'

The unfortunate girl paused. 'Oh! Collogue, Collogue, if you would but come with me. Oh! Collogue, come with me, if it be but to the bottom of the castle-hill.'

'If I went with you, dear, we should never reach the top of it alive again, for there are them near that would tear us both in pieces.'

'Oh! Collogue, Collogue—let me turn back then, and go to my own room—I have advanced too far, and I have done too much.'

'And that's what you have, dear, and so you must go further, and do more still, unless, when you return to your own room, you would see the likeness of *some one* instead of a handsome young bridegroom.'

The young lady looked about her for a moment, terror and wild hope trembling at her heart—then, with a sudden impulse of supernatural courage, she darted like a bird from the terrace of the Castle, the fluttering of her white garments was seen for a few moments, and then the hag who had been shading the flickering light with her hand, bolted the postern and, placing the candle before a glazed loophole, sat down on a stone seat in the recess of the tower, to watch the event of the spell. It was an hour before the young lady returned; when her face was as pale, and her eyes as fixed, as those of a dead body, but she held in her grasp *a dripping garment*, a proof that her errand had been performed. She flung it into her companion's hands, and then stood panting and gazing wildly about her as if she knew not where she was. The hag herself grew terrified at the insane and breathless state of her victim, and hurried her to her chamber; but here the preparations for the terrible ceremonies of the night were the first objects that struck her and, shivering at the sight, she covered her eyes with her hands, and stood immovably fixed in the middle of the room.

It needed all the hag's persuasions (aided even by mysterious menaces), combined with the returning faculties and reviving curiosity of the poor girl, to prevail on her to go through the remaining business of the night. At length she said, as if in desperation, 'I *will* go through with it: but be in the next room; and if what I dread should happen, I will ring my father's little silver bell which I have secured for the night—and as you have a soul to be saved, Collogue, come to me at its very first sound.'

The hag promised, gave her last instructions with eager and jealous minuteness, and then retired to her own room, which was adjacent to that of the young lady. Her candle had burned out, but she stirred up the embers of her turf fire, and sat nodding over them, and smoothing her pallet from time to time, but resolved not to lie down while there was a chance of a sound from the lady's room, for which she herself, withered as her feelings were, waited with a mingled feeling of anxiety and terror.

It was now long past midnight, and all was silent as the grave throughout the Castle. The hag dozed over the embers till her head touched her knees, then started up as the sound of the bell seemed to tinkle in her ears, then dozed again, and again started as the bell appeared to tinkle more distinctly—suddenly she was roused, not by the bell, but by the most piercing and horrible cries from the neighbouring chamber. The Crone, aghast for the first time at the possible consequences of the mischief she might have occasioned, hastened to the room. Anne was in convulsions, and the hag was compelled reluctantly to call up the housekeeper (removing meanwhile the implements of the ceremony), and assist in applying all the specifics known at that day, burnt feathers, etc., to restore her. When they had at length succeeded, the house-keeper was dismissed, the door was bolted, and the Collogue was left alone with Anne; the subject of their conference might have been guessed at, but was not known until many years afterwards; but Anne that night held in her hand, in the shape of a weapon with the use of which neither of them was acquainted, an evidence that her chamber had been visited by a being of no earthly form. This evidence the hag importuned her to destroy, or to remove, but she persisted with fatal tenacity in keeping it. She locked it up, however, immediately, and seemed to think she had acquired a right, since she had grappled so fearfully with the mysteries of futurity, to know all the secrets of which that weapon might yet lead to the disclosure. But from that night it was observed that her character, her manner, and even her countenance, became altered. She grew stern and solitary, shrank at the sight of her former associates, and imperatively forbade the slightest allusion to the circumstances which had occasioned this mysterious change.

It was a few days subsequent to this event that Anne, who after dinner had left the Chaplain reading the life of St Francis Xavier to Sir Redmond, and retired to her own room to work and, per-haps, to muse, was surprised to hear the bell at the outer gate ring loudly and repeatedly—a sound she had never heard since her first residence in the Castle; for the few guests who resorted there came and departed as noiselessly as humble visitors at the house of a great man generally do. Straight way there rode up the avenue of elms, which we have already mentioned, a stately gentleman, followed by four servants, all mounted, the two former having pistols in their holsters, and the two latter carrying saddle-bags before them: though it was the first week in November, the dinner hour being one o'clock, Anne had light enough to notice all these circumstances. The arrival of the stranger seemed to cause much, though not unwelcome tumult in the Castle; orders were loudly and hastily given for the accommodation of the servants and horses—steps were heard traversing the numerous passages for a full hour—then all was still; and it was said that Sir Redmond had locked with his own hand the door of the room where he and the stranger sat, and desired that no one should dare to approach it. About two hours afterwards, a female servant came with orders from her master to have a plentiful supper ready by eight o'clock, at which he desired the presence of his daughter. The family establishment was on a handsome scale for an Irish house, and Anne had only to descend to the kitchen to order the roasted chickens to be well strewed with brown sugar according to the unrefined fashion of the day, to inspect the mixing of a bowl of sago with its allowance of a bottle of port wine and a large handful of the richest spices, and to order particularly that the pease pudding should have a huge lump of cold salt butter stuck in its centre; and then, her household cares being over, to retire to her room and array herself in a robe of white damask for the occasion. At eight o'clock she was summoned to the supper-room. She came in, according to the fashion of the times, with the first dish; but as she passed through the ante-room, where the servants were holding lights and bearing the dishes, her sleeve was twitched, and the ghastly face of the Collogue pushed close to hers; while she muttered 'Did not I say *he would come for you*, dear?' Anne's blood ran cold, but she advanced, saluted her father and the stranger with two low and distinct reverences, and then took her place at the table. Her feelings of awe and perhaps terror at the whisper of her associate were not diminished by the appearance of the stranger; there was a singular and mute solemnity in his manner during the meal. He ate nothing. Sir Redmond appeared constrained, gloomy and thoughtful. At length, starting, he said (without naming the stranger's name), 'You will drink my daughter's health?' The stranger intimated his willingness to have that honour, but absently filled his glass with water; Anne put a few drops of wine into hers, and bowed towards him. At that moment, for the first time since they had met, she beheld his face—it was pale as that of a corpse. The deadly whiteness of his cheeks and lips, the hollow and distant sound of his voice, and the strange lustre of his large, dark, moveless eyes, strongly fixed on her, made her pause and even tremble as she raised the glass to her lips; she set it down, and the with another silent reverence retired to her chamber.

There she found Bridget Dease, busy in collecting the turf that burned on the hearth, for there was no grate in the apartment. 'Why are you here?' she said, impatiently.

The hag turned on her, with a ghastly grin of congratulation. 'Did not I tell you that *he* would come for you?'

'I believe he has,' said the unfortunate girl, sinking into the huge wicker chair by her bedside; 'for never did I see mortal with such a look.'

'But is not he a fine stately gentleman?' pursued the hag.

'He looks as if he were not of this world,' said Anne.

'Of this world, or of the next,' said the hag, raising her bony forefinger, 'mark my words – so sure as the (here she repeated some of the horrible formularies of the 31st of October) so sure he will be your bridegroom.'

'Then I shall be the bride of a corpse,' said Anne; 'for he I saw tonight is no living man.'

A fortnight elapsed, and whether Anne became reconciled to the features she had thought so ghastly, by the discovery that they were the handsomest she had ever beheld—and that the voice, whose sound at first was so strange and unearthly, was subdued into a tone of plaintive softness when addressing her—or whether it is impossible for two young persons with unoccupied hearts to meet in the country, and meet often, to gaze silently on the same stream, wander under the same trees, and listen together to the wind that waves the branches, without experiencing an assimilation of feeling rapidly succeeding an assimilation of taste; or whether it was from all these causes combined, but in less than a month Anne heard the declaration of the stranger's passion with many a blush, though without a sigh. He now avowed his name and rank. He stated himself to be a Scottish Baronet, of the name of Sir Richard Maxwell; family misfortunes had driven him from his country, and for ever precluded the possibility of his return: he had transferred his property to Ireland, and purposed to fix his residence there for life. Such was his statement. The courtship of those days was brief and simple. Anne became the wife of Sir Richard, and, I believe, they resided with her father till his death, when they removed to their estate in the North. There they remained for several years, in tranquillity and happiness, and had a numerous family. Sir Richard's conduct was marked by but two peculiarities: he not only shunned the intercourse, but the sight of any of his countrymen, and, if he happened to hear that a Scotsman had arrived in the neighbouring town, he shut himself up till assured of the stranger's departure. The other was his custom of retiring to his own chamber, and remaining invisible to his family on the anniversary of the 30th of October. The lady, who had her own associations connected with that period, only questioned him once on the subject of this seclusion, and was then solemnly and even sternly enjoined never to repeat her inquiry.

Matters stood thus, somewhat mysteriously, but not unhappily, when on a sudden, without any cause assigned or assignable, Sir Richard and Lady Maxwell parted, and never more met in this world, nor was she ever permitted to see one of her children to her dying hour. He continued to live at the family mansion, and she fixed her residence with a distant relative in a remote part of the country. So total was the disunion, that the name of either was never heard to pass the other's lips, from the moment of separation until that of dissolution.

Lady Maxwell survived Sir Richard forty years, living to the great age of 96; and, according to a promise, previously given, disclosed to a descendant with whom she had lived, the following extraordinary circumstances.

She said that on the night of the 30th of October, about seventy-five years before, at the instigation of her ill-advising attendant, she had washed one of her garments in a place where four streams met, and performed other unhallowed ceremonies under the direction of the Collogue, in the expectation that her future husband would appear to her in her chamber at twelve o'clock that night. The critical moment arrived, but with it no lover-like form. A vision of indescribable horror approached her bed, and flinging at her an iron weapon of a shape and construction unknown to her, bade her 'recognise her future husband by *that*.' The terrors of this visit soon deprived her of her senses; but on her recovery, she persisted, as has been said, in keeping the fearful pledge of the reality of the vision which, on examination, appeared to be incrusted with blood. It remained concealed in the inmost drawer of her cabinet till the morning of her separation. On that morning, Sir Richard Maxwell rose before daylight to join a hunting party. He wanted a knife for some accidental purpose and, missing his own, called to Lady Maxwell, who was still in bed, to lend him one. The lady, who was half asleep, answered, that in such a

drawer of her cabinet he would find one. He went, however, to
another, and the next moment she was fully awakened by seeing
her husband present the terrible weapon to her throat, and
threaten her with instant death unless she disclosed how she came
by it. She supplicated for life, and then, in an agony of horror and
contrition, told the tale of that eventful night. He gazed at her for
a moment with a countenance which rage, hatred, and despair
converted, as she avowed, into a living likeness of the demon-
visage she had once beheld (so singularly was the fated resemblance fulfilled), and then exclaiming, 'You won me by the devil's
aid, but you shall not keep me long,' left her—to meet no more
in this world. Her husband's secret was not unknown to the lady,
though the means by which she became possessed of it were wholly
unwarrantable. Her curiosity had been strongly excited by her
husband's aversion to his countrymen, and it was so stimulated by
the arrival of a Scottish gentleman in the neighbourhood some
time before, who professed himself formerly acquainted with Sir
Richard, and spoke mysteriously of the causes that drove him from
his country, that she contrived to procure an interview with him
under a feigned name, and obtained from him the knowledge of
circumstances which embittered her after-life to its latest hour.
His story was this:

Sir Richard Maxwell was at deadly feud with a younger brother;
a family feast was proposed to reconcile them, and as the use of
knives and forks was then unknown in the Highlands, the company
met armed with their dirks for the purpose of carving. They drank
deeply; the feast, instead of harmonising, began to inflame their
spirits; the topics of old strife were renewed; hands, that at first
touched their weapons in defiance, drew them at last in fury, and
in the fray, Sir Richard mortally wounded his brother. His life was
with difficulty saved from the vengeance of the clan, and he was
hurried towards the sea-coast, near which the house stood, and
concealed there till a vessel could be procured to convey him to
Ireland. He embarked *on the night of the 30th of October*, and
while he was traversing the deck in unutterable agony of spirit,
his hand accidentally touched the dirk which he had unconsciously
worn ever since the fatal night. He drew it, and, praying 'that the
guilt of his brother's blood might be as far from his soul as he
could fling that weapon from his body', sent it with all his strength
into the air. This instrument he found secreted in the lady's

cabinet, and whether he really believed her to have become possessed of it by supernatural means, or whether he feared his wife was a secret witness of his crime, has not been ascertained, but the result was what I have stated.

The reparation took place on the discovery: for the rest,

> I know not how the truth may be,
> I tell the Tale as 'twas told to me.

THE CHILD WHO LOVED
A GRAVE

Fitz-James O'Brien

Fitz-James O'Brien (1828–1862), who has been called 'the Celtic Poe', led a life as colourful and short-lived as that of Charles Maturin, and like him left an indelible mark on horror fiction. He, too, was a flamboyant character with a taste for the high life and hard-drinking which left him constantly in debt and forever dodging his creditors—yet he was still able to put pen to paper from time to time and dash off brilliantly original and influential tales. It was all rather a contrast to what life might have had in store for him. Born Michael Fitz-James DeCourcy O'Brien, the son of a lawyer in County Cork, he grew up in comfortable surroundings in Cork city and later in the village of Castleconnel in County Limerick. When he was 16, he was a witness to the effects of the terrible Great Famine on the people living all around him and was so moved that he wrote a poem, 'Oh, Give a Desert Life to Me', which effectively began his writing career when it was published in The Nation *in 1845. In 1849, however, he inherited a fortune of £8,000 and promptly began to squander the money on lavish entertaining. He still wrote occasionally, and in 1850 published his first short story, 'The Phantom Light', which revealed his interest in the supernatural. Two years later, with all his money spent, he decided to start a new life in America and turned his back on Ireland, never to return.*

Across the Atlantic, O'Brien was again unable to resist the allure of high living, yet for a while was able to sustain this through his extensive output of plays, stories, essays, satires and poetry. Among his tales were several which have since been described as being as influential in their own right as those of Edgar Allan Poe who is credited with having anticipated almost every element of detective fiction in just four short stories. O'Brien's contributions, however, were to fantasy fiction: in 'The Diamond Lens' (1858) he anticipated the microcosmic world; in 'What Was It?' (1859) the invisible being; and in 'The Wondersmith' (1859) evil mannikins. At a stroke he swept aside the Gothic fiction which his fellow countryman, Charles Maturin, had developed, and founded a completely new school of fantasy.

Yet for all his achievements and his good-fellowship which made him such a popular companion, O'Brien was often inclined to be truculent and always enjoyed a good fight. It seems his nature made him unable to resist the challenge of joining in the Civil War on the Union side. His reckless bravery quickly raised him to the rank of Captain, but in a skirmish with Confederate troops in February 1862 he was shot and fatally wounded. He was just 33 years old.

'The Child Who Loved a Grave' is one of O'Brien's rarest short stories and undeniably drawn from his Irish childhood. It has never appeared in his collected works and is here reprinted from Harper's New Monthly Magazine *of August 1861 as a fitting tribute to a writer whose Irish origins have often been overlooked.*

*   *   *

Far away in the deep heart of a lonely country there was an old solitary churchyard. People were no longer buried there, for it had fulfilled its mission long, long ago, and its rank grass now fed a few vagrant goats that clambered over its ruined wall and roamed through the sad wilderness of graves. It was bordered all round with willows and gloomy cypresses; and the rusty iron gate, seldom if ever opened, shrieked when the wind stirred it on its hinges as if some lost soul, condemned to wander in that desolate place forever, was shaking its bars and wailing at the terrible imprisonment.

In this churchyard there was one grave unlike all the rest. The stone which stood at the head bore no name, but instead the curious device, rudely sculptured, of a sun uprising out of the sea. The grave was very small and covered with a thick growth of dock and nettle, and one might tell by its size that it was that of a little child.

Not far from the old churchyard a young boy lived with his

parents in a dreary cottage; he was a dreamy, dark-eyed boy, who never played with the children of the neighbourhood, but loved to wander in the fields and lie by the banks of rivers, watching the leaves fall and the waters ripple, and the lilies sway their white heads on the bosom of the current. It was no wonder that his life was solitary and sad, for his parents were wild, wicked people who drank and quarrelled all day and all night, and the noises of their quarrels where heard in calm summer nights by the neighbours that lived in the village under the brow of the hill.

They boy was terrified at all this hideous strife, and his young soul shrank within him when he heard the oaths and the blows echoing through the dreary cottage, so he used to fly out into the fields where everything looked so calm and pure, and talk with the lilies in a low voice as if they were his friends.

In this way he came to haunt the old churchyard, roaming through its half-buried headstones, and spelling out upon them the names of people that had gone from earth years and years ago. The little grave, nameless and neglected, however, attracted him more than all others. The strange device of the sun uprising out of the sea was to him a perpetual source of mystery and wonder; and so, whether by day or night, when the fury of his parents drove him from his home, he used to wander there and lie amidst the thick grass and think who was buried beneath it.

In time his love for the little grave grew so great that he adorned it after his childish fashion. He cleared away the docks and the nettles and the mulleins that grew so sombrely above it, and clipped the grass until it grew thick and soft as the carpet of heaven. Then he brought primroses from the green banks of dewy lanes where the hawthorn rained its white flowers, and red poppies from the cornfields, and bluebells from the shadowy heart of the forest, and planted them around the grave. With the supple twigs of the silver osier he hedged it round with a little simple fence, and scraped the creeping mosses from the grey head-stone until the little grave looked as if it might have been the grave of a good fairy.

Then he was content. All the long summer days he would lie upon it with his arms clasping its swelling mound, while the soft wind with wavering will would come and play about him and timidly lift his hair. From the hillside he heard the shouts of the village boys at play, and sometimes one of them would come and ask him to join in their sports; but he would look at him with his calm, dark eyes and gently answer no; and the boy, awed and hushed, would steal back to his companions and speak in whispers about the child that loved a grave.

In truth, he loved the little graveyard better than all play. The stillness of the churchyard, the scent of the wild flowers, the golden chequers of the sunlight falling through the trees and playing over the grass were all delights to him. He would lie on his back for hours gazing up at the summer sky and watching the white clouds sailing across it, and wondering if they were the souls of good people sailing home to heaven. But when the black thunder-clouds came up bulging with passionate tears, and bursting with sound and fire, he would think of his bad parents at home, and, turning to the grave, lay his little cheek against it as if it were a brother.

So the summer went passing into autumn. The trees grew sad and shivered as the time approached when the fierce wind would strip them of their cloaks, and the rains and the storms buffet their naked limbs. The primroses grew pale and withered, but in their last moments seemed to look up at the child smilingly, as if to say, 'Do not weep for us. We will come again next year.' But the sadness of the season came over him as the winter approached, and he often wet the little grave with his tears, and kissed the grey head-stone, as one kisses a friend that is to depart for years.

One evening towards the close of autumn, when the woods looked brown and grim, and the wind as it came over the hills had a fierce, wicked growl, the child heard, as he was sitting by the grave, the shriek of the old gate swinging upon its rusty hinges, and looking up he saw a strange procession enter. There were five men. Two bore between them what seemed to be a long box covered with black cloth, two more carried spades in their hands, while the fifth, a tall stern-faced man clad in a long cloak, walked at their head. As the child saw these men pass to and fro through the graveyard, stumbling over half-buried head-stones, or stooping down and examining half-effaced inscriptions, his little heart almost ceased to beat, and he shrank behind the grey stone with the strange device in mortal terror.

The men walked to and fro, with the tall one at their head, searching steadily in the long grass, and occasionally pausing to consult. At last the leader turned and walked towards the little grave, and stooping down gazed at the grey stone. The moon had just risen, and its light fell on the quaint sculpture of the sun rising out of the sea. The tall man then beckoned to his companions. 'I have found it,' he said, 'it is here.' With that the four men came along, and all five of them stood by the grave. The child behind the stone could no longer breathe.

The two men bearing the long box laid it down in the grass, and taking off the black cloth, the child saw a little coffin of shining ebony covered with silver ornaments, and on the lid, wrought in silver, was the device of a sun uprising out of the sea, and the moon shone over all.

'Now to work!' said the tall man; and straightaway the two that held the spades plunged them into the little grave. The child thought his heart would break; and, no longer able to restrain himself, he flung his body across the mound, and cried out to the strange leader.

'Oh, Sir!' he cried, sobbing, 'do not touch my little grave! It is all I have to love in the world. Do not touch it; for all day long I lie here with my arms about it, and it seems like my brother. I tend it, and keep the grass short and thick, and I promise you, if you will leave it to me, that next year I will plant about it the finest flowers in the meadows.'

'Tush, child, you are a fool!' answered the stern-faced man. 'This is a sacred duty that I have to perform. He who is buried here was a child like you; but he was of royal blood, and his ancestors dwelt in palaces. It is not meet that bones like his should rest in common soil. Across the sea a grand mausoleum awaits them, and I have come to take them with me and lay them in vaults of porphyry and marble. Take him away, men, and to your work.'

So the men dragged the child from the grave by main force, and laid him nearby in the grass, sobbing as if his heart would break; and then they dug up the grave. Through his tears he saw the small white bones gathered up and put in the ebony coffin, and heard the lid shut down, and saw the men shovel back the earth into the empty grave, and he felt as if they were robbers. Then they took up the coffin and retraced their steps. The gate shrieked once more on its hinges, and the child was alone.

He returned home silent, and tearless, and white as any ghost. When he went to his little bed he called his father, and told him he was going to die, and asked him to have him buried in the little grave that had a grey head-stone with a sun rising out of the sea carved upon it The father laughed, and told him to go to sleep; but when morning came the child was dead!

They buried him where he wished; and when the sod was patted smooth, and the funeral procession departed, that night a new star came out in heaven and watched above the grave.

THE DIPLOMATIST'S STORY

Shane Leslie

Sir John Randolph Shane Leslie (1885–1971) is yet another larger-than-life Irishman who has contributed substantially to both the horror and supernatural genres. He is also famed for his close friendship with Tolstoy and for having lived for a period of his life as a tramp! The details of his life have, in fact, become as clouded by mystery as many of his stories and are worth setting straight. He was born on the family estate of Glaslough in County Monaghan, Ulster, right on the border between the Irish Republic and Northern Ireland. His family were staunch Unionists, but after taking his degree at Belfast University in 1907, he went to Russia where he met Tolstoy and became a devotee. Soon after this he converted to Catholicism and began supporting the cause of Irish independence. In 1910 he stood as a parliamentary candidate for the Irish Nationalist Party in Derry City against the Duke of Abercorn's son and lost by just 57 votes. There is another famous story about him that on one night he slipped quietly out of the family house at Glaslough to go and inspect the local company of the Irish Volunteers (the IRA) when he suddenly came face to face with his father going out to review the British regiment of which he was the colonel! Apocryphal or not, there is no doubt that Shane Leslie was formally disinherited by his father for becoming a Catholic and a nationalist, in favour of his younger brother. However, the death of Norman Leslie in the First World War led to Shane inheriting the baronetcy in 1944 when Sir John Leslie died. He was also for a time a teacher (at the University of Pennsylvania) and editor of the Dublin Review.

Shane Leslie's interest in the supernatural stemmed from his childhood, and much of his later life was dedicated to the painstaking collection of stories of the unknown, which he used as the raw

material for both factual and fictional works. His play, Lord
Mulroy's Ghost, *was successfully performed at the Abbey Theatre,
Dublin, in 1954; while the following year he published* Shane
Leslie's Ghost Book, *a classic collection of supernatural occur-
rences which has remained in print ever since. Among his books
of fictional horror stories the best are* Masquerades, Studies in the
Morbid *(1924) and* Fifteen Odd Stories *(1935); and his full-length
novel,* The Skull of Swift *(1928), is also worthy of mention. Curiously, 'The Diplomatist's Story' did not appear in any of Shane
Leslie's collections, but I am very pleased to include it here as it
offers a unique variation on one of the more fearsome creatures to
be found in Irish horror fiction . . . the Banshee.*

*   *   *

The diplomatic race are expected to go through life telling excel-
lent and wisely conceived falsehoods for the benefit of their
country. In the art of elegant lying there is a call for proficiency
whenever the world seeks to soften the display of its own powers
of intrigue and corruption. It has been noticed that any country
which breeds efficient horse-dealers can generally produce a good
average diplomatist. This may possibly be a reason why so many
Irishmen from North or South have excelled in the glittering paths
which lead from the gates of the British Foreign Office.

During the reign of Victoria no Irishman excelled more deserv-
edly in British diplomacy than the late Lord Monaghan, whose
breeding was a pleasant mixture of the dour Ulsterman and the
kindlier cunning of the South. Anglo-Irish writers and Dublin
Court beauties figured in his pedigree. At an early age he had
been inveigled into the Foreign Office by the promise of a career.
Post had followed post over nearly half a century. At the end of
it he had stepped into a Victorian peerage and retired to an ancient
Irish demesne, which like many Irish demesnes was composed
chiefly of Lough water and even more so in the rainy weather.

Lord Monaghan was socially much sought in the North of Ireland since his retirement. No garden-party or county function was
considered complete without his appearance. He always wore a
carefully prepared costume of the Third Empire based on the
tailoring of the Emperor whom he had known and entertained in
his later days of exile. This facial resemblance, of which he was a

little proud on the Continent, was completed by a tiny tuft of hair under his lip. During each autumn he paid visits to the big houses of the North. There was only one castle which he seemed anxious to avoid. He refused invitations thereto, whether for the afternoon or for a prolonged stay. He always refused and would never give reasons. It was known that he had paid a visit there in his youth nearly half a century before but that he had never returned. The countryside decided that he must have been refused in marriage by a daughter of the house and had retained an acute memory of the sting. He himself would never say why, and there was a natural delicacy in questioning him in his own country.

Towards the end of his life an uncle of mine met him in the train travelling from Paris to the Riviera. It was in the days before the hordes of English who either had no income or else had to dodge an income tax, began pouring into the sunshine of the Mediterranean. Invalids and retired diplomatists chiefly composed the mixed company to be found grilling under the cloudless heat. Strangers in the train were generally found to be distinguished and worthy of conversation. Accidentally my uncle mentioned that he had been staying at Mullymore Castle. Then he remembered where Lord Monaghan never went and with some secret reason for his conduct. The old diplomatist never as much as raised the hair of an eyebrow. But my uncle must have caught his thought, for a minute later he knew that he had been tactless and danced back over the conversational Tom Tiddler's ground. Feeling he had left some memory awake that had better been left to slumber he tried to turn conversation into another channel, but, as is often the way, his mental reservation, not to mention the name of Mullymore, led him to blurting it out again ten minutes later.

'What does Mullymore Castle look like today?' asked Lord Monaghan quickly, as though to release my uncle from the embarrassment into which he had fallen. My uncle described it much as he had seen it a month previously. Lord Monaghan, flitting back nearly half a century, listened quietly to his account, only observing at the end: 'It was much the same in the old days, but I don't remember the whitewash of which you speak.'

'Yes, it is whitewashed now like a peasant's cottage,' said my uncle, 'one of the English wives found it gloomy so they tried to cheer things up. And they have changed the entrance drive from the porch side into garden-beds.'

For the first time Lord Monaghan made a sign of interest. 'May I ask why they did that?'

'Same reason, I suppose.'

Both of them relapsed into dreamy silence bolstered by the cushions of a French express. It was the same picture of Irish landscape which both men were visioning behind their closing eyelids: a three-storeyed grey old castle with a windowless tower at the back, and a heavy porch on the west or windward side. Large sash-windows opened out of the walls. Whatever had been the ancient castellation it had given way to battered chimneys built of brick. But no repairs or additions could make it appear modern. It had a bare and bleak aspect and even after dark when it was illuminated by oil lamps within, it resembled a skull with lucifer matches burning behind the grey partitions of the bonework.

It was the same old building which both men visioned until the agreeable call came for lunch and they both moved down the corridor into the restaurant. Conversation broke out afresh. My uncle kept it to subjects which he thought must be agreeable as well as interesting to Lord Monaghan. It was the old diplomat who suddenly brought the talk back to Mullymore. They had been talking about the coincidences that were most difficult to explain in life but such as are bound to occur once or twice in everybody's experience. Lord Monaghan said that in his long career only once had the inexplicable crossed him, but with results which had reappeared during his life like an echo. It bordered on the supernatural and had convinced him that there could be occasions when four and four would fail to total eight. In other words there were times when the rules of mathematics did not apply to the logic of life.

'When I was a young man struggling between the University and the Foreign Office,' continued Lord Monaghan, 'I went to stay at Mullymore. It was a very long time ago. The old Dowager was still alive and her four daughters were in waiting upon her, and perhaps in waiting for husbands as well, though they did not seem to mind whether they ever got away from the old castle. It appeared to have laid a hand of possession on them all. People may claim that they own houses out of the past, but I have often known such houses entirely possess their inhabitants. Mullymore was one of them.

'I was entertained with old-world hospitality. The son of the family acted as my host. I was not worried to play games. I was left entirely to myself, for which I was grateful. I recall it all as though it were yesterday. The old Dowager sitting there with her ear-trumpet clashing against her soiled old family jewellery. She directed me to the Porch room, a long, chilly chamber, which looked out upon the drive as it used to be. You say that it has been changed around, do you not? Well, hereby may hang a tale. Towards the end of my last afternoon we were all sitting in the drawing-room. The five ladies were delicately administering tea to the two men present when we all heard the sound of carriage wheels on the drive, but so clearly that it raised no doubt. There was a noise of solid gravel being crunched and the regular stroke of horses' hoofs. All came to a halt outside the porch.

'The old lady looked up and mentioned that she could not imagine who would want to be calling that day. Nobody was invited or expected. And if I remember correctly, she added that nobody was wanted. A few minutes passed without anybody appearing. She rang the bell for the major-domo and ordered him to show in whoever the visitors might be. He returned to say that there was none waiting in the porch and that the bell had never been rung from the outside. At this the old lady turned pale but maintained her courage. 'This,' she said, 'is very sad for our family', before she relapsed into silence. You can guess from other stories you have heard that it was a manner of death-warning.

'But the supernatural aspect did not dawn on me until an hour later, though the warning by ghostly carriage wheels is told of more than one Irish family. It is only the sequel which is interesting in this case. The old lady refused to be upset, sitting over her tea for an hour but still looking as white as her cap of white lace. The young ladies continued to make tea assiduously for the non-arriving guests and I myself carried on a faint conversation until the usual hour for retiring to our rooms, when the gong rang bidding us to dress for dinner. On our way upstairs my host observed to me that he had very distinctly heard the carriage wheels on the drive, and asked me my opinion. I answered that I had heard them no less. He then casually informed me that they had a family Banshee: that whenever a member of their family was about to die, however distantly related, a carriage was always rolling up the drive, although it was never seen.

'The legend went back several generations. The origin was simple enough. An ancestor had been killed returning home from

Dublin when his high carriage crashed behind drunken postillions. It those days travellers were as much in the hands of their postillions as they are in the power of chauffeurs today. His wife had been expecting him all day and when she heard, as she believed, his wheels outside the porch she had run out eagerly to find nobody. The same day her husband had been killed the other side of Drogheda.'

Lord Monaghan recalled the deep impression this simple and not uncommon story of the supernatural had made upon him. But he had never learnt which member of the family had perished in answer to the particular warning he had heard. Some very distant cousin possibly, but he had not stayed to hear. That was his last night at Mullymore. What happened after dinner was as follows. He went to bed in the Porch room the same as on preceding nights, when he was awakened by the same chariot wheels on the gravel which had disturbed the house-party at the tea hour. He turned over to sleep but was roused by the same sound again. He sat up and realised that he was far from dreaming. The noise of horses on the gravel was as distinct as the ticking of his watch. He had the strength of nerve to find his way to the window and, as he might have expected, he caught sight of an old-fashioned coach poised on its high wheels. Uncertain whether it was an optical illusion caused by the glass or not, he opened the window. There could be little doubt of the reality presented to his visual senses, for the sound of voices reached him from below. He watched and saw two men carrying a shapeless mass from the porch into the carriage. He was caught in the fascination of the moment which seemed to be drawn out timelessly. It might have taken a few seconds and it might have occupied half an hour, but he kept his senses. When the black mass, which he vaguely recognised as a coffin, had been pushed on board the chariot, the two men climbed to the seats behind and gave the order to proceed.

Then Lord Monaghan observed that there was a coachman on the box who turned deliberately round and looking up caught him full in the eye, and said in words never to be forgotten: *Il y a place encore pour un.* Every word was clearly enunciated in French, but why in French? Lord Monaghan thought that he must have been more receptive in that language at that time, for he had been working very hard for his examinations at the Foreign Office. All those days he was thinking and dreaming in French. This might account for any subconscious revelation reaching him in that language. But to the end of his life he believed he had been awake all the time. He distinctly remembered walking round and round the room long after the carriage had disappeared, rumbling away like any other carriage on its wheels. The next morning he had left Mullymore never to return.

Fifty years had passed since he had enjoyed as great a career as a man with good fortune and fair talents could expect. He had had all that the world could offer him. He had accepted the standards, the conventions, and the diplomacy of the world. Even the religion of the world he found matter of fact and accepted as part of the international structure it was his duty to preserve. But there was something running through his life, it was true with considerable gaps, which was not matter of fact. It was simply that those words which he had heard uttered in the Porch room in that distant Irish castle had not exactly haunted him, but from time to time he had heard them re-uttered with no little import to his career. For intervals of years he entirely forgot the words. He might hear and use them himself without recalling anything strange in the past, but there were strange occasions when they sounded like an echo of destiny.

He would give a few instances. When he was a young Secretary at the Foreign Office, he was intensely anxious to be included in an embassage which was being sent out at the time to the East. It was a joint expedition shared by the French and promised some months of novelty in the East as well as assuring a step to all who were its partakers. Feeling that his career might pivot from his inclusion he applied for even the lowest position. There were two Secretaries to be chosen to accompany the English plenipotentiaries. He relied on his record, his examinations and his hard work, but he had no string he could pull in his own favour. An anxious moment arrived when the Minister for Foreign Affairs himself decided who were to go. So anxious was he that he spent the morning pacing the passage outside the Minister's room in mingled dread and hope. He watched the French representatives arrive and depart. An Under-Secretary had promised to let him know as soon as the decision was made in the inner councils. Well, his friend had appeared and told him that the other two Secretaries had been chosen over his head, but that his claims had been highly considered. As he stifled his disappointment and walked down the corridor he met the French representative returning on his tracks to tell the Foreign Secretary that as the French were including a Commercial Secretary beyond their quota of two there was room for another Englishman. He heard him as he disappeared behind the door say to his friend the Under-Secretary: '*Mais il y a place encore pour un.*'

The moment he heard those syllables he felt no more doubt, anxiety or disappointment. The words seemed to ring in his ears like the bell of good luck. He felt no surprise the following day when he was asked officially to join the embassage, and from that moment in his career he had never looked back.

There were a dozen other times in his life when those same words had rung out and always by the necessity of circumstances in French. He had always been able to associate their occurrence with some startling event in his life: at least every time that the words affected him. There must have been many unimportant occasions when he had heard the phrase as a phrase during his many years spent in Paris, but these he did not remember.

But the strangest occasion of all had been in Paris and that he could never forget. He had gone out to pay a visit to some French friends living in the fifth storey of an apartment house. It was a good many years back and the new system of American elevators had been recently introduced into European capitals. The liftman had taken him successfully up. It was almost a novel sensation in those days. After using this mechanical means of ascent to the fifth floor Lord Monaghan paid his intended visit and an hour later prepared to return to the Embassy, where he was quartered. The lift was descending from a higher floor. The lift appeared to be already full, and though the gates were swung open he had hesitated to enter. The people in the lift had shuffled a little, and the liftman called out in the most natural voice: '*Il y a place encore pour un!*' So quietly and naturally did the liftman pronounce his words that they raised no immediate tremor of memory in Lord Monaghan's mind. He already had one foot in the lift and was raising himself on the other when he caught sight of the liftman's face, and their eyes met full. Thoughts and memories passed with colliding force in the space of a hundredth of a second. It was a face he had seen before, and those were eyes into which he had once looked with wondering fear, but how long ago? And where? Was it an ancient dream? . . . And there swam back into memory an old Irish castle with a carriage drive running up to the porch. Thirty or forty years were as yesterday, and he remembered the features of the driver on the box of the phantom coach at Mullymore Castle. His second foot was already in the air but not in the lift, but he had the strength of mind subconsciously exerted to hurl himself backwards and to remain on the landing while the lift with quickly closing doors sped swiftly downward. There was a broken brake and the lift crashed . . . Everybody in the lift, including the liftman, was killed . . .

THE PORTRAIT OF
ROISIN DHU

Dorothy Macardle

In the history of horror movies, The Uninvited, *which was made in 1944 and based on a novel by Dorothy Macardle, has a unique place. For after the ground-breaking series of hugely successful films made by Universal Pictures in the early Thirties—including* Dracula, Frankenstein *and* The Invisible Man—The Uninvited *was 'the first major horror film released by a big studio since the 1930s', according to Timothy Sullivan in* The Penguin Encyclopedia of Horror and the Supernatural *(1986). The story concerns a brother and sister who rent a house and discover it is haunted by the ghost of a dead woman. When all attempts to explain the haunting by logic have failed, the couple are forced to call in an exorcist to get rid of the spirit which finally materialises in the terrifying final scenes as a glowing blob of ectoplasm. Ray Milland, Ruth Hussey and Gail Russell starred as the central characters in the film which remained remarkably faithful to Dorothy Macardle's original novel.*

Dorothy Marguerita Callan Macardle (1899–1958) was born in Dundalk and led a rousing and frequently dramatic life as a social and political activist. From her youth she was deeply committed to nationalism as a result of meeting W. B. Yeats and George Russell. Later she took part in the Irish Nationalist Movement and in 1922 was imprisoned in Mountjoy Gaol for her activities. It was there that she first began to write a number of ghost stories, and although her fame was to come from a 1,000-page history of Ireland, The Irish Republic *(1951), with its preface by the Prime Minister Eamon de Valera, the supernatural and horror were themes to which she returned regularly during the rest of her life in plays, novels and short stories. Another of her major works was* Children of Europe *(1949) which she wrote after travelling all over Europe investigating the plight of refugees in the aftermath of the Second World War. Apart from the success of* The Uninvited, *which sold over half a million copies before and after the film, she also wrote* Fantastic Summer *(1946), about extra-sensory perception, and* Dark Enchantment *(1953), a story of sorcery set in the French Alps. Here she is represented by one of the stories she wrote while in Mountjoy, a haunting tale about a mysterious painting and the effect it has on both the artist and his model . . .*

*   *   *

It was a year after the artist was drowned that the loan exhibition of Hugo Blake's paintings was opened in Philadelphia by Maeve. 'Whom the gods love die young,' people said.

To remember those paintings is like remembering a dream-life spent with the Ever-living in an Ireland untrodden by men.

Except once he never painted a human face or any form of life, human or fairy, yet the very light and air of them thrilled with life—it was as though he had painted life itself. There was the great 'Sliav Gullion'—stony, austere—the naked mountain against the northern sky, and to look at it was to be filled with a young, fierce hunger for heroic deeds, with the might of Cuchulain and Fionn. There was 'Loch Corrib' like a mirage from the first day of Creation—there was Una's 'Dawn' . . .

The critics, inarticulate with wonder, made meaningless phrases: 'Blake paints as a seer,' 'He paints on the astral plane.'

At the end of the room, alone on a grey wall, hung the 'Portrait of Roisin Dhu'. Before her, Irish men and women stood worshipping, the old with tears, the young with fire in their eyes. There were men whom it sent home.

Had Blake seen, anywhere on earth, others were asking, that heart-breaking, entrancing face? Knowledge of the secrets of God was in the eyes; on the lips was the memory, the endurance and the foreknowledge of endless pain; yet from the luminous, serene face shone out a beauty that made one crave for the spaces beyond death.

No woman in the world, we said, had been Hugo's Roisin Dhu; no mortal face had troubled him when he painted that immortal dream—that ecstasy beyond fear, that splendour beyond anguish—that wild, sweet holiness of Ireland for which men die.

Maeve, as we knew, had been his old friend. When strangers clamoured, 'Was there a woman?' she would not tell. But one evening when we were five only around Una's fire she told us the strange, incredible tale.

'I will not tell everyone for a while,' she said, 'because so few would understand, and Hugo, unless one understood to the heights and depths, might seem to have been . . . unkind. But I will tell you: There was a girl.'

'It is almost impossible to believe,' Liam said; 'It is not a human body he has painted; nor even a human soul!'

'That is true in a way,' Maeve answered, hesitating; 'I will try to make you understand.

'He was the loneliest being I have ever known. He was a little atom of misery and rebellion when my godmother rescued him in France. She bought the child from a drunkard who was starving him almost to death. His mother, you know, was Nora Raftery, the actress; she ran away from her husband with François Raoul, taking the child, and died. Poor Blake rode over a precipice while hunting—mad with grief, and the boy was left without a friend in the world. It was I who taught him to read and write: already he could draw.

To the end he was the same passionate, lonely child. The anguish of pity and love he had had for his mother he gave to her country when he came home: he suffered unbearable 'heim-weh' all the years he was studying abroad. The 'Dark Tower' as we called it, of our godmother's house on Loch Corrib was the place he loved best.

I have known no one who lived in such extremes, always, of misery or of joy. In any medium but paint he was helpless— chaotic or dumb, yet I think that his pictures came to him first not visually at all, but as intense perceptions of a *mood*. And between that moment of perception and the moment when it took form and colour in his mind he used to be like a wild creature in pain. He would prowl day and night around the region he meant to paint, waiting in a rage of impatience for the right moment of light and shadow to come, the incarnation of the soul . . . Then, when he had found it, the blessed mood of contentment would come and he would paint, day after day, until it was done. At those times, in the evenings, he would be exhausted and friendly and grateful like a child.

For all the vehemence that you feel in his work he painted very slowly, with intense, exquisite care, like a man in love. That is indeed what he was—in love, obliviously, with whatever spirit had enthralled his imagination at the time. And when the picture was finished and the vision gone he fell into a mood of desolation in which he wanted to die. He was very young.

I tried to scold Hugo out of those moods. I was with him in April just after he had finished his 'Loch Corrib'—you know the innocence, the angelic tranquillity in it, like the soul of a child. He would not go near the lake: 'It is nothing to me now,' he said sombrely, 'I have done with it.'

'Hugo!' I said, laughing, 'you are a vampire! The loch has given you its soul.' He answered, 'Yes: that is true; corpses are ugly things.'

For a month that empty, dead mood lasted and Hugo hated all the world. I took him to London to give him something to hate. After two days he fled back to his tower and breathed the smell of the peat and sea-wind, and the sweet, home-welcome of burning turf, and looked out on Ireland with eyes of love. The next morning he came in from a bathe in the loch with the awakened, wondering look I had longed to see and said, 'I am going to paint Roisin Dhu.' Then he went off to walk the west of Ireland seeking a woman for his need.

I was astonished and excited beyond words; he had been so contemptuous of human subjects, although I remembered, in his student days, studies for heads and hands that had made one artist whisper, 'Leonardo!' under his breath.

I wondered what woman he would bring home.

They came about two weeks later, after dark, rowing over the loch, Hugo and the girl alone.

After supper, sitting over the turf fire in the round hall of the tower, Hugo told me that she was the daughter of a king.

She smiled at him, knowing that he spoke of her although she had no English at all, and I told her in Irish what he had said. She answered gravely, 'It is true.'

I looked at her then as she moved from the window to her chair, and I felt almost afraid—her beauty was so delicate and so remote . . .

'Those red lips with all their mournful pride' . . . Poems of Yeats were haunting me while I looked at her. But it was the beauty of one asleep, unaware of life or of sorrow or of love . . . the face of a woman whose light is hidden . . .

She sat in the shadowed corner, brooding, while Hugo talked. He was at his happiest, overflowing with childish delight in his achievement and with eagerness for tomorrow's sun.

Nuala was her name. The King of the Blasket Isles was her father—a superstitious, tyrannical old man. Hugo had been able to make no way with him or his sons.

'I invited one of them to come too, and take care of her,' he said, 'but they would not hear of it at all.

'The old man was as dignified as a Spanish Grandee.

' "It is not that I would be misdoubting you, honest man," says he, "but my daughter is my daughter and there is no call for her to be going abroad to the world."

'And her brothers was as obstinate:

' " 'Tis not good to be put in a picture: it takes from you," they said.'

'They got me into a boat by a ruse, rowed me "back to Ireland", and when they had landed me pulled off.

' "The blessing of God on your far travelling!" they called to me gravely: a hint that I would not be welcome to the island again.

'You can imagine the frenzy I was in!' he said. And I could, well. He had walked night after night on the rocks of the mainland planning some desperate thing, but one night Nuala came to him, rowed out through the darkness by some boys who braved the vengeance of the old king for her sake. He rewarded them extravagantly and brought Nuala home.

He told it all triumphantly, and Nuala looked up at him from time to time with a gentle gaze full of content and rest. But my heart sank: there was only one possible end to this; Hugo, at his best, was loving and kind and selfless—all might be well—but I knew my Hugo after work.

She slept in my room and talked to me, softly, in the dark, asking me questions about Hugo's work. 'He told me you were his sister-friend,' she said.

I told her about his childhood, his suffering and his genius: she listened and sighed.

'It is a pity of him to be so long lonely,' she said, 'but he will not be lonely any more.'

'Why, Nuala?' I asked, my heart heavy with dread for her. Her answer left me silent.

'I myself will be giving him love.'

Hugo had found a being as lost to the world as himself. How would it end for her, I wondered. She slept peacefully, but I lay long awake.

The next morning work began in the studio at the top of the tower. I gave up all thought of going home. Nuala would need me.

Hugo was working faster than usual it seemed, beginning as soon as the light was clear and never pausing until it failed. I marvelled at Nuala's endurance, but I dared not plead for her. I had wrecked a picture of Hugo's once by going into his studio while he painted: his vision fled from him at the least intrusion and I had learned to keep aloof.

Day after day, when they came down at last to rest and eat, I could measure his progress by the sombre glow of power in his eyes. I could imagine some young druid when his spells proved potent, looking like that.

But the change that came over Nuala frightened me; he was wearing her away: her face had a clear, luminous look, her eyes were large and dark; I saw an expression in them sometimes as of one gazing into an abyss of pain. The change that might come to a lovely woman in years, seemed to come to her in days: the beauty of her, as she sat in the candle-light, gazing at her own thoughts in the shadows, would still your breathing. It grew more wonderful, more tragic, from day to day.

One night after she had stolen away to bed, exhausted, while Hugo sat by the fire in a kind of trance, I forced myself to question him.

'Hugo,' I said, as lightly as I could, with my heart throbbing: 'Is it that you are in love with your Roisin Dhu?'

He looked up suddenly, with a dark fire in his eyes. 'Love,' he whispered in a voice aching with passion. He rose and threw back his head and cried out in tones like deep music—

'I could plough the blue air!
I could climb the high hills!

O, I could kneel all night in prayer
To heal your many ills!'

Then he sighed and went away.

Nuala's look was becoming, day by day, a look of endurance and resignation that I could not bear, as of one despairing of all human happiness yet serene.

At last I questioned him again:

'Will you be marrying your Roisin Dhu?'

He turned on me startled, with a laugh, both angry and amazed.

'What a question! What an outrageous question, Maeve!'

I was unanswered still.

When seven weeks had gone I grew gravely anxious. I feared that Nuala would die: she had the beauty you could imagine in a spirit new-awakened from death, a look of anguish and ecstasy in one . . . She was frail and spent; she scarcely spoke to me or seemed to know me; she slept always in the garden alone.

It was towards the end of June that I said to Hugo, 'You are wearing your model out.'

'I am painting her better than God created her,' he answered. Then he said, contentedly, 'I shall have done with her very soon.'

I cannot express the dread that fell on me then; I was torn with irresolution. To interfere with Hugo—to break the spell of his vision, would not only sacrifice the picture, it might destroy him. I thought his reason would not survive the laceration, the passion that would follow the shattering of that dream.

That night I found Nuala utterly changed. She came down from the studio dull-eyed and ugly and went straight to bed in my room.

Hugo told me he did not want her any more.

I rowed her out next morning across the loch: it was one of those grey, misty days when it is loveliest; the Twelve Bens in the distance looked like mountains of Hy Breasail, the weeds and sedges glimmering silvery-gold . . . but she had no eyes for its beauty, no beauty of her own, no light . . . she lay drowsy and unresponsive on her cushions; her hands and face were like wax.

I would have rebelled that night, taken any risk, to make Hugo undo what he had done. She lay down to sleep under a willow by the water's edge and I went to him in the hall. He was standing by the fire and turned to me as I came in; there was a look of wondering humility in his face, as if his own achievement were a thing to worship—a thing he could not understand.

'Tomorrow!' he said: 'It will be finished in an hour: you shall see it.' Then he came and took my hands in his old, affectionate way and said:

'You have been such a good sister-friend!'

One hour more! She must endure it: I would not sacrifice him for that. But I lay awake all night oppressed with a sense of fear and cruelty and guilt.

At breakfast time there was no Hugo: he had eaten and started work. Old Kate rang the bell in the garden but Nuala did not come. My fears had vanished with the sweet air and sunshine of the early morning: larks were singing; it was mid-June: the joy of Hugo's triumph was my own joy. I went down to the willow where I had left Nuala asleep. She was lying there still; she never stirred when I touched her. She was cold.

I called no one, I ran madly up the spiral stair to Hugo's studio in the tower. Outside his door I paused: the memory of the last time I had broken in and the devastating consequences arrested me even then. I pushed the door open without a sound and stood inside, transfixed.

I looked for a moment and grew dizzy, so amazing was the thing I saw. Hugo stood by his easel: before him on the dais, glimmering in the misty silver light, stood Nuala, gazing at him, all a radiance of consummated sacrifice and sweet, unconquerable love—Nuala, as you have seen her in the portrait of Roisin Dhu.

Hugo stumbled, laid down his brush, drew his hand over his eyes, then turned and, seeing me, said, 'It is done.'

When I looked again at the dais she was gone.

I was shaken to the heart with fear. I cried out, 'Come to her! She is dead.'

He ran with me down to the water's edge.

I believe I had hoped that he would be able to waken her, but she was cold and dead, lying with wide-open eyes.

Hugo knelt down and touched her, then rose quickly and turned away: 'How unbeautiful!' he said.

I called out to him sternly, angrily, and he looked down at her again, then stooped and lifted her in his arms.

'Maeve, Maeve!' he cried then, piteously: 'Have I done this?'

He brought her home with state to the Island, told them she

had been his bride and gave her such a burial as the old King's heart approved. Then he came home again to his lonely house. I left it before he came; he had told me he wanted to be alone.

I heard nothing of him then for a long time and felt uneasy and afraid. After I had written many anxious letters a strange, disjointed answer came.

'She has never left me,' he wrote. 'She is waiting, near, quite near. But what can I do? This imprisoning body—this suffocating life—this burdenous mortality—this dead world.

'The picture is for you, Sister-friend, and for Ireland when you die.'

Before I could go to him the picture came and with it the news that he was drowned.

They found the boat far out on the loch.'

Maeve's face was pale when she ended: she covered her eyes for a moment with her hand.

'He had seen the hidden vision . . .' one of us said.

Nesta was looking into the fire, her dark eyes wide with foreboding.

'It is written in Destiny,' she said: 'the lovers of Roisin Dhu must die.'

DANSE MACABRE

L. A. G. Strong

*For years a familiar voice to radio listeners was that of L. A. G.
Strong reading short stories—many of them his own—and cleverly
employing the dialects of his native Ireland. He had a similar facility
for imitating the Scottish accent and, later, that of the Devonshire
folk among whom he settled during the closing years of his life. All
Strong's broadcasts were unmistakable for their brilliant bursts of
description and a breathless robustness which caused one critic to
declare of him, 'He has a variety of talents, clear simplicity of style,
passion, wit and shrewd observation.' He was also a superlative
short story writer and, according to another reviewer, 'a master of
stories about murder and sudden death'.*

*Leonard Alfred George Strong (1896–1958) came from an Irish
Protestant family and, after graduating, wrote a novel,* Dewer Rides
*(1929), which was an overnight success. He followed this with a
string of crime novels featuring Chief Detective Inspector McKay,
'the composer detective', and his assistant Inspector Bradstreet, as
well as biographies of such leading Irish literary figures as Tom
Moore, J. M. Synge and James Joyce, which earned him membership of the Irish Academy of Letters. But it is for his short fiction
that L. A. G. Strong undoubtedly remains best known in Ireland
and elsewhere. A number of his tales were first published in American periodicals such as* Harper's Magazine, The Century *and*
Atlantic Monthly, *and one of them, 'Breakdown', about a murder
in suburban England, was a favourite of the horror film star Boris
Karloff (himself English-born), who said of it that he 'never
expected to read a more truly shocking description of a simple
stabbing.' Strong's talent as a raconteur was shared by one of
his most enduring characters, Mr Mangan, an Irishman with a
seemingly endless store of tales, many of them with a horror or*

supernatural content, which he related at any opportunity. 'Danse Macabre' is one such yarn and starts in the pleasant surroundings of an Irish village dance—but soon begins to build inexorably to a finale that would surely also have impressed the great Boris Karloff . . .

*   *   *

'Tell me,' said Mr Mangan, 'do you dance?'

'Seldom,' I answered. 'They discourage me.'

'Who discourage ye?'

'My female relatives.'

Mr Mangan made no comment on this. Evidently he was not interested in my performance, and had only raised the subject in order to introduce some reminiscence of his own.

'Now, you are an observant man, too damned observant I think sometimes. Did you ever observe old Flanagan?'

'You mean the shopkeeper down there in the village?'

'Yerra, who else would I mean?'

Mr Mangan filled his pipe and lit it.

Some thirty years ago—he said—that same Flanagan was the handsomest-looking young divil, the most indefatigable sower of wild oats, in ten parishes. He dressed to distraction, he spent like a lord, and half the girls in the place were crazy about him. He laughed from morning to night, he danced like a puma, you saw him at every race-meeting, aye, and he was lucky too. It was a series of solid wins that set him up in the hardware business.

One night we'd a Red Cross dance above in the school. Mrs Mangan and I were there in our official capacity, and there was young Flanagan, in a six-guinea suit and gloves, and bedamn, it was a treat to see him. He danced with a dozen different girls, and there were their mothers, sitting over against the walls, like old pike watching a school of innocent young migratory frogs.

We'd a kind of a bar rigged up where the schoolmaster usually presides, with ices, mineral waters, tea, and such. As for the intelligentsia, all they had to do was to sneak out of the back door and up the lane into the 'Coach and Horses'.

Mrs Mangan was dispensing at the bar, and I seemed to be achieving little except getting in young people's way, when suddenly I noticed a new face. I thought I knew everyone in the room, but this particular city-bred-looking piece of feminine fragility seemed a new-comer. I find it hard to describe her, except that she had a Burne-Jones look—pre-Raphaelite—you know, the sort that the lachrymose artists of that time loved to depict floating on their back in green swamps, or streeling by the dozen up interminable staircases dressed in limp nightshirts.

This girl wore a long gauze sort of a frock with a necklace of imitation pearls. She had golden shoes on, with high heels, and to tell you the truth I thought she looked a bit out of date. She was leaning against the far end of the bar counter, and she seemed breathless, though I hadn't noticed her dancing.

I made my way along to the wife.

'Who's that pretty girl?' I asked her. 'The one with the yellow frock. Look—over there.'

Mrs Mangan took one look and went on serving out the tea.

'Listen to me,' she said, out of the side of her mouth. 'This is a highly respectable dance. It's been got up in aid of the Red Cross, and not for the benefit of the "Coach and Horses".'

Well, there were too many people around, and I couldn't argue with her. But for the moment she gave me quite a turn, as she often can.

However, I was sober all right, I know that. The girl was there in front of me; she was no hallucination. I resolved to go and speak to her, ask if she was enjoying herself, or could I get her something. I hoped the wife would see me, too. It would serve her right.

Before I could get to the girl, however, young Flanagan swept down on her with a flash and a smile, and before you could say snipe he had her swirling around to the strains of the 'Destiny' waltz.

I watched them going round the floor, the girl and young Flanagan, he laughing and talking and bending over her, and she half-responding, but with a sort of a look—I thought maybe it was my fancy—as if it wasn't of this night she was thinking, but of other nights long past, other partners, other waltzes. It's hard to be sure, afterwards, what you remember and what you put in from later knowledge.

Towards the end of the evening I was busy with my official duties, and couldn't keep an eye on them. I didn't see them again till the dance was done. There were but two motor-cars in the place then, and one of them still survives—Sheehy the baker's. The other belonged to Flanagan, a red, noisy, rackety affair which he got second-hand in town for seventy-five pounds. As I left the school-room, after putting out the lights, I saw Flanagan, and the lady beside him, crash off in the car with a sound of guns and thunder, and he with his handsome head thrown back, roaring with laughter.

Do ye know the road from here to town? Ye do? Then ye'll know the little cemetery, perched on the top of the hill: a few tombstones and a rusty iron gate. You may have wondered in your innocence why that spot was chosen for a graveyard. Rural economy, me boy. There's little to be got by ploughing and growing swedes or potatoes on a stony hill, but sure, it'll be a handy spot for a take-off when Gabriel blows his horn.

Well—to come back to Flanagan. I didn't see him for ten days or a fortnight after the dance. I heard afterwards he went on a jag up in town, and it was over a week before he came back, with no red car. It must have been the father and mother of a jag, I thought, for he seemed to have sobered up for good. He bought the shop where he is now, and settled down very seriously to business. But it didn't look to be doing him much benefit: before the year was out everyone was talking about the change in his appearance. His hair was greying, indeed it was going white on him; his face was yellow and wrinkled like a turkey's neck, his good looks fled before your eyes, and faith, now that financially he was a real sound catch, it seemed plain that he was safe from matrimony for ever.

After he'd been settled down into a busy confirmed shopkeeper for two or three years he became one of four typhoid cases we had in the village, the only cases we ever had that I remember. Aye, and he was the only one who survived. The sickness didn't improve his looks, as you can believe.

Listen now to what I'm going to tell ye. Ye know Mrs Mangan, and ye'll know I'm speaking without prejudice when I say that she's never so happy as when she's helping some poor divil who can't help himself. Well, Flanagan was over the killing part of the sickness, but he was very feeble, he'd no one to tend him, and it didn't look as if he'd stay the course. So Mrs Mangan persuaded him to come to our place and lie about and convalesce; and she got a cousin of hers, a lad with a red beard as long as your arm, who'd been in the grocery business and made a packet and retired to enjoy it, only being a miserable sort of a divil he didn't enjoy anything very much—she persuaded this boyo to come and look after Flanagan's business while he was laid by. By the same token, the cousin got rid of four gross of tin plates that had been duds with Flanagan ever since he opened the place. The long bearded lad sent them away, had them enamelled white, then splattered the whole window with them at sixpence apiece, and bedad in a week there wasn't one left.

But Flanagan. The wife fed him like a prize-fighter, and after six weeks he was able to be up and out and taking the air in my donkey-and-trap. The donkey got more exercise than he was used to or indeed tolerated, and yet he grew fat as a barrel. I couldn't make it out. Then I found Flanagan used to buy carrots and apples and sugar-sticks for his trips, and feed the donkey.

One autumn night, we were sitting in front of the fire, the wife and I and Flanagan, with his big forgetting eyes staring into last year. There'd been something in the paper about a fire at a dance hall, and all of sudden the wife speaks to him, without looking up from her sewing.

'Tell me, Mr Flanagan,' says she. 'I've often wondered. Mangan here had a story of you driving away, after that last Red Cross dance we had, with a pretty girl in yellow. He insists that he pointed her out to me at the time, but, faith, I thought he'd been to the "Coach and Horses".'

Flanagan had gone stiff as she spoke. Then he relaxed and let a long sigh out of him.

'I'm glad you asked me that, Mrs Mangan. It'll be a relief to tell someone. Oh yes, she was with me all right. I danced several dances with her. She was queer and absent, but she excited me, she was different from any other girl I'd met. At first she was so vague and elusive, I wondered, God forgive me, I wondered if her vagueness came from some young man's hip pocket. I asked her name and address, and she gave me them: Maud Gillie was the name, and an address in—well, never mind the address.

'I was smitten and piqued: I wasn't used to being treated in this offhand way, and when the dance was over I asked might I drive her home. Yes, she said, yes; just like that; more of a shrug of the shoulders.

'I tucked her up in my rug, and we set off. She didn't speak. When we'd driven maybe ten minutes in the white moonlight, at the top of the hill there, at Finstown, a bit short of the graveyard, she turned to me. "Let me down here," she said.

'We're not home yet, I said. I thought she was half asleep. "Let me down, please," she repeated. What? I said. Here, by the old graveyard? "Let me down at once," she said, "or I'll go."

'I pulled up, there was such strain in her voice. Maybe she was feeling ill, I thought. We were right by the graveyard gate. I jumped out, and hurried round to open the door for her and let her out. For three seconds, maybe, I had my eyes off her. You won't believe me, either of you—but when I got round to open the door, the car was empty.'

Mrs Mangan and I stared at him. I felt my spine creep.

'Empty,' he said. 'There was the seat, cold, filled with moonlight. I looked around, Not a sign or sound. Maud Gillie had gone. Disappeared. Evaporated.

'I don't know how long I stood there, like a frozen man. Silence. Clear, cold moonlight. I think I must have lost my head. I told myself there was an explanation. I jumped back into the car, and drove like mad to town. I drove to the address she'd given me, and pulled the bell, but there was no answer. Almost out of my mind, I looked for an hotel. I found one, ill lit. I parked the car outside, I got a bed. Did I sleep? Faith I did not. I tossed and tumbled and shivered the night through.

'Morning came, and a fine dismal rain, the rain you get at a funeral. I could eat no breakfast. As soon as I decently could, I went out and came to Maud Gillie's house. I rang, and rang, and I knocked. At last a slatternly girl opened the door, but she showed no disposition to let me in. While we parleyed on the step, an elderly woman came down the hall. She was dressed in faded and shabby black, with a sort of filmy wrap round her neck.

'"Well," she said, "and what do you want, young man, at this hour of the morning?"

'"You are Mrs Gillie, ma'am, are you?"

'"I am. And what of it, pray?"

'Then I told her about the dance, and how I'd started to drive her daughter home, and had somehow lost her.

'"She made me let her down there, at Finstown, by the grave-yard, ma'am. I couldn't find her again. I was terribly anxious. I—

I came to see if in some miraculous way she had got home."

'I backed away then, for the grim old woman had advanced till her chest was almost touching my own. Her face was convulsed and terrifying. She gave a shrill, thin squeal, like a rabbit caught by a stoat.

'"Get out of this, you infernal young blackguard!" she cried.

'"Ma'am! ma'am!" I backed down the steps. "I'm sorry. I only came to inquire was your daughter all right."

'"All right? All right?"

'She came out after me, and stood on the top step. I could see the drizzle falling against her black dress.

'"The fine daughter she was, with her dances and her gallivantings. I told her she'd pay for it. She was killed, you young fool, killed in a drunken car crash, and I buried her in that cemetery at Finstown. Now get out of here, or I'll call the police.'

'I fled,' said Flanagan to us. 'I sold the car, and spent the money in a way I'm bitterly ashamed of: but I had to try to forget, or I'd have lost my reason, I think. Look at my hair, Mrs Mangan. You see what that night did for me. I was never the same after it.

'Well, I'm glad to have told you both. You've been the soul of kindness to me. I'm nearly well again now. I'll be able to relieve your cousin next Monday, Mrs Mangan, I hope. And now, if you'll excuse me, I'll go up to my bed.'

'He went up,' said Mr Mangan, 'and he left the two of us staring at each other across the fireplace. Well—you'll come to the dance next week, won't you?'

THE HAPPY AUTUMN FIELDS

Elizabeth Bowen

Writing in the preface to a collection of her stories, A Day In The Dark *(1965), Elizabeth Bowen admitted, 'I do not make use of the supernatural as a get-out; it is inseparable (whether or not it comes to the surface) from my sense of life.' This confession has a particular relevance to the events that occur in 'The Happy Autumn Fields' which, despite its sunny title, is infused with dark elements of lurking unease that grow with every page. The tale was originally written for* The Cornhill Magazine *in 1944 and reflects Elizabeth Bowen's life at the time which was split between war-time London, then suffering from the Blitz, and her ancestral home, Bowen's Court, in County Cork. The reason for these journeys was a closely guarded secret: she was actually making the trips as part of her work for the British Ministry of Information to ascertain Irish attitudes towards the war then nearing its final, decisive period. In London, Mrs Bowen also served as an air raid warden in Blooms-bury and must have valued these visits to Ireland as a welcome respite from the terrors of the nightly German raids. 'The Happy Autumn Fields' is, indeed, about a woman in bombed-out London who finds an album of Victorian photographs and through it is mysteriously linked to a young girl in a nineteenth-century land-scape, who is preoccupied with fears about the future. Although the Irish location is not specifically given, Elizabeth Bowen remarked years later, 'to me it is unshakeably County Cork.'*

Elizabeth Bowen (1899–1973) was born in Dublin but grew up primarily in England after her father suffered a nervous breakdown in 1906. She became a prominent figure in English literary circles, where her short stories and novels such as The Death of the Heart *(1938) were widely praised and very popular with the reading public. However, she regularly renewed her Irish connections by returning to Bowen's Court, and these continued until she was forced to sell her old home in 1959. Sadly, the following year the building was demolished by its new owner. After her death, however, Elizabeth's body was returned to Ireland and buried at Farahay churchyard on the Court's former estate. There are probably few other stories which better demonstrate her mastery of weird fiction than 'The Happy Autumn Fields', and W. J. McCormack has intriguingly suggested in his essay* Irish Gothic and After *(1991) that it 'may well owe something to Sheridan Le Fanu's far more lurid double narrative involving women—the vampire tale,* Camilla . . .'

* * *

The family walking party, though it comprised so many, did not deploy or straggle over the stubble but kept in a procession of threes and twos. Papa, who carried his Alpine stick, led, flanked by Constance and little Arthur. Robert and Cousin Theodore, locked in studious talk, had Emily attached but not quite abreast. Next came Digby and Lucius, taking, to left and right, imaginary aim at rooks. Henrietta and Sarah brought up the rear.

It was Sarah who saw the others ahead on the blond stubble, who knew them, knew what they were to each other, knew their names and knew her own. It was she who felt the stubble under her feet, and who heard it give beneath the tread of the others a continuous different more distant soft stiff scrunch. The field and all these outlying fields in view knew as Sarah knew that they were Papa's. The harvest had been good and was now in: he was satisfied—for this afternoon he had made the instinctive choice of his most womanly daughter, most nearly infant son. Arthur, whose hand Papa was holding, took an anxious hop, a skip and a jump to every stride of the great man's. As for Constance—Sarah could often see the flash of her hat feather as she turned her head, the curve of her close bodice as she turned her torso. Constance gave Papa her attention but not her thoughts, for she had already been sought in marriage.

The landowner's daughters, from Constance down, walked with their beetle-green, mole or maroon skirts gathered up and carried clear of the ground, but for Henrietta, who was still ankle-free. They walked inside a continuous stuffy sound, but left silence behind them. Behind them, rooks that had risen and circled, sun striking blue from their blue-black wings, planed one by one to the earth and settled to peck again. Papa and the boys were dark-clad as the rooks but with no sheen, but for their white collars.

It was Sarah who located the thoughts of Constance, knew what a twisting prisoner was Arthur's hand, felt to the depths of Emily's pique at Cousin Theodore's inattention, rejoiced with Digby and Lucius at the imaginary fall of so many rooks. She fell back, how-ever, as from a rocky range, from the converse of Robert and Cousin Theodore. Most she knew that she swam with love at the nearness of Henrietta's young and alert face and eyes which shone with the sky and queried the afternoon.

She recognised the colour of valediction, tasted sweet sadness, while from the cottage inside the screen of trees wood smoke rose melting pungent and blue. This was the eve of the brothers' return to school. It was like a Sunday; Papa had kept the late afternoon free; all (all but one) encircling Robert, Digby and Lucius, they walked the estate the brothers would not see again for so long. Robert, it could be felt, was not unwilling to return to his books; next year he would go to college like Theodore; to all this they saw he was not the heir. But in Digby and Lucius aiming and popping hid a bodily grief, the repugnance of victims, though these two were further from being heirs than Robert.

Sarah said to Henrietta: 'To think they will not be here tomorrow!'

'*Is* that what you are thinking about?' Henrietta asked, with her subtle taste for the truth.

'More, I was thinking that you and I will be back again by one another at table . . .'

'You know we are always sad when the boys are going, but we are never sad when the boys have gone.' The sweet reciprocal guilty smile that started on Henrietta's lips finished on those of Sarah. 'Also,' the young sister said, 'we know this is only some-thing happening again. It happened last year, and it will happen next. But oh how should I feel, and how should you feel, if it were something that had not happened before?'

'For instance, when Constance goes to be married?'

'Oh, I don't mean *Constance*!' said Henrietta.

'So long,' said Sarah, considering, 'as whatever it is, it happens to both of us?' She must never have to wake in the early morning except to the birdlike stirrings of Henrietta, or have her cheek brushed in the dark by the frill of another pillow in whose hollow did not repose Henrietta's cheek. Rather than they should cease to lie in the same bed she prayed they might lie in the same grave. 'You and I will stay as we are,' she said, 'then nothing can touch one without touching the other.'

'So you say; so I hear you say!' exclaimed Henrietta, who then, lips apart, sent Sarah her most tormenting look. 'But I cannot forget that you chose to be born without me; that you would not wait—' But here she broke off, laughed outright and said: 'Oh, see!'

Ahead of them there had been a dislocation. Emily took advantage of having gained the ridge to kneel down to tie her bootlace so abruptly that Digby all but fell over her, with an exclamation. Cousin Theodore had been civil enough to pause beside Emily, but Robert, lost to all but what he was saying, strode on, head down, only just not colliding into Papa and Constance, who had turned to look back. Papa, astounded, let go of Arthur's hand, whereupon Arthur fell flat on the stubble.

'Dear me,' said the affronted Constance to Robert.

Papa said: 'What is the matter there? May I ask, Robert, where you are going, sir? Digby, remember that is your sister Emily.'

'Cousin Emily is in trouble,' said Cousin Theodore.

Poor Emily, telescoped in her skirts and by now scarlet under her hatbrim, said in a muffled voice: 'It is just my bootlace, Papa.'

'Your bootlace, Emily?'

'I was just tying it.'

'Then you had better tie it.—Am I to think,' said Papa, looking round them all, 'that you must all go down like a pack of ninepins because Emily has occasion to stoop?'

At this Henrietta uttered a little whoop, flung her arms round Sarah, buried her face in her sister and fairly suffered with laughter. She could contain this no longer; she shook all over. Papa who found Henrietta so hopelessly out of order that he took no notice of her except at table, took no notice, simply giving the signal for the others to collect themselves and move on. Cousin Theodore, helping Emily to her feet, could be seen to see how her heightened colour became her, but she dispensed with his hand chillily, looked elsewhere, touched the brooch at her throat and said: 'Thank you, I have not sustained an accident.' Digby apologised to Emily, Robert to Papa and Constance. Constance righted Arthur, flicking his breeches over with her handkerchief. All fell into their different steps and resumed their way.

Sarah, with no idea how to console laughter, coaxed, 'Come, come, come,' into Henrietta's ear. Between the girls and the others the distance widened; it began to seem that they would be left alone.

'And why not?' said Henrietta, lifting her head in answer to Sarah's thought.

They looked around them with the same eyes. The shorn uplands seemed to float on the distance, which extended dazzling to tiny blue glassy hills. There was no end to the afternoon, whose light went on ripening now they had scythed the corn. Light filled the silence which, now Papa and the others were out of hearing, was complete. Only screens of trees intersected and knolls made islands in the vast fields. The mansion and the home farm had sunk for ever below them in the expanse of woods, so that hardly a ripple showed where the girls dwelled.

The shadow of the same rook circling passed over Sarah then over Henrietta, who in their turn cast one shadow across the stubble. 'But, Henrietta, He cannot stay here for ever.'

Henrietta immediately turned her eyes to the only lonely plume of smoke, from the cottage. 'Then let us go and visit the poor old man. He is dying and the others are happy. One day we shall pass and see no more smoke; then soon his roof will fall in, and we shall always be sorry we did not go today.'

'But he no longer remembers us.'

'All the same, he will feel us there in the door.'

'But can we forget this is Robert's and Digby's and Lucius's goodbye walk? It would be heartless of both of us to neglect them.'

'Then how heartless Fitzgeorge is!' smiled Henrietta.

'Fitzgeorge is himself, the eldest and in the Army. Fitzgeorge I'm afraid is not an excuse for us.'

A resigned sigh, or perhaps the pretence of one, heaved up Henrietta's still narrow bosom. To delay matters for just a moment more she shaded her eyes with one hand, to search the distance like a sailor looking for a sail. She gazed with hope and zeal in every direction but that in which she and Sarah were bound to go. Then—'Oh, but Sarah, here *they* are, coming—they are!' she

cried. She brought out her handkerchief and began to fly it, drawing it to and fro through the windless air.

In the glass of the distance, two horsemen came into view, can-
tering on a grass track between the fields. When the track dropped
into a hollow they dropped with it, but by now the drumming of
hoofs was heard. The reverberation filled the land, the silence and
Sarah's being; not watching for the riders to reappear she instead
fixed her eyes on her sister's handkerchief which, let hang limp
while its owner intently waited, showed a bitten corner as well as
a damson stain. Again it became a flag, in furious motion.—'Wave
too, Sarah, wave too! Make your bracelet flash!'

'They must have seen us if they will ever see us,' said Sarah,
standing still as a stone.

Henrietta's waving at once ceased. Facing her sister she
crunched up her handkerchief, as though to stop it acting a lie. 'I
can see you are shy,' she said in a dead voice. 'So shy you won't
even wave to *Fitzgeorge*?'

Her way of not speaking the *other* name had a hundred mean-
ings; she drove them all in by the way she did not look at Sarah's
face. The impulsive breath she had caught stole silently out again,
while her eyes—till now at their brightest, their most speaking—
dulled with uncomprehending solitary alarm. The ordeal of awaiting Eugene's approach thus became for Sarah, from moment to
moment, torture.

Fitzgeorge, Papa's heir, and his friend Eugene, the young neighbouring squire, struck off the track and rode up at a trot with their
hats doffed. Sun striking low turned Fitzgeorge's flesh to coral and
made Eugene blink his dark eyes. The young men reined in; the
girls looked up the horses. 'And my father, Constance, the others?'
Fitzgeorge demanded, as though the stubble had swallowed them.

'Ahead, on the way to the quarry, the other side of the hill.'

'We heard you were all walking together,' Fitzgeorge said, seeming dissatisfied.

'We are following.'

'What, alone?' said Eugene, speaking for the first time.

'Forlorn!' glittered Henrietta, raising two mocking hands.

Fitzgeorge considered, said 'Good' severely, and signified to
Eugene that they would ride on. But too late: Eugene had dis-
mounted. Fitzgeorge saw, shrugged and flicked his horse to a trot;
but Eugene led his slowly between the sisters. Or rather, Sarah

walked on his left hand, the horse on his right and Henrietta the other side of the horse. Henrietta, acting like somebody quite alone, looked up at the sky, idly holding one of the empty stirrups. Sarah, however, looked at the ground, with Eugene inclined as though to speak but not speaking. Enfolded, dizzied, blinded as though inside a wave, she could feel his features carved in brightness above her. Alongside the slender stepping of his horse, Eugene matched his naturally long free step to hers. His elbow was through the reins; with his fingers he brushed back the lock that his bending to her had sent falling over his forehead. She recorded the sublime act and knew what smile shaped his lips. So each without looking trembled before an image, while slow colour burned up the curves of her cheeks. The consummation would be when their eyes met.

At the other side of the horse, Henrietta began to sing. At once her pain, like a scientific ray, passed through the horse and Eugene to penetrate Sarah's heart.

We surmount the skyline: the family come into our view, we into theirs. They are halted, waiting, on the decline to the quarry. The handsome statufied group in strong yellow sunshine, aligned by Papa and crowned by Fitzgeorge, turn their judging eyes on the laggards, waiting to close their ranks round Henrietta and Sarah and Eugene. One more moment and it will be too late; no further communication will be possible. Stop oh stop Henrietta's heartbreaking singing! Embrace her close again! Speak the only possible word! Say—oh, say what? Oh, the word is lost!

'Henrietta . . .'

A shock of striking pain in the knuckles of the outflung hand—Sarah's? The eyes, opening, saw that the hand had struck, not been struck: there was a corner of a table. Dust, whitish and gritty, lay on the top of the table and on the telephone. Dull but piercing white light filled the room and what was left of the ceiling; her first thought was that it must have snowed. If so, it was winter now.

Through the calico stretched and tacked over the window came the sound of a piano: someone was playing Tchaikovsky badly in a room without windows or doors. From somewhere else in the hollowness came a cascade of hammering. Close up, a voice: 'Oh, *awake*, Mary?' It came from the other side of the open door, which jutted out between herself and the speaker—he on the threshold, she lying on the uncovered mattress of a bed. The speaker added: 'I had been going away.'

Summoning words from somewhere she said: 'Why? I didn't know you were here.'

'Evidently—Say, who is "Henrietta"?'

Despairing tears filled her eyes. She drew back her hurt hand, began to suck at the knuckle and whimpered, 'I've hurt myself.'

A man she knew to be 'Travis,' but failed to focus, came round the door saying: 'Really I don't wonder.' Sitting down on the edge of the mattress he drew her hand away from her lips and held it: the act, in itself gentle, was accompanied by an almost hostile stare of concern. 'Do listen, Mary,' he said. 'While you've slept I've been all over the house again, and I'm less than ever satisfied that it's safe. In your normal senses you'd never attempt to stay here. There've been alerts, and more than alerts, all day; one more bang anywhere near, which may happen at any moment, could bring the rest of this down. You keep telling me that you have things to see to—but do you know what chaos the rooms are in? Till they've gone ahead with more clearing, where can you hope to start? And if there *were* anything you could do, you couldn't do it. Your own nerves know that, if you don't: it was almost frightening, when I looked in just now, to see the way you were sleeping—you've shut up shop.'

She lay staring over his shoulder at the calico window. He went on: 'You don't like it here. Your self doesn't like it. Your will keeps driving your self, but it can't be driven the whole way—it makes its own get-out: sleep. Well, I want you to sleep as much as you (really) do. But *not* here. So I've taken a room for you in a hotel; I'm going now for a taxi; you can practically make the move without waking up.'

'No, I can't get into a taxi without waking.'

'Do you realise you're the last soul left in the terrace?'

'Then who is that playing the piano?'

'Oh, one of the furniture-movers in Number Six. I didn't count the jaquerie; of course *they're* in possession—unsupervised, teeming, having a high old time. While I looked in on you in here ten minutes ago they were smashing out that conservatory at the other end. Glass being done in in cold blood—it was brutalising. You never batted an eyelid; in fact, I thought you smiled.' He listened.

'Yes, the piano—they are highbrow all right. You know there's a workman downstairs lying on your blue sofa looking for pictures in one of your French books?'

'No,' she said, 'I've no idea who is there.'

'Obviously. With the lock blown off your front door anyone who likes can get in and out.'

'Including you.'

'Yes. I've had a word with a chap about getting that lock back before tonight. As for you, you don't know what is happening.'

'I did,' she said, locking her fingers before her eyes.

The unreality of this room and of Travis's presence preyed on her as figments of dreams that one knows to be dreams can do. This environment's being in semi-ruin struck her less than its being some sort of device or trap; and she rejoiced, if anything, in its decrepitude. As for Travis, he had his own part in the conspiracy to keep her from the beloved two. She felt he began to feel he was now unmeaning. She was struggling not to condemn him, scorn him for his ignorance of Henrietta, Eugene, her loss. His possessive angry fondness was part, of course, of the story of him and Mary, which like a book once read she remembered clearly but with indifference. Frantic at being delayed here, while the moment awaited her in the cornfield, she all but afforded a smile at the grotesquerie of being saddled with Mary's body and lover. Rearing up her head from the bare pillow, she looked, as far as the crossed feet, along the form inside which she found herself trapped: the irrelevant body of Mary, weighted down to the bed, wore a short black modern dress, flaked with plaster. The toes of the black suède shoes by their sickly whiteness showed Mary must have climbed over fallen ceilings; dirt engraved the fate lines in Mary's palms.

This inspired her to say: 'But I've made a start; I've been pulling out things of value or things I want.'

For answer Travis turned to look down, expressively, at some object out of her sight, on the floor close by the bed. '*I* see,' he said, 'a musty old leather box gaping open with God knows what—junk, illegible letters, diaries, yellow photographs, chiefly plaster and dust. Of all things, Mary!—after a missing will?'

'Everything one unburies seems the same age.'

'Then what are these, where do they come from—family stuff?'

'No idea,' she yawned into Mary's hand. 'They may not even

be mine. Having a house like this that had empty rooms must have made me store more than I knew, for years. I came on these, so I wondered. Look if you like.'

He bent and began to go through the box—it seemed to her, not unsuspiciously. While he blew grit off packets and fumbled with tapes she lay staring at the exposed laths of the ceiling, calculating. She then said: 'Sorry if I've been cranky, about the hotel and all. Go away just for two hours, then come back with a taxi, and I'll go quiet. Will that do?'

'Fine—except why not now?'

'*Travis* . . .'

'Sorry. It shall be as you say . . . You've got some good morbid stuff in this box, Mary—so far as I can see at a glance. The photographs seem more your sort of thing. Comic but lyrical. All of one set of people—a beard, a gun and a pot hat, a schoolboy with a moustache, a phaeton drawn up in front of a mansion, a group on the steps, a *carte de visite* of two young ladies hand-in-hand in front of a painted field—'

'*Give that to me!*'

She instinctively tried and failed, to unbutton the bosom of Mary's dress: it offered no hospitality to the photograph. So she could only fling herself over on the mattress, away from Travis, covering the two faces with her body. Racked by that oblique look of Henrietta's she recorded, too, a sort of personal shock at having seen Sarah for the first time.

Travis's hand came over her, and she shuddered. Wounded, he said: 'Mary . . .'

'Can't you leave *me* alone?'

She did not move or look till he had gone out saying: 'Then, in two hours.' She did not therefore see him pick up the dangerous box, which he took away under his arm, out of her reach.

They were back. Now the sun was setting behind the trees, but its rays passed dazzling between the branches into the beautiful warm red room. The tips of the ferns in the jardinière curled gold, and Sarah, standing by the jardinière, pinched at a leaf of scented geranium. The carpet had a great centre wreath of pomegranates, on which no tables or chairs stood, and its whole circle was between herself and the others.

No fire was lit yet, but where they were grouped was a hearth.

Henrietta sat on a low stool, resting her elbow above her head on the arm of Mamma's chair, looking away intently as though into a fire, idle. Mamma embroidered, her needle slowed down by her thoughts; the length of tatting with roses she had already done over-flowed stiffly over her supple skirts. Stretched on the rug at Mamma's feet, Arthur looked through an album of Swiss views, not liking them but vowed to be very quiet. Sarah, from where she stood, saw fuming cataracts and null eternal snows as poor Arthur kept turning over the pages, which had tissue paper between.

Against the white marble mantelpiece stood Eugene. The dark red shadows gathering in the drawing-room as the trees drowned more and more of the sun would reach him last, perhaps never: it seemed to Sarah that a lamp was lighted behind his face. He was the only gentleman with the ladies: Fitzgeorge had gone to the stables, Papa to give an order; Cousin Theodore was consulting a dictionary; in the gunroom Robert, Lucius and Digby went through the sad rites, putting away their guns. All this was known to go on but none of it could be heard.

This particular hour of subtle light—not to be fixed by the clock, for it was early in winter and late in summer and in spring and autumn now, about Arthur's bedtime—had always, for Sarah, been Henrietta's. To be with her indoors or out, upstairs or down, was to share the same crepitation. Her spirit ran on past yours with a laughing shiver into an element of its own. Leaves and branches and mirrors in empty rooms became animate. The sisters rustled and scampered and concealed themselves where nobody else was in play that was full of fear, fear that was full of play. Till, by dint of making each other's hearts beat violently, Henrietta so wholly and Sarah so nearly lost all human reason that Mamma had been known to look at them searchingly as she sat instated for evening among the calm amber lamps.

But now Henrietta had locked the hour inside her breast. By spending it seated beside Mamma, in young imitation of Constance the Society daughter, she disclaimed for ever anything else. It had always been she who with one fierce act destroyed any toy that might be outgrown. She sat with straight back, poising her cheek remotely against her finger. Only by never looking at Sarah did she admit their eternal loss.

Eugene, not long returned from a foreign tour, spoke of travel, addressing himself to Mamma, who thought but did not speak of her wedding journey. But every now and then she had to ask Henrietta to pass the scissors or tray of carded wools, and Eugene seized every such moment to look at Sarah. Into eyes always brilliant with melancholy he dared begin to allow no other expression. But this in itself declared the conspiracy of still undeclared love. For her part she looked at him as though he, transfigured by the strange light, were indeed a picture, a picture who could not see her. The wallpaper now flamed scarlet behind his shoulder. Mamma, Henrietta, even unknowing Arthur were in no hurry to raise their heads.

Henrietta said: 'If I were a man I should take my bride to Italy.'

'There are mules in Switzerland,' said Arthur.

'Sarah,' said Mamma, who turned in her chair mildly, 'where are you, my love; do you never mean to sit down?'

'To Naples,' said Henrietta.

'Are you not thinking of Venice?' said Eugene.

'No,' returned Henrietta, 'why should I be? I should like to climb the volcano. But then I am not a man, and am still less likely ever to be a bride.'

'Arthur . . .' Mamma said.

'Mamma?'

'Look at the clock.'

Arthur sighed politely, got up and replaced the album on the circular table, balanced upon the rest. He offered his hand to Eugene, his cheek to Henrietta and to Mamma; then he started towards Sarah, who came to meet him. 'Tell me, Arthur,' she said, embracing him, 'what did you do today?'

Arthur only stared with his button blue eyes. 'You were there too; we went for a walk in the cornfield, with Fitzgeorge on his horse, and I fell down.' He pulled out of her arms and said: 'I must go back to my beetle.' He had difficulty, as always, in turning the handle of the mahogany door. Mamma waited till he had left the room, then said: 'Arthur is quite a man now; he no longer comes running to me when he has hurt himself. Why, I did not even know he had fallen down. Before we know, he will be going away to school too.' She sighed and lifted her eyes to Eugene. 'Tomorrow is to be a sad day.'

Eugene with a gesture signified his own sorrow. The sentiments of Mamma could have been uttered only here in the drawing-room, which for all its size and formality was lyrical and almost exotic. There was a look like velvet in darker parts of the air; sombre window draperies let out gushes of lace; the music on the pianoforte bore tender titles, and the harp though unplayed gleamed in a corner, beyond sofas, whatnots, armchairs, occasional tables that all stood on tottering little feet. At any moment a tinkle might have been struck from the lustres' drops of the brighter day, a vibration from the musical instruments, or a quiver from the fringes and ferns. But the towering vases upon the consoles, the albums piled on the tables, the shells and figurines on the flights of brackets, all had, like the alabaster Leaning Tower of Pisa, an equilibrium of their own. Nothing would fall or change. And everything in the drawing-room was muted, weighted, pivoted by Mamma. When she added: 'We shall not feel quite the same', it was to be understood that she would not have spoken thus from her place at the opposite end of Papa's table.

'Sarah,' said Henrietta curiously, 'what made you ask Arthur what he had been doing? Surely you have not forgotten today?'

The sisters were seldom known to address or question one another in public; it was taken that they knew each other's minds. Mamma, though untroubled, looked from one to the other. Henrietta continued: 'No day, least of all today, is like any other— Surely that must be true?' she said to Eugene. 'You will never forget my waving my handkerchief?'

Before Eugene had composed an answer, she turned to Sarah: 'Or *you*, them riding across the fields?'

Eugene also slowly turned his eyes on Sarah, as though awaiting with something like dread her answer to the question he had not asked. She drew a light little gold chair into the middle of the wreath of the carpet, where no one ever sat, and sat down. She said: 'But since then I think I have been asleep.'

'Charles the First walked and talked half an hour after his head was cut off,' said Henrietta mockingly. Sarah in anguish pressed the palms of her hands together upon a shred of geranium leaf.

'How else,' she said, 'could I have had such a bad dream?'

'That must be the explanation!' said Henrietta.

'A trifle fanciful,' said Mamma.

However rash it might be to speak at all, Sarah wished she knew how to speak more clearly. The obscurity and loneliness of her trouble was not to be borne. How could she put into words the feeling of dislocation, the formless dread that had been with her since she found herself in the drawing-room? The source of both had been what she must call her dream. How could she tell the others with what vehemence she tried to attach her being to each second, not because each was singular in itself, each a drop condensed from the mist of love in the room, but because she apprehended that the seconds were numbered? Her hope was that the others at least half knew. Were Henrietta and Eugene able to understand how completely, how nearly for ever, she had been swept from them, would they not without fail each grasp one of her hands?—She went so far as to throw her hands out, as though alarmed by a wasp. The shred of geranium fell to the carpet.

Mamma, tracing this behaviour of Sarah's to only one cause, could not but think reproachfully of Eugene. Delightful as his conversation had been, he would have done better had he paid this call with the object of interviewing Papa. Turning to Henrietta she asked her to ring for the lamps, as the sun had set.

Eugene, no longer where he had stood, was able to make no gesture towards the bell-rope. His dark head was under the tide of dusk; for, down on one knee on the edge of the wreath, he was feeling over the carpet for what had fallen from Sarah's hand. In the inevitable silence rooks on the return from the fields could be heard streaming over the house; their sound filled the sky and even the room, and it appeared so useless to ring the bell that Henrietta stayed quivering by Mamma's chair. Eugene rose, brought out his fine white handkerchief and, while they watched, enfolded carefully in it what he had just found, then returning the handkerchief to his breast pocket. This was done so deep in the reverie that accompanies any final act that Mamma instinctively murmured to Henrietta: 'But you will be my child when Arthur has gone.'

The door opened for Constance to appear on the threshold. Behind her queenly figure globes approached, swimming in their own light: these were the lamps for which Henrietta had not rung, but these first were put on the hall tables. 'Why, Mamma,' exclaimed Constance, 'I cannot see who is with you!'

'Eugene is with us,' said Henrietta, 'but on the point of asking if he may send for his horse.'

'Indeed?' said Constance to Eugene. 'Fitzgeorge has been asking for you, but I cannot tell where he is now.'

The figures of Emily, Lucius and Cousin Theodore criss-crossed the lamplight there in the hall, to mass behind Constance's in the drawing-room door. Emily, over her sister's shoulder, said: 'Mamma, Lucius wishes to ask you whether for once he may take his guitar to school.'—'One objection, however,' said Cousin Theodore, 'is that Lucius's trunk is already locked and strapped.' 'Since Robert is taking his box of inks,' said Lucius, 'I do not see why I should not take my guitar.'—'But Robert,' said Constance, 'will soon be going to college.'

Lucius squeezed past the others into the drawing-room in order to look anxiously at Mamma, who said: 'You have thought of this late; we must go and see.' The others parted to let Mamma, followed by Lucius, out. Then Constance, Emily and Cousin Theodore deployed and sat down in different parts of the drawing-room, to await the lamps.

'I am glad the rooks have done passing over,' said Emily, 'they make me nervous.'—'Why?' yawned Constance haughtily, 'what do you think could happen?' Robert and Digby silently came in.

Eugene said to Sarah: 'I shall be back tomorrow.'

'But, oh—' she began. She turned to cry: 'Henrietta!'

'Why, what is the matter?' said Henrietta, unseen at the back of the gold chair. 'What could be sooner than tomorrow?'

'But something terrible may be going to happen.'

'There cannot fail to be tomorrow,' said Eugene gravely.

'*I* will see that there is tomorrow,' said Henrietta.

'You will never let me out of your sight?'

Eugene, addressing himself to Henrietta, said: 'Yes, promise her what she asks.'

Henrietta cried: 'She is never out of my sight. Who are you to ask me that, you Eugene? Whatever tries to come between me and Sarah becomes nothing. Yes, come tomorrow, come sooner, come—when you like, but no one will ever be quite alone with Sarah. You do not even know what you are trying to do. It is *you* who are making something terrible happen.—Sarah, tell him that that is true! Sarah—'

The others, in the dark on the chairs and sofas, could be felt to turn their judging eyes upon Sarah, who, as once before, could not speak—

The house rocked: simultaneously the calico window split and more ceiling fell, though not on the bed. The enormous dull sound

of the explosion died, leaving a minor trickle of dissolution still
to be heard in parts of the house. Until the choking stinging plaster
dust had had time to settle, she lay with lips pressed close, nostrils
not breathing and eyes shut. Remembering the box, Mary wondered if it had been again buried. No, she found, looking over the
edge of the bed: that had been unable to happen because the box
was missing. Travis, who must have taken it, would when he came
back no doubt explain why. She looked at her watch, which had
stopped, which was not surprising; she did not remember winding
it for the last two days, but then she could not remember much.
Through the torn window appeared the timelessness of an imper-
meably clouded late summer afternoon.

There being nothing left, she wished he would come to take her
to the hotel. The one way back to the fields was barred by Mary's
surviving the fall of ceiling. Sarah was right in doubting that there
would be tomorrow: Eugene, Henrietta were lost in time to the
woman weeping there on the bed, no longer reckoning who she
was.

At last she heard the taxi, then Travis hurrying up the littered
stairs. 'Mary, you're all right, Mary—*another*?' Such a helpless
white face came round the door that she could only hold out her
arms and say: 'Yes, but where have *you* been?'

'You said two hours. But I wish—'

'I have missed you.'

'Have you? Do you know you are crying?'

'Yes. How are we to live without natures? We only know incon-
venience now, not sorrow. Everything pulverises so easily because
it is rot-dry; one can only wonder that it makes so much noise.
The source, the sap must have dried up, or the pulse must have
stopped, before you and I were conceived. So much flowed
through people; so little flows through us. All we can do is imitate
love or sorrow.—Why did you take away my box?'

He only said: 'It is in my office.'

She continued: 'What has happened is cruel: I am left with a
fragment torn out of a day, a day I don't even know where or
when; and now how am I to help laying that like a pattern against
the poor stuff of everything else?—Alternatively, I am a person
drained by a dream. I cannot forget the climate of those hours.
Or life at that pitch, eventful—not happy, no, but strung like a
harp. I have had a sister called Henrietta.'

'And I have been looking inside your box. What else can you expect?—I have had to write off this day, from the work point of view, thanks to you. So could I sit and do nothing for the last two hours? I just glanced through this and that—still, I know the family.'

'You said it was morbid stuff.'

'Did I? I still say it gives off something.'

She said: 'And then there was Eugene.'

'Probably. I don't think I came on much of his except some notes he must have made for Fitzgeorge from some book on scientific farming. Well, there it is: I have sorted everything out and put it back again, all but a lock of hair that tumbled out of a letter I could not trace. So I've got the hair in my pocket.'

'What colour is it?'

'Ash-brown. Of course, it is a bit—desiccated. Do you want it?'

'No,' she said with a shudder. 'Really, Travis, what revenges you take!'

'I didn't look at it that way,' he said puzzled.

'Is the taxi waiting?' Mary got off the bed and, picking her way across the room, began to look about for things she ought to take with her, now and then stopping to brush her dress. She took the mirror out of her bag to see how dirty her face was. 'Travis—' she said suddenly.

'Mary?'

'Only, I—'

'That's all right. Don't let us imitate anything just at present.'

In the taxi, looking out of the window, she said: 'I suppose, then, that I am descended from Sarah?'

'No,' he said, 'that would be impossible. There must be some reason why you should have those papers, but that is not the one. From all negative evidence Sarah, like Henrietta, remained unmarried. I found no mention of either, after a certain date, in the letters of Constance, Robert or Emily, which makes it seem likely both died young. Fitzgeorge refers, in a letter to Robert written in his old age, to some friend of their youth who was thrown from his horse and killed, riding back after a visit to their home. The young man, whose name doesn't appear, was alone; and the evening, which was in autumn, was fine though late. Fitzgeorge wonders, and says he will always wonder, what made the horse shy in those empty fields.'

MR MURPHY AND THE ANGEL

Brian Cleeve

Brian Cleeve is one of the most ingenious of current Irish mystery story writers, mixing a sardonic sense of humour with unforeseen moments of fear—there is very often something lurking in his tales that will catch you totally unawares. His themes have ranged from the tranquillity of the Irish countryside to the brutal world of prison—'a number of which I have visited on business,' he admits, 'but what sort of uniform my business called for, I leave to your conjecture and my discretion!' Like L. A. G. Strong, Cleeve worked for a time for Radio Telefís Eireann before devoting his energies to the novels and short stories that have made him a familiar name to readers on both sides of the Atlantic.

Brian Talbot Cleeve (1921–) was born in Essex of Irish parents and for some years served with the Merchant Navy before settling in Ireland. Hist first novel, The Far Hills, *was published in 1952, but he was unable to interest any publisher in his first thriller. 'Eventually,' he recalls, 'I threw it into the dustbin. Ten minutes later, hearing the dustmen coming, I felt I couldn't let my brainchild die without one more effort and I fished it out and sent it away again.' That proved to be a very wise decision: for* Assignment to Vengeance *was not only accepted this time, but after publication in 1961 it became a major book club title, and was paperbacked and translated. Further novels, including* Dark Blood, Dark Tower *(1966),* Cry of Morning *(1971) and* The Dark Side of the Sun *(1973), have demonstrated his mastery of the thriller genre, while his insight into his native Ireland has been shown in books such as* Portrait of My City *(1953), short-story collections like* The Horse Thieves of Ballysaggert *(1966) and his deeply felt work,* For the Love of Crannagh Castle *(1975). He is also the co-author of the invaluable* Dictionary of Irish Writers *(1971). 'Mr Murphy and the Angel' is, as he explained when revising it for this collection, 'not the Stephen King kind of horror story'. But it does have its 'horrid bits' and he believes that every reader 'should feel horror at what lies ahead for the character'. On that intriguing note I leave you to find out just* what *lurks in Mr Cleeve's particular shadows . . .*

*   *   *

Once upon a time, and not a very long time ago, there was an angel who fell into the River Liffey with a broken wing. This sounds unusual, and so it was, except that this was only an apprentice angel, even though of the seventh class, and nearly matriculated to senior status. As you probably know, angels prefer to stay in Heaven, but now and then they are sent to earth to deliver messages, or warn sinners, or encourage good people to become saints, and this is what the angel of our story had been doing when she noticed the row of bridges over the river, from the Toll bridge near the mouth of the Liffey, to Heuston bridge a long way inland.

'What fun it would be,' she thought, 'to fly under all those bridges, with one long swoop!' And spreading her wings as wide as possible, she made a tremendous dive—under one bridge and two and three and four, when she met a seagull coming the other way. She had a swift choice—either to obliterate the poor innocent gull, or zoom sideways, and hit the stone wall of the quays at ninety miles an hour.

Being an angel, she chose to sacrifice herself in order to spare the seagull. And also because she was an angel, the impact didn't kill her—but it did break her wing. Angelic feathers fell like snow flakes into the dark and dirty water, and she fell with them, making a tremendous splash.

This happened at two o'clock in the morning. Not a soul was about. Not even a policeman, except for one disreputable and drunken man trying to find his way home. Hearing the splash he staggered to the river wall and peered over.

'Help!' cried the angel. 'Help me please! I've broken my wing and I'm going to drown.' (It should be mentioned here that when angels play silly tricks like flying under bridges—a thing they seldom do of course—they must suffer the consequences just like human beings. As an immediate penance their angelic powers are withdrawn for so many days—ten in this particular case.)

So there was the angel, trying to swim in the horribly dirty river with her broken wing trailing beside her and her beautiful white gown clinging to her in a most immodestly revealing way like a soaking wet nightdress—and there above her was the drunken reprobate staring down at her in disbelief.

'Holy Mother!' cried the drunk. 'It's an angel! In the Liffey! I swear before God I'll never touch another drop!' and he turned away in horror, thinking that delirium tremens had caught up with him at last.

'Please, please!' the angel called after him, 'don't leave me to drown! I'll reward you with anything you ask for if only you'll help me. Look. You could climb down those steps.'

The word 'reward' struck home to the drunken man's intelligence. Delusions don't offer rewards. Whatever or whoever it was down there in the river must be real after all. So back he turned and down he climbed and at the cost of getting very wet and almost sober he managed to pull the angel out of the water, and hoisting her onto his back carried her up to the roadway.

'And now, miss,' he said, 'how about this reward you were promising me?' But look as he would, he could see neither handbag nor pocket in which she could be keeping it.

'If we could go somewhere where I could get dry,' she answered him, her teeth chattering, 'we could talk about it in more comfort. What kind of reward would you like?'

'How about ten pounds?' the man suggested, quite sober now. A young one from Trinity College, he was guessing, on her way home from a fancy dress party dressed up as an angel, and probably as drunk as he had been ten minutes ago. Drunk enough to fall in the river, God love her. He felt quite a kinship for her as a fellow drunk, and was sorry for sounding so mercenary. 'If that's too much, well a fiver would be a help.'

'Five pounds?' the angel said. 'I was thinking of something much more valuable. Long life. Health. Wealth. You've only to name it, and it's yours. But please, if I don't get dry soon I'll catch pneumonia.'

'Long life? Health? Wealth?' the man wondered, shaking his head to see if he was still drunk. 'She's still drunk, and that's for certain!' But he brought her at a good pace to the street where he lived, not far away, and into the house where he had two rooms at the very top, in the attics, and there he turned on the gas fire and made her a pot of strong tea on a little gas ring he used for cooking, and found her some digestive biscuits, and a blanket to wrap herself in while her heavenly robe dried in front of the gas fire.

Now you'll easily understand that to have an angel in one's sitting-room, even an angel dressed in one of your blankets and suffering a penance for flying under bridges, is an experience that creates a powerful impression on anyone, even a drunken scally-wag like the man in our story. And to have her there for ten whole days, while her wing mended and her lost feathers were replaced with soft, downy new ones, and the days of her penance were counted out, was an experience to change his life and his whole way of thinking.

First of all, he gave her his bed, and slept himself on the couch in the living-room, in spite of its broken springs. He fed her on fish and chips, and pizzas from the Italian café round the corner. He gave up drinking, and bought her the morning and evening news-papers every day, and hired a television set to keep her amused while he was out collecting the dole. (He couldn't restrain himself from telling a few of his friends that he was looking after an angel with a broken wing, and she was sitting in his flat at that moment watching TV, but they all knew him too well to believe him, and wouldn't waste their energy climbing the stairs to see her.)

On Sunday he suggested going to Mass with her—he hadn't been for twenty years, so you can imagine the effect she was having on him—but she said she couldn't go, her wings would upset the priest, let alone the congregation, so they stayed in the flat and read the Sunday papers, and had ice cream with their lunch. When-ever he thought about the way he had asked her for five pounds—no, be honest, ten at first!—for saving her out of the river, he grew hot with shame, and on the ninth day he went out and bought an expensive clothes brush so that he could brush her new feathers.

Then it was the tenth day—her penance was almost over and in another hour she would be free to leave. 'You have been very good and kind,' she said to him, 'and I really appreciated having my feathers brushed. Now, the reward I promised you—'

'No, no!' he protested. 'I'll never forget these last ten days so long as I live. That'll be reward enough.'

'I insist,' she said. 'I really do. How about a passport to Heaven? In another hour I can write you one.'

'Heaven? Me?' the man asked her, amazed. 'I'm afraid I haven't lived what they call a good life.'

'I know that,' she told him. 'But suppose I bend the rules a little? I can copy the recording angel's hand-writing so well that poor old St Peter will never tell the difference—he's got very short-sighted these last few hundred years. I can write that you've lived a saintly life, admired by your parish priest as an example to everyone.'

'And no one would cop on? None of them up there? Our Lord and so on?'

She shook her golden head. 'Once you're in, you're in. Everyone assumes St Peter has checked you in as having been truly good.'

'But *you'll* know,' he said, 'and worse still, *I'll* know.' He too shook his own far from golden head—rather balding in fact, and dingy grey and dandruffy. 'No, no it's very kind of you. More than kind. But I couldn't do it. Every time I saw one of *Them* my knees'd knock and I'd want to confess. And that'd get you into trouble. No. Just leave me—leave me one of your feathers,' he suggested. 'I'll be able to look at it and remember you being here, and you watching the TV and reading the sports results and eating ice cream with me—and—and I'll feel life isn't so bad after all.'

She took a new, downy feather out of one of her wings and laid it on the mantelpiece, beside the alarm clock. 'I'll tell you what. It will be more than a souvenir. It will help you live a good enough life to enter Heaven on your own merits, with a genuine passport. So long as you behave well, it will stay beautifully white, the way it is now. But if you—well—if you backslide a little, the feather will turn grey, while, Heaven forbid! but if you were to behave really badly it will turn black as a raven's feather, until you start behaving well again. It will be like a thermometer for your *real* health, your soul.' And with that the alarm clock struck twice— two in the morning of the tenth day of her penance. She opened the window, climbed out on the sill, spread her mended wing like a white sail and away with her into the night sky, with never a downward glance at the river or its wretched stone bridges tempting angels to destruction.

The no longer drunken man gazed after her, feeling his heart swelling with pride, and cracking with sadness, until she was no more than a little white dot in the darkness among the pale Irish stars. At last he closed the window and looked at the feather. 'My thermometer!' he told himself. 'By all that's holy, I'll get into Heaven along with the best of 'em! My poor mother'll be proud of me!'

But the years are long and memory is short—and good resolutions even shorter. It began with a pint or two on St Patrick's Day. It continued with a good many whiskies—or one ought to say a bad many whiskies—over the Easter holiday. And before very long the reprobate was back in his old ways and the poor feather on the mantelpiece was black as pitch. Now and then the remembrance of the angel would overcome the love of drink, and the drunken man would sober up and make new resolutions. The black feather would turn seagull grey, and almost white—but then there would be a new fall from grace and the feather would turn black again, seeming to reproach the man as if the angel herself were saying to him, 'Shame on you! Oh shame on you!'

Until one day, in a passion of guilty rage and drunkenness the man seized the feather and flung it at the gas fire, which he had just lit. 'Damn you,' he shouted at it as it began to burn, 'may the Devil take you!'

And with that there was a great roar of flame, a clap of thunder to deafen an elephant, and the Devil was there, horns, hooves and tail and a broad grin of delight.

'My fine fellow!' he said in an insinuating voice. 'My joy! My dear friend! What a gift you've just given me! An angel's feather, no less! A bit singed, admittedly, but practically as good as new. What *can* I do for you in return?' He smiled at the drunken man, who was cowering in the corner like a mouse hiding from the cat. 'Why, I know! The very thing for you! What was it you turned down? A passport—a *forged* passport to Heaven? I don't blame you in the least. What a shabby gift! Don't you believe that story about Peter being half-blind. The moment you showed him that forgery you'd have been on your way down to me faster than you could blink. Now me, I don't deal in forgeries. When I give anyone gold, it's 24 carat genuine. And when I give you a passport to Heaven, *that* will be genuine too. Stolen, yes, but one hundred per cent genuine.'

He cracked his tail like a whip. Sparks flew and a passport appeared in his claws, shining white, with the Papal Arms stamped on the cover in gold leaf. 'Here you are, my good fellow, catch!'

And he threw it to the poor soul quivering behind the broken-springed couch, who dropped it on the bare floorboards from his trembling hands.

'Me? A genuine passport? To Heaven,' he quavered. 'I thought—'

'That I'd want you down there?' the Devil said with a smile that sent shivers up the drunken man's spine and into his stomach. 'Oh no, I'm in a generous mood. Don't bother to thank me—all you need do is read page one—'

The drunken man picked up the passport and read the page. 'To admit ten perfect souls' was written on it in a fine flowing educated hand.

'Ten?' the drunken man asked in amazement? 'D'you mean I can take in nine of me pals?'

'Well, not exactly,' the Devil said, half of him disappearing into the gas fire. 'I'll choose the other nine. Don't worry your head about that. Just live your life, a little drop of the hard stuff now and then never hurt anyone—just live your horrible little life to its natural end. A bit before that the other nine will join you. All you've got to do is keep that passport safe. Put it by the alarm clock there.' He had almost entirely disappeared by now. Only his rather chilly smile remained visible, and his black moustache. 'Oh, there's one more thing—it won't change colour, no matter what you do.'

Then he was gone, leaving behind the white passport and a rather strong smell of sulphur as the only traces of his visit.

At first, the terrified wretch swore that he would never touch another pint of stout or gill of whiskey so long as he lived. But then he looked at the passport, white and shining beside the alarm clock, with its promise to admit 'ten perfect souls' and he wondered if there'd be any harm in say half a pint of light ale. After which he examined the cover, with the Papal Arms embossed on it in real gold. The Papal Tiara over a pair of crossed keys. The keys of Heaven, the man vaguely remembered from long, long ago catechism lessons.

He also remembered the hearty smack of the brother's leather strap for not knowing the answers. 'Religion is all a load of bosh,' he told himself, and he went out to get a drink to steady his nerves, which certainly needed steadying after such an experience.

One drink followed another, and he finished the night in the

Garda station, under arrest for assaulting another drunk and telling him he could get anyone into Heaven that he liked. It wasn't
exactly that that got him arrested, but the language he used
together with the assault.

Things went from bad to worse. His nose turned a nasty shade
of purple from the drink. His hands began to shake. He saw horrible visions on the stairs at night, and had to have another drink
to recover from them. At last one winter's night he staggered
home to find not visions on the stairs outside his flat, but a crowd
of terrible-looking men and women, and a peculiar-looking little
dog who tried to bite him.

'Who are you all?' he asked them muzzily. 'What do you want?'
The dog barked and sank its sharp little teeth in his ankle. A
young man with his hair in pink spikes and a black leather coat
with metal studs all over it banged him on the shoulder.

'You Mr Murphy?'

The drunken man admitted that he was.

'Then we're here. The nine of us. For the passport, remember?
Plus the dog.'

A girl in a black plastic skirt that hid next to nothing of what it
was supposed to hide shoved her face into the drunken man's with
a look so threatening it drove him back against the wall of the
landing with a thud. 'Don't tell us you've forgot,' she said, 'or
we'll do you over.' She took the key out of Mr Murphy's hand,
where he had been holding it ready as he climbed the stairs, and
opened his door, banging it back as if she meant to break it. All
nine of them and the little dog poured into the sitting-room.

'What a muck heap,' the girl said. The little dog raised its leg
against the gas fire. Three young men in dirty jeans flung themselves onto the couch. Another girl with very thick arms and legs
rooted in the cupboard and pulled out two cans of lager and a half
bottle of whiskey that poor Mr Murphy had been keeping for
emergencies.

'This all you got, you mean little squeaker?'

The first girl began frying his rashers on his gas-ring. The dog
barked. The nine young people yelled insults at one another and
worse insults at their bewildered host, who you now know was
called Mr Murphy. He tried to get hold of his half bottle of whiskey, to have at least one swallow out of it, but it was already
empty.

'We been waiting for you,' one of the young men yelled. 'A right old age pensioner you are—we thought you was never going to kick the bucket—two years I been waiting for tonight—' and he threw an empty beer can at the dog. 'Shurrup!'

'Who are you all?' pleaded Mr Murphy. 'Why are you here?'

'To go to effing Heaven with you, stupid!' the fat girl shouted. She had found the Heavenly passport on the mantelpiece and was trying to read it. 'Ad—mit ten—per—fick—souls—ha ha ha! That's us, eh? Nine of us at least. Plus Fido here—' and she took a kick at the little dog. 'My effing sister's. It just came along. Want to go to Heaven, Fido?'

'But why—how—?' Mr Murphy cried. 'I mean I'm not dying— am I?' He had suddenly felt very ill, his heart beating too fast, and a queer noise in his ears. The room seemed to be going round and round.

'I bin waiting six months,' the first girl said, 'and I'm not waiting any longer.' She picked up the bread knife from beside the gas ring and looked at Mr Murphy in a very meaningful way. 'Are you ready or not?'

'Of course I'm not ready!' he cried in desperation. 'I'm not ill—I need a priest—a doctor—it's not the time yet—' The girl advanced on him, and he backed against the window. 'Please! No! Don't touch me! Why d'you all want to go to Heaven?'

'To have fun,' the girl said. 'Just wait till we get there, we'll turn it upside bloody down. Start a Rock group—heavy metal—'

'Pushin' drugs!' one of the boys on the couch yelled. 'Teach the effing angels to smoke pot—'

'Cocaine!'

'Heroin!'

'Smack!'

'Perfick souls!'

'Sex orgies!'

'Gay rights for the effing saints!'

'P . . . on earth an' ill will to all men—'

'—an' all effing women too—'cept us!'

The little dog barked, frantic with excitement, and bit the fat girl in the calf.

'No no no!' cried Mr Murphy in terror. The vision of his own angel came back to him in a blinding flash of contrition. These monsters invading Heaven. Because of him. Pushing drugs on the angels. She was exactly the one who'd try them, just to see what they were like—the way she had flown under the bridges. His beautiful, golden angel spaced out on smack. Little cherubs sniffing glue in corners. Rock music instead of hymns. And all his fault. For throwing her feather into the gas fire. With a sudden lunge he grabbed hold of the passport from a boy who was examining it with a sneer, tore it in half and quarters and flung it out of the window.

'You'll not go!' he cried, and dropped to the floor with a heart attack as if he had been shot. There was a sudden blaze of whiteness at the window, and his angel was climbing through into the room, tall and splendid and furious. The nine invaders took one look at her and fled for the door, crushing each other in their anxiety to escape. Inside twenty seconds they were all outside and pounding down the stairs. Only the little dog had stayed behind. Not even barking, but gazing at the angel in wonder, and what seemed very like the beginnings of devotion.

'You can get up now,' the angel told Mr Murphy. 'They've gone.'

'I can't,' Mr Murphy answered her. 'I'm dead.'

The angel pulled him to his feet and dusted him down a little. 'I know that.'

To his amazement Mr Murphy found that he could stand up quite well. And yet there he was too, lying on the floor. There were two of him. One dead on the floor with a silly expression. And one standing up beside the angel. The little dog rolled on its back at the angel's feet and waved its paws in ecstasy, its tongue lolling out of its mouth like a pink sausage.

'Those—those people—' Mr Murphy quavered. 'Were—are—they dead too?'

The angel nodded indifferently. 'They've been waiting for you. One dead here, one there—We were wondering what you'd do when the time came.'

'Could they—have got in?'

'On your passport, yes.'

'And—done all those things?'

The angel nodded, slowly. 'Why not? He's succeeded down here. Now he's trying up there.'

'But—but *Them*? They'd *allow* it?'

The angel stared out of the window for a moment, before answering. 'Every one has free will.'

'You mean the Fall an' all that?' More memories of catechism classes floated back to Mr Murphy. 'But that was ages ago.'

'Nothing is ages ago,' the angel said, her voice suddenly very sad. 'Everything is now.'

Mr Murphy tried to make sense of that and failed. But the word 'now' woke him to immediate concerns. Or at least, his immediate concerns. 'What about me? I suppose—I suppose I've got to—' and unable to say the words he pointed to the floor.

The angel shook her head. 'You're to come with me.'

'With you?' Hope fluttered in what had been Mr Murphy's heart, and what indeed felt as if it still was his heart.

'To—to Heaven?'

She shook her head again. 'Neither of us,' she said. 'I've been expelled.'

He stared at her. 'Expelled? You?'

'Yes. They weren't a bit pleased about my offering you a forged passport. The Recording Angel made a formal complaint.'

'But I didn't accept it!'

The angel sighed. 'That was recorded in your favour. Not in mine.'

'How did they find out?'

'They know everything. It makes life difficult.' The little dog was licking her toes. 'Good Fido,' she said, bending down to rub its ears. Its tail came up like a white plume, and it danced on its back paws. 'We'd better be going.'

'Going where?'

'You'll see,' she told him.

'Is it far?' He was looking round the room, trying to believe he was really dead.

She drew him towards the doorway, and down the narrow, smelly stairs. The little dog followed them, and out into the street. It was empty, and suddenly unfamiliar. The buildings across the way wavered as if he was seeing them under water. Mr Murphy screwed his eyes shut to steady his vision. When he opened them again the buildings were gone. And the street. And his own house. Only himself and the angel remained standing together, and the little dog at their feet. A grey expanse stretched in front of them, featureless, barren, seemingly endless, the line where it must meet the equally grey sky so distant that it was invisible.

'Where is this!' Mr Murphy whispered. 'Why are we here?'

'This is nowhere,' the angel said, a touch of anxiety in her voice, 'or at least, the edge of nowhere. And we're here to find ten perfect spirits. Remember?'

'You—you mean the—the ones back in my room?' He jerked his thumb over his shoulder rather than look round, for fear of what he might see behind him.

'Those ones? Of course not,' she said. 'They're for someone else to look after. Ours are waiting for us out there,' and she pointed into the grey distance. 'Nine of them. And you too. To match your passport.'

Mr Murphy looked down at his old brown boots with the cracks across the insteps, and the legs of his shabby blue suit. Ten perfect souls, the passport had said. He had been mad to accept it, stark mad. If he only *looked* like a perfect soul! Handsome. With curly black hair and good teeth.

'One thing I have to warn you about,' the angel was saying, but he was too intent on the sudden vision of himself as young and handsome to listen. A good suit, and a hat with a curly brim, and a walking stick with a gold knob. And the landlord of Dillon's treating him with respect and calling him Mr Murphy, and the parish priest asking his advice—

'No no!' cried the angel, 'listen to me! Don't start wishing!'

'Why not?' said Mr Murphy. 'All I'm wishing is that I looked a bit better—you know, a bit of all right, curly hair and that—and a bit younger—' He was ashamed to tell her the rest of what he had wished, or why. 'I *do* wish it,' and he had a sudden, dizzy sensation as if all his wishes were really coming true. Even his hair seemed to be growing and his legs getting younger. And there in his hand was a handsome malacca cane with a gold handle. The landlord's voice seemed to be echoing in his ears—'You're a right one, Mr Murphy, a real high flyer!' And the parish priest catching him by the arm saying, 'I've been wondering if you could help me, James. I've this problem with the bishop, and—'

He struck a pose for her, his head tilted, putting up his hand to caress the brim of his smart new hat. But his fingers found themselves touching long furry ears. And instead of thick black curls, harsh dusty fur. 'What—what's happened!' he cried, and his voice came out in a donkey's dreadful bray. The malacca cane in his hand turned to a length of old straw rope that was twisted round his monstrous donkey's neck.

'Braaaa!' he cried in terror. The angel reached into the pocket of his new blue suit and took out a handful of silver pebbles. She threw them into the air with an expression of near despair on her face. 'Eight promises!' she cried furiously. 'All your promises wasted!' As she said it they exploded into eight tiny puffs of silver smoke. He felt the weight of his donkey's ears vanish, along with his new suit and restored youth and everything else he had wished for. He stood staring at his old, familiar boots, feeling sullenly rebellious.

'What's wrong with wishes?' he said. It was only then, stealing a sideways glance at her, that he saw the change in her appearance. Her wings were gone, and she was dressed in a rough brown tunic with a rope girdle. Her golden hair had been shorn close to her head and she looked like a young boy, with her legs bare from the knees down. Handsome, yes. But no longer an angel. And all his fault!

'No,' she said, reading his thoughts. 'All my fault. But you're kind to try and take the blame. I'm sorry I shouted at you about your wishes, but you see, here in the real world wishes come true. Only not the way you'd like them to. They come *really* true. And use up your promises.'

'What promises? Those pebbles?'

'Yes. I was given twelve and you were given eight, not for ourselves, but for the people we're being sent to rescue. As promises of help if they get into really desperate trouble.'

She took him by the arm and they started walking. He was afraid to ask her any more questions. Even though she no longer had her wings, or her splendid white dress, there was still an air of authority about her that overawed him. The little dog trotted beside them, its pink tongue hanging out with joyous excitement, every now and then giving the angel a look of adoration.

And you, dear reader, who may have been reading this tale with condescending contempt for its lack of horror—asking yourself when the monster rats might appear, or the demons—let me whisper it to you. The real horror of this story is that it is true. And, God forbid, may one day become true for you, too.

Finding yourself in a grey, featureless, endless desert, in search of some means, however impossible, of gaining your entry into Paradise. If that should happen to you—and again, God forbid it—may you at least have a little dog and even a fallen angle to keep you company.

2
WAKE NOT THE DEAD

'The Cemetery That Moved', a woodcut by John Farleigh for
'The Miraculous Revenge' by George Bernard Shaw.

THE RAISING OF
ELVIRA TREMLETT

William Trevor

*Horror stories based on fears about death and the departed are
another long-standing Irish tradition, which can be traced back to
the early nineteenth-century tales of Gerald Griffin, one of Ireland's
first writers of fiction in English, right through to leading contemporary authors such as William Trevor whose grim fables have
brought him widespread comparison with Edgar Allan Poe and
Charles Dickens. The two men are, indeed, linked across the years
by their desire to portray the terrors that are forever just on the edge
of everyday life. William Trevor Cox (1928–   ) was born in County
Cork and was actually a sculptor before turning to writing and
thereby earning an international reputation for the quality of his
stage plays, television scripts, novels and short stories. He has won
several major literary awards for his fiction, was made a CBE in
1977 and is a member of the Irish Academy of Letters.*

*William Trevor has been fascinated with horror since his child-
hood, and throughout his career has written tales in which the
ghastly and the horrible frequently occur. As James F. Kilroy has
noted, 'He is like a phlegmatic Poe, and perhaps even more perni-
cious because no one ever takes Poe's romances seriously. To a
Poe or a Hawthorne, or to a Monk Lewis or an Ann Radcliffe,
horror was romantic or glamorous or at least interestingly odd—
but to Trevor horror is the dull, realistic stuff of everyday life.' This
can be seen in his stories such as 'Miss Smith' in which a baby is
maliciously killed by a fiendish schoolboy; 'An Evening with John
Joe Dempsey' about a town's crazed, sex-obsessed dwarf; and
'Attracta' in which the head of a young man killed by the IRA is*

*sent to his wife in a plastic bag, after which her horror is com-
pounded when she is raped by seven men. There are certainly similar elements of awfulness in 'The Raising of Elvira Tremlett',
a story that in less skilful and accomplished hands might well
have become simply revolting, but is actually an example of the
traditional horror story at its very finest . . .*

* * *

My mother preferred English goods to Irish, claiming that the
quality was better. In particular she had a preference for English
socks and vests, and would not be denied in her point of view.
Irish motor-car assemblers made a rough-and-ready job of it, my
father used to say, the Austins and Morrises and Vauxhalls that
came direct from British factories were twice the cars. And my
father was an expert in his way, being the town's single garage-
owner. *Devlin Bros.* it said on a length of painted wood, black
letters on peeling white. The sign was crooked on the red corrugated iron of the garage, falling down a bit on the left-hand side.

In all other ways my parents were intensely of the country that
had borne them, of the province of Munster and of the town they
had always known. When she left the Presentation convent my
mother had been found employment in the meat factory, working
a machine that stuck labels on to tins. My father and his brother
Jack, finishing at the Christian Brothers', had automatically passed
into the family business. In those days the only sign on the corrugated façade had said *Raleigh Cycles*, for the business, founded
by my grandfather, had once been a bicycle one. 'I think we'll
make a change in that,' my father announced one day in 1933
when I was five, and six months or so later the rusty tin sheet that
advertised bicycles was removed, leaving behind an island of grey
in the corrugated red. 'Ah, that's grand,' my mother approved
from the middle of the street, wiping her chapped hands on her
apron. The new sign must have had a freshness and a gleam to it,
but I don't recall that. In my memory there is only the peeling
white behind the letters and the drooping down at the left-hand
side where a rivet had fallen out. 'We'll paint that in and we'll be
dandy,' my Uncle Jack said, referring to the island that remained,
the contours of Sir Walter Raleigh's head and shoulders. But the
job was never done.

We lived in a house next door to the garage, two storeys of cement that had a damp look, with green window-sashes and a green hall-door. Inside, a wealth of polished brown linoleum, its pattern faded to nothing, was cheered here and there by the rugs my mother bought in Roche's Stores in Cork. The votive light of a crimson Sacred Heart gleamed day and night in the hall. Christ blessed us halfway up the stairs; on the landing the Virgin Mary was coy in garish robes. On either side of a narrow trodden carpet the staircase had been grained to make it seem like oak. In the dining-room, never used, there was a square table with six rexine-seated chairs around it, and over the mantelpiece a mirror with chromium decoration. The sitting-room smelt of must and had a picture of the Pope.

The kitchen was where everything happened. My father and Uncle Jack read the newspaper there. The old Phillips wireless, the only one in the house, stood on one of the window-sills. Our two nameless cats used to crouch by the door into the scullery because one of them had once caught a mouse there. Our terrier, Tom, mooched about under my mother's feet when she was cooking at the range. There was a big scrubbed table in the middle of the kitchen, and wooden chairs, and a huge clock, like the top bit of a grandfather clock, hanging between the two windows. The dresser had keys and bits of wire and labels hanging all over it. The china it contained was never used, being hidden behind bric-à-brac: broken ornaments left there in order to be repaired with Seccotine, worn-out parts from the engines of cars which my father and uncle had brought into the kitchen to examine at their leisure, bills on spikes, letters and Christmas cards. The kitchen was always rather dusky, even in the middle of the day: it was partially a basement, light penetrating from outside only through the upper panes of its two long windows. Its concrete floor had been reddened with Cardinal polish, which was renewed once a year, in spring. Its walls and ceiling were a sooty white.

The kitchen was where we did our homework, my two sisters and two brothers and myself. I was the youngest, my brother Brian the oldest. Brian and Liam were destined for the garage when they finished at the Christian Brothers', as my father and Uncle Jack had been. My sister Effie was good at arithmetic and the nuns had once or twice mentioned accountancy. There was a commercial college in Cork she could go to, the nuns said, the same

place that Miss Madden who did the books for Bolger's Medical
Hall had attended. Everyone said my sister Kitty was pretty: my
father used to take her on his knee and tell her she'd break some
fellow's heart, or a dozen hearts or maybe more. She didn't know
what he was talking about at first, but later she understood and
used to go red in the face. My father was like that with Kitty. He
embarrassed her without meaning to, hauling her on to his knee
when she was much too old for it, fondling her because he liked
her best. On the other hand, he was quite harsh with my brothers,
constantly suspicious that they were up to no good. Every evening
he asked them if they'd been to school that day, suspecting that
they might have tricked the Christian Brothers and would the next
day present them with a note they had written themselves, saying
they'd had stomach trouble after eating bad sausages. He and my
Uncle Jack had often engaged in such ploys themselves, spending
a whole day in the field behind the meat factory, smoking
Woodbines.

My father's attitude to my sister Effie was coloured by Effie's
plainness. 'Ah, poor old Effie,' he used to say, and my mother
would reprimand him. He took comfort from the fact that if the
garage continued to thrive it would be necessary to have someone
doing the increased book-work instead of himself and Uncle Jack
trying to do it. For this reason he was in favour of Effie taking a
commercial course: he saw a future in which she and my two
brothers would live in the house and run the business between
them. One or other of my brothers would marry and maybe move
out of the house, leaving Effie and whichever one would still be
a bachelor: it was my father's way of coming to terms with Effie's
plainness. 'I wonder if Kitty'll end up with young Lacy?' I once
heard him enquiring of my mother, the Lacy he referred to being
the only child of another business in the town—Geo. Lacy and
Sons, High-Class Drapers—who was about eight at the time. Kitty
would do well, she'd marry whom she wanted to, and somehow
or other she'd marry money: he really believed that.

For my part I fitted nowhere into my father's vision of the
family's future. My performance at school was poor and there
would be no place for me in the garage. I used to sit with the
others at the kitchen table trying to understand algebra and Irish
grammar, trying without any hope to learn verses from *Ode to the
West Wind* and to improve my handwriting by copying from a

headline book. 'Slow,' Brother Flynn had reported. 'Slow as a dying snail, that boy is.'

That was the family we were. My father was bulky in his grey overalls, always with marks of grease or dirt on him, his fingernails rimmed with black, like fingers in mourning, I used to think. Uncle Jack wore similar overalls but he was thin and much smaller than my father, a ferrety little man who had a way of looking at the ground when he spoke to you. He, too, was marked with grime and had the same rimmed fingernails, even at weekends. They both brought the smell of the garage into the kitchen, an oily smell that mingled with the fumes of my uncle's pipe and my father's cigarettes.

My mother was red-cheeked and stout, with waxy black hair and big arms and legs. She ruled the house, and was often cross: with my brothers when they behaved obstreperously, with my sisters and myself when her patience failed her. Sometimes my father would spend a long time on a Saturday night in Keogh's, which was the public house he favoured, and she would be cross with him also, noisily shouting in their bedroom, telling him to take off his clothes before he got into bed, telling him he was a fool. Uncle Jack was a teetotaller, a member of the Pioneer movement. He was a great help to Canon O'Keefe in the rectory and in the Church of the Holy Assumption, performing chores and repairing the electric light. Twice a year he spent a Saturday night in Cork in order to go to greyhound racing, but there was more than met the eye to these visits, for on his return there was always a great silence in the house, a fog of disapproval emanating from my father.

The first memories I have are of the garage, of watching my father and Uncle Jack at work, sparks flying from the welding apparatus, the dismantling of oil-caked engines. A car would be driven over the pit and my father or uncle would work underneath it, lit by an electric bulb in a wire casing on the end of a flex. Often, when he wasn't in the pit, my father would drift into conversation with a customer. He'd lean on the bonnet of a car, smoking continuously, talking about a hurling match that had taken place or about the dishonesties of the Government. He would also talk about his children, saying that Brian and Liam would fit easily into the business and referring to Effie's plans to study commerce and Kitty's prettiness. 'And your man here?' the customer might remark, inclining his head in my direction. To this question my father always replied in the same way. The Lord, he said, would look after me.

As I grew up I became aware that I made both my father and my mother uneasy. I assumed that this was due to my slowness at school, an opinion that was justified by a conversation I once overheard coming from their bedroom: they appeared to regard me as mentally deficient. My father repeated twice that the Lord would look after me. It was something she prayed for, my mother replied, and I imagined her praying after she'd said it, kneeling down by their bed, as she'd taught all of us to kneel by ours. I stood with my bare feet on the linoleum of the landing, believing that a plea from my mother was rising from the house at that very moment, up into the sky where God was. I had been on my way to the kitchen for a drink of water, but I returned to the bedroom I shared with Brian and Liam and lay awake thinking of the big brown-brick mansion on the Mallow road. Once it had been owned and lived in by a local family. Now it was the town's asylum.

The town itself was small and ordinary. Part of it was on a hill, the part where the slum cottages were, where three or four shops had nothing in their windows except pasteboard advertisements for tea and Bisto. The rest of the town was flat, a single street with one or two narrow streets running off it. Where they met there was a square of a kind, with a statue of Daniel O'Connell. The Munster and Leinster Bank was here, and the Bank of Ireland, and Lacy and Sons, and Bolger's Medical Hall, and the Home and Colonial. Our garage was at one end of the main street, opposite Corrigan's Hotel. The Electric Cinema was at the other, a stark white façade not far from the Church of the Holy Assumption. The Protestant church was at the top of the hill, beyond the slums.

When I think of the town now I can see it very clearly: cattle and pigs on a fair-day, always a Monday; Mrs Driscoll's vegetable shop, Vickery's hardware, Phelan's the barber's, Kilmartin's the turf accountant's, the convent and the Christian Brothers', twenty-nine public houses. The streets are empty on a sunny afternoon, there's a smell of bread. Brass plates gleam on the way home from school: Dr Thos. Garvey M.D., R.C.S., Regan and O'Brien, Commissioners for oaths, W. Tracy, Dental Surgeon.

But in my thoughts our house and our garage close in on everything else, shadowing and diminishing the town. The bedroom I shared with Brian and Liam had the same nondescript linoleum as the hall and the landing had. There was a dressing-table with a wash-stand in white-painted wood, and a wardrobe that matched. There was a flowery wallpaper on the walls, but the flowers had all faded to a uniform brown, except behind the bedroom's single picture, of an ox pulling a cart. Our three iron bedsteads were lined against one wall. Above the mantelpiece Christ on his cross had already given up the ghost.

I didn't in any way object to this bedroom and, familiar with no alternative, I didn't mind sharing it with my brothers. The house itself was somewhere I was used to also, accepted and taken for granted. But the garage was different. The garage was a kind of hell, its awful earth floor made black with sump oil, its huge indelicate vices, the chill of cast iron, the grunting of my father and my uncle as they heaved an engine out of a tractor, the astringent smell of petrol. It was there that my silence, my dumbness almost, must have begun. I sense that now, without being able accurately to remember. Looking back, I see myself silent in a classroom, taught first by nuns and later by Christian Brothers. In the kitchen, while the others chattered at mealtimes, I was silent too. I could take no interest in what my father and uncle reported about the difficulties they were having in getting spare parts or about some fault in a farmer's carburettor. My brothers listened to all that, and clearly found it easy to. Or they would talk about sport, or tease Uncle Jack about the money he lost on greyhounds and horses. My mother would repeat what she had heard in the shops, and Uncle Jack would listen intently because although he never himself indulged in gossip he loved to hear it. My sisters would retail news from the convent, the decline in the health of an elderly nun, or the inability of some family to buy Lacy's more expensive First Communion dresses. I often felt, listening at mealtimes, that I was scarcely there. I didn't belong and I sensed it was my fault; I felt I was a burden, being unpromising at school, unable to hold out hopes for the future. I felt I was a disgrace to them and might even become a person who was only fit to lift cans of paraffin about in the garage. I thought I could see that in my father's eyes, and in my uncle's sometimes, and in my mother's. A kind of shame it was, peering back at me.

*   *   *

I turned to Elvira Tremlett because everything about her was quiet. 'You great damn clown,' my mother would shout angrily at my father. He'd smile in the kitchen, smelling like a brewery, as she used to say. 'Mind that bloody tongue of yours,' he'd retort, and then he'd eye my uncle in a belligerent manner. 'Jeez, will you look at the cut of him?' he'd roar, laughing and throwing his head about. My uncle would usually be sitting in front of the range, a little to one side so as not to be in the way of my mother while she cooked. He'd been reading the *Independent* or *Ireland's Own*, or trying to mend something. 'You're the right eejit,' my father would say to him. 'And the right bloody hypocrite.'

It was always like that when he'd been in Keogh's on a Saturday evening and returned in time for his meal. My mother would slap the plates on to the table, my father would sing in order to annoy her. I used to feel that my uncle and my mother were allied on these occasions, just as she and my father were allied when my uncle spent a Saturday night in Cork after the greyhound racing. I much preferred it when my father didn't come back until some time in the middle of the night. 'Will you look at His Nibs?' he'd say in the kitchen, drawing attention to me. 'Haven't you a word in you, boy? Bedad, that fellow'll never make a lawyer.' He'd explode with laughter and then he'd tell Kitty that she was looking great and could marry the crowned King of England if she wanted to. He'd say to Effie she was getting fat with the toffees she ate; he'd tell my brothers they were lazy.

They didn't mind his talk the way I did; even Kitty's embarrassment used to evaporate quite quickly because for some reason she was fond of him. Effie was fond of my uncle, and my brothers of my mother. Yet in spite of all this family feeling, whenever there was quarrelling between our parents, or an atmosphere after my uncle had spent a night away, my brothers used to say the three of them would drive you mad. 'Wouldn't it make you sick, listening to it?' Brian would say in our bedroom, saying it to Liam. Then they'd laugh because they couldn't be bothered to concern themselves too much with other people's quarrels, or with atmospheres.

The fact was, my brothers and sisters were all part of it, whatever it was—the house, the garage, the family we were—and they could take everything in their stride. They were the same as our parents and our uncle, and Elvira Tremlett was different. She was a bit like Myrna Loy, whom I had seen in the Electric, in *Test*

Pilot and *Too Hot to Handle* and *The Thin Man*. Only she was more beautiful than Myrna Loy, and her voice was nicer. Her voice, I still consider, was the nicest thing about Elvira Tremlett, next to her quietness.

*   *   *

'What do you want?' the sexton of the Protestant church said to me one Saturday afternoon. 'What're you doing here?'

He was an old, hunched man in black clothes. He had rheumy eyes, very red and bloody at the rims. It was said in the town that he gave his wife an awful time.

'It isn't your church,' he said.

I nodded, not wanting to speak to him. He said:

'It a sin for you to be coming into a Protestant church. Are you wanting to be a Protestant, is that it?' He was laughing at me, even though his lips weren't smiling. He looked as if he'd never smiled in his life.

I shook my head at him, hoping he might think I was dumb.

'Stay if you want to,' he said, surprising me, even though I'd seen him coming to the conclusion that I wasn't going to commit some act of vandalism. I think he might even have decided to be pleased because a Catholic boy had chosen to wander among the pews and brasses of his church. He hobbled away to the vestry, breathing noisily because of his bent condition.

Several months before that Saturday I had wandered into the church for the first time. It was different from the Church of the Holy Assumption. It had a different smell, a smell that might have come from mothballs or from the tidy stacks of hymn-books and prayer-books, whereas the Church of the Holy Assumption smelt of people and candles. It was cosier, much smaller, with dark-coloured panelling and pews, and stained-glass windows that seemed old, and no cross on the altar. There were flags and banners that were covered with dust, all faded and in shreds, and a bible spread out on the wings of an eagle.

The old sexton came back. I could feel him watching me as I read the tablets on the walls, moving from one to the next, pretending that each of them interested me. I might have asked him: I might have smiled at him and timidly enquired about Elvira Tremlett because I knew he was old enough to remember. But I didn't. I walked slowly up a side-aisle, away from the altar, to the back of the church. I wanted to linger there in the shadows, but I could feel his rheumy eyes on my back, wondering about me. As I slipped away from the church, down the short path that led through black iron gates to the street at the top of the hill, I knew that I would never return to the place.

'Well, it doesn't matter,' she said. 'You don't have to go back. There's nothing to go back for.'

I knew that was true. It was silly to keep on calling in at the Protestant church.

'It's curiosity that sends you there,' she said. 'You're much too curious.'

I knew I was: she had made me understand that. I was curious and my family weren't.

She smiled her slow smile, and her eyes filled with it. Her eyes were brown, the same colour as her long hair. I loved it when she smiled. I loved watching her fingers playing with the daisies in her lap, I loved her old-fashioned clothes, and her shoes and her two elaborate earrings. She laughed once when I asked her if they were gold. She'd never been rich, she said.

There was a place, a small field with boulders in it, hidden on the edge of the wood. I had gone there the first time, after I'd been in the Protestant church. What had happened was that in the church I had noticed the tablet on the wall, the left wall as you faced the altar, the last tablet on it, in dull grey marble.

> Near by this Stone
> Lies Interred the Body
> of Miss Elvira Tremlett
> Daughter of Wm. Tremlett
> of Tremlett Hall
> in the County of Dorset.
> She Departed this Life
> August 30 1873
> Aged 18.

Why should an English girl die in our town? Had she been passing through? Had she died of poisoning? Had someone shot her? Eighteen was young to die.

On that day, the first day I read her tablet, I had walked from the Protestant church to the field beside the wood. I often went there because it was a lonely place, away from the town and from people. I sat on a boulder and felt hot sun on my face and head, and on my neck and the backs of my hands. I began to imagine her, Elvira Tremlett of Tremlett Hall in the county of Dorset, England. I gave her her long hair and her smile and her elaborate earrings, and I felt I was giving her gifts. I gave her her clothes, wondering if I had got them right. Her fingers were delicate as straws, lacing together the first of her daisy-chains. Her voice hadn't the edge that Myrna Loy's had, her neck was more elegant.

'Oh, love,' she said on the Saturday after the sexton had spoken to me. 'The tablet's only a stone. It's silly to go gazing at it.'

I knew it was and yet it was hard to prevent myself. The more I gazed at it the more I felt I might learn about her: I didn't know if I was getting her right. I was afraid even to begin to imagine her death because I thought I might be doing wrong to have her dying from some cause that wasn't the correct one. It seemed insulting to her memory not to get that perfectly correct.

'You mustn't want too much,' she said to me on that Saturday afternoon. 'It's as well you've finished with the tablet on the wall. Death doesn't matter, you know.'

I never went back to the Protestant church. I remember what my mother had said about the quality of English goods, and how cars assembled in England were twice the ones assembled in Dublin. I looked at the map of England in my atlas and there was Dorset. She'd been travelling, maybe staying in a house near by, and died somehow: she was right, it didn't matter.

Tremlett Hall was by a river in the country, with Virginia creeper all over it, with long corridors and suits of armour in the hall, and a fire-place in the hall also. In *David Copperfield*, which I had seen in the Electric, there might have been a house like Tremlett Hall, or in *A Yank at Oxford*: I couldn't quite remember. The gardens were beautiful: you walked from one garden to another, to a special rose-garden with a sundial, to a vegetable garden with high walls around it. In the house someone was always playing a piano. 'Me,' Elvira said.

My brothers went to work in the garage, first Brian and then Liam. Effie went to Cork, to the commercial college. The boys at the Christian Brothers' began to whistle at Kitty and sometimes would give me notes to pass on to her. Even when other people

were there I could feel Elvira's nearness, even her breath sometimes, and certainly the warmth of her hands. When Brother Flynn
hit me one day she cheered me up. When my father came back
from Keogh's in time for his Saturday tea her presence made it
easier. The garage I hated, where I was certain now I would one
day lift paraffin cans from one corner to another, was lightened
by her. She was in Mrs Discroll's vegetable shop when I bought
cabbage and potatoes for my mother. She was there while I waited
for the Electric to open, and when I walked through the animals
on a fair-day. In the stony field the sunshine made her earrings
glitter. It danced over a brooch she had not had when first I imagined her, a brooch with a scarlet jewel, in the shape of a dragon.
Mist caught in her hair, wind ruffled the skirts of her old-fashioned
dress. She wore gloves when it was cold, and a green cloak that
wrapped itself all around her. In spring she often carried daffodils,
and once—one Sunday in June—she carried a little dog, a grey
Cairn that afterwards became part of her, like her earrings and
her brooch.

I grew up but she was always eighteen, as petrified as her tablet
on the wall. In the bedroom which I shared with Brian and Liam
I came, in time, to take her dragon's brooch from her throat and
to take her earrings from her pale ears and to lift her dress from
her body. Her limbs were warm, and her smile was always there.
Her slender fingers traced caresses on my cheeks. I told her that
I loved her, as the people told one another in the Electric.

'You know why they're afraid of you?' she said one day in the
field by the wood. 'You know why they hope that God will look
after you?'

I had to think about it but I could come to no conclusion on my
own, without her prompting. I think I wouldn't have dared; I'd
have been frightened of whatever there was.

'You know what happens,' she said, 'when your uncle stays in
Cork on a Saturday night? You know what happened once when
your father came back from Keogh's too late for his meal, in the
middle of the night?'

I knew before she told me. I guessed, but I wouldn't have if she
hadn't been there. I made her tell me, listening to her quiet voice.
My Uncle Jack went after women as well as greyhounds in Cork.
It was his weakness, like going to Keogh's was my father's. And
the two weaknesses had once combined, on Saturday night a long

time ago when my uncle hadn't gone to Cork and my father was a long time in Keogh's. I was a child of my Uncle Jack and my mother, born of his weakness and my mother's anger as she waited for the red bleariness of my father to return, footless in the middle of the night. It was why my father called my uncle a hypocrite. It was maybe why my uncle was always looking at the ground, and why he assisted Canon O'Keefe in the rectory and in the Church of the Holy Assumption. I was their sin, growing in front of them, for God to look after.

'They have made you,' Elvira said. 'The three of them have made you what you are.'

I imagined my father returning that night from Keogh's, stumbling on the stairs, and haste being made by my uncle to hide himself. In these images it was always my uncle who was anxious and in a hurry: my mother kept saying it didn't matter, pressing him back on to the pillows, wanting him to be found there.

My father was like a madman in the bedroom then, wild in his crumpled Saturday clothes. He struck at both of them, his befuddled eyes tormented while my mother screamed. She went back through all the years of their marriage, accusing him of cruelty and neglect. My uncle wept. 'I'm no more than an animal to you,' my mother screamed, half-naked between the two of them. 'I cook and clean and have children for you. You give me thanks by going out to Keogh's.' Brian was in the room, attracted by the noise. He stood by the open door, five years old, telling them to be quiet because they were waking the others.

'Don't ever tell a soul,' Brian would have said, years afterwards, retailing that scene for Liam and Effie and Kitty, letting them guess the truth. He had been sent back to bed, and my uncle had gone to his own bed, and in the morning there had begun the pretending that none of it had happened. There was confession and penance, and extra hours spent in Keogh's. There were my mother's prayers that I would not be born, and my uncle's prayers, and my father's bitterness when the prayers weren't answered.

On the evening of the day that Elvira shared all that with me I watched them as we ate in the kitchen, my father's hands still smeared with oil, his fingernails in mourning, my uncle's eyes bent over his fried eggs. My brothers and sisters talked about events that had taken place in the town; my mother listened without interest, her large round face seeming stupid to me now. It was a cause for celebration that I was outside the family circle. I was glad not to be part of the house and the garage, and not to be part of the town with its statue and its shops and its twenty-nine public houses. I belonged with a figment of my imagination to an English ghost who had acquired a dog, whose lips were soft, whose limbs were warm, Elvira Tremlett who lay beneath the Protestant church.

'Oh, love,' I said in the kitchen, 'thank you.'

The conversation ceased, my father's head turned sharply. Brian and Liam looked at me, so did Effie and Kitty. My mother had a piece of fried bread on a fork, on the way to her mouth. She returned it to her plate. There was grease at the corner of her lips, a little shiny stream from some previous mouthful, running down to her chin. My uncle pushed his knife and fork together and stared at them.

I felt them believing with finality now, with proof, that I was not sane. I was fifteen years old, a boy who was backward in his ways, who was all of a sudden addressing someone who wasn't in the room.

My father cut himself a slice of bread, moving the bread-saw slowly through the loaf. My brothers were as valuable in the garage now as he or my uncle; Effie kept the books and sent out bills. My father took things easy, spending more time talking to his older customers. My uncle pursued the racing pages; my mother had had an operation for varicose veins, which she should have had years ago.

I could disgrace them in the town, in all the shops and public houses, in Bolger's Medical Hall, in the convent and the Christian Brothers' and the Church of the Holy Assumption. How could Brian and Liam carry on the business if they couldn't hold their heads up? How could Effie help with the petrol pumps at a busy time, standing in her wellington boots on a wet day, for all the town to see? Who would marry Kitty now?

I had spoken by mistake, and I didn't speak again. It was the first time I had said anything at a meal in the kitchen for as long as I could remember, for years and years. I had suddenly felt that she might grow tired of coming into my mind and want to be left alone, buried beneath the Protestant church. I had wanted to reassure her.

'They're afraid of you,' she said that night. 'All of them.'

She said it again when I walked in the sunshine to our field. She kept on saying it, as if to warn me, as if to tell me to be on the look-out. 'They have made you,' she repeated. 'You're the child of all of them.'

I wanted to go away, to escape from the truth we had both instinctively felt and had shared. I walked with her through the house called Tremlett Hall, haunting other people with our footsteps. We stood and watched while guests at a party laughed among the suits of armour in the hall, while there was waltzing in a ballroom. In the gardens dahlias bloomed, and sweet-pea clung to wires against a high stone wall. Low hedges of fuchsia bounded the paths among the flower-beds, the little dog ran on in front of us. She held my hand and said she loved me; she smiled at me in the sunshine. And then, just for a moment, she seemed to be different; she wasn't wearing the right clothes; she was wearing a tennis dress and had a racquet in her hand. She was standing in a conservatory, one foot on a cane chair. She looked like another girl, Susan Peters in *Random Harvest*.

I didn't like that. It was the same kind of thing as feeling I had to speak to her even though other people were in the kitchen. It was a muddle, and somewhere in it I could sense an unhappiness I didn't understand. I couldn't tell if it was hers or mine. I tried to say I was sorry, but I didn't know what I was sorry for.

*   *   *

In the middle of one night I woke up screaming. Brian and Liam were standing by my bed, cross with me for waking them. My mother came, and then my father. I was still screaming, unable to stop. 'He's had some type of nightmare,' Brian said.

It wasn't a nightmare because it continued when I was awake. She was there, Elvira Tremlett, born 1855. She didn't talk or smile: I couldn't make her. Something was failing in me: it was the same as Susan Peters suddenly appearing with a tennis racquet, the same as my desperation in wanting to show gratitude when we weren't in private.

My mother sat beside my bed. My brothers returned to theirs. The light remained on. I must have whispered, I must have talked about her because I remember my mother's nodding head and her voice assuring me that it was all a dream. I slept, and when I woke up it was light in the room and my mother had gone and my brothers were getting up. Elvira Tremlett was still there, one eye half-closed in blindness, the fingers that had been delicate misshapen now. When my brothers left the room she was more vivid, a figure by the window, turning her head to look at me, a gleam of fury in her face. She did not speak but I knew what she was saying. I had used her for purposes of my own, to bring solace. What right, for God's sake, had I to blow life into her decaying bones? Born 1855, eighty-nine years of age.

I closed my eyes, trying to imagine her as I had before, willing her young girl's voice and her face and hair. But even with my eyes closed the old woman moved about the room, from the window to the foot of Liam's bed, to the wardrobe, into a corner, where she stood still.

She was on the landing with me, and on the stairs and in the kitchen. She was in the stony field by the wood, accusing me of disturbing her and yet still not speaking. She was in pain from her eye and her arthritic hands: I had brought about that. Yet she was no ghost, I knew she was no ghost. She was a figment of my imagination, drawn from her dull grey tablet by my interest. She existed within me, I told myself, but it wasn't a help.

Every night I woke up screaming. The sheets of my bed were sodden with my sweat. I would shout at my brothers and my mother, begging them to take her away from me. It wasn't I who had committed the sin, I shouted, it wasn't I who deserved the punishment. All I had done was to talk to a figment. All I'd done was to pretend, as they had.

Canon O'Keefe talked to me in the kitchen. His voice came and went, and my mother's voice spoke of the sheets sodden with sweat every morning, and my father's voice said there was terror in my eyes. All I wanted to say was that I hadn't meant any harm in raising Elvira Tremlett from the dead in order to have an imaginary friend, or in travelling with her to the house with Virginia creeper on it. She hadn't been real, she'd been no more than a flicker on the screen of the Electric Cinema: I wanted to say all that. I wanted to be listened to, to be released of the shame that I felt like a shroud around me. I knew that if I could speak my imagination would be free of the woman who haunted it now. I tried, but they were afraid of me. They were afraid of what I was going to say and between them they somehow stopped me. 'Our

Father,' said Canon O'Keefe, 'Who art in heaven, Hallowed be
Thy Name . . .'

Dr Garvey came and looked at me: in Cork another man looked
at me. The man in Cork tried to talk to him, telling me to lie
down, to take my shoes off if I wanted to. It wasn't any good, and
it wasn't fair on them, having me there in the house, a person in
some kind of nightmare. I quite see now that it wasn't fair on
them, I quite see that.

Because of the unfairness I was brought, one Friday morning
in a Ford car my father borrowed from a customer, to this brown-
brick mansion, once the property of a local family. I have been
here for thirty-four years. The clothes I wear are rough, but I have
ceased to be visited by the woman who Elvira Tremlett became
in my failing imagination. I ceased to be visited by her the moment
I arrived here, for when that moment came I knew that this was
the house she had been staying in when she died. She brought me
here so that I could live in peace, even in the room that had been
hers. I had disturbed her own peace so that we might come here
together.

*   *   *

I have not told this story myself. It has been told by my weekly
visitor, who has placed me at the centre of it because that, of
course, is where I belong. Here, in the brown-red mansion, I have
spoken without difficulty. I have spoken in the garden where I
work in the daytime; I have spoken at all meals; I have spoken to
my weekly visitor. I am different here. I do not need an imaginary
friend, I could never again feel curious about a girl who died.

I have asked my visitor what they say in the town, and what the
family say. He replies that in the bar of Corrigan's Hotel commercial travellers are told of a boy who was haunted, as a place or a
house is. They are drawn across the bar to a window: Devlin Bros.,
the garage across the street, is pointed out to them. They listen
in pleasurable astonishment to the story of nightmares, and hear
the name of an English girl who died in the town in 1873, whose
tablet is on the wall of the Protestant church. They are told of the
final madness of the boy, which came about through his visions of
this girl, Elvira Tremlett.

The story is famous in the town, the only story of its kind the town possesses. It is told as a mystery, and the strangers who hear it sometimes visit the Protestant church to look up at the tablet that commemorates a death in 1873. They leave the church in bewilderment, wondering why an uneasy spirit should have lighted on a boy so many years later. They never guess, not one of them, that the story as it happened wasn't a mystery in the least.

THE UNBURIED LEGS

Gerald Griffin

The stories of Gerald Griffin have been described as containing more than their share of murders and foul crimes, as well as portraying events which are firmly in the Gothic tradition that was so popular with readers when Griffin began his career. As a pioneer in Irish literature, his work was to prove influential to many subsequent generations of writers—not least Bram Stoker who was familiar with his famous collection, Holland-Tide; *or* Munster Popular Tales *(1827) which contained 'The Brown Man', a gruesome tale about the ravages of an undead creature not unlike a vampire. The similarities between this story and some of the elements in Stoker's* Dracula, *which was written seventy years later, have been commented upon by a number of literary critics.*

Gerald Griffin (1803–1840) was a contemporary of that other great horror story pioneer, Edgar Allan Poe, and like him was to endure a hopeless love affair and die tragically young. Born into a large Catholic farming family in Limerick, he developed in his teens a passionate desire to write, and subsequently went to London where he met up with a group of expatriate Irish journalists who helped him to get his early stories and essays published. His first book, Holland-Tide, *was enthusiastically reviewed and sold extremely well. His reputation was further enhanced when he published* The Collegians *(1829), a novel of the darker side of Irish life which James M. Cahalan has described in* The Irish Novel: A Critical History *(1988) as 'the best and most popular full-length Irish novel up until that date.'*

But fame did nothing to ease the young author's hopeless passion for a married Protestant lady, Lydia Fisher, or help his almost pathological reclusiveness. In a desperate attempt to resolve these conflicts, Griffin retreated for two years into service as a Christian Brother in Cork, but within eighteen months of leaving the order he contracted typhus fever and died. He was just 37, but his influence would live on in the work of writers such as Stoker, Dion Boucicault, Flann O'Brien (who took his famous pseudonym, Myles na Coppaleen, from a character in The Collegians), *and James Plunkett. Another of his admirers, Brian Cleeve, has even compared him to Dostoyevski. 'The Unburied Legs', first published in 1827, is just one of Griffin's several unique horror tales in which he demonstrates how the Irish sense of humour can exist side by side with cruelty and violence.*

*   *   *

In the cool grey of a fine Sunday morning in the month of June, Shoresha Hewer, dressed out in a new *shoot* of clothes, and with a pair of runner leather brogues that had never been on the foot of man before, set out from his father's little cabin, romantically situated amidst a little group of elder and ash trees, on the banks of the river Flesk, to overtake an early mass in the village of Abbeydorney. Such, at least, to the old couple, was represented as the ostensible object of Shoresha's long walk, though they did not fail to hint to one another, with half-suppressed smiles, as he closed the door after him, that his views were not altogether limited to that sacred ceremony. What was really uppermost in his thoughts on that auspicious morning, as he brushed along with a light and springing step over heather or tussock—whether the chapel, where he was to kneel by the side of a little blue-eyed, fair-haired devotee, during the service, and the long and digressive exhortation; or the barn at Abbeydorney cross, where he was to commence the evening dance with her, it would be invidious to scrutinise, and was especially of little consequence on this occasion, as both his love and his devotion fell prostrate before a master-feeling which suddenly usurped an absolute command over the events of the day.

As he was trudging along a low monotonous heath-covered country, whistling the old air of *Thau me en a hulla agus na dhusig me,** he came to a high double ditch, covered with blackthorn bushes, with here and there the decaying trunk of an old oak or beech, throwing forth a few weakly shoots, which still waved their

---

* I am asleep, and don't wake me.

slender boughs in the wind, as if almost in mimicry of the mighty arms it once stretched forth over the fields. He looked along the bank, and observing a spot where the ascent was likely to prove easy, caught hold of a branch to assist him in mounting, when he heard a noise at the other side, and a rustling among the bushes, as if someone was making his way through; he got his foot, however, on a tuft of rushes in the ditch side to proceed, when suddenly with a loud exclamation he tumbled backward into the field; for what should he see walking upon the top of the ditch, and just preparing to jump down, but two well-shaped, middle-sized legs, without either hip, body, or head. It was just as if they had been cut off a little above the knee, and though there was nothing to connect or regulate their movements, they climbed, jumped and progressed along the moor, in as well adjusted steps as if the first dancing-master of the county of Kerry had been superintending their movements. They evidently belonged to a man, as appeared not only from their figure and size, but from the portion of the white kerseymere garment which buckled at the knee, over a neat silk stocking. The shoes were square-toed, of Spanish leather, and were ornamented with old-fashioned silver buckles, such as had not been used in that part of the country for some generations. They had slowly paced by Shoresha, and already left him staring behind, at the distance of a good stone-throw, before he recovered from his astonishment sufficiently to think of rising, which he accomplished slowly, and almost involuntarily, never taking his eyes off the legs, but ejaculating to himself, 'Blessed mother in heaven! is it awake or dreaming I am?' They had now got on so far, that he perceived they would be soon out of sight if he did not move in pursuit; so abandoning Abbeydorney and its inducements, he, without hesitation, adopted that resolution.

It would be vain to detail all the ohs! the Dhar a dieus! the monoms! that escaped from Shoresha, time after time, as the legs hopped over a trench, picked their steps through a patch of bog, or pushed through a thicket. He was before long joined by a neighbour who was on his way to Listowel, for the priest to christen his child, but who could not resist the temptation of following and ascertaining how this extraordinary phenomenon should end. A smith, and a little boy who had been despatched to fetch him from the cross-road by a traveller to get a few nails driven into a loosened shoe, soon after fell in with them. A milkmaid laid down her can and spancill, and some ragged gorçoons gave over their early game of goal, as they came up, and so great were the numbers collected when they approached Listowel, even at that dewy hour of the morning, that it seemed like the congregation of some little village chapel moving along at prayer time.

It was amusing enough, when they arrived at the waters of the Flesk, to observe with what delicacy and elegance the legs tripped over it, from stepping stone to stepping stone, without getting spot or speck on the beautiful silk stockings. They now cut across the country at a nimble gait, the procession behind lengthening every hour, and increasing in clamorous exclamations of wonder as it proceeded.

After some hard walking, they descended into a wooded glen, where the tangled underwood, and wild briar, and close and stooping branches of the older timber, rendered it no pleasant travelling to such as were under the heavy disadvantage of a superincumbent body. To the subjects of our narrative, which were annoyed by no such lumber, of course no difficulties presented themselves; they hopped over the dense brushwood, or ducked under the branchy arms of oak or elm stretched across the path, with equal activity, while the most eager of the crowd behind were eternally knocking their foreheads and noses against some unobserved bough, or dragging their tattered clothes through blackthorn and briar: several, wearied and fretted with the chase, soon fell behind, while others, seeing no probability of any immediate termination to it, and altogether ignorant to what it might lead, gave up in apprehension. A thousand surmises about it were already afloat; some saying, they saw them going to stop once or twice, and that they certainly would not go much farther; others swearing out, that ' 'twas faster and faster they were walking every moment, and that the dickens a one of 'em would stop or stay until they got to the banks of the Shannon.' Many suggested that it wasn't they at all that were there, but only, as it were, the shapes of 'em; and that they'd keep going, going, ever, until it was night, and lead 'em all into some wood or desert place; and then, maybe, the ground to open beneath 'em, or a gust of wind to come by and sweep 'em away in one *gwall*, so that they'd never be heard of after. The legs had, meantime, crossed a shallow part of the river Gale that stole noiselessly through the bottom of the glen, and pressed on with renewed vigour at the opposite side. A flat, moorish, uninteresting looking country fell fast behind them; and, as they invariably pursued the most direct route to Tarbert, the tired followers, which now consisted chiefly of boys and young men, began in good earnest to suspect that town to be their real destination. They were, however, soon relieved from these disagreeable anticipations, when the legs arrived opposite a place called Newtownsands, made a sudden stop, wheeled the toes round to the right, and almost instantly sprang across a little trench; they then advanced rapidly towards the remains of an old church, which are still to be seen there, within one or two fields of the road. There are but three roofless walls now standing; and close to where the west gable formerly stood is one solitary tree which, in that unwooded and almost uninhabited region, only adds to the universal loneliness. There are a few graves about, but even these are only observable on a very close approach, so buried are they in the long rank grass and weeds, and in the fallen rubbish of the building. To one of these, which lay close to the south wall, our heroes moved on, but at a more measured, and it would seem, reverential pace than before; and kneeling slowly down beside it, remained in that position before the wondering eyes of the few who had persevered in the pursuit, and had now, one after another, come up. As their courage grew in contemplating the pacific and holy attitude of the legs, they began gradually to contract their circle, and creep nearer and nearer; but the closer they approached, the more shadowy did the objects become, until the resemblance was only to be distinguished by a fleecy, almost transparent outline, which moment after moment was less defined, and at last melted away into thin air.

Such was the story that occupied the thoughts and tongues of all the gossips from Newtownsands to Abbeydorney, for months and years after. As the occurrence was in itself quite unique in its kind, even those who pretended to the most intimate communication with the spiritual world, as well as the confessed and best accredited agents of the *gentlemen*, were wholly unable to offer anything like a probable explanation of it. One old blind woman, who was, indeed, the Lord knows how old, and was wrinkled and grey in the memory of the baldest inhabitant of Abbeydorney, called to mind a tale that had been told her when a child, which perhaps may be said to give some clue to it.

'There lived,' she said, 'in former times, a lady of immense wealth, who had a strong castle not far from Abbeydorney, though no one could now tell where; and two great lords came to propose for her: one a fair-haired, blue-eyed youth, of a delicate make and graceful manner; the other a dark, stout, athletic figure, but proud and uncourtly. The lady liked the fair lad best, which made the other so jealous of him that he was determined, one way or another, to compass his death. So he engaged a fellow, by a large sum of money, to get access to his bedroom at night, and cut off his head with a hatchet. On the night the murder was to be committed, he made the lad, who never suspected him, drink more wine than usual after dinner, that he might be wholly incapable of resistance. In this state he retired to his room, where he threw himself on the bed without undressing, and, as it awkwardly enough happened, with his head towards the bed's feet. In a few minutes, in came the fellow with the hatchet, and struck a blow that he thought must have severed the head from the body, but it was the two legs he had cut off. Upon this the young lord groaned, and immediately after received another blow, which killed him. The corpse was put into a sack and carried that night to Newtownsands, where it got Christian burial; but the legs were thrown into a hole in the castle garden, and covered up with earth. The lord who had procured the murder, the next day pretended to the lady that the blue-eyed lad had returned home; upon which, not knowing the deceit, she became quite offended, and in a few weeks after agreed to marry his rival. But in the midst of the joy and feasting on the bridal night, there was a horn blown outside the castle, and soon after, steps were heard ascending the grand staircase, and the doors of the bridal-hall flew open, and in walked two bodyless legs. Then there was screaming, and running, and the bride fainted; but the legs followed the bridegroom about everywhere, until he quitted the castle; and it was said that wherever he looked or turned to, from that hour, he saw them stalking before, or beside, or behind him, until he wasted and fell into a decay. And when he was dying he confessed the whole, and desired the assassin might be searched for everywhere, to ascertain from him where the legs were thrown, that they might be dug up, and get Christian burial; but the villain was never found from that day to this, and maybe,' continued the old woman, 'the legs are in punishment this way, and get leave to walk the country of an odd time, to show what's happening to them, and make some good soul search them out, and have them removed to Newtownsands.'

THE MAN FROM SHORROX'

Bram Stoker

The elements which went into the creation of Bram Stoker's
Dracula—*undeniably the most famous horror story written by any
Irishman—have been slavishly detailed, from the casual comments
about vampires which were made to the author during a dinner
he had with the Hungarian folklore expert, Professor Arminius
Vambery, to his own researches into Transylvanian folklore carried
out in the British Museum before he began to write his masterpiece.
The influence of Gerald Griffin, however, has been less studied but
is equally valid. Stoker had a life-long fascination with the weird,
which had been sown in him by his mother who delighted in telling
him grisly tales from Irish folklore, and also of the real-life horrors
associated with the outbreak of cholera that had occurred in Sligo
in 1832. This love of the gruesome was evident in his earliest
attempts at fiction, as was the fact that he was subconsciously working towards his great novel in certain of these tales—in particular
'The Man From Shorrox''*, *which was originally published in the*
Pall Mall Magazine *in February 1894, some three years before*
Dracula *was completed. According to Harry Ludlam in his book*
A Biography of Dracula: The Life Story of Bram Stoker *(1962),*
'"The Man From Shorrox'" *is clearly a stepping stone to Dracula.'*
  *Abraham Stoker (1847–1912) was born in Dublin and although
a sickly infant, grew up to be a hulking, red-bearded man who
revelled in sports and threw up his first job as a civil servant to enter
the hectic world of the theatre. He was for many years the manager
of the great thespian, Sir Henry Irving, a demanding job which
makes his creation of numerous short stories and various other
horror novels after* Dracula—*including* The Mystery of the Sea
(1902), The Jewel of the Seven Stars *(1903),* The Lady of the
Shroud *(1909), and* The Lair of the White Worm *(1911)—all the*

more remarkable. Small wonder, perhaps, that his death in London at the age of 65 should have been ascribed to exhaustion.

Although the majority of Stoker's short stories were collected after his death by his widow into a volume entitled Dracula's Guest *(1914), 'The Man From Shorrox" was not among these. A curious omission, certainly, for it is a traditional tale of terror, about a traveller and his bizarre encounter with a dead man, that is the equal of anything else in the published collection. It is of particular relevance to the present anthology as the original idea was given to Bram during a visit to Dublin in 1893, when he and Henry Irving dined with his older brother, Thornley. A bluff and exuberant man, Thornley Stoker had travelled extensively throughout Ireland and loved telling stories about the places he had visited and the unusual customs he had seen. During their meal together, he entertained his brother and Sir Henry with a story about a traveller and a corpse which at once provided the attentive Bram with the idea for a short story. Recounted in an intimate, dialect style, 'The Man From Shorrox" represents yet another facet of the extraordinary talent of Ireland's great master of horror.*

*   *   *

'Throth, yer 'ann'rs, I'll tell ye wid pleasure; though, trooth to tell, it's only poor wurrk telling the same shtory over an' over agin. But I niver object to tell it to rale gintlemin, like yer 'ann'rs, what don't forget that a poor man has a mouth on to him as much as Creeshus himself has.

'The place was a market-town in Kilkenny—or maybe King's County, or Queen's County. At all events, it was wan of them counties what Cromwell—bad cess to him!—gev his name to. An' the house was called after him that was the Lord Liftinint an' invinted the polis—God forgive him! It was kep' be a man iv the name iv Misther Mickey Byrne an' his good lady—at laste it was till wan dark night whin the bhoys mistuk him for another gintleman, an unknown man, what had bought a contagious property— mind ye the impidence iv him. Mickey was comin' back from the Curragh Races wid his skin that tight wid the full of the whisky inside of him that he couldn't open his eyes to see what was goin' on, or his mouth to set the bhoys right afther he had got the first tap on the head wid wan of the blackthorns what they done such jobs wid. The poor bhoys was that full of sorra for their mishap whin they brung him home to his widdy that the crather hadn't the hearrt to be too sevare on thim. At the first iv course she was wroth, bein' only a woman afther all, an' weemin not bein' gave to rayson like min is. Millia murdher! but for a bit she was like a madwoman, and was nigh to have cut the heads from aff av thim wid the mate chopper, till, seein' thim so white and quite, she all at wance flung down the chopper an' knelt down be the corp.

'"Lave me to me dead," she sez. "Oh min! it's no use more people nor is needful bein' made unhappy over this night's terrible wurrk. Mick Byrne would have no man worse for him whin he was living, and he'll have harm to none for his death! Now go; an', oh bhoys, be dacent and quite, an' don't thry a poor widdied sowl too hard!"

'Well, afther that she made no change in things ginerally, but kep' on the hotel jist the same; an' whin some iv her friends wanted her to get help, she only sez:

'"Mick an' me run this house well enough; an' whin I'm thinkin' of takin' help I'll tell yez. I'll go on be meself, as I mane to, till Mick an' me comes together agin.'

'An', sure enough, the ould place wint on jist the same, though, more betoken, there wasn't Mick wid his shillelagh to kape the pace whin things got pretty hot on fair nights, an' in the gran' ould election times, when heads was bruk like eggs—glory be to God!

'My! but she was the fine woman, was the Widdy Byrne! A gran' crathur intirely: a fine upshtandin' woman, nigh as tall as a modherate-sized man, wid a forrm on her that'd warrm yer hearrt to look at, it sthood out that way in the right places. She had shkin like satin, wid a warrm flush in it, like the sun shinin' on a crock iv yesterday's crame; an' her cheeks an' her neck was that firrm that ye couldn't take a pinch iv thim—though sorra wan iver dar'd to thry, the worse luck! But her hair! Begor, that was the finishing touch that set all the min crazy. It was just wan mass iv red, like the hearrt iv a burnin' furze-bush whin the smoke goes from aff iv it. Musha! but it'd make the blood come up in yer eyes to see the glint iv that hair wid the light shinin' on it. There was niver a man, what was a man at all at all, iver kem in be the door that he didn't want to put his two arrms round the widdy an' giv' her a hug immadiate. They was fine min too, some iv thim—and warrm

men—big graziers from Kildare, and the like, that counted their
cattle be scores, an' used to come ridin' in to market on huntin'
horses what they'd refuse hundhreds iv pounds for from officers
in the Curragh an' the quality. Begor, but some iv thim an' the
dhrovers was rare min in a fight. More nor wance I seen them,
forty, maybe half a hundred, strong, clear and market-place at
Banagher or Athy. Well do I remimber the way the big, red, hairy
wrists iv thim'd go up in the air, an' down'd come the springy
ground-ash saplins what they carried for switches. The whole lot
iv thim wanted to come coortin' the widdy; but sorra wan iv her'd
look at thim. She'd flirt an' be coy an' taze thim and make thim
mad for love iv her, as weemin likes to do. Thank God for the
same! for mayhap we min wouldn't love thim as we do only for
their thricky ways; an' thin what'd become iv the counthry wid
nothin' in it at all except single min an' ould maids jist dyin', and
growin' crabbed for want iv childher to kiss an' tache an' shpank
an' make love to? Shure, yer 'ann'rs, 'tis childher as makes the
heart iv man green, jist as it is fresh wather than makes the grass
grow. Divil a shtep nearer would the widdy iver let mortial man
come. "No," she'd say; "whin I see a man fit to fill Mick's place,
I'll let yez know iv it; thank ye kindly"; an' wid that she'd shake
her head till the beautiful red hair iv it'd be like shparks iv fire—
an' the min more mad for her nor iver.

'But, mind ye, she wasn't no shpoil-shport; Mick's wife knew
more nor that, an' his widdy didn't forgit the thrick iv it. She'd
lade the laugh herself if 'twas anything a dacent woman could
shmile at; an' if it wasn't, she'd send the girrls aff to their beds,
an' tell the min they might go on talkin' that way, for there was
only herself to be insulted; an' that'd shut thim up pretty quick
I'm tellin' yez. But av any iv thim'd thry to git affectionate, as min
do whin they've had all they can carry, well, thin she had a playful
way iv dalin' wid thim what'd always turn the laugh agin' thim.
She used to say that she larned the beginnin' iv it at the school
an' the rest iv it from Mick. She always kep by her on the counther
iv the bar wan iv thim rattan canes wid the curly ends, what the
soldiers carries whin they can't borry a whip, an' are goin' out wid
their cap on three hairs, an' thim new oiled, to scorch the girrls.
An' thin whin any iv the shuitors'd get too affectionate she'd lift
the cane an' swish them wid it, her laughin' out iv her like mad
all the time. At first wan or two iv the min'd say that a kiss at

the widdy was worth a clip iv a cane; an' wan iv thim, a warrm horse-farmer from Poul-a-Phoka, said he'd complate the job av she was to cut him into ribbons. But she was a handy woman wid the cane—which was shtrange enough, for she had no childer to be practisin' on—an' whin she threw what was left iv him back over the bar, wid his face like a gridiron, the other min what was laughin' along wid her tuk the lesson to hearrt. Whinniver afther that she laid her hand on the cane, no matther how quitely, there'd be no more talk iv thryin' for kissin' in that quarther.

'Well, at the time I'm comin' to there was great divarshuns intirely goin' on in the town. The fair was on the morra, an' there was a power iv people in the town; an' cattle, an' geese, an' tur-keys, an' butther, an' pigs, an' vegetables, an' all kinds iv divil-ment, includin' a berryin'—the same bein' an ould attorneyman, savin' yer prisince; a lone man widout friends lyin' out there in the gran' room iv the hotel what they call the "Queen's Room". Well, I needn't tell yer 'ann'rs that the place was pretty full that night. Musha, but it's the fleas thimselves what had the bad time iv it, wid thim crowded out on the outside, an' shakin', an' thrim-blin' wid the cowld. The widdy, av coorse, was in the bar passin' the time iv the day wid all that kem in, an' keepin' her eyes afore an' ahint her to hould the girrls up to their wurrk an' not to be thriflin' wid the min. My! but there was a power iv min at the bar that night; warrm farmers from four counties, an' graziers wid their ground-ash plants an' big frieze coats, an' plinty iv commer-cials, too. In the middle iv it all, up the shtreet at a hand gallop comes an Athy carriage wid two horses, an' pulls up at the door wid the horses shmokin'. An' begor', the man in it was smokin' too, a big cygar nigh as long as yer arrm. He jumps out an' walks up as bould as brass to the bar, jist as if there was niver a livin' sowl but himself in the place. He chucks the widdy undher the chin at wanst, an', taking aff his hat, sez:

'"I want the best room in the house. I travel for Shorrox', the greatest long-cotton firrm in the whole worrld, an' I want to open up a new line here! The best is what I want, an' that's not good enough for me!"

'Well, gintlemin, ivery wan in the place was spacheless at his impidence; an', begor! that was the only time in her life I'm tould whin the widdy was tuk back. But, glory be, it didn't take long for her to recover herself, an' sez she quietly:

'"I don't doubt ye, sur! The best can't be too good for a gintle-man what makes himself so aisy at home!" an' she shmiled at him till her teeth shone like jools.

'God knows, gintlemin, what does be in weemin's minds whin they're dalin' wid a man! Maybe it was that Widdy Byrne only wanted to kape the pace wid all thim min crowdin' roun' her, an' thim clutchin' on tight to their shticks an' aiger for a fight wid any man on her account. Or maybe it was that she forgive him his impidence; for well I know that it's not the most modest man, nor him what kapes his distance, that the girrls, much less the widdies, likes the best. But anyhow she spake out iv her to the man from Manchesther:

'"I'm sorry, sur, that I can't give ye the best room—what we call the best—for it is engaged already."

'"Then turn him out!" sez he.

'"I can't," she says—"at laste not till tomorra; an' ye can have the room thin iv ye like."

'There was a kind iv a sort iv a schnicker among some iv the min, thim knowin' iv the corp, an' the Manchesther man tuk it that they was laughin' at him; so he sez:

'"I'll shleep in that room tonight; the other gintleman can put up wid me iv I can wid him. Unless," sez he, oglin' the widdy, "I can have the place iv the masther iv the house, if there's a priest or a parson handy in this town—an' sober," sez he.

'Well, tho' the widdy got as red as a Claddagh cloak, she jist laughed an' turned aside, sayin':

'"Throth, sur, but it's poor Mick's place ye might have, an' welkim, this night."

'"An' where might that be now, ma'am?" sez he, lanin over the bar; an' him would have chucked her under the chin agin, only that she moved her head away that quick.

'"In the churchyard!" she sez. "Ye might take Mick's place there, av ye like, an' I'll not be wan to say ye no."

'At that the min round all laughed, an' the man from Manchesther got mad, an' shpoke out, rough enough too it seemed:

'"Oh, he's all right where he is. I daresay he's quieter times where he is than whin he had my luk out. Him an' the devil can toss for choice in bein' lonely or bein' quite."

'Wid that the widdy blazes up all iv a suddint, like a live sod shtuck in the thatch, an' sez she:

'"Who are ye that dares to shpake ill iv the dead, an' to couple his name wid the divil, an' to his widdy's very face? It's aisy seen that poor Mick is gone!" an' wid that she threw her apron over her head an' sot down an' rocked herself to and fro, as widdies do whin the fit is on thim iv missin' the dead.

'There was more nor wan man there what'd like to have shtud opposite the Manchesther man wid a bit iv a blackthorn in his hand; but they knew the widdy too well to dar to intherfere till they were let. At length wan iv thim—Mr Hogan from nigh Portarlington, a warrm man, that'd put down a thousand pounds iv dhry money any day in the week—kem over to the bar an' tuk aff his hat, an' sez he:

'"Mrs Byrne, ma'am, as a friend of poor dear ould Mick, I'd be glad to take his quarrel on meself on his account, an' more than proud to take it on his widdy's, if, ma'am, ye'll only honour me be saying the wurrd."

'Wid that she tuk down the apron from aff iv her head an' wiped away the tears in her jools iv eyes wid the corner iv it.

'"Thank ye kindly," sez she; "but, gintlemin, Mick an' me run this hotel long together, an' I've run it alone since thin, an' I mane to go on runnin' it be meself, even if new min from Manchesther itself does be bringin' us new ways. As to you, sur," sez she, turnin' to him, "it's powerful afraid I am that there isn't accommodation here for a gintlemin what's so requireful. An' so I think I'll be askin' ye to find convanience in some other hotel in the town."

'Wid that he turned on her an' sez, "I'm here now, an' I offer to pay me charges. Be the law ye can't refuse to resave me or refuse me lodgmint, especially whin I'm on the primises."

'So the Widdy Byrne drewed herself up, an' sez she, "Sur, ye ask yer legal rights; ye shall have them. Tell me what it is ye require."

'Sez he sthraight out: "I want the best room."

'""I've tould you already," sez she, "there's a gintleman in it."

'"Well," sez he, "what other room have ye vacant?"

'"Sorra wan at all,' sez she. "Every room in the house is tuk. Perhaps, sur, ye don't think or remimber that there's a fair on tomorra."

'She shpoke so polite that ivery man in the place knew there was somethin' comin'—later on. The Manchesther man felt that the laugh was on him; but he didn't want for impidence, so he up, an' sez he:

'"Thin, if I have to share wid another, I'll share wid the best! It's the Queen's Room I'll be shleepin' in this night."

'Well, the min shtandin' by wasn't too well plazed wid what was going on; for the man from Manchesther he was plumin' himself for all the worrld like a cock on a dunghill. He laned agin over the bar an' began makin' love to the widdy hot an' fast. He was a fine, shtout-made man, wid a bull neck on to him an' short hair, like wan iv thim "two-to-wan-bar-wans" what I've seen at Punchestown an' Fairy House an' the Galway races. But he seemed to have no manners at all in his coortin', but done it as quick an' business-like as takin' his commercial ordhers. It was like this: "I want to make love; you want to be made love to, bein' a woman. Hould up yer head!"

'We all could see that the widdy was boilin' mad; but, to do him fair, the man from Manchesther didn't seem to care what any wan thought. But we all seen what he didn't see at first, that the widdy began widout thinkin' to handle the rattan cane on the bar. Well, prisintly he began agin to ask about his room, an' what kind iv a man it was that was to share it wid him.

'So sez the widdy, "A man wid less wickedness in him nor you have, an' less impidence."

'"I hope he's a quite man," sez he.

'So the widdy began to laugh, an' sez she: "I'll warrant he's quite enough."

'"Does he shnore? I hate a man—or a woman ayther—what shnores."

'"Throth," sez she, "there's no shnore in him"; an' she laughed agin.

'Some iv the min round what knew iv the ould attorney-man— saving yer prisince—began to laugh too; and this made the Manchesther man suspicious. When the likes iv him gets suspicious he gets rale nasty; so he sez, wid a shneer:

'"You seem to be pretty well up in his habits, ma'am!"

'The widdy looked round at the graziers, what was clutchin' their ash plants hard, an' there was a laughin' divil in her eye that kep' thim quite; an' thin she turned round to the man, and sez she:

'"Oh, I know that much, anyhow, wid wan thing an' another, begor!"

'But she looked more enticin' nor iver at that moment. For sure the man from Manchesther thought so, for he laned nigh his whole body over the counther, an' whispered somethin' at her, puttin' out his hand as he did so, an' layin' it on her neck to dhraw her to him. The widdy seemed to know what was comin', an' had her hand on the rattan; so whin he was draggin' her to him an' puttin' out his lips to kiss her—an' her first as red as a turkey-cock an' thin as pale as a sheet—she ups wid the cane and gev him wan skelp across the face wid it, shpringin' back as she done so. Oh jool! but that was a skelp! A big wale iv blood riz up as quick as the blow was shtruck, jist as I've seen on the pigs' backs whin they do be prayin' aloud not to be tuk where they're wanted.

'"Hands off, Misther Impidence!" sez she. The man from Manchesther was that mad that he ups wid the tumbler forninst him an' was goin' to throw it at her, whin there kem an odd sound from the graziers—a sort of "Ach!" as whin a man is workin a sledge, an' I seen the ground-ash plants an' the big fists what held thim, and the big hairy wrists go up in the air. Begor, but polis thimselves wid bayonets wouldn't care to face thim like that! In the half of two twos the man from Manchesther would have been cut in ribbons, but there came a cry from the widdy what made the glasses ring:

'"Shtop! I'm not goin' to have any fightin' here; an' besides, there's bounds to the bad manners iv even a man from Shorrox'. He wouldn't dar to shtrike me—though I have no head! Maybe I hit a thought too hard; but I had rayson to remimber that somethin' was due on Mick's account too. I'm sorry, sur," sez she to the man, quite polite, "that I had to defind meself; but whin a gintleman claims the law to come into a house, an' thin assaults th' owner iv it, though she has no head, it's more restrainful he should be intirely!"

'"Hear, hear!" cried some iv the min, an' wan iv thim sez "Amen," sez he, an' they all begin to laugh. The Manchesther man he didn't know what to do; for begor he didn't like the look of thim ash plants up in the air, an' yit he was not wan to like the laugh agin' him or to take it aisy. So he turns to the widdy an' he lifts his hat an' sez he wid mock politeness:

'"I must complimint ye, ma'am, upon the shtrength iv yer arrm,

as upon the mildness iv yer disposition. Throth, an' I'm thinkin'
that it's misther Mick that has the best iv it, wid his body lyin'
paceful in the churchyard, anyhow; though the poor sowl doesn't
seem to have much good in changin' wan devil for another!' An'
he looked at her rale spiteful.

'Well, for a minit her eyes blazed, but thin she shmiled at him,
an made a low curtsey, an' sez she—oh! mind ye, she was a gran'
woman at givin' back as good as she got—

' "Thank ye kindly, sur, for yer polite remarks about me arrm.
Sure me poor dear Mick often said the same; only he said more
an' wid shuparior knowledge! 'Molly,' sez he—'I'd mislike the
shtrength iv yer arrm whin ye shtrike, only that I forgive ye for it
whin it comes to the huggin'!' But as to poor Mick's prisint condition I'm not goin' to argue wid ye, though I can't say that I
forgive ye for the way you've shpoke iv him that's gone. Bedad,
it's fond iv the dead y'are, for ye seem onable to kape thim out
iv yer mouth. Maybe ye'll be more respectful to thim before ye
die!"

' "I don't want no sarmons!" sez he, wery savage. "Am I to
have me room to-night, or am I not?"

' "Did I undherstand ye to say," sez she, "that ye wanted a
share iv the Queen's Room?"

' "I did! an' I demand it."

' "Very well, sur," sez she very quietly, "ye shall have it!" Jist
thin the supper war ready, and most iv the min at the bar thronged
into the coffee-room an among thim the man from Manchesther,
what wint bang up to the top iv the table an sot down as though
he owned the place, an' him niver in the house before. A few iv
the bhoys shtayed a minit to say another word to the widdy, an'
as soon as they was alone Misther Hogan up, an' sez he:

' "Oh, darlint! but it's a jool iv a woman y'are! Do ye raly mane
to put him in the room wid the corp?"

' "He said he insisted on being in that room!" she says, quite
sarious; an' thin givin' a look undher her lashes at the bhoys as
made thim lep, sez she:

' "Oh! min, an ye love me give him his shkin that full that he'll
tumble into his bed this night wid his sinses obscurified. Dhrink
toasts till he misremimbers where he is! Whist! Go, quick, so that
he won't suspect nothin'!"

'That was a warrm night, I'm telling ye! The man from Shorrox' had wine galore wid his mate; an' afther, whin the plates an' dishes was tuk away an the nuts was brought in, Hogan got up an' proposed his health, an wished him prosperity in his new line. Iv coorse he had to dhrink that; an' thin others got up, an' there was more toasts dhrunk than there was min in the room, till the man, him not bein' used to whisky punch, began to git onsartin in his shpache. So they gev him more toasts—"Ireland as a nation", an' "Home Rule", an' "The mimory iv Dan O'Connell", an' "Bad luck to Boney", an' "God save the Queen", an' "More power to Manchesther", an' other things what they thought would plaze him, him bein' English. Long hours before it was time for the house to shut, he was as dhrunk as a whole row of fiddlers, an' kep shakin' hands wid ivery man an' promisin' thim to open a new line in Home Rule, an' sich nonsinse. So they tuk him up to the door iv the Queen's Room an' left him there.

'He managed to undhress himself all except his hat, and got into bed wid the corp iv th' ould attorney-man, an' thin an' there fell asleep widout noticin' him.

'Well, prisintly he woke wid a cowld feelin' all over him. He had lit no candle, an' there was only the light from the passage comin' in through the glass over the door. He felt himself nigh fallin' out iv the bed wid him amost on the edge, an' the cowld shtrange gintleman lyin' shlap on the broad iv his back in the middle. He had enough iv the dhrink in him to be quarrelsome.

'"I'll throuble ye,' sez he, "to kape over yer own side iv the bed—or I'll soon let ye know the rayson why." An' wid that he give him a shove. But iv coorse the ould attorney-man tuk no notice whatsumiver.

'"Y'are not that warrm that one'd like to lie contagious to ye," sez he. "Move over, I say, to yer own side!" But divil a shtir iv the corp.

'Well, thin he began to get fightin' angry, an' to kick an' shove the corp; but not gittin' any answer at all at all, he turned round an' hit him a clip on the side iv the head.

'"Git up," he sez, "iv ye're a man at all, an' put up yer dooks."

'Then he got more madder shtill, for the dhrink was shtirrin' in him, an' he kicked an' shoved an' grabbed him be the leg an' the arrm to move him.

'"Begor!" sez he, "but ye're the cowldest chap I iver kem anigh iv. Musha! but yer hairs is like icicles."

'Thin he tuk him be the head, an' shuk him an' brung him to the bedside, an' kicked him clane out on to the flure on the far side iv the bed.

'"Lie there," he sez, "ye ould blast furnace! Ye can warrm yerself up on the flure till to-morra."'

'Be this time the power iv the dhrink he had tuk got ahoult iv him agin, an' he fell back in the middle iv the bed, wid his head on the pilla an' his toes up, an' wint aff ashleep, like a cat in the frost.

'By-an'-by, whin the house was about shuttin' up, the watcher from th' undhertaker's kem to sit be the corp till the mornin', an' th' attorney him bein' a Protestan' there was no candles. Whin the house was quite, wan iv the girrls, what was coortin' wid the watcher, shtole into the room.

'"Are ye there, Michael?" sez she.

'"Yis, me darlint!" he sez, comin' to her; an' there they shtood be the door, wid the lamp in the passage shinin' on the red heads iv the two iv thim.

'"I've come," sez Katty, "to kape ye company for a bit, Michael; for it's crool lonesome worrk sittin' there alone all night. But I mustn't shtay long, for they're all goin' to bed soon, when the dishes is washed up."

'"Give us a kiss," sez Michael.

'"Oh, Michael!" sez she: "kissin' in the prisince iv a corp! It's ashamed iv ye I am."

'"Sorra cause, Katty. Sure, it's more respectful than any other way. Isn't it next to kissin' in the chapel?—an' ye do that whin ye're bein' married. If ye kiss me now, begor but I don't know as it's mortial nigh a weddin' it is! Anyhow, give us a kiss, an' we'll talk iv the rights an' wrongs iv it afterwards."

"Well, somehow, yer 'ann'rs, that kiss was bein' gave—an' a kiss in the prisince iv a corp is a sarious thing an' takes a long time. Thim two was payin' such attintion to what was going on betune thim that they didn't heed nothin', whin suddint Katty stops, and sez:

'"Whist! what is that?"

'Michael felt creepy too, for there was a quare sound comin' from the bed. So they grabbed one another as they shtud in the doorway an' looked at the bed almost afraid to breathe till the hair on both iv thim began to shtand up in horror; for the corp rose up in the bed, an' they seen it pointin' at thim, an' heard a hoarse voice say—

'"It's in hell I am!—Divils around me! Don't I see thim burnin' wid their heads like flames? an' it's burnin' I am too—burnin', burnin', burnin'! Me throat is on fire, an' me face is burnin'! Wather! wather! Give me wather, if only a dhrop on me tongue's tip!"

'Well, thin Katty let one screetch out iv her, like a wake the dead, an' tore down the passage till she kem to the shtairs, and tuk a flyin' lep down an' fell in a dead faint on the mat below; and Michael yelled 'murdher' wid all his might.

'It wasn't long till there was a crowd in that room, I tell ye; an' a mighty shtrange thing it was that sorra wan iv the graziers had even tuk his coat from aff iv him to go to bed, or laid by his shtick. An' the widdy too, she was as nate an' tidy as iver, though seemin' surprised out iv a sound shleep, an' her clothes onto her, all savin' a white bedgown, an' a candle in her hand. There was some others what had been in bed, min an' wimin wid their bare feet an' slippers on to some iv thim, wid their bracers down their backs, an' their petticoats flung on anyhow. An' some iv thim in big nightcaps, an' some wid their hair all screwed up in knots wid little wisps iv paper, like farden screws iv Limerick twist or Lundy Foot snuff. Musha! but it was the ould weemin what was afraid iv things what didn't alarrm the young wans at all. Divil resave me! but the sole thing they seemed to dhread was the min—dead or alive it was all wan to thim—an' 'twas ghosts an' corpses an' mayhap divils that the rest was afraid iv.

'Well, whin the Manchesther man seen thim all come tumblin into the room he began to git his wits about him; for the dhrink was wearin' aff, an' he was thryin' to remimber where he was. So whin he seen the widdy he put his hand up to his face where the red welt was, an' at wance seemed to undhershtand, for he got mad agin an' roared out:

'"What does this mane? Why this invasion iv me chamber? Clear out the whole kit, or I'll let yez know!" Wid that he was goin' to jump out of bed, but the moment they seen his toes the ould weemin let a screech out iv thim, an' clung to the min an' implored thim to save thim from murdher—an' worse. An' there was the Widdy Byrne laughin' like mad; an' Misther Hogan shtepped out, an' sez he:

'"Do jump out, Misther Shorrox! The boys has their switches, an' it's a mighty handy costume ye're in for a leatherin'!"

'So wid that he jumped back into bed an' covered the clothes over him.

'"In the name of God," sez he, "what does it all mane?"

'"It manes this," sez Hogan, goin' round the bed an' draggin' up the corp an' layin' it on the bed beside him. "Begorra! but it's a cantankerous kind iv a scut y'are. First nothin' will do ye but sharin' a room wid a corp: an' thin ye want the whole place to yerself.'

'"Take it away! Take it away," he yells out.

'"Begorra," sez Mister Hogan, "I'll do no such thing. The gintleman ordhered the room first, an' it's he has the right to ordher you to be brung out!"

'"Did he shnore much, sur?" says the widdy; an' wid that she burst out laughin' an' cryin' all at wanst. "That'll tache ye to shpake ill iv the dead agin!" An' she flung her petticoat over her head an run out iv the room.

'Well, we turned the min all back to their own rooms; for the most part iv thim had plenty iv dhrink on board, an' we feared for a row. Now that the fun was over, we didn't want any unplisintness to follow. So two iv the graziers wint into wan bed, an' we put the man from Manchesther in th' other room, an' gev him a screechin' tumbler iv punch to put the hearrt in him agin.

'I thought the widdy had gone to her bed; but whin I wint to put out the lights I seen one in the little room behind the bar, an' I shtepped quite, not to dishturb her, and peeped in. There she was on a low shtool rockin' herself to an' fro, an' goin' on wid her laughin' an' cryin' both together, while she tapped wid her fut on the flure. She was talkin' to herself in a kind iv a whisper, an' I heerd her say:

'"Oh, but its the crool woman I am to have such a thing done in me house—an' that poor sowl, wid none to weep for him, knocked about that a way for shport iv dhrunken min—while me poor dear darlin' himself is in the cowld clay!—But oh! Mick, Mick, if ye were only here! Wouldn't it be you—you wid the fun iv ye an' yer merry hearrt—that'd be plazed wid the doin's iv this night!"'

A HOUSE POSSESSED

Sax Rohmer

Sax Rohmer was the creator of another of the immortal figures of horror fiction—the vile and villainous Fu Manchu, whose attempts at world domination were recounted in a total of thirteen novels, from Dr Fu Manchu, *published in 1913, to the final adventure,* Emperor Fu Manchu, *which appeared in 1958. The evil oriental mastermind employed all manner of horrifying weapons in his battles with his great adversary, Nayland Smith, including man-eating plants, poison gases, deadly fungi and even poisonous spiders. The success of the Fu Manchu stories, in print and later in films, on radio and TV, has tended to obscure Rohmer's other outstanding macabre and horror stories which appeared in collections such as* Tales of Secret Egypt *(1918),* The Haunting of Low Fennel *(1920) and* Tales of East and West: Thirteen Little Masterpieces of Death and Fear and Terror *(1933), as well as his novels* Brood of the Witch Queen *(1918),* The Green Eyes of Bast *(1920) and* The Bat Flies Low *(1935).*

Sax Rohmer (1883–1959) was the pseudonym of Arthur Sarsfield Ward, whose parents were both Irish and came from two of the most distinguished Irish families. His middle name, Sarsfield, was from the great seventeenth-century Irish general, and Ward was the anglicised version of Mac an Bhaird, the son of the bard. Arthur initially set his sights on becoming a journalist, but having failed to make an impact he turned to writing crime and mystery stories for the many popular magazines on sale at the turn of the century. His initial stories were published as by 'A. Sarsfield Ward', but he invented the more exotic Sax Rohmer for his tales of Fu Manchu and the pair became world-famous almost overnight. The author's desire for authenticity in his stories—especially those with an occult or supernatural background—caused him to join the secretive

*Order of the Golden Dawn which harboured a membership includ-
ing the notorious Aleister Crowley. Sax Rohmer used his experi-
ences with this group as the basis for a series of stories about Moris
Klaw, a London antique dealer and expert on the occult known as
the Dream Detective, who investigated crimes which had supernatural connotations. Among his numerous short tales, 'A House Possessed', which he contributed to* The New Magazine *in December
1912, is undoubtedly the most suitable for this book. It is all about
the return of a man from the dead and features a genial, red-bearded
Irish monk named Father Bernard—shades of Bram Stoker here!
The story was also apparently based on a seventeenth-century Irish
legend handed down to Sax Rohmer by the Sarsfield family, about
a group of devil worshippers who dabbled in black magic. Like
Bram Stoker's story, too, 'A House Possessed' was never included
in the author's collected works and has been unavailable for almost
a quarter of a century.*

* * *

I strode briskly up the long beech avenue. The snow that later
was to carpet the drive and to clothe the limbs of the great trees,
now hung suspended in dull grey cloud banks over Devrers Hall.
This I first set eyes upon the place.

Earl Ryland had seen it from the car when motoring to Strat-
ford, had delayed one hour and twenty-five minutes to secure the
keys and look over the house, and had leased it for three years.
That had been two days ago. Now, as I passed the rusty, iron
gates and walked up the broad stairs of the terrace to the front
door, the clatter of buckets and a swish of brushes told me that
the workmen were busy within. It is, after all, a privilege to be
the son of a Wall Street hustler.

Faithful to my promise, I inspected the progress made by the
decorating contractor, and proceeded to look over the magnificent
old mansion. Principally, I believe, it was from designs by Vanbrugh. The banqueting hall impressed me particularly with its fret-
work ceiling, elaborate mouldings, and its large, stone-mullioned
windows with many-hued, quarrel-pane lattices.

I had this wing of the building quite to myself, and passing
through into what may have been a library, I saw at the farther
end a low, arched door in the wall. It was open, and a dim light

showed beyond. I approached it, passed down six stone steps and found myself in a small room, evidently of much earlier date than the rest of the house.

It had an elaborately carved chimney piece reaching to the ceiling, and the panelling was covered with extraordinary designs. One small window lighted the room. Before the window, his back towards me, stood a cowled monk!

At my gasp of mingled fear and surprise, he turned a red, bearded face to me. To my great amazement, I saw that the mysterious intruder was smoking a well coloured briar!

'Did I frighten you?' he inquired, with a strong Irish brogue. 'I'm sorry! But it's years since I saw over Devrers, and so I ventured to trespass. I'm Father Bernard from the monastery yonder. Are you Mr Ryland?'

I gasped again, but with relief. Father Bernard, broad-shouldered and substantial, puffing away at his briar, was no phantom after all, but a very genial mortal.

'No,' I replied. 'He will be down later. I am known as Cumberly.'

He shook my hand very heartily; he seemed on the point of speaking again, yet hesitated.

'What a grand old place it is,' I continued. 'This room surely, is older than the rest?'

'It is part of the older mansion,' he replied, 'Devereaux Hall. Devrers is a corruption.'

'Devereaux Hall,' I said. 'Did it belong to that family?'

Father Bernard nodded.

'Robert Devereaux, Earl of Essex, owned it. There's his crest over the door. He never lived here himself, but if you can make out medieval Latin, this inscription here will tell you who did.'

He watched me curiously while I struggled with the crabbed characters.

'Here by grace of his noble patron, Robert Devereaux, my lord of Essex,' I read, 'laboured Maccabees Nosta of Padua, a pupil of Michel de Notredame, seeking the light.'

'Nosta was a Jewish astrologer and magician,' explained the monk, 'and according to his own account, as you see, a pupil of the notorious Michel de Notredame, or Nostradamus. He lived here under the patronage of the Earl until 1601, when Essex was executed. Legend says that he was not the pupil of Nostradamus, but his master the devil, and that he brought about the fall of his patron. What became of Nosta of Padua nobody knows.'

He paused, watching me with something furtive in his blue eyes.

'I'm a regular guidebook, you're thinking?' he went on. 'Well, so I am. We have it all in the old records at the monastery. A Spanish family acquired the place after the death of Robert Devereaux—the Miguels, they called themselves. They were shunned by the whole country, and it's recorded that they held Black Masses and Devil's Sabbaths here in this very room!'

'Good heavens!' I cried, 'the house has an unpleasant history!'

'The last of them was burned for witchcraft in the market-place at Ashby, as late as 1640!'

I suppose I looked as uncomfortable as I felt, glancing apprehensively about the gloomy apartment.

'When Devereaux or Devrers Hall was pulled down and rebuilt, this part was spared for some mysterious reason. But let me tell you that from 1640 till 1863—when a Mr Nicholson leased it—nobody has been able to live here!'

'What do you mean? Ghosts?'

'No, fires!'

'Fires!'

'That same! If you'll examine the rooms closely, you'll find that some of them have been rebuilt and some partially rebuilt, at dates long after Vanbrugh's day. It's where the fires have been! Seven poor souls have burned to death in Devrers since the Miguels' time, but the fires never spread beyond the rooms they broke out in!'

'Father Bernard,' I said, 'tell me no more at present! This is horrible! Some of the best friends I have are coming to spend Christmas here!'

'I'd have warned Mr Ryland if he'd given me time,' continued the monk. 'But it's likely he'd have laughed at me for my pains! All you can do now, Mr Cumberly, is to say nothing about it until after Christmas. Then induce him to leave. I'm not a narrow-minded man, and I'm not a superstitious one, I think, but if facts are facts, Devrers Hall is *possessed!*'

The party that came together that Christmas at Devrers Hall was quite the most ideal that one could have wished for or imagined. There was no smart set boredom, for Earl's friends were not smart set bores. Old and young there were, and children too. What Christmas gathering is complete without children?

Mr Ryland, Sr, and Mrs Ryland were over from New York, and the hard-headed man of affairs proved the most charming old gentleman one could have desired at a Christmas party. A Harvard friend of Earl's, the Rev. Lister Hanson, Mrs Hanson, Earl's sister, and two young Hansons were there. They, with Mrs Van Eyck, a pretty woman of thirty whose husband was never seen in her company, completed the American contingent.

But Earl had no lack of English friends, and these, to the round number of twenty, assisted at the Christmas house-warming.

On the evening of the twenty-third of December, as I entered the old banqueting hall bright with a thousand candles, the warm light from the flaming logs danced upon the oak leaves, emblems of hospitality which ornamented the frieze. Searching out strange heraldic devices upon the time-blackened panelling, I stood in the open door in real admiration.

A huge Christmas tree occupied one corner by the musicians' gallery, and around this a group of youngsters had congregated, looking up in keen anticipation at the novel gifts which swung from the frosted branches. My Ryland, Sr, his wife and another grey-haired lady, with Father Bernard from the monastery, sat upon the black oak settles by the fire; they were an oddly assorted, but merry group. In short, the interior of the old hall made up a picture that would have delighted the soul of Charles Dickens.

'It's just perfect, Earl!' came Hanson's voice.

I turned, and saw that he and Earl Ryland stood at my elbow.

'It will be, when Mona comes!' was the reply.

'What has delayed Miss Verek?' I asked. Earl's fiancée, Mona Verek, and her mother were to have joined us that afternoon.

'I can't quite make out from her wire,' he answered quietly, a puzzled frown ruffing his forehead. 'But she will be here by tomorrow, Christmas Eve.'

Hanson clapped him on the back and smiled. 'Bear up, Earl,' he said. 'Hello! here comes Father Bernard, and he's been yarning again. Just look how your governor is laughing.'

Earl turned, as with a bold gait the priest came towards them, his face radiating with smiles, his eyes alight with amusement. It was certainly a hilarious group the monk had left behind him. As he joined us, he linked his arm in that of the American clergyman and drew him aside for a private chat, I thought what a broad-minded company we were. When the two, in intimate conversation, walked off together, they formed one of the most pleasant pictures imaginable. The true spirit of Christmas reigned.

I passed to an oak settee where Justin Grinley, his wife and small daughter were pulling crackers with Mrs Hanson, just as young Lawrence Bowman appeared from a side door.

'Have you seen Mrs Van Eyck?' he inquired quickly.

No one had seen her for some time, and young Bowman hurried off upon his quest.

Grinley raised quizzical eyebrows, but said nothing. In point of fact, Bowman's attentions to the lady had already excited some comment; but Mrs Van Eyck was an old friend of the Rylands, and we relied upon her discretion to find a nice girl among the company—there were many—to take the romantic youth off her hands.

Father Bernard presently beckoned to me from the door beneath the musicians' gallery.

'You have, of course, said nothing of the matters we know of?' he asked, as I joined him.

I shook my head, and the monk smiled around on the gathering.

'The old sorcerer's study is fitted up as a cozy corner, I see,' he continued, 'but between ourselves, I shouldn't let any of the young people stay long in there!' He met my eyes seriously.

'If, indeed, the enemy holds power within Devrers, I think there is no likely victim among you tonight. The legend of Devrers Hall, you must know, Mr Cumberly, is that Maccabees Nosta, or the arch enemy in person, appears here in response to the slightest evil thought, word or deed within the walls! If any company could hope to exclude him, it is the present!' This he said half humorously and with his eyes roaming again over the merry groups about the great lighted room. 'But, please God, the evil has passed.'

He was about to take his leave, for he came and went at will, a privileged visitor, as others of the Brotherhood. I walked with him along the gallery, lined now with pictures from Earl Ryland's collection. One of the mullioned windows was open.

Out of the darkness we looked for a moment over the dazzling white carpet which lay upon the lawn, to where a fairy shrubbery, backed by magical, white trees, glittered as though diamond-dusted under the frosty moon. A murmur of voices came, and two figures passed across the snow: a woman in a dull red cloak with a furred collar and a man with a heavy travelling coat worn over his dress clothes. His arm was about the woman's waist.

The monk made no sign, leaving me at the gallery door with a deep 'Good night.'

But I saw his cowled figure silhouetted against a distant window, and his hand was raised in the ancient form of benediction.

Alone in the long gallery, something of the gaiety left me. By the open window, I stood for a moment looking out, but no one was visible now. The indiscreet dalliance of Mrs Van Eyck with a lad newly down from Cambridge seemed so utterly out of the picture. The lawn on that side of the house was secluded, but I knew that Father Bernard had seen and recognised them. I knew, too, the thought that was in his mind. As I passed slowly back towards the banqueting hall, my footsteps striking hollowly upon the oaken floor, that thought grew in significance. Free as I was, or as I thought I was, from the medieval superstitions which possibly were part of the monk's creed, I shuddered at remembrance of the unnamable tragedies which this gallery might have staged.

It was very quiet. As I came abreast of the last window, the moonlight through a stained quarrel pane spread a red patch across the oaken floor, and I passed it quickly. It had almost the look of a fire burning beneath the woodwork!

Then, through the frosty, night air, I distinctly heard the great bell tolling out, from up the beech avenue at the lodge gate.

I was anxious to know what it meant myself. But Earl, whose every hope and every fear centred in Mona Verek, outran me easily. I came up to the lodge gates just as he threw them open in his madly impulsive way. The lodge was unoccupied, for the staff was incomplete, and a servant had fastened the gates for the night after Father Bernard had left.

The monk could not have been gone two minutes, but now in the gateway stood a tall man enveloped in furs, who rested one hand upon the shoulder of a chauffeur. It had begun to snow again.

'What's the matter?' cried Ryland anxiously, as the man who attended to the gates tardily appeared. 'Accident?'

The stranger waved his disengaged hand with a curiously foreign gesture, and showed his teeth in a smile. He had a black, pointed

beard and small moustache, with fine, clear-cut features and commanding eyes.

'Nothing serious,' he replied. Something in his voice reminded
me of a note in a great organ, it was so grandly deep and musical.
'My man was blinded by a drive of snow and ran us off the road.
I fear my ankle is twisted, and the car being temporarily
disabled . . .'

With the next house nearly two miles away, that was explanation
enough for Earl Ryland. Very shortly we were assisting the distin-
guished-looking stranger along the avenue, Earl pooh-poohing his
protests and sending a man ahead to see that a room would be
ready. The snow was falling now in clouds, and Ryland and I
were covered. At the foot of the terrace stairs, with cheery light
streaming out through the snowladen air, I noted something that
struck me as odd, but at the time as no more than that.

Not a flake of snow rested upon the stranger, from the crown
of his black fur cap to the edge of his black fur coat!

Before I had leisure to consider this circumstance, which a
moment's thought must have shown to be a curious phenomenon,
our unexpected visitor spoke.

'I have a slight face wound, occasioned by broken glass,' he
said. For the first time, I saw that it was so. 'I would not alarm
your guests unnecessarily. Could we enter by a more private door?'

'Certainly!' cried Ryland heartily. 'This way, sir.'

So, unseen by the rest of the party, we entered by the door in
the tower of the south wing and lodged the stranger in one of the
many bedrooms there. He was profuse in his thanks, but declined
any medical aid other than that of his saturnine man. When the
blizzard had somewhat abated, he said, the man could proceed to
the wrecked car and possibly repair it well enough to enable them
to continue their journey. He would trespass upon our good nature
no longer; an hour's rest was all that he required.

'You must not think of leaving tonight,' said Ryland cordially.
'I will see that your wants are attended to.'

His man entered, carrying a bag; we left him descending again
to the hall.

'Why!' cried Earl, 'I never asked him his name and never told
him mine!'

He laughed at his own absentmindedness, and we rejoined his
guests. But an indefinable change had come over the party. The

blizzard was increasing in violence, so that now it shrieked around Devrers Hall like a regiment of ghouls. The youthful members, numbering five, had been sent off to bed, and into the hearts of the elders of the company had crept a general predilection for the fireside. Our entrance created quite a sensation.

'Why,' cried Ryland, 'I believe you took us for bogeys. Who's been telling ghost stories?'

Mrs Van Eyck stretched a dainty foot to the blaze and writhed her white shoulders expressively.

'Mr Hanson has been talking about the Salem witch trials,' she said, turning her eyes to Earl. 'I don't know why he likes to frighten us!'

'There was an alleged witch burned at Ashby, near here, as recently as 1640,' continued Hanson. 'I remember reading about it in a work on the subject; a young Spanish woman, of great beauty, too, called Isabella de Miguel, I believe.'

I started. The conversation was turning in a dangerous direction. Old Mr Ryland laughed, but not mirthfully.

'Quit demons and witches,' he said. 'Let's find a more humorous topic, not that I stand for such nonsense.'

Three crashing blows, sounding like those of a titanic hammer on an anvil, rang through the house. An instant's silence followed, then a frightened chorus: 'What was that?'

No one could imagine, and Earl had been as startled as the rest of us. He ran from the room, and I followed him. The wind howled and whistled with ever increasing violence. At the low arched door leading to the domestic offices, we found a group of panic-stricken servants huddled together.

'What was that noise?' asked Earl sharply.

His American butler, Knowlson, who formed one of the group, came forward. 'It seemed to come from upstairs, sir,' he said. 'But I don't know what can have caused it.'

'Come and look, then.'

Up the massive staircase we went, Knowlson considerably in the rear. But though we searched everywhere assiduously, there was nothing to show what had occasioned the noise. Leaving Ryland peeping in at his two small nephews, who proved to be slumbering peacefully, I went up three steps and through a low archway, and found myself in the south wing. The only occupant, as far as I knew, was the injured stranger. A bright light shone

under his door, and I wondered how many candles he had burning.
I knocked.

A gust of wind shrieked furiously around the building, then
subsided to a sound like the flapping of wings.

The door was opened a few inches. The light almost dazzled
me. I had a glimpse of the unbidden guest, and saw that he wore
a loose dressing gown of an unusual shade of red.

'Has anything disturbed you?' I asked.

'No,' he replied, with much concern in his deep, organ voice,
yet his black eyes were laughing. 'Why do you ask?'

'We heard a strange noise,' I answered shortly. 'Is your ankle
better?'

'I thank you—very much,' he said, 'I am awaiting my man's
report respecting the state of the car.'

There was nothing in his handsome dark face, in his deep voice,
or even in his laughing eyes to justify it, but at that moment I felt
certain, beyond any possibility of doubt, that the noise had come
from his room. I wanted to run! In fact, I do not know how I
might have acted, if Ryland hadn't joined me.

'Sorry to have disturbed you,' came his jovial tones, 'but the
house is full of funny noises! By the way, I forgot to mention that
my name is Wilbur Earl Ryland, and I hope you'll stay just as
long as it suits you!'

'I thank you,' was the unemotional reply. 'You are more than
kind. I am Count de Stano of Padua. Good night.'

He closed the door.

Again came the wind, shrieking around the end of the wing like
a troop of furies; and again came an uncanny flapping. Earl caught
at my arm.

'What is it?'

'Did you hear—someone laughing?'

'No,' I said unsteadily. 'It was the howling of the blizzard.'

At the landing, he turned to me again.

'What had the Count burning in his room?' he muttered. 'That
wasn't candlelight!'

We found a crowd awaiting us at the foot of the staircase. No
one was anxious to go to bed, and arrangements were made by
several of the more nervous to share rooms.

'Has the Count's chauffeur returned?' Earl asked Knowlson.

'He's just come into the servants' hall now, sir. He—'

'Lock up, then.'

'He'd been out in all that snow, sir . . .'

'Well?'

'There wasn't a sign of any on his coat.'

The man's voice shook and he glanced back at the group of servants, none of whom seemed disposed to return to their quarters.

'He wore another over it, ass!' snapped Ryland. 'Set about your business, all of you! You are like a pack of children.'

We experienced no further alarms, save from the uncanny howling of the wind, but there were no more ghost stories. Those who went to bed ascended the great oak staircase in parties. Mr Ryland, Earl and I were the last to go, and we parted at last without reference to the matter, of which, I doubt not, all of us were thinking.

Sleep was almost impossible. My quaint little oak-panelled room seemed to rock in a tempest which now had assumed extraordinary violence. For hours I lay listening for that other sound which was not the voice of the blizzard and which, although I had belittled, I had heard as clearly as Earl had heard it.

I detected it at last, just once—a wild, demoniacal laugh.

I leaped to the floor. The sound had not been within the house, I thought, but outside. Clenching my teeth in anticipation of the icy gust which would sweep into the room, I slightly opened the heavily leaded window. The south wing was clearly visible.

Out from the small, square window of the study of Maccabees Nosta poured a beam of fiery light, staining the snow flakes as they swirled madly through its redness.

A moment it shone, and was gone.

I pulled the window fast.

Strange needs teach us strange truths. I was sure in that hour that the simple faith of Father Bernard was greater than all our wisdom, and I would have given much for his company.

For me the pleasures and entertainments of the ensuing day were but gnawing anxieties and fruitless vigils. Who was the man calling himself de Stano? *Stano* was merely a play on *Nosta*. To what place had his chauffeur taken his car to be repaired? Why did he avoid Father Bernard, as that morning I had seen him do? De Stano claimed acquaintance with mutual friends, all of them absent. Earl was too hospitable. A man who could walk, even with the aid of a big ebony stick, could reach the station in a borrowed car and proceed on his journey.

Devrers Hall was nearly empty, but by one pretext or another I had avoided joining any of the parties. As I stood smoking on the terrace, Mrs Van Eyck came out, dressed in a walking habit which displayed her lithe figure almost orientally.

'Mr Bowman and I are walking over to the monastery. Won't you join us, Mr Cumberly?' she said.

'Thank you, but some unexpected work has come to hand and I fear I must decline! Have you seen our new guest recently?'

'The Count? Yes, just a while ago. What a strange man! Do you know, Mr Cumberly, he almost frightens me.'

'Indeed!'

'He is a most accomplished hypnotist! Oh, I must show you! He was angry with me for being sceptical, you know, and suddenly challenged me to touch him, even with my little finger. I did, look!'

She had pulled off her glove and held out her hand. The top of one finger was blistered, as by contact with fire!

'Hypnotic suggestion, of course,' she said laughingly. 'He is not always red hot.'

She laughed gaily as young Bowman came out; the two walking off together.

I re-entered the house.

None of the servants had seen the Count, and when I knocked at his door there was no reply. Passing back along the corridor I met Lister Hanson.

'Hello!' I said. 'I thought you were out with the others.'

'No. I had some trivial matters to attend to; Majorie and the youngsters have gone skating.'

I hesitated.

'Is Earl with them?'

Hanson laughed.

'He has motored over to the station. Mona Verek is due some time within the next three hours.'

Should I confide in him? Yes, I decided, for I could contain my uncanny suspicions no longer.

'What is your opinion of this de Stano?' I asked abruptly.

Hanson's face clouded.

'Curiously enough, I have not met him,' he replied. 'He patently avoids me. In fact, Cumberly, very few of the folks *have* met him. You must have noticed that on one pretence or another he has avoided being present at meals? Though he is living under the same roof, I assure you the bulk of us *have never seen him.*'

It was sufficient. I at any rate felt assured of a hearing, and, drawing Hanson into my own room, I unfolded to him the incredible suspicions which I dared to harbour and which were shared by Father Bernard.

At the end of my story, the young clergyman sat looking out the window. When he turned his face to me, it was unusually serious.

'It is going back to the Middle Ages,' he said, 'but there is nothing in your story that a Churchman may not believe. I have studied the dark pages of history which deal with witchcraft, demonology and possession. I have seen in Germany the testimonies of men as wise as any we have today. Although I can see your expected incredulity and scepticism, I assure you I am at one with Father Bernard upon this matter. The Count de Stano, whoever or whatever he is, must quit this house.'

'But what weapons have we against—'

'Cumberly, if some awful thing in the shape of man is among us, that thing has come in obedience to a summons. Do you know the legend of Devrers Hall, the dreadful history of the place?'

I nodded, greatly surprised.

'You wonder where I learned it? You forget that I have dipped deeply into these matters. Directly after the party broke up, I had intended to induce Earl to leave. Cumberly, the place is unclean.'

'Is there no way of ridding it of—'

'Only by defeating the thing which legend says first appeared here as Maccabees Nosta. And which of us, being human, can hope to brave that ordeal?'

I was silent for some time.

'We must remember, Hanson,' I said, 'that, regarding certain undoubtedly weird happenings in the light of what we know of Devrers, we may have deceived ourselves.'

'We may,' he agreed. 'But we dare not rest until we know that we *have.*'

So together we searched the house for Count de Stano, but failed to meet with him. The storm of the previous night had subsided, and dusk came creeping upon a winter landscape which spoke only of great peace. The guests began to return, in parties, and presently Earl Ryland arrived, looking very worried.

'Mona's missed her train,' he said. 'There seems to be a fatality about the thing.'

Hanson said nothing at the time, but when Earl had gone upstairs to dress, he turned to me.

'You know Mona Verek, of course?'

'Quite well.'

'She justifies all his adoration, Cumberly. She is the nearest thing to an angel that a human can be. I agree with Earl that there is a fatality in her delay! He is going off again after dinner. You know how dreadfully impulsive he is, and I have always at the back of my brain the idea that we may be deluding ourselves.'

It was close to the dinner hour now, and I hurried to my room to dress. The quaint little window, as I already have mentioned, commanded a view of the south wing, and as I stooped to the oaken window seat, groping for the candles, my gaze strayed across the snow-carpeted lawns to where the shrubbery loomed greyly in the growing December dusk.

Two figures passed hurriedly in by the south entrance, Lawrence Bowman and Marie Van Eyck. They would have quick work to dress. I found the candles, then dropped them and stood peering from the window with a horror upon me greater than any I yet had known in that house.

A few paces behind the pair, footsteps were forming in the snow—the footsteps of one invisible, who followed, who came to the southern door and who entered after them. Faint wreaths as of steam floated over the ghostly trail.

'My God!' I whispered. 'My God!'

How I dressed, Heaven only knows. I have no recollection of anything until, finding myself at the foot of the great staircase, I said to Knowlson, struggling to make my voice sound normal, 'Is the Count de Stano in?'

'I think not, sir. I believe he is leaving this evening. But I have never seen the Count personally, sir.'

Looking in at the door of the long apartment which Earl had had converted into a billiard room, I found Bowman adjusting his tie before a small mirror.

'Have you seen the Count?' I asked shortly.

'Yes. He is talking to Marie—to Mrs Van Eyck—in the lounge.'

I set off briskly. There was but one door to the old study, now the lounge. I hoped (and feared, I confess) to meet the Count there face to face.

The place was only lighted by the crackling wood fire on the great hearth and Mrs Van Eyck alone stood leaning against the mantelpiece, the red gleam of the fire upon her bare shoulders.

'I had hoped to find the Count here,' I said, as she turned to me.

'Surely you passed him? He couldn't have reached farther than the library as you came in.'

I shook my head, and for a moment Mrs Van Eyck looked almost afraid.

'Are you sure?' she asked. 'I can't understand it. He is leaving almost immediately, too.'

Her hands were toying with a curious little ornament suspended by a chain about her neck. She saw me looking at it and held it up for my inspection.

'Isn't it odd?' she laughed rather uneasily. 'The Count tells me that it is an ancient Assyrian love charm.'

It was a tiny golden calf, and, unaccountably, I knew that I paled as I looked at it.

The gong sounded.

I met Lister Hanson at the door of the banqueting hall. His quest had proved as futile as mine.

We were a very merry dinner party. Again it seemed impossible to credit the idea that malign powers were at work in our midst. Earl Ryland made himself the object of much good-humoured jest by constantly glancing at his watch.

'I know it's rude,' he said, 'but you don't know how anxious I am about Mona.'

When at last dinner was over, he left the old people to do the honours and rushed away in his impetuous, schoolboy fashion to the waiting car, and so off to the station.

Hanson touched me on the shoulder.

'To the Count's room first,' he whispered.

We slipped away unnoticed and mounted the staircase. On the landing we met Mrs Van Eyck's maid carrying an armful of dresses.

'Are you packing?' rapped Hanson, with a sudden suspicion in his voice.

'Yes, sir,' replied the girl. 'My lady has had a message and must leave tonight.'

'Have you seen the Count de Stano?'

'A tall, dark gentleman, carrying a black stick? He has just gone along the passage, sir.'

Hanson stood looking after the maid for a moment.

'I have heard of no messenger,' he said, 'and Van Eyck is due on Christmas morning.'

Along the oak-lined passage and up into the south wing we went. The Count's room was empty. There was no fire in the hearth, but the heat of the place was insupportable, although the window was open.

Something prompted me to glance out. From the edge of the lawn below, across to the frosted shrubbery, extended a track of footprints.

'Look, Hanson!' I said and grasped his arm. 'Look! and tell me if I dream!'

A faint vapour was rising from the prints.

'Let's get our coats and see where they lead,' he said quietly.

It was with an indescribable sense of relief that I quitted the room which the Count de Stano had occupied. We got our coats and prepared to go out. With a suddenness which was appalling, the wind rose and, breaking in upon the frozen calm of the evening, shrieked about Devrers Hall with all the fury of a high gale. With it came snow.

Through that raging blizzard, we fought our way around the angle of the house, leaving the company preparing for the dance in the banqueting hall.

Not a track was to be seen, and the snow was falling in swirling clouds.

We performed a complete circuit of the hall, and in the huge yard we found lamps and lanterns burning. Lawrence Bowman's man was preparing his car for the road; he was driving Mrs Van Eyck to the station, the man said. But both Hanson and I quickly noted that young Bowman's luggage was strapped in place.

Retracing our steps, we saw two snow-covered figures ahead of us, a woman in a dull-red cloak and a man in a big motor coat. They passed on to the terrace, and into the light streaming from the open doors. Earl Ryland had returned. His big Panhard stood at the steps.

'My God! Look!' gasped Hanson, and dragged me back.

I knew what to expect, yet at sight of it my heart stood still.

Steaming footprints appeared, hard upon those of Mrs Van Eyck and Bowman. They pursued a supernatural course on the terrace steps, stopped, and passed away around the north angle of the hall.

'May Heaven protect all here tonight!' prayed the clergyman fervently. 'Follow, follow, Cumberly? At all costs we must follow!' he continued hoarsely.

Which of us trembled the more violently, I do not know. Passing the cheery light of the open doors, we traced the devilish tracks before us. The wind had dropped as suddenly as it had arisen, but snow still fell lightly. Then, from the angle of the great house, we saw a sight which robbed us of what little courage we retained.

Glaring in at the window of the room known as the lantern room, with the light of a great log fire and many candles playing fully upon its malignant face, crouched a red-robed figure. A demon of the Dark Ages it seemed, that clutched and mewed and muttered as it glared. It crouched lower, and lower, then drew back and held its arms before its awful face, thrusting away from it that which approached the window from within. It turned and fled with a shriek unlike anything human or animal, and was gone, leaving behind it steaming footprints in the snow.

A slim shape showed darkly behind the lattice, and the cold light reflected from the snow touched the pure, oval face of Mona Verek.

We fought our way back to the terrace.

'The curse of Devrers Hall in its true form,' muttered Hanson, 'in the red robe of Maccabees Nosta, the Uniform of Satan!'

We could not and dared not, speak of what we had seen, but the gaieties of the night left us cold. As the hours passed and still nothing occurred to break the serenity of the happy gathering, my forebodings grew keener.

Yet, whenever I looked at Mona Verek, fair and fragile, with wonderful blue eyes—which often made me fear that already she was more than half a creature of another sphere—I found new courage.

It was Hanson who first noticed that Mrs Van Eyck and Bowman were missing.

He drew my attention to it at the instant when the tempest, for a while quiescent, awoke to renewed fury.

'Did you hear that?' he whispered.

I saw Earl glance up quickly from an intimate chat with Mona.

Mingled with the song of the storm had arisen fiendish laughter again and the sound of dull flapping. It seemed like the signal for what was to befall.

Knowlson, ghastly white, rushed into the hall.

'Mr Ryland! Mr Ryland!' he cried unceremoniously.

In an instant we were all flocking about the door. Bowman's man, trembling, stood outside.

'I don't know what's become of him, sir,' he said tremulously. 'He and Mrs Van Eyck were to have started at eleven-thirty, and, going in to look for him in the lounge—Oh, my God, sir!—I saw something like a great owl go in at the window.'

We delayed no longer. Out into the blizzard we poured and over the snow to the south wing.

Blue, spirituous flames were belching from the window of the astrologer's study! One shrill scream reached our ears, to be drowned by the mighty voices of the wind.

'Impossible to get in the window,' cried Ryland. 'Around through the library. Form up a line to pass buckets, Knowlson!'

As we rushed up the snow-carpeted terrace steps, Hanson fell. Someone stayed to attend to him. Ryland and I ran on through the house and entered the library together. It was in darkness, but the ancient, iron-studded door leading down into the study was outlined in blue light.

I leapt forward in the gloom, my hand outstretched, and something interposed between me and the door—something fiery. With a muffled yell, I drew back.

Ryland passed me. His form vaguely silhouetted against that weird glow, I saw him raise his arms as if to shield his face. An evidently irresistible force hurled him back, and he fell with a crash at the feet of those who crowded the entrance to the library.

'Oh! my God!' he groaned, struggling to his feet. '*What* is before that door?'

A sound like the roaring of a furnace came from within, with a dull beating on the oak. We stood there in the dark, watching the door. Someone pushed to the front of the group.

'Keep back, Masters,' said Ryland huskily. 'My arms are burned to the elbows. Some hellish thing stands before that door. Keep back, man, till we get lights. Bring lights! Bring lights!'

At that we withdrew from the dark library, until we all stood outside in the hall. Some of us muttered what prayers we knew, while the furnace roared inside and the storm shrieked outside.

There have been some with whom I have discussed these events, who were convinced that these were the result of hallucination combined with the unsuspected presence of an accomplished illusionist and remorseless jester, but I am convinced otherwise.

Mona Verek approached from the direction of the banqueting hall, two trembling servants following with lights. She was very pale, but quite composed.

'Mona!' began Earl huskily, 'there's devil's work! This is no place—'

She stopped him with a quiet little gesture, and took a lamp from one of the men.

'Mr Hanson has explained to me, Earl,' she said. 'He is disabled, or he would be here. I quite understand that there is nothing in the library that can harm me. It can only harm those who fear it. I will unlock the door, Earl, I have promised.'

'Mona! Hanson has asked *you*—'

'You don't understand. He has asked me, because for me there is no danger.'

He would have stopped her, but he forgot his injured arms, and was too late. She went in, believing she would be protected.

Protected she was.

No invisible flame seared her, nothing contested her coming. Entering behind her, he saw her stoop and unlock the door. A cloud of oily, blue-black smoke belched out.

We had thought to find those within past aid, but up the steps Lawrence Bowman staggered, dragging the insensible form of Marie Van Eyck.

'Thank God!' said old Mr Ryland devoutly.

There was a piercing, frenzied shriek. All heard it with horror. One of the Library windows banged open, and a cloud of snow poured into the room.

'There's someone getting out,' cried a man's voice.

'De Stano!' yelled Earl.

Several of us leaped to the window. In the stormy darkness, a red something was racing over the snow towards the beech avenue. The wind dropped, and from the monastery a bell rang.

'The midnight service,' I said.

At the first stroke the red figure stopped dead, turned, and seemed to throw up its arms. It was at that moment, I was told by those near the door, that the strange flames died away in the ancient study, leaving only some charred woodwork to show where the fire had been. The blizzard howled again madly. I was not the only one there who heard amid its howling the sound as of flapping wings.

Mona Verek and Bowman were bending over the insensible woman. Upon her flesh was burned a clear impression of a calf, but the little image itself was missing.

The wind died away, no more snow fell and suddenly, as if a curtain had been raised from before it, the moon sailed into the skies. Marie Van Eyck opened her eyes and looked about her with an expression I shall never forget.

'The fire!' she whispered, 'the fire! What is it?'

The bell ceased tolling.

'It is Christmas morning!' said Mona Verek.

THE MIRACULOUS REVENGE

George Bernard Shaw

George Bernard Shaw (1856–1950), whom the distinguished critic Vivian Mercier described as the 'Irish International', is perhaps a surprising figure to find in a collection of horror stories. Yet his body of writings including the earlier novels like Cashel Byron's Profession *(1886), about the brutal world of boxing, and his plays such as* The Devil's Disciple *(1900) and* John Bull's Other Island *(1904) are full of instances of his Irish 'gallows humour'. Particular examples of this can be found in the famous trial scene in* The Devil's Disciple *and the fearful episode in* John Bull's Other Island *where a runaway car endangers several lives, leaves a trail of wreckage as it careers along and finally mangles a pig to death. As one of the characters in the play, Barney Doran, explains with almost sadistic glee: 'There is danger, destruction, torment! What more do we need to make us merry!' Shaw, in fact, once declared that he regarded himself as a tragic writer, 'perpetually tripped up by a comic one.'*

Shaw was born in Dublin, the son of an improvident father and an energetic and musically-minded mother, and it was from her that he inherited the strength of character which shaped his life. After his education at Wesley College, Dublin, he worked for almost five years in a firm of land agents and tried, generally unsuccessfully, to write. In 1876 he followed his mother and sister to London and after a lengthy period of struggle and impoverishment slowly began to make his impact on the world of letters. It was the critical acclaim which greeted his series of Plays Pleasant and Unpleasant *(1898) which at last began to establish his reputation as a major dramatist and literary figure. 'The Miraculous Revenge' is a rare short story and appeared originally in* Time *magazine in March 1885. It is Irish to the core: featuring a dark, satanic character known as*

'Brimstone Billy' and what happens in the wake of the extraordinary discovery that a graveyard in the little community of Four Mile Water has seemingly moved one night, bodies and all, across a river . . .

* * *

I arrived in Dublin on the evening of the 5th of August, and drove to the residence of my uncle, the Cardinal Archbishop. He is, like most of my family, deficient in feeling, and consequently cold to me personally. He lives in a dingy house, with a side-long view of the portico of his cathedral from the front windows, and of a monster national school from the back. My uncle maintains no retinue. The people believe that he is waited upon by angels. When I knocked at the door, an old woman, his only servant, opened it, and informed me that her master was then officiating in the cathedral, and that he had directed her to prepare dinner for me in his absence. An unpleasant smell of salt fish made me ask her what the dinner consisted of. She assured me that she had cooked all that could be permitted in His Holiness's house on a Friday. On my asking her further why on a Friday, she replied that Friday was a fast day. I bade her tell His Holiness that I had hoped to have the pleasure of calling on him shortly, and drove to a hotel in Sackville Street, where I engaged apartments and dined.

After dinner I resumed my eternal search—I know not for what: it drives me to and fro like another Cain. I sought in the streets without success. I went to the theatre. The music was execrable, the scenery poor. I had seen the play a month before in London, with the same beautiful artist in the chief part. Two years had passed since, seeing her for the first time, I had hoped that she, perhaps, might be the long-sought mystery. It had proved otherwise. On this night I looked at her and listened to her for the sake of that bygone hope, and applauded her generously when the curtain fell. But I went out lonely still. When I had supped at a restaurant, I returned to my hotel, and tried to read. In vain. The sound of feet in the corridors as the other occupants of the hotel went to bed distracted my attention from my book. Suddenly it occurred to me that I had never quite understood my uncle's character. He, father to a great flock of poor and ignorant Irish;

an austere and saintly man, to whom livers of hopeless lives daily appealed for help heavenward; who was reputed never to have sent away a troubled peasant without relieving him of his burden by sharing it; whose knees were worn less by the altar steps than by the tears and embraces of the guilty and wretched: *he* had refused to humour my light extravagances, or to find time to talk with me of books, flowers, and music. Had I not been mad to expect it? Now that I needed sympathy myself, I did him justice. I desired to be with a true-hearted man, and to mingle my tears with his.

I looked at my watch. It was nearly an hour past midnight. In the corridor the lights were out, except one jet at the end. I threw a cloak upon my shoulders, put on a Spanish hat, and left my apartment, listening to the echoes of my measured steps retreating through the deserted passages. A strange sight arrested me on the landing of the grand staircase. Through an open door I saw the moonlight shining through the windows of a saloon in which some entertainment had recently taken place. I looked at my watch again: it was but one o'clock and yet the guests had departed. I entered the room, my boots ringing loudly on the waxed boards. On a chair lay a child's cloak and a broken toy. The entertainment had been a children's party. I stood for a time looking at the shadow of my cloaked figure upon the floor, and at the disordered decorations, ghostly in the white light. Then I saw that there was a grand piano, still open, in the middle of the room. My fingers throbbed as I sat down before it, and expressed all that I felt in a grand hymn which seemed to thrill the cold stillness of the shadows into a deep hum of approbation, and to people the radiance of the moon with angels. Soon there was a stir without too, as if the rapture were spreading abroad. I took up the chant triumphantly with my voice, and the empty saloon resounded as though to the thunder of an orchestra.

'Hallo, sir!' 'Confound you, sir—' 'Do you suppose that this—' 'What the deuce—?'

I turned; and silence followed. Six men, partially dressed, and with dishevelled hair, stood regarding me angrily. They all carried candles. One of them had a bootjack, which he held like a truncheon. Another, the foremost, had a pistol. The night porter was behind trembling.

'Sir,' said the man with the revolver, coarsely, 'may I ask

whether you are mad, that you disturb people at this hour with such an unearthly noise?'

'Is it possible that you dislike it?' I replied, courteously.

'Dislike it!' said he, stamping with rage. 'Why—damn everything—do you suppose we were enjoying it?'

'Take care: he's mad,' whispered the man with the bootjack.

I began to laugh. Evidently they did think me mad. Unaccustomed to my habits, and ignorant of music as they probably were, the mistake, however absurd, was not unnatural. I rose. They came closer to one another; and the night porter ran away.

'Gentlemen,' I said, 'I am sorry for you. Had you lain still and listened, we should all have been the better and happier. But what you have done, you cannot undo. Kindly inform the night porter that I am gone to visit my uncle, the Cardinal Archbishop. Adieu!'

I strode past them, and left them whispering among themselves. Some minutes later I knocked at the door of the Cardinal's house. Presently a window on the first floor was opened; and the moonbeams fell on a grey head, with a black cap that seemed ashy pale against the unfathomable gloom of the shadow beneath the stone sill.

'Who are you?'

'I am Zeno Legge.'

'What do you want at this hour?'

The question wounded me. 'My dear uncle,' I exclaimed, 'I know you do not intend it, but you make me feel unwelcome. Come down and let me in, I beg.'

'Go to your hotel,' he said sternly. 'I will see you in the morning. Goodnight.' He disappeared and closed the window.

I felt that if I let this rebuff pass, I should not feel kindly towards my uncle in the morning, nor, indeed, at any future time. I therefore plied the knocker with my right hand, and kept the bell ringing with my left until I heard the door-chain rattle within. The Cardinal's expression was grave nearly to moroseness as he confronted me on the threshold.

'Uncle,' I cried, grasping his hand, 'do not reproach me. Your door is never shut against the wretched. I am wretched. Let us sit up all night and talk.'

'You may thank my position and not my charity for your admission, Zeno,' he said. 'For the sake of the neighbours, I had rather you played the fool in my study than upon my doorstep at this hour. Walk upstairs quietly, if you please. My housekeeper is a hard-working woman: the little sleep she allows herself must not be disturbed.'

'You have a noble heart, uncle. I shall creep like a mouse.'

'This is my study,' he said, as we entered an ill-furnished den on the second floor. 'The only refreshment I can offer you, if you desire any, is a bunch of raisins. The doctors have forbidden you to touch stimulants, I believe.'

'By heaven—!' He raised his finger. 'Pardon me: I was wrong to swear. But I had totally forgotten the doctors. At dinner I had a bottle of *Graves*.'

'Humph! You have no business to be travelling alone. Your mother promised me that Bushy should come over here with you.'

'Pshaw! Bushy is not a man of feeling. Besides, he is a coward. He refused to come with me because I purchased a revolver.'

'He should have taken the revolver from you, and kept to his post.'

'Why will you persist in treating me like a child, uncle? I am very impressionable, I grant you; but I have gone round the world alone, and do not need to be dry-nursed through a tour in Ireland.'

'What do you intend to do during your stay here?'

I had no plans; and instead of answering I shrugged my shoulders and looked round the apartment. There was a statuette of the Virgin upon my uncle's desk. I looked at its face, as he was wont to look in the midst of his labours. I saw there eternal peace. The air became luminous with an infinite network of the jewelled rings of Paradise descending in roseate clouds upon us.

'Uncle,' I said, bursting into the sweetest tears I had ever shed, 'my wanderings are over. I will enter the Church, if you will help me. Let us read together the third part of *Faust*; for I understand it at last.'

'Hush, man,' he said, half rising with an expression of alarm. 'Control yourself.'

'Do not let my tears mislead you. I am calm and strong. Quick, let us have Goethe:

> Das Unbeschreibliche,
> Hier ist gethan;
> Das Ewig-Weibliche,
> Zieht uns hinan.'

'Come, come. Dry your eyes and be quiet. I have no library here.'

'But I have—in my portmanteau at the hotel,' I said, rising. 'Let me go for it, I will return in fifteen minutes.'

'The devil is in you, I believe. Cannot—'

I interrupted him with a shout of laughter. 'Cardinal,' I said noisily, 'you have become profane; and a profane priest is always the best of good fellows. Let us have some wine; and I will sing you a German beer song.'

'Heaven forgive me if I do you wrong,' he said; 'but I believe God has laid the expiation of some sin on your unhappy head. Will you favour me with your attention for a while? I have something to say to you, and I have also to get some sleep before my hour for rising, which is half-past five.'

'My usual hour for retiring—when I retire at all. But proceed. My fault is not inattention, but over-susceptibility.'

'Well, then, I want you to go to Wicklow. My reasons—'

'No matter what they may be,' said I, rising again. 'It is enough that you desire me to go. I shall start forthwith.'

'Zeno! will you sit down and listen to me?'

I sank upon my chair reluctantly. 'Ardour is a crime in your eyes, even when it is shown in your service,' I said. 'May I turn down the light?'

'Why?'

'To bring on my sombre mood, in which I am able to listen with tireless patience.'

'I will turn it down myself. Will that do?'

I thanked him, and composed myself to listen in the shadow. My eyes, I felt, glittered. I was like Poe's raven.

'Now for my reasons for sending you to Wicklow. First, for your own sake. If you stay in town, or in any place where excitement can be obtained by any means, you will be in Swift's Hospital in a week. You must live in the country, under the eye of one upon whom I can depend. And you must have something to do to keep you out of mischief, and away from your music and painting and poetry, which, Sir John Richards writes to me, are dangerous for you in your present morbid state. Second, because I can entrust you with a task which, in the hands of a sensible man, might bring discredit on the Church. In short, I want you to investigate a miracle.'

He looked attentively at me. I sat like a statue.

'You understand me?' he said.

'Nevermore,' I replied, hoarsely. 'Pardon me,' I added, amused at the trick my imagination had played me, 'I understand you perfectly. Proceed.'

'I hope you do. Well, four miles distant from the town of Wicklow is a village called Four Mile Water. The resident priest is Father Hickey. You have heard of the miracles at Knock?'

I winked.

'I did not ask you what you think of them, but whether you have heard of them. I see you have. I need not tell you that even a miracle may do more harm than good to the Church in this country, unless it can be proved so thoroughly that her powerful and jealous enemies are silenced by the testimony of followers of their heresy. Therefore, when I saw in a Wexford newspaper last week a description of a strange manifestation of the Divine Power which was said to have taken place at Four Mile Water, I was troubled in my mind about it. So I wrote to Father Hickey, bidding him give me an account of the matter if it were true, and, if not, to denounce from the altar the author of the report, and to contradict it in the paper at once. This is his reply. He says—well, the first part is about Church matters: I need not trouble you with it. He goes on to say—'

'One moment. Is that his own handwriting? It does not look like a man's.'

'He suffers from rheumatism in the fingers of his right hand; and his niece, who is an orphan, and lives with him, acts as his amanuensis. Well—'

'Stay. What is her name?'

'Her name? Kate Hickey.'

'How old is she?'

'Tush, man, she is only a little girl. If she were old enough to concern you, I should not send you into her way. Have you any more questions to ask about her?'

'None. I can fancy her in a white veil at the rite of confirmation, a type of faith and innocence. Enough of her. What says the Reverend Hickey of the apparitions?'

'They are not apparitions. I will read you what he says. Ahem! "In reply to your inquiries concerning the late miraculous event in this parish, I have to inform you that I can vouch for its truth, and that I can be confirmed not only by the inhabitants of the place, who are all Catholics, but by every person acquainted with the former situation of the graveyard referred to, including the Protestant Archdeacon of Baltinglas, who spends six weeks annually in the neighbourhood. The newspaper account is incomplete and inaccurate. The following are the facts: About four years ago, a man named Wolfe Tone Fitzgerald settled in this village as a farrier. His antecedents did not transpire; and he had no family. He lived by himself; was very careless of his person; and when in his cups, as he often was, regarded the honour neither of God nor man in his conversation. Indeed if it were not speaking ill of the dead, one might say that he was a dirty, drunken, blasphemous blackguard. Worse again, he was, I fear, an atheist; for he never attended Mass, and gave His Holiness worse language even than he gave the Queen. I should have mentioned that he was a bitter rebel, and boasted that his grandfather had been out in '98, and his father with Smith O'Brien. At last he went by the name of Brimstone Billy, and was held up in the village as the type of all wickedness.

' "You are aware that our graveyard, situate on the north side of the water, is famous throughout the country as the burial-place of the nuns of St Ursula, the hermit of Four Mile Water, and many other holy people. No Protestant has ever ventured to enforce his legal right of interment there, though two have died in the parish within my own recollection. Three weeks ago, this Fitzgerald died in a fit brought on by drink; and a great hullabaloo was raised in the village when it became known that he would be buried in the graveyard. The body had to be watched to prevent its being stolen and buried at the cross-roads. My people were greatly disappointed when they were told I could do nothing to stop the burial, particularly as I of course refused to read any service on the occasion. However, I bade them not interfere; and the interment was effected on the 14th of July, late in the evening, and long after the legal hour. There was no disturbance. Next morning, the graveyard was found moved to the south side of the water, with the one newly-filled grave left behind on the north side; and thus they both remain. The departed saints would not lie with the reprobate. I can testify to it on the oath of a Christian priest; and if this will not satisfy those outside the Church, everyone, as I said before, who remembers where the graveyard was two months ago, can confirm me.

' "I respectfully suggest that a thorough investigation into the truth of this miracle be proposed to a committee of Protestant gentlemen. They shall not be asked to accept a single fact on hearsay from my people. The ordnance maps show where the graveyard was; and anyone can see for himself where it is. I need not tell your Eminence what a rebuke this would be to those enemies of the holy Church that have sought to put a stain on her by discrediting the late wonderful manifestations at Knock Chapel. If they come to Four Mile Water, they need cross-examine no one. They will be asked to believe nothing but their own senses.

' "Awaiting your Eminence's counsel to guide me further in the matter,

' "I am, etc." '

'Well, Zeno,' said my uncle: 'what do you think of Father Hickey now?'

'Uncle: do not ask me. Beneath this roof I desire to believe everything. The Reverend Hickey has appealed strongly to my love of legend. Let us admire the poetry of his narrative, and ignore the balance of probability between a Christian priest telling a lie on his oath and a graveyard swimming across a river in the middle of the night and forgetting to return.'

'Tom Hickey is not telling a lie, sir. You may take my word for that. But he may be mistaken.'

'Such a mistake amounts to insanity. It is true that I myself, awaking suddenly in the depth of night, have found myself convinced that the position of my bed had been reversed. But on opening my eyes the illusion ceased. I fear Mr Hickey is mad. Your best course is this. Send down to Four Mile Water a perfectly sane investigator; an acute observer; one whose perceptive faculties, at once healthy and subtle, are absolutely unclouded by religious prejudice. In a word, send me. I will report to you the true state of affairs in a few days; and you can then make arrangements for transferring Hickey from the altar to the asylum.'

'Yes, I had intended to send you. You are wonderfully sharp; and you would make a capital detective if you could only keep your mind to one point. But your chief qualification for this business is that you are too crazy to excite the suspicion of those whom you may have to watch. For the affair may be a trick. If so, I hope and believe that Hickey has no hand in it. Still, it is my duty to take every precaution.'

'Cardinal: may I ask whether traces of insanity have ever appeared in our family?'

'Except in you and in my grandmother, no. She was a Pole; and you resemble her personally. Why do you ask?'

'Because it has often occurred to me that you are, perhaps, a little cracked. Excuse my candour; but a man who has devoted his life to the pursuit of a red hat; who accuses everyone else beside himself of being mad; and who is disposed to listen seriously to a tale of a peripatetic graveyard, can hardly be quite sane. Depend upon it, uncle, you want rest and change. The blood of your Polish grandmother is in your veins.'

'I hope I may not be committing a sin in sending a ribald on the Church's affairs,' he replied, fervently. 'However, we must use the instruments put into our hands. Is it agreed that you go?'

'Had you not delayed me with this story, which I might as well have learned on the spot, I should have been there already.'

'There is no occasion for impatience, Zeno. I must first send to Hickey to find a place for you. I shall tell him that you are going to recover your health, as, in fact, you are. And, Zeno, in Heaven's name be discreet. Try to act like a man of sense. Do not dispute with Hickey on matters of religion. Since you are my nephew, you had better not disgrace me.'

'I shall become an ardent Catholic, and do you infinite credit, uncle.'

'I wish you would, although you would hardly be an acquisition to the Church. And now I must turn you out. It is nearly three o'clock; and I need some sleep. Do you know your way back to your hotel!'

'I need not stir. I can sleep in this chair. Go to bed, and never mind me.'

'I shall not close my eyes until you are safely out of the house. Come, rouse yourself, and say goodnight.'

* * *

The following is a copy of my first report to the Cardinal:

Four Mile Water, County Wicklow,
10th August.

My Dear Uncle,

The miracle is genuine. I have affected perfect credulity
in order to throw the Hickeys and the countryfolk off their
guard with me. I have listened to their method of convincing
sceptical strangers. I have examined the ordnance maps, and
cross-examined the neighbouring Protestant gentlefolk. I
have spent a day upon the ground on each side of the water,
and have visited it at midnight. I have considered the up-
heaval theories, subsidence theories, volcanic theories and
tidal wave theories which the provincial *savants* have suggested. They are all untenable. There is only one scoffer in
the district, an Orangeman; and he admits the removal of
the cemetery, but says it was dug up and transplanted in the
night by a body of men under the command of Father Tom.
This also is out of the question. The interment of Brimstone
Billy was the first which had taken place for four years; and
his is the only grave which bears a trace of recent digging.
It is alone on the north bank; and the inhabitants shun it
after nightfall. As each passer-by during the day throws a
stone upon it, it will soon be marked by a large cairn. The
graveyard, with a ruined stone chapel still standing in its
midst, is on the south side. You may send down a committee
to investigate the matter as soon as you please. There can
be no doubt as to the miracle having actually taken place,
as recorded by Hickey. As for me, I have grown so accustomed to it that if the county Wicklow were to waltz off
with me to Middlesex, I should be quite impatient of any
expressions of surprise from my friends in London.

Is not the above a businesslike statement? Away, then,
with this stale miracle. If you would see for yourself a miracle
which can never pall, a vision of youth and health to be
crowned with garlands for ever, come down and see Kate
Hickey, whom you suppose to be a little girl. Illusion, my
lord cardinal, illusion! She is seventeen, with a bloom and a
brogue that would lay your asceticism in ashes at a flash. To
her I am an object of wonder, a strange man bred in wicked
cities. She is courted by six feet of farming material, chopped
off a spare length of coarse humanity by the Almighty, and

flung into Wicklow to plough the fields. His name is Phil Langan; and he hates me. I have to consort with him for the sake of Father Tom, whom I entertain vastly by stories of your wild oats sown at Salamanca. I exhausted all my authentic anecdotes the first day; and now I invent gallant escapades with Spanish donnas, in which you figure as a youth of unstable morals. This delights Father Tom infinitely. I feel that I have done you a service by thus casting on the cold sacerdotal abstraction which formerly represented you in Kate's imagination a ray of vivifying passion.

What a country this is! A Hesperidean garden: such skies! Adieu, uncle.

Zeno Legge.

Behold me, then, at Four Mile Water, in love. I had been in love frequently; but not oftener than once a year had I encountered a woman who affected me as seriously as Kate Hickey. She was so shrewd, and yet so flippant! When I spoke of art she yawned. When I deplored the sordidness of the world she laughed, and called me 'poor fellow'! When I told her what a treasure of beauty and freshness she had she ridiculed me. When I reproached her with her brutality she became angry, and sneered at me for being what she called a fine gentleman. One sunny afternoon we were standing at the gate of her uncle's house, she looking down the dusty road for the detestable Langan, I watching the spotless azure sky, when she said:

'How soon are you going back to London?'

'I am not going back to London, Miss Hickey. I am not yet tired of Four Mile Water.'

'I'm sure Four Mile Water ought to be proud of your approbation.'

'You disapprove of my liking it, then? Or is it that you grudge me the happiness I have found there? I think Irish ladies grudge a man a moment's peace.'

'I wonder you have ever prevailed on yourself to associate with Irish ladies, since they are so far beneath you.'

'Did I say they were beneath me, Miss Hickey? I feel that I have made a deep impression on you.'

'Indeed! Yes, you're quite right. I assure you I can't sleep at night for thinking of you, Mr Legge. It's the best a Christian can do, seeing you think so mighty little of yourself.'

'You are triply wrong, Miss Hickey: wrong to be sarcastic with me, wrong to pretend that there is anything unreasonable in my belief that you think of me sometimes, and wrong to discourage the candour with which I always avow that I think constantly of myself.'

'Then you had better not speak to me, since I have no manners.'

'Again! Did I say you had no manners? The warmest expressions of regard from my mouth seem to reach your ears transformed into insults. Were I to repeat the Litany of the Blessed Virgin, you would retort as though I had been reproaching you. This is because you hate me. You never misunderstand Langan, whom you love.'

'I don't know what London manners are, Mr Legge; but in Ireland gentlemen are expected to mind their own business. How dare you say I love Mr Langan?'

'Then you do not love him?'

'It is nothing to you whether I love him or not.'

'Nothing to me that you hate me and love another?'

'I didn't say I hated you. You're not so very clever yourself at understanding what people say, though you make such a fuss because they don't understand you.' Here, as she glanced down the road again, she suddenly looked glad.

'Aha!' I said.

'What do you mean by "Aha!"'

'No matter. I will now show you what a man's sympathy is. As you perceived just then, Langan—who is too tall for his age, by the bye—is coming to pay you a visit. Well, instead of staying with you, as a jealous woman would, I will withdraw.'

'I don't care whether you go or stay, I'm sure. I wonder what you would give to be as fine a man as Mr Langan.'

'All I possess: I swear it! But solely because you admire tall men more than broad views. Mr Langan may be defined geometrically as length without breadth; altitude without position; a line on the landscape, not a point in it.'

'How very clever you are!'

'You do not understand me, I see. Here comes your lover, stepping over the wall like a camel. And here go I, out through the gate like a Christian. Good afternoon, Mr Langan. I am going because Miss Hickey has something to say to you about me which she would rather not say in my presence. You will excuse me?'

'Oh, I'll excuse you,' said he boorishly. I smiled, and went out. Before I was quite out of hearing, Kate whispered vehemently to him, 'I *hate* that fellow.'

I smiled again; but I had scarcely done so when my spirits fell. I walked hastily away with a coarse threatening sound in my ears like that of the clarionets whose sustained low notes darken the woodland in 'Der Freischütz'. I found myself presently at the graveyard. It was a barren place, enclosed by a mud wall with a gate to admit funerals, and numerous gaps to admit the peasantry, who made short cuts across it as they went to and fro between Four Mile Water and the market town. The graves were mounds overgrown with grass: there was no keeper; nor were there flowers, railings or any of the conventionalities that make an English grave-yard repulsive. A great thorn bush, near what was called the grave of the holy sisters, was covered with scraps of cloth and flannel, attached by peasant women who had prayed before it. There were three kneeling there as I entered; for the reputation of the place had been revived of late by the miracle; and a ferry had been established close by, to conduct visitors over the route taken by the graveyard. From where I stood I could see on the opposite bank the heap of stones, perceptibly increased since my last visit, marking the deserted grave of Brimstone Billy. I strained my eyes broodingly at it for some minutes, and then descended the river bank and entered the boat.

'Good evenin t'your honour,' said the ferryman, and set to work to draw the boat hand over hand by a rope stretched across the water.

'Good evening. Is your business beginning to fall off yet?'

'Faith, it never was as good as it mightabeen. The people that comes from the south side can see Billy's grave—Lord have mercy on him!—across the wather; and they think bad of payin' a penny to put a stone over him. It's them that lives towrst Dublin that makes the journey. Your honour is the third I've brought from south to north this blessed day.'

'When do most people come? In the afternoon, I suppose?'

'All hours, sur, except afther dusk. There isnt a sowl in the counthry ud come within sight of that grave wanst the sun goes down.'

'And you! do you stay here all night by yourself?'

'The holy heavens forbid! Is it me stay here all night? No, your honour: I tether the boat at siven o'hlyock, and lave Brimstone Billy—God forgimme!—to take care of it t'll mornin'.'

'It will be stolen some night, I'm afraid.'

'Arra, who'd dar come next or near it, let alone stale it? Faith, I'd think twice before lookin' at it meself in the dark. God bless your honour, and gran'che long life.'

I had given him sixpence. I went to the reprobate's grave and stood at the foot of it, looking at the sky, gorgeous with the descent of the sun. To my English eyes, accustomed to giant trees, broad lawns, and stately mansions, the landscape was wild and inhospitable. The ferryman was already tugging at the rope on his way back (I had told him I did not intend to return that way), and presently I saw him make the painter fast to the south bank; put on his coat; and trudge homeward. I turned towards the grave at my feet. Those who had interred Brimstone Billy, working hastily at an unlawful hour, and in fear of molestation by the people, had hardly dug a grave. They had scooped out earth enough to hide their burden, and no more. A stray goat had kicked away a corner of the mound and exposed the coffin. It occurred to me, as I took some of the stones from the cairn, and heaped them so as to repair the breach, that had the miracle been the work of a body of men, they would have moved the one grave instead of the many. Even from a supernatural point of view, it seemed strange that the sinner should have banished the elect, when, by their superior numbers, they might so much more easily have banished him.

It was almost dark when I left the spot. After a walk of half a mile, I recrossed the water by a bridge, and returned to the farmhouse in which I lodged. Here, finding that I had had enough of solitude, I only stayed to take a cup of tea. Then I went to Father Hickey's cottage.

Kate was alone when I entered. She looked up quickly as I opened the door, and turned away disappointed when she recognised me.

'Be generous for once,' I said. 'I have walked about aimlessly for hours in order to avoid spoiling the beautiful afternoon for you by my presence. When the sun was up I withdrew my shadow from your path. Now that darkness has fallen, shed some light on mine. May I stay half an hour?'

'You may stay as long as you like, of course. My uncle will soon be home. He is clever enough to talk to you.'

'What! More sarcasms! Come, Miss Hickey, help me to spend a pleasant evening. It will only cost you a smile. I am somewhat cast down. Four Mile Water is a paradise; but without you, it would be a little lonely.'

'It must be very lonely for you. I wonder why you came here.'

'Because I heard that the women here were all Zerlinas, like you, and the men Masettos, like Mr Phil—where are you going to?'

'Let me pass, Mr Legge. I had intended never speaking to you again after the way you went on about Mr Langan today; and I wouldn't either, only my uncle made me promise not to take any notice of you, because you were—no matter; but I won't listen to you any more on the subject.'

'Do not go. I swear never to mention his name again. I beg your pardon for what I said: You shall have no further cause for complaint. Will you forgive me?'

She sat down, evidently disappointed by my submission. I took a chair, and placed myself near her. She tapped the floor impatiently with her foot. I saw that there was not a movement I could make, not a look, not a tone of my voice, which did not irritate her.

'You were remarking,' I said, 'that your uncle desired you to take no notice of me because—'

She closed her lips, and did not answer.

'I fear I have offended you again by my curiosity. But indeed, I had no idea that he had forbidden you to tell me the reason.'

'He did not forbid me. Since you are so determined to find out—'

'No: excuse me. I do not wish to know, I am sorry I asked.'

'Indeed! Perhaps you would be sorrier still to be told. I only made a secret of it out of consideration for you.'

'Then your uncle has spoken ill of me behind my back. If that be so, there is no such thing as a true man in Ireland. I would not have believed it on the word of any woman alive save yourself.'

'I never said my uncle was a backbiter. Just to show you what he thinks of you, I will tell you, whether you want to know it or not, that he bid me not mind you because you were only a poor mad creature, sent down here by your family to be out of harm's way.'

'Oh, Miss Hickey!'

'There now! you have got it out of me; and I wish I had bit my tongue out first. I sometimes think—that I maytr't sin!—that you have a bad angel in you.'

'I am glad you told me this,' I said gently. 'Do not reproach yourself for having done so, I beg. Your uncle has been misled by what he has heard of my family, who are all more or less insane. Far from being mad, I am actually the only rational man named Legge in the three kingdoms. I will prove this to you, and at the same time keep your indiscretion in countenance, by telling you something I ought not to tell you. It is this. I am not here as an invalid or a chance tourist. I am here to investigate the miracle. The Cardinal, a shrewd if somewhat erratic man, selected mine from all the long heads at his disposal to come down here, and find out the truth of Father Hickey's story. Would he have entrusted such a task to a madman, think you?'

'The truth of—who dared to doubt my uncle's word? And so you are a spy, a dirty informer.'

I started. The adjective she had used, though probably the commonest expression of contempt in Ireland, is revolting to an Englishman.

'Miss Hickey,' I said: 'there is in me, as you have said, a bad angel. Do not shock my good angel—who is a person of taste—quite away from my heart, lest the other be left undisputed monarch of it. Hark! The chapel bell is ringing the angelus. Can you, with that sound softening the darkness of the village night, cherish a feeling of spite against one who admires you?'

'You come between me and my prayers,' she said hysterically, and began to sob. She had scarcely done so, when I heard voices without. Then Langan and the priest entered.

'Oh, Phil,' she cried, running to him, 'take me away from him: I can't bear—' I turned towards him, and showed him my dog-tooth in a false smile. He felled me at one stroke, as he might have felled a poplar-tree.

'Murdher!' exclaimed the priest. 'What are you doin', Phil?'

'He's an informer,' sobbed Kate. 'He came down here to spy on you, uncle, and to try and show that the blessed miracle was a make-up. I knew it long before he told me, by his insulting ways. He wanted to make love to me.'

I rose with difficulty from beneath the table, where I had lain motionless for a moment.

'Sir,' I said, 'I am somewhat dazed by the recent action of Mr Langan, whom I beg, the next time he converts himself into a fulling-mill, to do so at the expense of a man more nearly his equal in strength than I. What your niece has told you is partly true. I am indeed the Cardinal's spy; and I have already reported to him that the miracle is a genuine one. A committee of gentlemen will wait on you tomorrow to verify it, at my suggestion. I have thought that the proof might be regarded by them as more complete if you were taken by surprise. Miss Hickey: that I admire all that is admirable in you is but to say that I have a sense of the beautiful. To say that I love you would be mere profanity. Mr Langan: I have in my pocket a loaded pistol, which I carry from a silly English prejudice against your countrymen. Had I been the Hercules of the ploughtail, and you in my place, I should have been a dead man now. Do not redden: you are safe as far as I am concerned.'

'Let me tell you before you leave my house for good,' said Father Hickey, who seemed to have become unreasonably angry, 'that you should never have crossed my threshold if I had known you were a spy: no, not if your uncle were his Holiness the Pope himself.'

Here a frightful thing happened to me. I felt giddy, and put my hand to my head. Three warm drops trickled over it. Instantly I became murderous. My mouth filled with blood, my eyes were blinded with it; I seemed to drown in it. My hand went involuntarily to the pistol. It is my habit to obey my impulses instantaneously. Fortunately the impulse to kill vanished before a sudden perception of how I might miraculously humble the mad vanity in which these foolish people had turned upon me. The blood receded from my ears; and I again heard and saw distinctly.

'And let *me* tell you,' Langan was saying, 'that if you think yourself handier with cold lead than you are with your fists, I'll exchange shots with you, and welcome, whenever you please. Father Tom's credit is the same to me as my own; and if you say a word against it, you lie.'

'His credit is in my hands,' I said. 'I am the Cardinal's witness. Do you defy me?'

'There is the door,' said the priest, holding it open before me. 'Until you can undo the visible work of God's hand your testimony can do no harm to me.'

'Father Hickey,' I replied, 'before the sun rises again upon Four Mile Water, I will undo the visible work of God's hand, and bring the pointing finger of the scoffer upon your altar.'

I bowed to Kate, and walked out. It was so dark that I could not at first see the garden-gate. Before I found it, I heard through the window Father Hickey's voice, saying, 'I wouldn't for ten pound that this had happened, Phil. He's as mad as a march hare. The Cardinal told me so.'

I returned to my lodging, and took a cold bath to cleanse the blood from my neck and shoulder. The effect of the blow I had received was so severe, that even after the bath and a light meal I felt giddy and languid. There was an alarm-clock on the mantel-piece: I wound it; set the alarm for half-past twelve; muffled it so that it should not disturb the people in the adjoining room; and went to bed, where I slept soundly for an hour and a quarter. Then the alarm roused me, and I sprang up before I was thoroughly awake. Had I hesitated, the desire to relapse into per-fect sleep would have overpowered me. Although the muscles of my neck were painfully stiff, and my hands unsteady from my nervous disturbance, produced by the interruption of my first slum-ber, I dressed myself resolutely, and, after taking a draught of cold water, stole out of the house. It was exceedingly dark; and I had some difficulty in finding the cow-house, whence I borrowed a spade, and a truck with wheels, ordinarily used for moving sacks of potatoes. These I carried in my hands until I was beyond earshot of the house, when I put the spade on the truck, and wheeled it along the road to the cemetery. When I approached the water, knowing that no one would dare to come thereabout as such an hour, I made greater haste, no longer concerning myself about the rattling of the wheels. Looking across to the opposite bank, I could see a phosphorescent glow, marking the lonely grave of Brimstone Billy. This helped me to find the ferry station, where, after wandering a little and stumbling often, I found the boat, and embarked with my implements. Guided by the rope, I crossed the water without difficulty; landed; made fast the boat; dragged the truck up the bank; and sat down to rest on the cairn at the grave. For nearly a quarter of an hour I sat watching the patches of jack-o'-lantern fire, and collecting my strength for the work before me. Then the distant bell of the chapel clock tolled one. I rose; took the spade; and in about ten minutes uncovered the coffin, which smelt horribly. Keeping to windward of it, and using the spade as a lever, I contrived with great labour to place it on the truck. I wheeled it without accident to the landing-place, where, by placing the shafts of the truck upon the stern of the boat and lifting the foot by main strength, I succeeded in embarking my load after twenty minutes' toil, during which I got covered with clay and perspiration, and several times all but upset the boat. At the southern bank I had less difficulty in getting truck and coffin ashore, and dragging them up to the graveyard.

It was now past two o'clock, and the dawn had begun; so that I had no further trouble from want of light. I wheeled the coffin to a patch of loamy soil which I had noticed in the afternoon near the grave of the holy sisters. I had warmed to my work; my neck no longer pained me; and I began to dig vigorously, soon making a shallow trench, deep enough to hide the coffin with the addition of a mound. The chill pearl-coloured morning had by this time quite dissipated the darkness. I could see, and was myself visible, for miles around. This alarmed me, and made me impatient to finish my task. Nevertheless, I was forced to rest for a moment before placing the coffin in the trench. I wiped my brow and wrists, and again looked about me. The tomb of the holy women, a massive slab supported on four stone spheres, was grey and wet with dew. Near it was the thornbush covered with rags, the newest of which were growing gaudy in the radiance which was stretching up from the coast on the east. It was time to finish my work. I seized the truck; laid it alongside the grave; and gradually prised the coffin off with the spade until it rolled over into the trench with a hollow sound like a drunken remonstrance from the sleeper within. I shovelled the earth round and over it, working as fast as possible. In less than a quarter of an hour it was buried. Ten minutes more sufficed to make the mound symmetrical, and to clear the traces of my work from the adjacent sward. Then I flung down the spade; threw up my arms; and vented a sigh of relief and triumph. But I recoiled as I saw that I was standing on a barren common, covered with furze. No product of man's handiwork was near me except my truck and spade and the grave of Brimstone Billy, now as lonely as before. I turned towards the water. On the opposite bank was the cemetery, with the tomb of the holy women, the thornbush with its rags stirring in the morning breeze, and the broken mud wall. The ruined chapel was there too, not a stone shaken from its crumbling walls, not a sign to show that it and its precinct were less rooted in their place than the eternal hills around.

I looked down at the grave with a pang of compassion for the unfortunate Wolfe Tone Fitzgerald, with whom the blessed would not rest. I was even astonished, though I had worked expressly to this end. But the birds were astir, and the cocks crowing. My landlord was an early riser. I put the spade on the truck again, and hastened back to the farm, where I replaced them in the cow-house. Then I stole into the house, and took a clean pair of boots, an overcoat, and a silk hat. These, with a change of linen, were sufficient to make my appearance respectable. I went out again, bathed in the Four Mile Water, took a last look at the cemetery, and walked to Wicklow, whence I travelled by the first train to Dublin.

*   *   *

Some months later, at Cairo, I received a packet of Irish newspapers and a leading article, cut from *The Times*, on the subject of the miracle. Father Hickey had suffered the meed of his inhospitable conduct. The committee, arriving at Four Mile Water the day after I left, had found the graveyard exactly where it had formerly stood. Father Hickey, taken by surprise, had attempted to defend himself by a confused statement, which led the committee to declare finally that the miracle was a gross imposture. *The Times*, commenting on this after adducing a number of examples of priestly craft, remarked, 'We are glad to learn that the Rev. Mr Hickey has been permanently relieved of his duties as the parish priest of Four Mile Water by his ecclesiastical superior. It is less gratifying to have to record that it has been found possible to obtain two hundred signatures to a memorial embodying the absurd defence offered to the committee, and expressing unabated confidence in the integrity of Mr Hickey.'

FIVE POUNDS OF FLESH

J. M. Synge

*It is perhaps not altogether surprising that the dramatist and poet
J. M. Synge should have had a taste for traditional stories of terror.
His grandfather had owned a towering neo-Gothic Castle, Glan-
more, near Ashford in County Wicklow, and though it had passed
from the family's hands by the time Synge was a child, he frequently
stayed at a nearby farmhouse where its gloomy battlements dominated the skyline. When he later began to write, many of his early
experiments were melancholic and filled with dark images and old
Irish superstitions which that building had very probably fostered
in his mind.*

*John Millington Synge (1871–1909) was born at Rathfarnham in
County Dublin and educated at Trinity College, Dublin. Fascinated
by travel, he spent some time in Germany and France, and while
in Paris was introduced to W. B. Yeats who encouraged him
to write. Much of his raw material was drawn from his travels
in Wicklow, Kerry and the Aran Islands. His stay on the lonely
and desolate islands resulted in one of his best known books,* The
Aran Islands *(1907). It was his plays, however, produced at
the Abbey Theatre in Dublin, which made Synge's reputation as Ireland's leading dramatist—in particular* Riders to the Sea *(1904)
and* The Playboy of the Western World *(1907). The story
of 'Five Pounds of Flesh' was inspired by his time in the Aran
Islands and is as stark and terrifying a tale as any to be found in
this collection.*

*   *   *

When I was going out this morning to walk round the island with
Michael, the boy who is teaching me Irish, I met an old man

making his way down to the cottage. He was dressed in miserable black clothes which seemed to have come from the mainland, and was so bent with rheumatism that, at a little distance, he looked more like a spider than a human being.

Michael told me it was Pat Dirane, the storyteller old Mourteen had spoken of on the other island. I wished to turn back, as he appeared to be on his way to visit me, but Michael would not hear of it.

'He will be sitting by the fire when we come in,' he said: 'let you not be afraid, there will be time enough to be talking to him by and by.'

He was right. As I came down into the kitchen some hours later old Pat was still in the chimney-corner, blinking with the turf-smoke.

He spoke English with remarkable aptness and fluency, due, I believe, to the months he spent in the English provinces working at the harvest when he was a young man.

After a few formal compliments he told me how he had been crippled by an attack of the 'old hin' (*i.e.*, the influenza), and had been complaining ever since in addition to his rheumatism.

While the old woman was cooking my dinner he asked me if I liked stories, and offered to tell one in English, though, he added, it would be much better if I could follow the Gaelic. Then he began:

There were two farmers in County Clare. One had a son, and the other, a fine rich man, had a daughter.

The young man was wishing to marry the girl, and his father told him to try and get her if he thought well, though a power of gold would be wanting to get the like of her.

'I will try,' said the young man.

He put all his gold into a bag. Then he went over to the other farm, and threw in the gold in front of him.

'Is that all gold?' said the father of the girl.

'All gold,' said O'Conor (the young man's name was O'Conor).

'It will not weigh down my daughter,' said the father.

'We'll see that,' said O'Conor.

Then they put them in a scales, the daughter in one side and the gold in the other. The girl went down against the ground, so O'Conor took his bag and went out on the road.

As he was going along he came to where there was a little man, and he standing with his back against the wall.

'Where are you going with the bag?' said the little man.

'Going home,' said O'Conor.

'Is it gold you might be wanting?' said the man.

'It is, surely,' said O'Conor.

'I'll give you what you are wanting,' said the man, 'and we can bargain in this way—you'll pay me back in a year the gold I give you, or you'll pay me with five pounds cut off your own flesh.'

That bargain was made between them. The man gave a bag of gold to O'Conor, and he went back with it, and was married to the young woman.

They were rich people, and he built her a grand castle on the cliffs of Clare, with a window that looked out straightly over the wild ocean.

One day when he went up with his wife to look out over the wild ocean, he saw a ship coming in on the rocks, and no sails on her at all. She was wrecked on the rocks, and it was tea that was in her, and fine silk.

O'Conor and his wife went down to look at the wreck, and when the lady O'Conor saw the silk she said she wished a dress of it.

They got the silk from the sailors, and when the Captain came up to get the money for it, O'Conor asked him to come again and take his dinner with them. They had a grand dinner, and they drank after it, and the Captain was tipsy. While they were still drinking, a letter came to O'Conor, and it was in the letter than a friend of his was dead, and that he would have to go away on a long journey. As he was getting ready the Captain came to him.

'Are you fond of your wife?' said the Captain.

'I am fond of her,' said O'Conor.

'Will you make me a bet of twenty guineas no man comes near her while you'll be away on the journey?' said the Captain.

'I will bet it,' said O'Conor, and he went away.

There was an old hag who sold small things on the road near the castle, and the lady O'Conor allowed her to sleep up in her room in a big box. The Captain went down on the road to the old hag.

'For how much will you let me sleep one night in your box?' said the Captain.

'For no money at all would I do such a thing,' said the hag.

'For ten guineas?' said the Captain.

'Not for ten guineas,' said the hag.

'For twelve guineas?' said the Captain.

'Not for twelve guineas,' said the hag.

'For fifteen guineas?' said the Captain.

'For fifteen I will do it,' said the hag.

Then she took him up and hid him in the box. When night came the lady O'Conor walked up into her room, and the Captain watched her through a hole that was in the box. He saw her take off her two rings and put them on a kind of board that was over her head like a chimney-piece, and take off her clothes, except her shift, and go up into her bed.

As soon as she was asleep the Captain came out of his box, and he had some means of making a light, for he lit the candle. He went over to the bed where she was sleeping without disturbing her at all, or doing any bad thing, and he took the two rings off the board, and blew out the light, and went down again into the box.

He paused for a moment, and a deep sigh of relief rose from the men and women who had crowded in while the story was going on, till the kitchen was filled with people.

As the Captain was coming out of his box the girls, who had appeared to know no English, stopped their spinning and held their breath with expectation.

The old man went on—

When O'Conor came back the Captain met him, and told him that he had been a night in his wife's room, and gave him the two rings.

O'Conor gave him the twenty guineas of the bet. Then he went up into the castle, and he took his wife up to look out of the window over the wild ocean. While she was looking he pushed her from behind, and she fell down over the cliff into the sea.

An old woman was on the shore, and she saw her falling. She went down then to the surf and pulled her out all wet and in great disorder, and she took the wet clothes off of her, and put on some old rags belonging to herself.

When O'Conor had pushed his wife from the window he went away into the land.

After a while the lady O'Conor went out searching for him, and when she had gone here and there a long time in the country, she heard that he was reaping in a field with sixty men.

She came to the field and she wanted to go in, but the gate-man would not open the gate for her. Then the owner came by, and she told him her story. He brought her in, and her husband was there, reaping, but he never gave any sign of knowing her. She showed him to the owner, and he made the man come out and go with his wife.

Then the lady O'Conor took him out on the road where there were horses, and they rode away.

When they came to the place where O'Conor had met the little man, he was there on the road before them.

'Have you my gold on you?' said the man.

'I have not,' said O'Conor.

'Then you'll pay me the flesh off your body,' said the man.

They went into a house, and a knife was brought, and a clean white cloth was put on the table, and O'Conor was put upon the cloth.

Then the little man was going to strike the lancet into him, when says lady O'Conor—

'Have you bargained for five pounds of flesh?'

'For five pounds of flesh,' said the man.

'Have you bargained for any drop of his blood?' said lady O'Conor.

'For no blood,' said the man.

'Cut out the flesh,' said lady O'Conor, 'but if you spill one drop of his blood I'll put that through you.' And she put a pistol to his head.

The little man went away, and they saw no more of him.

When they got home to their castle they made a great supper, and they invited the Captain and the old hag, and the old woman that had pulled the lady O'Conor out of the sea.

After they had eaten well the lady O'Conor began, and she said they would all tell their stories. Then she told how she had been saved from the sea, and how she had found her husband.

Then the old woman told her story, the way she had found the lady O'Conor wet, and in great disorder, and had brought her in and put on her some old rags of her own.

The lady O'Conor asked the Captain for his story, but he said they would get no story from him. Then she took her pistol out of her pocket, and she put it on the edge of the table, and she said that any one that would not tell his story would get a bullet into him.

Then the Captain told the way he had got into the box, and come over to her bed without touching her at all, and had taken away the rings.

Then the lady O'Conor took the pistol and shot the hag through the body, and they threw her over the cliff into the sea.

THE WATCHER O' THE DEAD

John Guinan

The Abbey Theatre, which promoted so many other talented writers in the wake of J. M. Synge, was where John Guinan, the author of this next story, also made his mark, with the play Black Oliver *which was produced in Dublin in 1927. Apart from his work for the theatre, Dublin-born Guinan (1894–n.d.) wrote stories and essays for Irish periodicals such as* The Bell *and the* Dublin Magazine, *and in England was published by* The Cornhill Magazine *which printed the work of a number of Ireland's leading short story writers during the first half of the twentieth century, including Elizabeth Bowen's story 'The Happy Fields of Autumn' which appears in Part One of this book. 'The Watcher o' the Dead' is perhaps the best of Guinan's horror stories—it was certainly highly regarded by the curious English priest-anthologist of Gothic and horror fiction, the Reverend Montague Summers—and makes full use of the old Irish folklore with which the writer was familiar. In this instance, his theme is the gruesome old belief that the last person to be buried in a churchyard is doomed to fetch and carry for all the older residents . . .*

* * *

It is now the fall of the night. The last of the neighbours are hitting the road for home. The time they went out through that door together, for the sake of the company on the way, as they said, did they give e'er a thought at all to myself, left alone here in this desolate house? To be sure, they asked me more than once why I refuse to leave the place, and the day is in it, by the same token. But I have no call to answer them, though what I am about to set down here in black and white will settle the question, at least for myself.

A few hours ago, and the corpse of Tim McGowan was taken from under this roof and buried deep in the clay. They laid the spade and the shovel like a rude cross on the fresh sod of his grave, and they went down on their knees and said a few hasty prayers for the good of his soul. One or two, and their faces hidden in their hats, took good care not to rise from the wet ground till they got sight of others already on their two feet. Letting on that their thoughts were on higher things, they kept in mind the old belief that the first one to leave the churchyard warm in life would not be the last to come back cold in death.

The little groups moving out began to talk of the man who was gone. Their talk ran in whispers, for fear they might trouble his long sleep. They all knew, though none had the rights of it, that he was after earning his rest dearly. An old man, whose face was hard, even for his years, took a white clay pipe from the pocket of his body coat.

'God rest your soul, Tim McGowan,' he cried. It was the custom to pray for the dead before taking a 'draw' from a wake pipe. 'God rest you in the grave,' he added, 'for it's little peace or ease you had and you in the world that we know!'

The bulk of those who heard his words caught, a little gladly, a mocking undertone which stole through the kindly feeling that had at first shaken his voice. A young man, with eager eyes and a desire to know and talk of things that should be left hidden, took courage and spoke out bluntly:

'For him to be haunting the graveyard like a ghost, and he a living man! That was a strange vagary, for sure.'

'It was the death of the good woman a year ago,' the old man went on, speaking more openly, in his turn. 'It was her loss turned his poor head.'

'There's no denying there was a queer strain in him already,' the young man said to that. 'Sure they say all of that family were a bit touched!'

They did not scruple to speak like this before myself, and I of the one blood with the man who was dead, if any of them could know or suspect that. They were after doing their duty towards his mortal remains: if there was a kink in his nature or a mystery about his life why, they might fairly ask, should it not fill the gossip of the idle hour? But it was myself only, the stranger amongst them, who knew the true reason of Tim McGowan's nightly vigils in Gort na Marbh, why he, a living man, as was said, chose to become the Watcher o' the Dead in the lonesome graveyard. It was ere yesterday morning he told me his secret. Tim was lying there in the settle-bed from which his stark body was carried feet foremost this day. I was trying to get ready a little food by the fire on the hearth, for Tim had not been able to rise, let alone to do a hand's turn for himself. Our wants were simple, and it was not for the first time that I had turned my poor endeavours to homely use.

'There are times,' I made bold to remark, 'there are times I feel this house to be haunted': for every night during the short spell since I came to see my kinsman, I was sure I heard the fall of footsteps on the floor after the pair of us had gone to our beds. The rattling of the door, if it was not a troubled dream, had also startled me in my sleep. I had begun to ask myself was it one of these houses where the door must be left on the latch and the hearth swept clean for Those who come back. Always at a certain hour Tim was in a hurry to rake the fire and get shut of me out of the kitchen. A pang now shot through my breast. With the poor man hardly able to raise hand or foot, it was not kind to draw down such a thing. But he looked glad that I had given him the chance to speak out.

'As you make mention of it,' he said eagerly, 'I want to let you know the house is haunted, surely! But it is not by any spirit of good or evil from beyond the grave. That is a strange thing, you will be saying.'

'It is a strange thing,' I agreed. I had no doubt what he was going to disclose. He had already given me the story of a house built, and not without warning, on a 'fairy pass', through which the Sluagh Sidhe in their hosting and revels swept gaily every night. This was the house for sure: The Gentle Folk had never passed the gates of death and know nothing of the grave.

'But,' he went on, 'there is one other thing as strange again. It is that same you will now be hearing, if you pay heed to me.'

'You mean that this is the house'—I began, intending to say that it was the house of the story, but I checked myself—'that it is a case of a fallen angel, hanging between heaven and hell, who never had to pay the penalty of death?'

'If you let me,' he made answer, 'I will tell you the truth. The place is haunted by a mortal man!'

'One still in the world, one who goes about in his clothes, one to be seen by daylight?' I asked, without drawing breath.

'In troth,' he declared, 'it is haunted by the man who tells it, and no other, if I am still in the flesh itself!'

I lifted him slightly in the bed, not knowing what to say or think. Was this his way of speaking about some common habit, or was his reason leaving him?

'Whisper!' he said, and his face was flushed. 'You came here to gather old stories out of the past, over and above seeing your last living relative in the world, leaving our Michael, my son, who should be here by this. I might do worse than give you the true version of my own trouble.'

This made a double reason why I should hear him out. There is no man but carries in his breast the makings of a story, which, though never told, comes more home to him than any the mind of another man can find and fashion in words.

'What harm if my story should turn out a poor thing in the telling?' he sighed. 'It will ease my mind, if it does only that. And who knows: but we will talk of that when the time comes.'

He turned aside from the food I was coaxing him to take, and started:

'It is now a year since herself was laid to rest. Laid to rest!' He laughed, a little bitterly. 'That is what they call it. A week after that again, call it what you like, the graveyard was closed by orders. There are people still to the fore who have their rights under the law; but it is hardly likely that many, if any of them, will try to make good their claim to be buried in Gort na Marbh.'

Gurthnamorrav, the Field of the Dead, that is what those around about call the lonely patch to this day. Though this generation of them are 'dull of' the ancient tongue, such names, of native savour, help to keep them one in soul with the proud children of Banbha who are in eternity. Vivid imagery, symbols drawn, in a manner of speaking, from the brown earth, words of strength and beauty that stud like gems of light and grace the common speech hold not merely an abiding charm in themselves. Such heritages of the mind of the Gael evoke through active fancy the fuller life of the race of kings no less surely than those relics of skill and handcraft found by chance in tilth or red bog, the shrine of bell or battle book, the bronze spear head, the torque of gold.

'But, surely,' I objected, 'those who are able would like to have their bones laid beside their own when their day of nature is past! Surely they would choose such a ground as the place of their resurrection, as the holy men of old used to say!'

'Time and time again,' he made answer, 'people have left it to their deaths not to be buried in Gort na Marbh. Man and wife have been parted, mother and child. What call have I to tell you the reason? You know it rightly. You know it is the lot of the last body brought to its long home to be from that time forth the Watcher o' the Dead?'

'I have heard tell of that queer—of that belief,' I replied. 'That the poor soul cannot go to its rest, if it took years itself, till another comes to fill its place; that it must wander about in the dead of the night amongst the graves where the mortal body is crumbling to dust; and, as one might say in a plain way, keep an eye over the place!'

'And who would care to be buried in ground that was shut up for ever?' he asked. 'Even at the best of times people try their best endeavours to be first through the gate with the corpse of their own friend and when two funerals happen to fall on the one day.'

And then he went on to tell me, and his voice failing at that, of all he was after going through thinking of his woman, his share of the world, making the weary, dreary, rounds of the graveyard during the best part of the changing year. And, bitter agony! he felt that she could not share in the Communion of Saints, that all his good works for her sake would not hasten her release. But the thing that made it the hardest for him to bear was this: It was through his veneration for the old customs, through his great respect even for the dead, that this awful tribulation had come to the pair of them.

'Let you not be laughing at what I'm going to tell you now,' he warned me: 'for I won't deny there have been times when I made merry over the like myself. It was a seldom thing two funerals to be the one day; nor would it have come to happen at the time it did if the other people had the proper spirit, like myself, or the right regard for the things good Christians hold highly. Listen! They knew the order to close the graveyard, the other people knew it was on the road, for the man who was dead and going to be buried on the same day as herself was himself on the Board of Guardians. That was why they waked him for one night only, and they people of means, and rushed with him in unseemly haste to Gort na Marbh. But we got wind of it, and would have been the first, for all that, only we followed the old road, the long road, and in a decent and becoming way walked in through the open gate while they took a short cut and got in over the stile. We did more than that, and so did they. While the savages, for they were little less, while they were trampling above the relics of the dead, we went round about the ground in the track of the sun till we came in the proper course to the side of the open grave.'

This set me thinking of the ancient ritual by which the corpse is brought round to pay its respects, as a body might say, to those who have gone before. I began to ask myself was it a fragment of Druid worship that had come down even to our own day. But this is what I said to my kinsman:

'You did what was right, and no one would be better pleased than the woman who was gone!'

'That is the way I felt myself at the first going off,' he agreed: 'but soon I began to question myself: When I did the right thing, that the neighbours gave me full credit for, was I thinking more of what was expected from the living or what was due to the dead? Was I thinking of myself, and the great name I'd be getting from the self-same neighbours, or of the woman going into the clay, who only wanted their prayers? Many's the long night this thought kept me on the rack till I was nigh gone astray in the head. In my mind I saw her, and her brown habit down to her feet, and she looking to me for help, and it my sin of human respect, as I felt, that kept her so long from walking on the sunny hills of Glory! Funeral after funeral went the way, for people have to die; but not a one but passed the rusty gate of Gort na Marbh as a poor woman of the road might give the go-by to a stricken house.

'At length and at last, I could stand it no longer, and one night I got up from my bed and made my way to the graveyard. 'Twas in the dark hour before the crowing of the cocks, when wandering spirits are warned home to their house of clay.'

'And did you half expect to see the Watcher o' the Dead?' I asked.

'Did I? And why not?' he asked in turn, by way of reply.

'With your mind disturbed that way,' I went on, 'the wonder is you didn't see her, if only in fancy.'

I meant to be kind. He faced me testily.

'I did see her, as sure as I'm a living man!' he declared.

I had not the heart to urge my view that it was only a brain-born figure.

'I no sooner crossed the stile,' he said softly, 'than I got clear sight of herself. She was moving through the graves she guarded, and a kindly look in her two eyes. The dead image I thought her of the Nuns you see in the sick ward of the poorhouse in Bally-brosna, and she taking a look at the beds in their little rows, and fearing to waken the tired sleepers in her charge. There she was, in truth, as I had seen her a thousand times in my own mind.'

'In your own mind!' I said after him. 'It was on your eyes, so to speak, and you merely saw what was in your mind already. Was it not more natural to see the figment that never left your sight than not to see it at all?'

It was all very clear to me, and I felt this was sound talk; and isn't it a caution the way the rage of battle will rise in a body and set the tongue loose! But Tim's reply put a stop to any dispute or war of words.

'It was in my mind, for sure,' he said. 'But tell me, you who have the book learning, why was it in my mind? When a man's brain begins to work, what gives it the start, or sets it going—or does it start to go of itself?'

I had to give in that I always left such vexed questions to wiser heads, adding, whimsically enough as it seems to me now, that I was not such a great fool as to attempt an answer where they failed. In a way I was put out by the reflection that this old man, who 'didn't know his letters', was making a mockery of me on the head of my few books and my small store of book learning.

'There is nothing hard about the case I am after putting before you,' he said. 'It was on my mind because the thing was taking place in Gort an Marbh night after night, was taking place in the Field of the Dead, though there was no living eye to see it!'

I had no reply to that, whether it was a head-made ghost or not. Where was the use of starting to argue that nothing really takes place if not within the knowledge of man? I told myself weakly that such visions were due to the queer strain in the old man the neighbours spoke about this day. It might be that, in his present state, all this had only come into his head as the two of us talked together. It did not occur to me then, and I have too much respect for the dead to credit it now, that he was 'taking a rise' out of me, as the plain saying is.

Tim became a little rambling in his speech and asked me to let him lie flat in the bed. I gathered from the words he mumbled and jumbled that he made a promise to the departed spirit to take her place till his own time came in real earnest: that he had bid her go to her rest, in the Name of God, much, I could not help but think, as one might banish an evil spirit to the 'red sea' to make ropes of the sand; that he had kept his word, which brought great peace to his breast: and that he never set eyes on her again from that hour, there or there else.

I had no doubt he had but laid the ghost of his own troubled thoughts. It is not every poor mortal can do that same, even by dint of hard sacrifice. Tim was growing worse. I tried hard to cheer him. It was all to no use. I talked of his son, Michael, who was far away on the fishing grounds. We had already sent word for him to come home, and he might be here any stroke, if it was a long ways off, itself.

'Michael will never be here in time!' the father groaned. 'That is my great trouble. I never could ask another to do it. It would be again' reason.'

'There is nothing you could name I would not gladly do!' I declared; and, in all fair speaking, I meant it.

'There are things no man should ask of his friend,' he said to that, with a slight shake of the head.

'And who else should he ask but his friend?' I laughed, trying to rouse him. 'But, first, I'll send for the Doctor—'

'The Doctor, how are ye!' he broke in on me. 'That is not what I want. What can the like of himself do for a body who has seen the Watcher o' the Dead?'

'What hark if you did itself?' I asked. 'The sign of a long life it is, as likely as not. It would be another story, entirely, one's "fetch" to be seen in the late hours of the day. An early death that would signify.'

'The man,' he made answer, 'the man who lays eyes on the Watcher o' the Dead, late or early, if the like could come to pass at all before dark, that man will soon be only a shadow himself. I am saying, he will soon be among the silent company. The time

I took the woman's place, the woman who held my heart for years, I knew rightly, it would not be for long. It is for that reason and no other I am after telling you my secret sorrow. I will never be able to put out this night, if I live through this night of the nights, or any night for the future; and if it was a thing I failed her, sure herself would be disturbed in her rest.'

I took a grip of his hand and looked down steadily into his eyes.

'Put your trust in me!' I said. 'I'll take your place till such time as you are laid in the clay!'

Who is it, though he might throw doubt on the very stars above his head, would not try to humour an old man or a little child?

'God sent you for a friend,' he said, 'praised be His holy Name! For all I know, I may not want you to do so much: I may want you to do a little more, but in another way. I want you to take my place till Michael comes, and not an hour more; I want you, as well as that, to tell him all I have told you and to give him my dying wish, if it is a thing he does not come before I go for ever. Whisper! You'll tell Michael, in case I'm too far through myself, that I am dying happy knowing he will not refuse a last favour to the father who reared him. It is this: That he will become the Watcher o' the Dead, though a living man, like myself, and let me, after so much fret and torment, go straight to herself, to his mother, in Heaven. Tell him I know he will do this, for the rest of his mortal days, if it comes to that. Tell him I know that, after that again, if he gets no release he will have his bones laid in Gort na Marbh and wait his own turn. I have done my share of watching, God knows!'

Some kind neighbours gathered during the course of the day, and the priest of the parish was sent for. Father Malachy was a man of the world, without being worldly. It is not for the knowing, and never will be in this world, whether Tim told him about the Watcher o' the Dead. As a man, his reverence knew all the customs and beliefs of the people, for he was one of them himself. Deep in his nature a body might expect to find a kindly toleration for the harmless 'superstitions', as some would call them, lingering from the pagan days of Firbolg or Tuatha de Danaan. As a priest, he had, no doubt, full knowledge of the rites of the Church for dealing with 'appearances' from the other world, which shows it to be no harm to give heed to such things.

Tim kept quiet till the night wore on. Then he got restless and began to mutter to himself. The use of his speech was wellnigh gone. I caught such words as 'Gort na Marbh', and 'Herself', and 'the Watcher o' the Dead'. His grip was tight on my fist when I said in his ear that I would not fail him, dead or alive, till Michael came. The kind neighbours did not let on to hear the pair of us, and I left him in their charge while I set out for the strange duty I had taken on myself so lightly, taken on, indeed, with a certain zest, in the vague hope of enlarging my experience. It was clear from Tim's behaviour that the hour of the night had come when he felt the 'call' to the graveyard, and still there was no sign of Michael. The moon was in the sky. The night was cold. There was no stir. The place held no terrors for me. I set little store by Tim's story, except as a 'study' in delusion. The old man was much in my thoughts, for he was passing rapidly away. I saw him in my mind, as he used to say, and he walking here and there through the graves that now held nothing but cold clay, passing by fallen stones, broken and moss-grown. I tried hard to banish such airy pictures, for I did not want to begin seeing sights.

What was that story Tim told me a few days ago as we stood before a headstone in Gort na Marbh? It was a true tale of revenge, revenge both on the living and the dead, and it was a poor sort of revenge at that. Before long I would be seeing again the spot where the dead man he spoke about was laid in the clay. His relations, in blood and law, hoped to benefit largely by his death. But he left all to his son. The boy was an only child whose mother died the hour he came into the world. He came home, a likely youth, to be at the father's funeral. For the first time in his young life he saw the place that was now to be his own. It was natural for him to ask why the usual black plumes did not wave above the hearse instead of white. The errors of the past, if any, should have been covered by charity. Feuds are forgiven, if not forgotten, in the hour of death. It is what they told him, with wild malice, that black plumes were only for people who were lawfully joined in wedlock.

Here I found the elements of tragedy, but the story only helped to keep the figure of Tim before me. I was stepping over the stile and thinking of the nights he spent walking about in the dreary waste, for, after so much neglect, that is what it had by now sunk to. I felt the nettles rank and dank as I set foot on the ground; and then—if it was not wild phantasy!—I got sight of Tim moving in the moonlight among the shadows of the headstones and the trees.

'In the Name of God!' I cried, profanely, I am half afraid, 'leave the place at once, and let me keep my promise in peace.'

I was furious with the neighbours for letting him rise and he in a fever. But were they to be blamed? I crossed hastily and found myself alone! This gave me a start, and I began to wonder whether in that strange ground—for, surely, the place was not 'right'!—I, in my turn, saw what was on my eyes only? Had Tim been there in the flesh or was it that I, in my turn, had laid but the ghost of a deranged imagination? Could it be that the queer strain of the family, if there is such a thing, runs in my own blood? Or does a sane man put such a question to himself? Without waiting for the crowing of the cocks, I made haste back to the house. My heart was beating loudly.

'We were going to call after you,' the neighbours said to me. 'Hardly was your back turned when the end came!'

Tim was stretched there in his long sleep, his features set free by the kindly touch of death!

Last night at the same hour we dug his grave. I was heartened by the presence of the neighbours and lingered over the work till the dawn broke, walking about from time to time, 'by way of no harm', trying to keep my promise to the dead man. More than once the shadows, moving with the shifting lanthorn, took a start out of me. There were a few of the neighbours would not put out with us. One was the strong young man who was so free of the tongue this day.

'Why do you want to choose such an unreasonable hour?' they grumbled. 'It is not lucky to turn up the sod in the dead of the night.'

'As likely as not,' I heard another make answer, 'he was waiting to see would Michael come on the long car.'

I did not put him right. If we were waiting for Michael only the work could have been left over till morning. It is the long wait we would have, for the same Michael, God rest the poor boy! God rest him! I say, for before Tim was taken out this day word came that the hardy young fisherman had been lost a week ago in the depths of the salt water. The hungry, angry sea did not give up its dead. And now his death comes home to me! Michael's bones will never be laid in Gort na Marbh. Michael will never, never, either in life or death, become the Watcher o' the Dead! And I have pledged my word to the man who is gone, the father, to take his place till such time as Michael should come home! That will be never, never!

What way can I break my word to the dead, whether I credit his story or doubt it? It was part of his own belief, part of himself. What odds does it make even if he was out of his mind, or if I am a madman myself? A promise, a promise to one passed away, is sacred.

Where is the good of talking of common sense! Half the world is stupid with common sense, if there is any such quality. But I see a dismal prospect before me, till the end of my days, as likely as not, let alone, for all I know, till the Day of Judgement itself! Already I feel there is a stir in my blood, the time has come for me to get up and make my lonely vigil: for I have been putting this down in black and white for many hours. It is a true word for Tim; every man has his own story, his own agony. But I set out to tell of his troubles, which, for sure, are at an end, and not of my own, which, for all a body can see, are only in their birth throes.

THE SAMHAIN FEIS

Peter Tremayne

*A leading historian of Gaelic history under his real name of Peter
Berresford Ellis (1943–   ), the author of this next story has also
written several acclaimed horror books and a number of widely
anthologised tales of terror. Best known among his works is the
trilogy of novels in which he continued Bram Stoker's adventures of
Dracula. Although published originally in three volumes,* Dracula
Unborn *(1977),* The Revenge of Dracula *(1978) and* Dracula, My
Love *(1980), the novels have recently been reissued together as*
Dracula Lives! *(1993). One American newspaper has written of
them, 'Tremayne weaves no less engrossing tales that Edgar Allan
Poe.'*

*Peter Berresford Ellis's family came from Cork City which
sparked his interest in Irish lore and legend. He says his fascination
with the horror genre was inspired by Bram Stoker's novel and one
of his proudest possessions is a rare Irish language edition of*
Dracula *which was translated in 1933 by Sean O Cuirren. 'The
Samhain Feis' is unique among his horror stories in being the only
one which was first published in the Irish language, under the title
'Feis na Samhna' in the Irish literary magazine* Feasta *of November
1984. Its evocative mixture of old traditions in a contemporary setting make it an ideal finale to Part Two of this collection.*

*   *   *

Katy Fantoni began to wonder whether she had made a mistake
almost as soon as she left the eastern suburbs of Dublin, taking
the western road by the small airport at Rathcoole. Yet she had
to get away from the stuffy city, away from the Victorian disapproval of Aunt Fand and her thin-lipped glances of reproach.

She needed peace; a place to relax and work out her problem without the narrow-minded condemnation of her only relative.

It had been the local shopkeeper, a kindly woman, who had suggested that Katy might like to stay in the holiday cottage which she owned up in the Slieve Aughty Mountains in County Clare. At first the idea of spending a week in a remote country area was attractive to Katy, especially with the alternative being a week with Aunt Fand. But now, as she drove the hire-car through Kildare, misgivings began to tumble through her mind. After all, what was she going to do in a remote cottage in an alien countryside except brood . . . brood about Mario and her busted marriage?

She glanced into the driving mirror and caught sight of her seven-year-old son, Mike, sitting quietly on the back seat playing with his teddy bear. Was it fair to him, she wondered? He had been restless staying in Aunt Fand's house but, in her eagerness to escape Aunt Fand, had she precipitated them into a worse situation? It was to be a whole week in the isolated country cottage. She tried to dispel the disquiet from her mind with a shake of her fair hair. No, she refused to turn back now. Something urged her onwards, perhaps pride. She had already earned the disfavour of Aunt Fand; no need to give her another example of what the old woman saw as her niece's fecklessness.

Katy Fantoni—or rather, Katy Byrne, as she was then—had been born in Dublin but, when she was five years old, her parents had emigrated to America and she had grown up in the Jamaica Bay area of Brooklyn. There was nothing special about her childhood; it was a common story of most immigrant Irish families. Not long after she had graduated from high school and secured a job in an advertising agency, however, her parents were killed in an automobile accident. Then she had met Mario Fantoni. Mario managed a chin of diners, owned by his father, Salvatore Fantoni, on Long Island. It was whispered that Salvatore Fantoni was 'connected' . . . a euphemism for membership in the Mafia. Katy Byrne's agency was owned by Gentile Alunno and it was doing a campaign for the Fantoni diners. That was how they met.

Mario was young, handsome, and good company. Katy was young, attractive, and very much alone with an emotional vacuum since the death of her parents. To both Katy and Mario, with their Catholic backgrounds, marriage was the next step. Mama and Papa Fantoni were not exactly happy that Mario was not marrying

'Italian', for they were Sicilians of an archaic type. But they consoled themselves with the fact that Katy Byrne was a good Catholic.

So Katy and Mario were married. Mama and Papa Fantoni bought them a house in Glen Cove, overlooking Long Island Sound. It was a large house and with it came Lise, a good-natured though coarse-looking Calabrian, who was the housekeeper. A year later they had a son, Mike. Katy mentally prepared herself to settle down to an indolent life. After all, working for his father, Mario Fantoni had no financial worries.

The honeymoon did not last long. As soon as Katy became noticeably pregnant she began to learn some unpleasant truths about Mario. Mama and Papa Fantoni had brought him up in some old-fashioned Sicilian philosophies where wives were concerned. Even after Mike was born Katy was expected to stay at home, act as hostess at a moment's notice when Mario decided to invite his friends to drop in, and not to develop any friendships of her own. Mario was always out on 'business dates' and it soon came to Katy's knowledge that his business colleagues were all about twenty years old, came in a variety of colourings and just one gender—female! When she contemplated her seven years with Mario, Katy did not really understand how the marriage had survived that period. She supposed it was unconscious pressure from her Catholic upbringing. Or maybe she had been waiting for Mario to mature, waiting for him to change . . .

Then Mario went off on a West Coast tour 'strictly for business' . . . and Katy was not long in discovering that the business sessions were taking place in Las Vegas night spots and motels and that his travelling companion was some TV starlet. That was when her Irish blood finally boiled over and she hopped on a plane for Dublin with little Mike in tow, telling Lise that she would return in a couple of weeks—probably!

Katy Byrne Fantoni had one surviving relative and that was Aunt Fand in Dublin. She was the elder sister of Katy's mother, and while they had exchanged cards from time to time, Katy had not seen her since she was five years old. She had thought to find in Aunt Fand some of her mother's caring nature, her broadmindedness and concern. Instead Aunt Fand was a bigot as only a spinster of fanatical religious disposition can be. Ostentatious piety was a substitute for Christian charity. Her narrowness was demonstrated by her enthusiastic support of Archbishop Lefevre, who refused the introduction of the modern vernacular Mass in his churches as being impious and adhered strictly to the sixteenth-century Latin Mass. Aunt Fand's ideas on divorce were more extreme than those of the Pope. She was parochial and narrow and threw up her hands in horror when Katy began to speak of her problems with Mario and hinted she was contemplating a legal separation. Aunt Fand was hardly the person to confide in.

After the first week living in Aunt Fand's house in the small Dublin suburb of Kimmage, Katy was feeling stifled and oppressed. Even young Mike asked her one bedtime whether Aunt Fand was their wicked stepmother. Katy had taken the boy to see Disney's *Cinderella* a few days before.

Katy felt that she just had to escape in order to think quietly and rationally about her situation.

It was when she was in the local grocery shop and fell to talking with Mrs MacMahon, the owner, that she mentioned she would like to get away for a few days to the west of Ireland. Mrs MacMahon promptly suggested that Katy might like to stay in a holiday cottage which she owned in County Clare.

Katy hesitated out of a certain respect for Aunt Fand's hospitality before agreeing.

'It's up in the Slieve Aughty Mountains,' smiled Mrs MacMahon. 'Near Lough Atorick. All you have to do is take the main road from Dublin to Portumna, drive past Lough Derg, turn south on the Ennis Road; turn off at Gorteeny for Derrygoolin, and then ask for Flaherty's farmstead. Ned Flaherty keeps the keys of the cottage and he'll let you in. There's a trackway from his farm which winds up into the mountains and you'll find the cottage by the lakeside about ten miles further on.'

Ned Flaherty was a man of indeterminate age. He had snow-white hair, a shrewd weatherworn face and sparkling deep blue eyes, almost violet in colour. Humour never seemed to be far from his features.

When Katy drove up to the farmstead, found him, and handed over Mrs MacMahon's scribbled note giving her permission to stay at the cottage, Flaherty was clearly astonished. He looked from Katy Fantoni to young Mike in surprise.

''Tis late for tourists,' he said in his slow, rolling County Clare drawl.

'I'm not really a tourist,' Katy replied. 'I just want a few days of quiet in a remote spot.'

He frowned. 'And you an American?' he pondered. 'Well, peace and quiet you'll be getting up at the croft and that's no lie.'

He turned into the farmhouse and reappeared with a bunch of keys. 'I'd best come and show you the croft.'

He climbed into the car beside her and directed her up a track, a single unpaved trackway that twisted itself into the mountains. It was obvious that this track was rarely used. Now and then they had to halt and push their way through sheep who stood indifferent to the angry blasts of the car horn. As they climbed upwards the scenery became spectacular. Katy had always believed that Ireland was at its best in the golds, russets, and muted greens of autumn. The gorse-strewn mountains were speckled in pale yellow.

Suddenly they came round the shoulder of a mountain onto a high plateau, a small valley with a large lake in its centre. By the lakeside stood a quaint thatched cottage with thick grey stone walls.

'Mrs MacMahon's croft,' gestured the old farmer with a jerk of his head.

She halted the car before the cottage, or croft as Flaherty called it, and the dismay must have registered on her face.

The croft was fronted with a garden, bordered by a low stone wall of the same grey granite as the house. The garden had become overgrown and wild.

'It's a lonely spot, right enough,' Flaherty said, observing her expression. 'No gas, no electricity, nor a telephone.'

Her spirits fell. 'What shall I do for light and heat?'

'There's oil lamps, a fire, and plenty of turf, and there'll be a primus stove as well for the cooking. I'll show you.'

She sighed as she climbed out of the car and followed him to the cottage door. Little Mike was running after them in ecstasy.

'Look, Mommy! Look! Can I play here? Is it ours?'

Well, it was certainly a beautiful spot. 'Isolated' was hardly the word for it, though. It seemed a million miles from anywhere. Flaherty seemed to read her mind.

'No one has lived here for many years. In winter, when it rains, the road gets cut off. The old croft was deserted until Mrs Mac-Mahon from Dublin bought it. She only comes for a fortnight in summer and then lets it from time to time. I've never known it to be occupied so late in the year, though.'

Katy turned and gazed about her as he fiddled with the keys.

The sun shone on the lake which reflected the pale blue of the sky. It seemed pleasant and inviting. To the side of the croft the mountain rose to a black jagged peak, looking more like a hill from this elevation on the high plateau. It was strewn with granite boulders, poking up in grotesque shapes through the black earth. It was a strange landscape, almost out of a fantasy world.

Flaherty caught her gaze.

'That's *Reilig na Ifreann*,' he said.

'What does that mean?'

'The Cemetery of Hell.'

Katy grinned.

'I see the likeness. The granite boulders do look a bit like tombstones.'

They left little Mike racing around the garden, finding curious things to do.

'Keep in the garden, Mike,' she admonished him as Flaherty conducted her inside. The door opened immediately into a large room which was apparently a combined kitchen, dining and living room. Two doors led off this large central room with its big open fireplace. One door led into a small bedroom which Katy immediately designated for Mike, while the other led into a larger bedroom which she took for herself. It was primitive but it was quaint. She knew many New York matrons who would pay a fortune to stay in such a place.

Flaherty proved to be a treasure. He laid a turf fire and lit it, showing her how to build it so that it would remain alight through the night. He showed her how the primus stove worked and how to light the oil lamps. The water was drawn by a pump which emptied into a big china sink. They managed to find a kettle and some tea bags and brew a cup of milkless, unsweetened tea.

'I'll have to collect some groceries from the village,' Katy reflected.

Flaherty nodded.

'At least you have a car,' he smiled. 'In the old days one had to walk the twelve miles to the village and return the same way carrying the shopping.'

'No wonder the place became deserted.'

They finally climbed back into the hire-car and drove back down the mountain road. Once again Flaherty shook his head as he gazed at them.

'I've never known the croft to be let so late in the year,' he said. ' 'Tis almost the Samhain Feis.' The words were pronounced 'Sowan Fesh'.

Katy gazed at him with a smile of puzzlement. 'What's that?'

'Hallowe'en. We still call it by its old name in these parts.'

Young Mike piped up from the back seat: 'Mommy! Mommy! Are we going to have a Hallowe'en party with pumpkin masks and candles and games?'

'We'll see.' Katy smiled at him in the driving mirror. 'Do they have any local Hallowe'en celebrations in the village, Mr Flaherty?'

Flaherty gave her a curious glance. 'The Samhain Feis is not a time to celebrate,' he replied in an almost surly manner.

'I thought everyone celebrated Hallowe'en,' Katy said with raised brows. 'In the States it's a great time for the kids.'

Flaherty sighed deeply.

'Samhain, which you call Hallowe'en, is an ancient festival celebrated among the pagan Irish centuries before the coming of Christianity.'

'Tell me about it,' said Katy. 'I'm interested, truly.'

'Samhain was one of the four great religious festivals among the pagan Irish. it started on the evening of October 31 and continued on November 1. It marked the end of one pastoral year and the beginning of the next. The name is derived from the words *Samred*, meaning summer, and *fuin*, meaning the end. Hence it was "end of summer", for Samhain was the first day of *Gemred*, the winter. It was the time when, according to the druids, the Otherworld became visible to mankind and when spiritual forces were loosed upon the human race.'

Katy chuckled. 'So that is the origin of the Hallowe'en idea? The night when evil marches across the world, when spirits and ghosts set out to wreak their vengeance on the living?'

Flaherty simply stared, obviously not sharing her merriment.

'Christianity was unable to suppress many of the old beliefs. A great many pagan beliefs and superstitions and even ceremonies were adopted by the early Christians. Samhain was renamed All

Saints' or All Hallows' Day so that the evening before became Hallowe'en.'

Katy smiled. 'You have quite a wealth of folkloric knowledge, Mr Flaherty.'

'When you live up in these mountains, the folk memory becomes an extension of your own experience.'

Within two days Katy had settled in the area and even grown used to the primitive living conditions of the croft. As for little Mike, he loved playing in the garden. Ned Flaherty seemed to take them under his personal protection and was always calling by for a brew of tea. He was a natural storyteller and had an amazing wealth of knowledge on many subjects. The English he spoke was slow and sedate and apparently Irish was his first language. In fact, Irish seemed to be quite widely spoken among the remote mountain folk.

It was on the third day that Katy suddenly realised that she had not once thought about Mario. Mario! It was high time that she sorted that mess out. After all, it was her whole reason for being in Ireland. But she had been so engrossed with learning to live in primitive style, with listening to Flaherty's stories and walking amidst the wild countryside, that the problem of Mario seemed remote and almost nothing to do with her.

It was surprising. She could not even blame the distraction on little Mike, for the boy was no burden at all. He loved playing by himself and, indeed, invented an imaginary playmate with whom he seemed quite content.

One day when Katy was cleaning the kitchen he came running into the croft to tell her about his playmate.

'He's called Seán Rua, Mommy. That means Red John,' added the little boy proudly.

Katy frowned, peering out of the window. 'And where is this Red John?' she demanded.

Mike pointed to the garden gate. 'There he is.'

Katy could see nothing except a bird perched on the gate post, a bird which looked like a raven, although the sun made its black feathers glow with a curious coppery colour.

It was at that point that Katy realised the situation. She had had an imaginary friend when she was Mike's age; it was a phase all children went through.

'I see.' She smiled and ruffled the boy's fair hair. 'Well, you run off and play for a while because I'm going to fix your supper.'

Dutifully, little Mike trotted off.

The next morning Mike was eager to play with his 'friend' and so Katy left him with strict orders not to move out of the cottage garden while she went to pick up a few necessary provisions from the village. As she drove by Flaherty's farmstead she saw the old man sitting on a stone bridge which spanned a gushing mountain stream. He was gazing moodily up at the darkening rain-laden skies while whittling a stick. He smiled when he saw her, and waved, so she halted the car and wound down the window.

'Settling in?' he asked.

'No problems,' she replied with a smile.

'And where is the *garsún*?'

Katy frowned. 'The gosoon?' she echoed.

'The boy. Isn't he with you?'

'Ah, no. He's having a game around the cottage. He's invented an imaginary friend to play with. He calls him Seán Rua.'

'*Nár lige Dia!*' whispered Flaherty, suddenly genuflecting with the sign of the Cross.

Katy gazed at his troubled face in surprise. 'What's wrong?' she demanded.

'Nothing,' muttered Flaherty. 'Will you be out long?'

'I'm just going down to the village to buy a few things.'

The old man peered at the sky. 'You realise that it is the Samhain Feis tonight?'

Katy couldn't quite grasp the abrupt change of topic.

Flaherty stood up, nodded to her, and walked briskly towards his tractor.

When Katy returned to the croft she found Flaherty sitting on the stone wall of the garden, whittling his stick and watching little Mike as he attempted to dam a stream which ran through the overgrown wilderness. Katy thought that the old man was being a little overprotective.

'You shouldn't have bothered to watch over Mike,' she said as she unloaded the car. 'He wouldn't have come to any harm in the garden.'

'Ah,' shrugged the old man, 'it's turned into a nice afternoon. The rain clouds have blown clear of the mountain and it's nice enough to sit in the sun.'

Katy nodded absently as little Mike came running up. She had promised to bring him some sweets. As she handed him a toffee he said, 'Mommy, may I have one for Seán Rua?' Inwardly she groaned. She would have to watch that. Imaginary friends were all right until two of everything was demanded. Just this once, she thought, as she handed Mike another toffee. He took them both and ran to the far side of the garden where he appeared to be in conversation with someone.

Flaherty, watching him, plucked at his lower lip thoughtfully.

'Strange that the *garsún* picked on that name,' he mused. 'There is an old tale hereabouts . . .'

'The whole place is riddled with old tales,' Katy interrupted as she heaved her shopping bags to the cottage.

Flaherty followed.

'One of the beliefs of the Samhain Feis is that on the stroke of midnight the fairy hills split wide open and from each fairy hill there emerges a spectral host . . . goblins, imps, bogeymen, demons, phantoms, and the like. They spill out to take revenge on the living. The local people stay indoors on that night of the Samhain Feis.'

Katy smiled tolerantly at him as she started to unpack. 'What has that got to do with the name Mike chose for his playmate?'

'Of all the goblins and imps who appear at the Samhain Feis, there is a small red-haired imp called the *Taibhse Derg*.'

'The Tavesher Derug?' Katy tried to repeat the name. 'What's that?'

'The Red Bogeyman,' replied Flaherty solemnly. 'Round these parts we call him Red John. It is said he eats the souls of children.'

Katy glanced at the old man, not sure whether he was joking with her. Flaherty's face was grave.

'Tonight is the Samhain Feis, Mrs Fantoni. Do you have a crucifix in the croft?'

Katy's jaw dropped a little. Then, trying to suppress a smile, she pointed above the cottage door where an ornate crucifix hung.

Flaherty nodded approvingly. 'That's a good place to hang it,' he said. 'But would you take notice of an old man? Mix a paste of oatmeal and salt and put it on your child's head before he goes to bed tonight.'

Katy could scarce keep from laughing. 'What would that do, Mr Flaherty, except make a mess for me to clean up?'

'It will keep the boy from harm,' he replied solemnly. Then the old man wished her a 'good night' and walked off towards his tractor.

Katy watched it trundle down the mountain path and suddenly realised how removed she had become from the superstitions of her Irish roots. The years in New York had taught her some sophistication. Oatmeal and salt indeed! Crucifixes! Goblins! Imps! The Samhain Feis!

A wild croaking made her peer upwards.

A flock of birds were wheeling around the roof of the cottage, their wings beating in the crisp air. She came out into the garden to stare upwards, attracted by their lamenting cacophony. She knew enough of birds to recognise ravens by their appearance, although the lowering sun seemed to make their feathers flicker with a coppery glow. Three times she watched them circle overhead and then fly upwards towards the distant peaks of the mountains.

She turned into the croft again and continued to sort her groceries.

Katy had just finished cooking supper when she noticed the chill in the air and realised that the sun was already disappearing over the mountain tops. It was nearly time to light the lamps.

She looked through the window and saw young Mike standing at the garden gate. She gazed in surprise for he was with another small boy, a boy with bright coppery hair which flickered with a thousand little pinpricks of light in the rays of the setting sun. Katy hurried to the door and opened it.

Was she cracking up? Mike was standing by the gate alone. Katy peered round. There was no one about.

'Mike!' she called 'Time to come in now.'

Mike turned and waved at the empty air and then trotted towards her.

'It's been a lovely day, Mommy.' He smiled.

'Mike.' Katy hesitated, feeling foolish. 'Were you with a small red-haired boy just a moment ago?'

'Of course,' came his prompt reply. 'I was with Seán Rua.'

Katy shuddered slightly. Perhaps she was cracking up?

'Seán Rua wants me to go out and play with him tonight because it's the Samhain Feis.'

Katy pulled herself together. 'Well, Mr Fantoni Junior,' she replied, 'I am sure that young Seán Rua's parents will have him tucked up in bed tonight and that is where you are going to be.'

Little Mike's lips drooped. 'Aw, Mom!'

'No buts or complaints, it's bed for you at your usual time, young man.'

Mike had finally settled to sleep in his room and Katy had put some more turf on the fire, then sat in the old carved chair before it, warming her feet and sipping a cup of hot chocolate. It was so peaceful, just sitting there with the music of the ticking clock on the mantelshelf and crackle of the fire in the hearth.

She supposed it was at that moment that she made up her mind finally about Mario Fantoni. It was ridiculous pretending that a relationship still existed. Separation or divorce was the only solution. Everything swam into crystal clarity. She set down her cup and sighed.

Abruptly she became aware that a curious thing had happened. A deathly silence pervaded the cottage. The loud ticking of the clock had stopped. The silence made her glance up in astonishment. It was one minute to midnight. She turned her eyes to the fire whose flames roared and crackled away . . . without any sound at all. God! Had she gone deaf?

Her heart began to beat wildly.

Then she heard a sibilant whispering which was incomprehensible at first but which grew in volume like the keening of a wind. It grew louder until she could hear the clear, melodic voice of a child.

'Mi-ike . . . ! Mi-ike . . . ! Come and play with me . . . come and play . . .'

She turned her head to see where the whispering came from.

The creak of a door caused her to start.

Across the room, the door of Mike's bedroom was swinging slowly open.

A shadow moved there.

Little Mike came stumbling forward, barefoot, clad in his striped pyjamas. His eyes were blurry and blinking from his sleep.

'Mi-ike! Mi-ike . . . come and play!'

She tried to stand up and found a great weight pressing her back in her chair. She tried to call out to Mike but her throat was suddenly constricted.

A sharp rasp of a bolt being drawn caused her to jerk her gaze over her shoulder towards the door of the cottage. She gazed fearfully as she saw the bolts being drawn back of their own volition! First one iron bolt and then the other was drawn aside, then the handle moved and the cottage door swung inwards.

The whispering voice grew louder.

'Mi-ike!'

Little Mike's eyes were wide open now and he was smiling.

'Seán Rua!' he cried. 'I knew you would come for me. I want to play, truly I do.'

Katy struggled to free herself from her strange paralysis while Mike, ignoring her, went trotting trustingly towards the door.

Katy turned her frantic gaze after him.

Just beyond the cottage door she could see the shadowy outline of a little boy.

Then a great chanting chorus filled the air and the earth seemed to quiver and shake under the cottage. It rocked as if there was an earthquake.

Through the open door she could see the outline of the oddly shaped peak which Flaherty had called *Reilig na Ifreann*—Hell's Cemetery.

Even as she watched, the earth seemed to spring apart as if opening a jagged tear down the side of the mountain. A pulsating red light shone forth into the night. The chanting grew exhilarated, increasing in volume until Katy felt her eardrums would burst with the vibration.

She saw Mike's little figure run through the doorway, saw the shadowy figure behind awaiting him with outstretched hand.

The light from the open hillside seemed to glow on the figure's red coppery hair, causing it to dance as if it were on fire. And the light from the cottage fell onto its face.

Oh God! That face!

Malevolent green eyes stared unblinking at her from slanted, almond shapes. The face was deathly white and its contours were sharp. The eyebrows also rose upwards. The cheekbones were sharp and jutting and the ears were pointed, standing almost at right angles to the head. It was an elfin head.

For a moment the face of the creature—what else was it?—stared at Katy and then, slowly, a malicious smile crossed those bizarre features.

Little Mike ran straight up to it, their hands grasped each other, and then the two tiny figures turned and ran towards the opening in the mountainside.

Katy's wildly beating heart increased its tempo until she could stand its beat no longer and fell into a merciful world of blackness.

She awoke still sitting in the chair, twisted uncomfortably before the dead fire. The oil lamp was spluttering and smelling on the table behind her. The room was terribly cold and the grey half-light of dawn seeped through the small windows of the croft.

She raised her itching eyes to the monotonously ticking clock. It was seven-thirty. She eased herself up, stretched, and stared at the dead embers of the fire.

Then she remembered.

Her eyes swung to the door of the croft. It was closed. The bolts were in place and nothing seemed out of order. She sprang from her chair and turned towards Mike's room. The door was closed. She hesitated before it, scared of what she might find on the other side.

Summoning her courage, she turned the door knob and peered in.

Mike's tousled fair head lay on the pillow, a hand to his mouth, thumb inserted between his lips. His breathing was deep and regular.

Katy could have wept with relief.

She turned back into the main room, shivering.

So it had been some grotesque nightmare after all? She must have fallen asleep in front of the fire and had the strangest dream! She supposed it was a mixture of fears; fears about Mike, her own fears . . . and all restated through Flaherty's folk talks. She shook her head in disgust and set to building a fire. She had just set the primus stove going when she heard the sound of Flaherty's tractor halting outside.

'I was just passing,' the old man said when she opened the door. 'I thought I'd call by . . .'

'I'm making tea.' Katy smiled as she gestured him to enter.

His bright eyes gazed keenly at her.

'You seem tired,' he observed.

'I fell asleep in front of the fire last night,' she confessed, 'and had a rather nasty nightmare.'

He pursed his lips thoughtfully. 'How's the *garsún*?'

'Mike? He's sleeping.'

'Ah.'

Katy glanced at the old man pityingly. She felt confident now in the morning light. 'Well, your Samhain Feis is over. Did anyone get their souls eaten last night?'

Flaherty sniffed. ' 'Tis not a thing to joke about. But, true, the Samhain Feis is over for another year, *búiochas le Dia* . . . thanks be to God,' he added piously.

'Mommy!'

Katy turned as Mike came stumbling from his bedroom, yawning and rubbing the sleep from his eyes. 'Mommy, I'm hungry!'

Flaherty slapped his thigh and laughed. 'Now that's the sign of a healthy lad. Here, *a mhic*,' he called to the boy, 'I've a little something for you.'

He reached into his coat pocket and handed little Mike a length of wood, the same wood piece that Katy had seen the old man whittling so often. It had been transformed into a beautiful ornate whistle.

' 'Tis called a *feadóg stáin*, a penny-whistle,' smiled Flaherty.

Mike held the whistle up and gave a few tentative blasts.

'*Go raibh maith agat*,' he said solemnly to the old man.

Flaherty chuckled. '*An-mhaith! Is rómhaith uait é sin!*' He clapped the boy on the shoulder and turned to Katy. 'I see you're making the boy fluent in Irish.'

Katy frowned. 'Not me. I don't know a word of the language. Where did you pick that up, Mike?'

'From my friend,' smiled Mike, retiring to a corner to practise on the whistle.

Flaherty apparently did not hear, nor did he see the troubled look which passed across Katy's face. He sipped appreciatively at his tea.

'I shall miss the *garsún* and yourself when you leave.'

Katy turned back to him and smiled. 'That's a nice thing to say. We'll be going back to Dublin in a day or so and then straight back to New York.'

The old man gazed shrewdly at her. 'And the problem you came here to think about? Is it resolved?'

Katy smiled, a little tightly. 'In my mind it is.'

Flaherty sighed. 'Then perhaps you'll come back here one day.'

'Perhaps.'

A week later the cab dropped Katy and Mike at the house in

Glen Cove. Mario was at home and he was drunk and angry at Katy's 'disappearance'. Almost before she stepped into the living room he started to scream abuse at her for taking *his* son out of the country without permission. He accused her of attempting to kidnap young Mike. Katy tried to keep calm; tried to keep her temper in check. In the end she let it all out: how she was sick of Mario's countless girl friends, his drunken boorish behaviour, his attitude towards her and, finally, how she was utterly sick of him and their relationship. She wanted a separation pending a divorce.

After his initial shock Mario grinned derisively. 'You try to divorce me and I'll countersue,' he sneered. 'What's more, I'll make sure that enough mud is thrown at you to ensure the courts give me custody of Mike so that you'll never see him again. No one walks out on me, baby!'

Katy stared at him aghast.

There was no use asking if he meant it. She could see by the triumphant leer in his eyes that he meant every word and was capable of carrying his threat through. She knew exactly how much power the Fantonis could wield. He would take Mike from her not because he cared for Mike but in order to spite her. That was when she picked up a china ornament and threw it straight into Mario's grinning, triumphant face. He dodged aside easily and called her a string of foul names.

'I wish you were dead!' she snarled in reply. 'I hope you rot in hell!'

She turned on her heel and found little Mike standing in the open doorway behind her. He was staring at his father with a curious expression on his face. There was a look of such malevolence in his eyes that it made Katy pause and shiver. Mario, too, saw the expression.

'Hey, kid, wipe that look off your goddamn face and show your old man some respect! Don't stare at me like that!'

Mike said nothing but continued to stare at his father.

Mario became really angry. 'Hey, what stories have you been filling the kid's head with about me, you bitch?' he snarled at Katy. 'Have you been feeding the kid with tales about me?'

'He only has to see the way you behave to know what kind of person you are,' replied Katy evenly. 'There's no need for tales.'

Mario was staring at the boy's hair.

'Have you been dying the kid's hair?'

Katy frowned, not understanding what he meant at first. Then she glanced at Mike's hair. The fair tousled curls were much darker than usual, a deeper brown, almost chestnut. She blinked. Maybe it was the lighting in the room. The hair seemed to verge on copper in colour.

'Quit staring at me, kid!' shouted Mario, suddenly lunging towards the boy.

Katy did not know how it happened, but as Mario moved forward he somehow tripped and fell on his face.

She glowered down at him.

'You drunken bum!' she said through clenched teeth. 'When you've sobered up, we'll talk about that divorce.'

'I'll see you in hell first!' swore Mario from the floor.

Katy grabbed little Mike and hurried upstairs.

It was early the next morning when Lise, the housekeeper, woke Katy from a deep sleep. Her face was pale and she was in a state of agitation.

'*Dio! Dio! Signore Fantoni è morto!*'

Katy rubbed the sleep from her eyes and stared at the woman who was waving her arms, repeating the words in her broad Calabrian accent.

'What is it?' demanded Katy. 'Is it Mike? Oh God, has something happened to Mike?'

'No, no.' The woman shook her head between her sobs. 'It is Signore Fantoni . . .'

'What's the matter?'

Lise was shivering hopelessly and pointed to the corridor.

Since their relationship became uneasy, Katy and Mario had had separate bedrooms. Mario's bedroom lay across the corridor opposite.

Katy threw on a dressing gown and strode to Mario's door with Lise sobbing in her wake.

The first thing Katy noticed was the blood. It was everywhere, staining the room streaky red. Mario lay on his back on the bed amidst the jumble of bedclothes. His eyes were wide and staring as if in fear.

Katy raised a hand to her mouth and felt nausea well from her stomach.

It looked as if part of Mario's throat had been torn out.

Behind her Lise breathed, '*Animale! Lupo mannaro!*'

Katy paused a moment longer, drew herself together, and pushed Lise from the room before her. Outside, in the corridor, she felt shivery and faint.

'Call the police, Lise,' she said. 'Get a hold on yourself and get the police.' Her voice was sharp and near hysteria.

Lise turned away.

'Mike!' Katy suddenly cried. 'We must keep him away from this. Where is he?'

Lise turned back, sniffing as she tried to control herself. 'He was playing when I started to make Signore Fantoni his breakfast. Just playing on the lawn, signora.'

Katy strode to her bedroom window and gazed down on the lawn below.

Sure enough, there was little Mike playing; running round and round in circles on the lawn, the sun glinting on his coppery hair. Katy caught her breath. His *coppery* hair!

Almost as if he heard her sharp intake of breath, he stopped and gazed up at the bedroom window.

Katy's heart began to pump wildly and she clutched for the window sill.

It was little Mike's face right enough, yet the features were somehow distorted, sharper. The eyes were almost almond-shaped. The ears were pointed and stood out at right angles. The face was malignant, elfin. He stared up and his green sparkling eyes gazed into Katy's. Then he smiled. A shy, mischievous smile. And she noticed there was blood on his lips.

3

TO MAKE THE FLESH CREEP

Chilling Tales

'Fly Away Finger, Fly Away Thumb', pen and ink drawing by
Francis Butterfield for Brian Moore's story.

FLY AWAY FINGER, FLY AWAY THUMB

Brian Moore

Like the tales in the previous two parts, the Irish 'chiller' story has a long tradition that can be traced back to the work of the great Joseph Sheridan Le Fanu and is currently evident in the work of modern masters like Brian Moore—a writer who has been compared with Graham Greene and was referred to in the Sunday Times *as 'the best living novelist of conscience'. Although he lived abroad for many years, a considerable proportion of Moore's books were set in Ireland or had Irish central characters, underlining the influence the country and its people always had on his work. In some of these he tended to move from realism and naturalism into fabulism, which further links him with the nation's traditions of the past.*

Among the most notable of these titles have been Judith Hearne *(1955), with its portrait of a Gothic lecher, which was banned in Ireland for its 'anti-clericalism' but has subsequently been filmed as* The Lonely Passion of Judith Hearne *(1987) with Bob Hoskins and Maggie Smith;* The Emperor of Ice-Cream *(1966), about the fantasy world of a young Belfast lad who wants to escape his pious father and join the Air Force; and* The Mangan Inheritance *(1979) in which an Irish-American would-be poet visiting the south of Ireland comes to believe that he is a reincarnation of the doomed nineteenth-century Irish poet Clarence James Mangan. In what proved to be one of his last novels,* Lies of Silence *(1990), he for the first time turned his attention to the troubles in his native Northern Ireland.*

Brian Moore (1921–99) was born in Belfast, one of a family of nine children, and educated at a strict Catholic School before transferring to the University of London in 1938. The advent of the Second World War put an end to his studies and he volunteered for the Belfast Air Raid Precautions Unit. Later he served with the Ministry of War Transport section in North Africa, Italy and France. In 1948 he moved to Canada and there began his writing career by producing a number of 'hardboiled' paperback murder mysteries, including Wreath for a Redhead *(1951)*, French for Murder *(1954)*, Bullet for my Lady *(1955) and* This Gun for Gloria *(1957), which are now much-prized collector's items. But following the success of his 'serious' novels, Moore moved to Los Angeles in 1965 and while there wrote the screenplay for Alfred Hitchcock's box office success,* Torn Curtain. *Soon becoming disillusioned with the life of a screenwriter, he returned to novels and his talent developed with each successive book. He wrote only a handful of short stories, of which 'Fly Away Finger, Fly Away Thumb' is undoubtedly the most suitable to demonstrate that, when it comes to making the reader's flesh creep, Brian Moore has few equals . . .*

*   *   *

This grotesque little story was told me by an old Sicilian whose face was brown and seamed like the bark of an oak, although his hair was as dark and as luxuriant as a young man's.

It is a weird story, indeed. Yet the narrator's manner carried conviction, even though he made no claim to first-hand knowledge. Perhaps it was the primitive atmosphere of that crudely furnished inn among the Sicilian mountains in which we sat which made reason capitulate. The firelight danced on the bare walls, the candles guttered, the four old olive growers listened and nodded. I was young, too—young enough to be carried away by the sincerity in a man's voice.

This is the story he told me:

In the days of the briganti there were two men who lived in these mountains whose names were Salvatore and Luigi. This was before my time, you understand, and before my father's time. They were estate owners, neighbours, and Salvatore made much money out of his vines and orange groves until he fell a victim to the vendetta. Then his house was burnt down, his vines and orange trees were destroyed, his family was butchered. And he himself would have perished had not his neighbour, Luigi—a brave, simple man who owned only a few poor vines—hidden him in his house until the danger had passed.

Salvatore, however, had friends. He took to the hills, and there he formed a powerful band of outlaws, led by himself, with Luigi as his right-hand man.

But times were bad. There were then too many outlaws in Sicily for brigandage to be a profitable occupation. You can imagine, therefore, how interested Salvatore and Luigi were when they heard that a rich troupe of entertainers had come to Sicily and were then playing in Messina. It was said that these performers, whose leader was a conjuror called *Il Potentato*, the potentate, wandered about Europe and made money by their performances or by any illegal method which came their way. The greatest criminals they were, those performers! Why else should they come to Sicily if not to take refuge where they could not easily be found? Moreover, it was clear that they intended to remain for a long time.

'If they are to stay a long while here in Sicily,' said Salvatore, 'they must have much money with them. Is it not true, Luigi?'

'Certainly it is true, Salvatore.'

'And if they stay here a long time, will they not steal much more money?'

'They will, indeed. There can be no doubt of that.'

'They will steal money, Luigi, from our poor countrymen, who are already so greatly afflicted by bandits that they can ill afford to lose money to foreigners as well.'

'Indeed, you are right, Salvatore!'

'Should we not, then, benefit our countrymen by relieving these strangers of their wealth, so that they will have to return to Italy or France, where they can make more money out of their entertaining?'

'Yes, Salvatore, we should if that is possible. But this man, this conjuror, *Il Potentato*—he must be a clever man—'

'Santa madre! It is true that he must be clever with his hands—to say "Ecco! here is a rabbit where there was no rabbit." But he cannot turn us all into rabbits, Luigi. He is a conjuror, not a magician.'

This discussion took place in the heart of the mountains, in the stronghold which Salvatore's band had made for themselves among the rocks and caves. It was determined forthwith to send two men, the very next day, to learn what they could about *Il Potentato*.

A few days later they returned. 'He is a man,' they said, 'at whom you cannot help laughing as soon as you see him. He has a white face which changes all the time as if it were made of putty, and his lips are thick like a negro's. He makes great fun of himself, and his friends also make fun of him—but when he tells them to do a thing they do it. We went to see him and his company give a performance, and *Il Potentato* put on a black robe and a pointed hat with moons and stars on it. He looked very mysterious then, but that was because he wore a black mask and a white beard. When, at the end, he took off his mask and hat and beard, everyone roared with laughter to see what a poor thing he was.'

'Did he make rabbits appear?' asked Luigi.

'He did many wonderful things. He made rabbits and frogs; he turned water into many colours; he sawed a woman in two halves, and yet each half was alive and felt no pain.'

'All that was trickery,' said Salvatore.

'Yes, it is true that it was all trickery. We have heard of these things before, although we have never seen them until now.'

'But when he is not performing,' asked Salvatore, 'what then?'

'Ah! There is a woman whom he goes to see in Milazzo—a woman named Maria Sganarelli. Gian here went to see her and made love to her.'

'She did not wish me to make love,' said Gian. 'She told me she already had a lover. I think she was afraid of him.'

'But he goes often to see this woman?'

'Many times. Sometimes there is a friend with him and sometimes he goes alone. Always he goes on horseback.'

'Amici,' said Salvatore, 'tomorrow night, or the next night perhaps, Signorina Sganarelli will wait in vain for her lover to come.'

*   *   *

The next night, Salvatore and Luigi helped themselves most skilfully and so made it easy for Heaven to help them too. They had to wait only for a little while before *Il Potentato* approached on his way from Messina to spend the night at Milazzo. He was surrounded and politely bidden to dismount. Then his hands were tied behind him, he was set on his horse again and led up into the mountains, between the horses of Salvatore and Luigi. There is no need to tell you that he was guarded very carefully, so that he might not escape by means of any conjuring tricks.

When he was once more inside his stronghold, Salvatore sent for his prisoner and looked at him for a long while before he spoke. He was indeed a strange man, *Il Potentato*. His nose turned up and his face was as if it were made of rubber. He had long, slender fingers like a woman's, and he clasped them together while he waited for Salvatore to speak. Then a little white mouse ran out of his pocket and climbed his arm. He apologised with a smile, put the little mouse in an empty pistol holster, and, after shaking the holster three times, returned it to its hook on the wall. Salvatore looked inside the holster and the mouse was gone.

Salvatore, however, took no more notice. He told the conjuror that he wanted money, much money, and that he must write a letter to his friends, telling them to bring 100,000 lire to a certain place at a certain time. Otherwise, *Il Potentato* would be killed. That was impossible, said the conjuror, for he could not write.

'Very well,' said Salvatore. 'I myself will send your friends a message, and they will know by your absence that what I say is true.' That also was impossible, said *Il Potentato*, for he must return to Messina the next day in time to give a performance. 'That shall not be,' Salvatore replied. 'You shall not leave here until I receive my 100,000 lire.'

Luigi took the conjuror away and locked him up. There was no danger of his escaping, for the room in which Salvatore and Luigi kept their prisoners was hollowed out of the solid rock. It had a heavy iron door in which there was one small peep-hole, and this door was secured by a lock and two bolts. Not even a conjuror could perform the impossible.

This night there was already a prisoner in the cell when *Il Potentato* was brought there. Paolo was the name of the other prisoner. He was a member of Salvatore's band, who was being punished for trying to steal more than his share of plunder. He was an indolent man and was not greatly unhappy at being a prisoner.

A few minutes after the door had closed behind the new prisoner, Paolo prepared to blow out the candle which, apart from a quantity of straw, was the only furniture of the cell.

'Wait!' said *Il Potentato*. 'You have a knife—is it not so?'

'Yes,' said Paolo.' But how—?'

'Because I see you have scraped a hollow in the ground for your hip-bone. Lend me your knife.'

Paolo thought he could be trusted and lent him the knife. 'But it is not a throwing knife,' he said. 'And the peep-hole is not large enough to throw a knife through it.'

'Grazie,' said *Il Potentato*. 'I do not need a throwing knife.'

Then he spread out his left hand on the ground before him, and he cut off the first finger and the thumb. Taking a handkerchief from his pocket, he wiped the blood from the knife and restored his property to Paolo, thereafter using the handkerchief to bandage his mutilated hand. He went to the door and looked through the peep-hole. Paolo knew that there was a guard posted a little way along the passage, but this guard, it seemed, was not looking at the door, for *Il Potentato* took his two severed fingers and dropped them out through the hole.

'It is time to sleep,' said this strange man; and, after blowing out the candle, he lay down on the straw and fell soundly asleep.

For Paolo sleep was out of the question. He lay staring at the doorway and watching the round hole grow brighter as his eyes accustomed themselves to the darkness. After a while, the hole flickered and became very dim—the guard's candle had gone out. It was a little while after this that Paolo heard a faint clinking sound—such a little sound that even his own breathing rendered it inaudible. Yet he was sure he was not mistaken. He rose and went to the peep-hole.

Save for a shaft of moonlight the passage was in darkness. At the far end Paolo could see the guard sitting with his back against the wall and his head lolling on his knees. He was fast asleep. And then, in the blue beam of moonlight, Paolo saw something else which made his knees shake so violently that they knocked against the door; for, on the moonlit ground, he saw a finger and a thumb painfully dragging a key, which emitted a slight metallic, scraping noise.

Paolo blundered back to his corner and buried himself so deeply in straw that only his eyes were uncovered. From time to time his ears caught the faint clink of metal—almost inaudible at first, but then louder as if the key were being dragged up the outside of the door. There followed a different kind of scraping—the key, he thought, being slowly turned in the lock. Then there was a sharp click, and after that the iron squeak of a bolt being drawn back. After this squeak had been repeated for the second bolt, there was silence.

Soon the straw rustled and told Paolo that his fellow prisoner had woken up.

'Amico,' he heard him whisper, 'you are awake?'

'S-sí,' replied Paolo.

'Then come with me. You are free to depart.'

'I will stay,' said Paolo.

'Very well, if you wish. In that case, I can leave a message with you. Tell your bandit chiefs that I intend to teach one of them a lesson. Tell them also that when *Il Potentato*'s flesh is severed, a soul is cut off from earth.'

He then went softly to the door and passed out of the cell. The last Paolo saw of him was his figure silhouetted against the moonlight as he picked up his finger and thumb and put them in his pocket.

When they heard this account next morning. Salvatore and Luigi whispered many times the phrase 'I intend to teach one of them a lesson.'

'He will teach one of us,' breathed Luigi,' *by killing the other*.'

That they believed Paolo's story, strange though that story was, is not surprising. They knew there was no normal means of escaping from the cell. Moreover, they found a little blood on the cell floor and a trail of red drops leading from the doorway to the guard's seat. On that seat they found the guard's dead body—strangled, with his pistol in his hand and in his empty holster a little white mouse.

*   *   *

Madre di dio! What a change one conjuror made in those two men! They dared scarcely eat or sleep or venture out of their stronghold for fear of—for fear of they knew not what.

'It was all trickery,' said Salvatore. 'He cannot harm us here.' Yet he did not believe what he said, nor did he convince Luigi.

It was their custom to keep sentinels posted at strategic points on the mountain-side. And one day two of their men brought to them a stranger whom they had captured as he rode up from the valley. This stranger gave his name as Enrico, and said he was a native of Ragusa in the south.

'A man,' he said, 'has paid me a large sum of money to come to you here and pay you the ransom which he said he owed you.'

'What is his name?' demanded Salvatore.

'His true name I do not know,' replied this man Enrico. 'But here in Sicily people call him *Il Potentato*. He is a conjuror from foreign parts. The ransom, he told me, is contained in this box. But I have carried the box for three days and three nights, and it seems to me that there is something inside it which lives. Sometimes you may hear it scratching. For fear it should contain a snake, I advise you, my friends, to be careful how you open it.'

Salvatore and Luigi looked at the little box that was no bigger than a man's hand and was tied most neatly with green ribbon.

'This man,' said Salvatore, 'this conjuror—had he—had he a bandaged hand?'

'It may have been so,' replied Enrico. 'I could not tell, for he was wearing gloves. On both his hands he wore gloves, although the weather is warm.'

'Luigi,' said Salvatore, 'we must burn this box. We will go to the charcoal burner's hut and we will burn the box. Pick it up, Luigi, and come with me.'

Luigi, however, would not touch the box. Salvatore called him many hard names for his cowardice, but he would not touch it either. So in the end they ordered one of their men to take the box, and then they all went, the three of them, to the charcoal burner's hut and stood in a ring round the brazier.

'Drop it in,' commanded Salvatore.

The man took the box, holding it by the emerald-green ribbon, and let it fall into the heart of the fire. There was a faint knocking sound as it lay in the flames, and that was followed by a hissing and a spluttering. They watched it until it was consumed, and then they rode back to their stronghold. Their hearts were lighter on the return journey, you may be sure, than when they had ridden forth. Their hearts were lighter, indeed, than they had ever been in their lives.

'Now,' said Luigi, 'we are safe.'

'Yes,' said Salvatore. 'Praised be the blessed saints! we are at last safe.'

The man Enrico asked their pardon when they returned, and

said he had wished them no harm. Indeed, it was he who had warned them about the box. The journey back, he said, was a long one, and he wished to stay the night if they would let him.

Salvatore and Luigi said he could stay if he wished; but they were not fools—he would have to be content with being locked in the cell. Then, when he had been locked up for the night, they caroused with their men until a late hour, and at last went to bed.

In the morning, when Luigi arose . . . But, Signore, I can see you know what Luigi found when he arose. He found his friend, Salvatore, quite dead—strangled, his eyes staring as if he had seen something horrible when he died, his tongue protruding from his mouth. On his throat were four marks—the impression of two thumbs and two index fingers. There were a few drops of blood on the ground beside him, and the trail of blood led to the cell door which was open. The guest, Enrico, had of course gone, leaving behind him nothing but a little box, the size of a man's hand, beside which lay a strip of ribbon—red ribbon. The inside of the box was stained with blood.

FOOTSTEPS IN THE LOBBY

Joseph Sheridan Le Fanu

To many critics, Joseph Sheridan Le Fanu is one of the most important and innovative writers of supernatural fiction in English, while the periodical which he edited, the Dublin University Magazine, *is recognised as one of the earliest publications that welcomed horror stories into its pages. Some of the very best of Le Fanu's work was written towards the end of his life when the sudden death of his wife had turned him into an eccentric recluse who shunned society. Instead he confined himself to bed in his Dublin home and there constructed some of the most chilling tales to come out of Ireland—or indeed anywhere else. Today few ghost story anthologies do not include at least one example of his work, and to M. R. James, who rescued a number of his tales from oblivion, he was, simply, 'the master'. Le Fanu was also one of the first writers to do away with the Gothic staples of haunted castles and heroines in peril in favour of stories in everyday surroundings in which the psychological intricacies of fear were explored. As another exponent of the ghost story, E. F. Benson, has put it, 'Le Fanu's stories begin quietly enough, the tentacles of terror applied so softly that the reader hardly notices them till they are sucking the courage from his blood.'*

Joseph Sheridan Le Fanu (1814–1873), who was a grand-nephew of the playwright Richard Brinsley Sheridan, was born into a middle class Dublin family of Huguenot descent. He graduated from Trinity College, Dublin, and thereafter worked for several newspapers and periodicals before becoming the editor of the Dublin University Magazine. *In 1858 his wife died and the previously gregarious man-of-letters locked himself behind the doors of his home. According to his son, Brinsley, Le Fanu would write at night by candlelight until he dropped asleep. Then around 2 a.m. he would waken, probably fresh from a nightmare, and continue his work.*

Among the products of this extraordinary method of creativity were his famous vampire tale, 'Carmilla'; the psychological classic of a man haunted by a monkey-like creature, 'Green Tea'; and Uncle Silas, *written in 1864, which E. F. Benson has called 'a masterpiece of alarm' and E. F. Bleiler 'the finest Victorian mystery novel'. It is a chilling tale about a young orphan girl who goes to live with her malevolent guardian, Uncle Silas, and gradually comes to suspect him of having been involved in the brutal murder of her father. The book has been adapted for the stage, radio and television: most recently in 1989 as a serial called* The Dark Angel, *with Peter O'Toole as a villainous, hypocritical Silas and Beatie Edney the demure heroine, Maud. The novel itself was actually inspired by the following story which Le Fanu had written for the November 1838 issue of the* Dublin University Magazine *and published with the sub-title 'A Passage in the Secret History of an Irish Countess'. A quarter of a century later, he utilised the same facts again for the chief incident in* Uncle Silas. *'Footsteps in the Lobby' introduces us to a young girl who has been left by her father as the ward of her uncle and has just refused the old man's wish that she should marry his son. Now read on . . .*

*   *   *

I went to my room early that night, but I was too miserable to sleep. At about twelve o'clock, feeling very nervous, I determined to call my cousin Emily, who slept in the next room, which communicated with mine by a second door. By this private entrance I found my way into her chamber, and without difficulty persuaded her to return to my room and sleep with me. We accordingly lay down together—she undressed, and I with my clothes on—for I was every moment walking up and down the room, and felt too nervous and miserable to think of rest or comfort. Emily was soon fast asleep, and I lay awake, fervently longing for the first pale gleam of morning, reckoning every stroke of the old clock with an impatience which made every hour appear like six.

It must have been about one o'clock when I thought I heard a slight noise at the partition door between Emily's room and mine, as if caused by somebody's turning the key in the lock. I held my breath, and the same sound was repeated at the second door of my room—that which opened upon the lobby—the sound was here distinctly caused by the revolution of the bolt in the lock, and it was followed by a slight pressure upon the door itself, as if to ascertain the security of the lock. The person, whoever it might be, was probably satisfied, for I heard the old boards of the lobby creak and strain, as if under the weight of somebody moving cautiously over them.

My sense of hearing became unnaturally, almost painfully acute. I suppose the imagination added distinctness to sounds vague in themselves. I thought that I could actually hear the breathing of the person who was slowly returning down the lobby; at the head of the staircase there appeared to occur a pause; and I could distinctly hear two or three sentences hastily whispered; the steps then descended the stairs with apparently less caution. I now ventured to walk quickly and lightly to the lobby door, and attempted to open it; but it was indeed fast locked upon the outside, as was also the other. I now felt that the dreadful hour was come; but one desperate expedient remained—it was to awaken Emily, and by our united strength, to attempt to force the partition door, which was slighter than the other, and through this to pass to the lower part of the house, whence it might be possible to escape to the grounds, and forth to the village.

I returned to the bedside, and shook Emily, but in vain; nothing that I could do availed to produce from her more than a few incoherent words—it was a death-like sleep. She had certainly drunk of some narcotic, as had I probably also, in spite of all the caution with which I had examined everything presented to us to eat or drink. I now attempted, with as little noise as possible, to force first one door, then the other—but all in vain. I believe no strength could have effected my object, for both doors opened inwards. I therefore collected whatever movables I could carry thither, and piled them against the doors, so as to assist me in whatever attempts I should make to resist the entrance of those without. I then returned to the bed and endeavoured again, but fruitlessly, to awaken my cousin. It was not sleep, it was torpor, lethargy, death. I knelt down and prayed with an agony of earnestness; and then seating myself upon the bed, I awaited my fate with a kind of terrible tranquillity.

I heard a faint clanking sound from the narrow court below, as if caused by the scraping of some iron instrument against stones or rubbish. I at first determined not to disturb the calmness which

I now felt, by uselessly watching the proceedings of those who sought my life; but as the sounds continued, the horrible curiosity which I felt overcame every other emotion, and I determined, at all hazards, to gratify it. I therefore crawled upon my knees to the window, so as to let the smallest portion of my head appear above the sill.

The moon was shining with an uncertain radiance upon the antique grey buildings, and obliquely upon the narrow court beneath, one side of which was therefore clearly illuminated, while the other was lost in obscurity, the sharp outlines of the old gables, with their nodding clusters of ivy, being at first alone visible. Whoever or whatever occasioned the noise which had excited my curiosity, was concealed under the shadow of the dark side of the quadrangle. I placed my hand over my eyes to shade them from the moonlight, which was so bright as to be almost dazzling, and, peering into the darkness, I first dimly, but afterwards gradually, almost with full distinctness, beheld the form of a man engaged in digging what appeared to be a rude hole close under the wall. Some implements, probably a shovel and pickaxe, lay beside him, and to these he every now and then applied himself as the nature of the ground required. He pursued his task rapidly, and with as little noise as possible.

'So,' thought I, as shovelful after shovelful the dislodged rubbish mounted into a heap, 'they are digging the grave in which, before two hours pass, I must lie, a cold, mangled corpse. I am *theirs*— I cannot escape.' I felt as if my reason was leaving me. I started to my feet, and in mere despair I applied myself again to each of the two doors alternately. I strained every nerve and sinew, but I might as well have attempted, with my single strength, to force the building itself from its foundation. I threw myself madly upon the ground, and clasped my hands over my eyes as if to shut out the horrible images which crowded upon me.

The paroxysm passed away. I prayed once more with the bitter, agonised fervour of one who feels that the hour of death is present and inevitable. When I arose I went once more to the window and looked out, just in time to see a shadowy figure glide stealthily along the wall. The task was finished. The catastrophe of the tragedy must soon be accomplished. I determined now to defend my life to the last; and that I might be able to do so with some effect, I searched the room for something which might serve as a weapon;

but either through accident, or from an anticipation of such a possibility, everything which might have been made available for such a purpose had been carefully removed. I must thus die tamely and without an effort to defend myself.

A thought suddenly struck me—might it not be possible to escape through the door, which the assassin must open in order to enter the room? I resolved to make the attempt. I felt assured that the door through which ingress to the room would be effected was that which opened upon the lobby. It was the more direct way, besides being, for obvious reasons, less liable to interruption than the other. I resolved then to place myself behind a projection of the wall, whose shadow would serve fully to conceal me, and when the door should be opened, and before they should have discovered the identity of the occupant of the bed, to creep noiselessly from the room, and then to trust to Providence for escape. In order to facilitate this scene, I removed all the lumber which I had heaped against the door; and I had nearly completed my arrangements, when I perceived the room suddenly darkened by the close approach of some shadowy object to the window. On turning my eyes in that direction, I observed at the top of the casement, as if suspended from above, first the feet, then the legs, then the body, and at length the whole figure of a man present itself.

It was Edward T——n. He appeared to be guiding his descent so as to bring his feet upon the centre of the stone block which occupied the lower part of the window; and having secured his footing upon this, he kneeled down and began to gaze into the room. As the moon was gleaming into the chamber, and the bed curtains were drawn, he was able to distinguish the bed itself and its contents. He appeared satisfied with his scrutiny, for he looked up and made a sign with his hand, upon which the rope by which his descent had been effected was slackened from above, and he proceeded to disengage it from his waist: this accomplished, he applied his hands to the window-frame, which must have been ingeniously contrived for the purpose, for with apparently no resistance the whole frame, containing casement and all, slipped from its position in the wall, and was by him lowered into the room. The cold night waved the bed-curtains, and he paused for a moment—all was still again—and he stepped in upon the floor of the room. He held in his hand what appeared to be a steel instrument, shaped something like a hammer, but larger and sharper at the extremities. This he held rather behind him, while, with three long *tip-toe* strides, he brought himself to the bedside.

I felt that the discovery must now be made, and held my breath in momentary expectation of the execration in which he would vent his surprise and disappointment. I closed my eyes—there was a pause—but it was a short one. I heard two dull blows, given in rapid succession: a quivering sigh, and the long-drawn, heavy breathing of the sleeper was for ever suspended. I unclosed my eyes, and saw the murderer fling the quilt across the head of his victim: he then, with the instrument of death still in his hand, proceeded to the lobby door, upon which he tapped sharply twice or thrice—a quick step was then heard approaching, and a voice whispered something from without—Edward answered, with a kind of chuckle, 'Her ladyship is past complaining; unlock the door, in the devil's name, unless you're afraid to come in, and help me to lift the body out of the window.' The key was turned in the lock—the door opened—and my uncle entered the room.

I have told you already that I had placed myself under the shade of a projection of the wall, close to the door. I had instinctively shrunk down cowering towards the ground on the entrance of Edward through the window. When my uncle entered the room, he and his son both stood so very close to me that his hand was every moment upon the point of touching my face. I held my breath, and remained motionless as death.

'You had no interruption from the next room?' said my uncle.

'No,' was the brief reply.

'Secure the jewels, Ned; the French harpy must not lay her claws upon them. You've a steady hand, by G—; not much blood—eh?'

'Not twenty drops,' replied his son, 'and those on the quilt.'

'I'm glad it's over,' whispered my uncle again; 'we must lift the—the *thing* through the window, and lay the rubbish over it.'

They then turned to the bedside, and, winding the bed-clothes round the body, carried it between them slowly to the window, and, exchanging a few brief words with someone below, they shoved it over the window sill, and I heard it fall heavily on the ground underneath.

'I'll take the jewels,' said my uncle; 'there are two caskets in the lower drawer.'

He proceeded, with an accuracy which, had I been more at ease, would have furnished me with matter of astonishment, to lay his hand upon the very spot where my jewels lay; and having possessed himself of them, he called to his son—

'Is the rope made fast above?'

'I'm not a fool—to be sure it is,' replied he.

They then lowered themselves from the window. I now rose lightly and cautiously, scarcely daring to breathe, from my place of concealment, and was creeping towards the door, when I heard my cousin's voice, in a sharp whisper, exclaim, 'Scramble up again; G—d d—n you, you've forgot to lock the door;' and I perceived, by the straining of the rope which hung from above, that the mandate was instantly obeyed.

Not a second was to be lost. I passed through the door, which was only closed, and moved as rapidly as I could, consistently with stillness, along the lobby. Before I had gone many yards I heard the door through which I had just passed double locked on the inside. I glided down the stairs in terror, lest, at every corner, I should meet the murderer or one of his accomplices. I reached the hall, and listened for a moment to ascertain whether all was silent around; no sound was audible; the parlour windows opened on the park, and through one of them I might, I thought, easily effect my escape. Accordingly, I hastily entered; but, to my consternation, a candle was burning in the room, and by its light I saw a figure seated at the dinner-table, upon which lay glasses, bottles, and the other accompaniments of a drinking party.

There was no other means of escape, so I advanced with a firm step and collected mind to the window. I noiselessly withdrew the bars and unclosed the shutters—I pushed open the casement, and, without waiting to look behind me, I ran with my utmost speed, scarcely feeling the ground under me, down the avenue, taking care to keep upon the grass which bordered it. I did not for a moment slack my speed, and I had now gained the centre point between the park gate and the mansion-house—here the avenue made a wider circuit, and in order to avoid delay, I directed my way across the smooth sward round which the pathway wound, intending, at the opposite side of the flat, at a point which I distinguished by a group of old birch trees, to enter again upon the beaten track, which was from thence tolerably direct to the gate.

I had, with my utmost speed, got about halfway across this broad flat when the rapid treading of a horse's hoofs struck upon my ear. My heart swelled in my bosom, as though I would smother. The clattering of galloping hoofs approached—I was pursued— they were now upon the sward on which I was running—there was not a bush or a bramble to shelter me—and, as if to render escape altogether desperate, the moon, which had hitherto been obscured, at this moment shone forth with a broad clear light, which made every object distinctly visible. The sounds were now close behind me. I felt my knees bending under me, with the sensation which torments one in dreams. I reeled—I stumbled— I fell—and at the same instant the cause of my alarm wheeled past me at full gallop. It was one of the young fillies which pastured loose about the park, whose frolics had thus all but maddened me with terror.

I scrambled to my feet, and rushed on with weak but rapid steps, my sportive companion still galloping round and round me with many a frisk and fling, until, at length, more dead than alive, I reached the avenue gate and crossed the stile, I scarce knew how. I ran through the village, in which all was silent as the grave, until my progress was arrested by the hoarse voice of a sentinel, who cried, 'Who goes there?' I felt that I was now safe. I turned in the direction of the voice, and fell fainting at the soldier's feet.

When I came to myself I was sitting in a miserable hovel, sur- rounded by strange faces, all bespeaking curiosity and compassion. Many soldiers were in it also; indeed, as I afterwards found, it was employed as a guard-room by a detachment of troops quartered for that night in the town. In a few words I informed their officer of the circumstances which had occurred, describing also the appear- ance of the persons engaged in the murder; and he, without loss of time, proceeded to the mansion-house of Carrickleigh, taking with him a number of his men. But the villains had discovered their mistake, and had effected their escape, before the arrival of the military.

Deep and fervent as must always be my gratitude to Heaven for my deliverance, effected by a chain of providential occur- rences, the failing of a single link of which must have insured my destruction, I was long before I could look back upon it with other feelings than those of bitterness, almost of agony. My cousin, the only being that had ever really loved me, my nearest dearest friend, ever ready to sympathise, to counsel, and to assist—the gayest, the gentlest, the warmest heart—the only creature on earth that cared for me—*her* life had been the price of my deliverance; and I then uttered the wish—which no event of my long and sorrowful life has taught me to recall—that she had been spared, and that in her stead *I* were mouldering in the grave forgotten and at rest.

THE CEDAR CLOSET

Patrick Lafcadio Hearn

The life of Patrick Lafcadio Hearn—much of whose work appeared under the shortened by-line Lafcadio Hearn—was so extraordinary that he could only have been Irish. Born of Irish-Greek parentage, he emigrated in his twenties to America where he rapidly earned a reputation as a writer of macabre fact and fiction. Abandoning this at the height of his fame, he migrated once again to Japan, whose culture and mythology had apparently started to fascinate him, and there married a Japanese girl and eventually took Japanese citizenship. Hearn's final years were spent as a writer of ghost stories and the Professor of English Literature at the Imperial University of Tokyo!

The full name of this remarkable man was Patrick Lafcadio Tessima Carlos Hearn (1850–1904), his father's name being an anglicised form of the old Irish name O hEachtighearne ('lord of the horse'), a family said to have descended from the High King Brian Boru. Patrick was educated in Dublin, but a childhood accident left him blind in the left eye and chronic myopia made him live in fear of going permanently blind. Nonetheless, he chose to follow the career of an itinerant journalist and first came to public attention in Cincinnati with stories of nauseating and horrific crimes—including cannibalism, graveyard robbery and violent cremation—which earned him a reputation of being a 'ghoulish writer', though one whose name on a story was guaranteed to sell extra copies of the paper. It was said he also took opium, concealed a white-handled razor in one of his socks in case of attack and carried a large telescope to enable him to peer into inaccessible spots—making him a forerunner of today's intrusive tabloid journalists! In true Irish fashion, he happily cultivated this notoriety and did nothing to disclaim one rumour that he actually enjoyed drinking blood!

It was while he was living a bohemian existence in New Orleans with a pretty mulatto girl that he wrote his first novel, Chita, *about a young female who survives a tidal wave on a small island; but he only achieved his unique place in the world of supernatural fiction after his wanderlust had taken him to Japan and he had begun to produce ghost and horror stories based on local legends. The subsequent collections of these stories, including* Stray Leaves from Strange Literatures *(1884),* Kwaidan *(1904) and* Fantastics *(1914) earned the highest praise, and in Japan Hearn is revered to this day as a Japanese writer. Sadly, his work is still undervalued in the West, although in Ireland his contributions have been recognised by several critics, including Paul Murray, a member of the Irish diplomatic service, who recently delivered a lecture at Clontarf, Dublin (Bram Stoker's birthplace!) entitled, 'Lafcadio Hearn and the Irish Tradition of Literary Horror.' The following story, 'The Cedar Closet', which he wrote in 1874, is just one example of his gift to that genre as well as being an outstandingly chilling tale . . .*

*   *   *

It happened ten years ago, and it stands out, and ever will stand out, in my memory like some dark, awful barrier dividing the happy, gleeful years of girlhood, with their foolish, petulant sorrows and eager, innocent joys, and the bright, lovely life which has been mine since. In looking back, that time seems to me shadowed by a dark and terrible brooding cloud, bearing in its lurid gloom what, but for love and patience the tenderest and most untiring, might have been the bolt of death, or, worse a thousand times, of madness. As it was, for months after 'life crept on a broken wing', if not 'through cells of madness', yet verily 'through haunts of horror and fear'. O, the weary, weary days and months when I longed piteously for rest! when sunshine was torture, and every shadow filled with horror unspeakable; when my soul's craving was for death; to be allowed to creep away from the terror which lurked in the softest murmur of the summer breeze, the flicker of the shadow of the tiniest leaf on the sunny grass, in every corner and curtain-fold in my dear old home. But love conquered all, and I can tell my story now, with awe and wonder, it is true, but quietly and calmly.

Ten years ago I was living with my only brother in one of the quaint, ivy-grown, red-gabled rectories which are so picturesquely scattered over the fair breadth of England. We were orphans, Archibald and I; and I had been the busy, happy mistress of his pretty home for only one year after leaving school, when Robert Draye asked me to be his wife. Robert and Archie were old friends, and my new home, Draye's Court, was only separated from the parsonage by an old grey wall, a low iron-studded door in which admitted us from the sunny parsonage dawn to the old, old park which had belonged to the Drayes for centuries. Robert was lord of the manor; and it was he who had given Archie the living of Draye in the Wold.

It was the night before my wedding day, and our pretty home was crowded with the wedding guests. We were all gathered in the large old-fashioned drawing-room after dinner. When Robert left us late in the evening, I walked with him, as usual, to the little gate for what he called our last parting; we lingered awhile under the great walnut-tree, through the heavy, sombre branches of which the September moon poured its soft pure light. With his last goodnight kiss on my lips and my heart full of him and the love which warmed and glorified the whole world for me, I did not care to go back to share in the fun and frolic in the drawing-room, but went softly upstairs to my own room. I say 'my own room', but I was to occupy it as a bedroom tonight for the first time. It was a pleasant south room, wainscoted in richly-carved cedar, which gave the atmosphere a spicy fragrance. I had chosen it as my morning room on my arrival in our home; here I had read and sung and painted, and spent long, sunny hours while Archibald was busy in his study after breakfast. I had had a bed arranged there as I preferred being alone to sharing my own larger bedroom with two of my bridesmaids. It looked bright and cosy as I came in; my favourite low chair was drawn before the fire, whose rosy light glanced and flickered on the glossy dark walls, which gave the room its name, 'The Cedar Closet'. My maid was busy preparing my toilet table, I sent her away, and sat down to wait for my brother, who I knew would come to bid me goodnight. He came; we had our last fireside talk in my girlhood's home; and when he left me there was an incursion of all my bridesmaids for a 'dressing-gown reception.'

When at last I was alone I drew back the curtain and curled myself up on the low wide window-seat. The moon was at its brightest; the little church and quiet churchyard beyond the lawn looked fair and calm beneath its rays; the gleam of the white headstones here and there between the trees might have reminded me that life is not all peace and joy—that tears and pain, fear and parting, have their share in its story—but it did not. The tranquil happiness with which my heart was full overflowed in some soft tears which had no tinge of bitterness, and when at last I did lie down, peace, deep and perfect, still seemed to flow in on me with the moonbeams which filled the room, shimmering on the folds of my bridal dress, which was laid ready for the morning. I am thus minute in describing my last waking moments, that it may be understood that what followed was not creation of a morbid fancy.

I do not know how long I had been asleep, when I was suddenly, as it were, wrenched back to consciousness. The moon had set, the room was quite dark; I could just distinguish the glimmer of a clouded, starless sky through the open window. I could not see or hear anything unusual, but not the less was I conscious of an unwonted, a baleful presence near; an indescribable horror cramped the very beatings of my heart; with every instant the certainty grew that my room was shared by some evil being. I could not cry for help, though Archie's room was so close, and I knew that one call through the death-like stillness would bring him to me; all I could do was gaze, gaze, gaze into the darkness. Suddenly—and a throb stung through every nerve—I heard distinctly from behind the wainscot against which the head of my bed was placed a low, hollow moan, followed on the instant by a cackling, malignant laugh from the other side of the room. If I had been one of the monumental figures in the little churchyard on which I had seen the quiet moonbeams shine a few hours before I could not have been more utterly unable to move or speak; every other faculty seemed to be lost in the one intent strain of eye and ear. There came at last the sound of a halting step, the tapping of a crutch upon the floor, then stillness, and slowly, gradually the room filled with light—a pale, cold, steady light. Everything around was exactly as I had last seen it in the mingled shine of the moon and fire, and though I heard at intervals the harsh laugh, the curtain at the foot of the bed hid from me whatever uttered it. Again, low but distinct, the piteous moan broke forth, followed by some words in a foreign tongue, and with the sound a figure started from behind the curtain—a dwarfed, deformed woman, dressed in a loose robe of black, sprinkled with golden stars, which gave forth a dull, fiery gleam, in the mysterious light; one lean, yellow hand clutched the curtain of my bed; it glittered with jewelled rings;—long black hair fell in heavy masses from a golden circlet over the stunted form. I saw it all clearly as I now see the pen which writes these words and the hand which guides it. The face was turned from me, bent aside, as if greedily drinking in those astonished moans; I noted even the streaks of grey in the long tresses, as I lay helpless in dumb, bewildered horror.

'Again!' she said hoarsely, as the sounds died away into indistinct murmurs, and advancing a step she tapped sharply with a crutch on the cedar wainscot; then again louder and more purposeful rose the wild beseeching voice; this time the words were English.

'Mercy, have mercy! not on me, but on my child, my little one; she never harmed you. She is dying—she is dying here in darkness; let me but see her face once more. Death is very near, nothing can save her now; but grant one ray of light, and I will pray that you may be forgiven, if forgiveness there be for such as you.'

'What, you kneel at last! Kneel to Gerda, and kneel in vain. A ray of light! Not if you could pay for it in diamonds. You are mine! Shriek and call as you will, no other ears can hear. Die together. You are mine to torture as I will; mine, mine, mine!' and again an awful laugh rang through the room. At the instant she turned. O the face of malign horror that met my gaze! The green eyes flamed, and with something like the snarl of a savage beast she sprang towards me; that hideous face almost touched mine; the grasp of the skinny jewelled hand was all but on me; then—I suppose I fainted.

For weeks I lay in brain fever, in mental horror and weariness so intent, that even now I do not like to let my mind dwell on it. Even when the crisis was safely past I was slow to rally; my mind was utterly unstrung. I lived in a world of shadows. And so winter wore by, and brought us to the fair spring morning when at last I stood by Robert's side in the old church, a cold, passive, almost unwilling bride. I cared neither to refuse nor consent to anything that was suggested; so Robert and Archie decided for me, and I allowed them to do with me as they would, while I brooded silently and ceaselessly on the memory of that terrible night. To my husband I told all one morning in a sunny Bavarian valley, and my weak, frightened mind drew strength and peace from his; by degrees the haunting horror wore away, and when we came home for a happy reason nearly two years afterwards, I was as strong and blithe as in my girlhood. I had learned to believe that it had all been, not the cause, but the commencement of my fever. I was to be undeceived.

Our little daughter had come to us in the time of roses; and now Christmas was with us, our first Christmas at home, and the house was full of guests. It was a delicious old-fashioned Yule; plenty of skating and outdoor fun, and no lack of brightness indoors. Towards New Year a heavy fall of snow set in which kept us all prisoners; but even then the days flew merrily, and somebody suggested tableaux for the evenings. Robert was elected manager; there was a debate and selection of subjects, and then came the puzzle of where, at such short notice, we could procure the dresses required. My husband advised a raid on some mysterious oaken chests which we knew had been for years stowed away in a turret-room. He remembered having, when a boy, seen the housekeeper inspecting them, and their contents had left a hazy impression of old stand-alone brocades, gold tissues, sacques, hoops and hoods, the very mention of which put us in a state of wild excitement. Mrs Moultrie was summoned, looked duly horrified at the desecration of what to her were relics most sacred; but seeing it was inevitable, she marshalled the way, a protest in every rustle and fold of her stiff silk dress.

'What a charming old place,' was the exclamation with variations as we entered the long oak-joisted room, at the further end of which stood in goodly array the chests whose contents we coveted. Bristling with unspoken disapproval, poor Mrs Moultrie unlocked one after another, and then asked permission to retire, leaving us unchecked to 'cry havoc'. In a moment the floor was covered with piles of silks and velvets.

'Meg,' cried little Janet Crawford, dancing up to me, 'isn't it a good thing to live in the age of tulle and summer silks? Fancy being imprisoned for life in a fortress like this!' holding up a thick crimson and gold brocade, whaleboned and buckramed at all points. It was thrown aside, and she half lost herself in another chest and was silent. Then—'Look, Major Fraude! This is the very thing for you—a true astrologer's robe, all black velvet and golden stars. If it were but long enough; it just fits me.'

I turned and saw—the pretty slight figure, the innocent girlish face dressed in the robe of black and gold, identical in shape, pattern and material with what I too well remembered. With a wild cry I hid my face and cowered away.

'Take it off! O, Janet—Robert—take it from her!'

Every one turned wondering. In an instant my husband saw, and catching up the cause of my terror, flung it hastily into the chest again, and lowered the lid. Janet looked half offended, but the cloud passed in an instant when I kissed her, apologising as well as I could. Rob laughed at us both, and voted an adjournment to a warmer room, where we could have the chests brought to us to ransack at leisure. Before going down, Janet and I went into a small anteroom to examine some old pictures which leaned against the wall.

'This is just the thing, Jennie, to frame the tableaux,' I said, pointing to an immense frame, at least twelve feet square. 'There is a picture in it,' I added, pulling back the dusty folds of a heavy curtain which fell before it.

'That can be easily removed,' said my husband, who had followed us.

With his assistance we drew the curtain quite away, and in the now fast waning light could just discern the figure of a girl in white against a dark background. Robert rang for a lamp, and when it came we turned with much curiosity to examine the painting, as to the subject of which we had been making odd merry guesses while we waited. The girl was young, almost childish—very lovely, but, oh, how sad! Great tears stood in the innocent eyes and on the round young cheeks, and her hands were clasped tenderly around the arms of a man who was bending towards her, and, did I dream?—no, there in hateful distinctness was the hideous woman of the Cedar Closet—the same in every distorted line, even to the starred dress and golden circlet. The swarthy hues of the dress and the face had at first caused us to overlook her. The same wicked eyes seemed to glare into mine. After one wild bound my heart seemed to stop its beating, and I knew no more. When I recovered from a long, deep swoon, great lassitude and intense nervous excitement followed; my illness broke up the party, and for months I was an invalid. When again Robert's love and patience had won me back to my old health and happiness, he told me all the truth, so far as it had been preserved in old records of the family.

It was in the sixteenth century that the reigning lady of Draye

Court was a weird, deformed woman, whose stunted body, hideous face, and a temper which taught her to hate and vilify everything good and beautiful for the contrast offered to herself, made her universally feared and disliked. One talent only she possessed; it was for music; but so wild and strange were the strains she drew from the many instruments of which she was mistress, that the gift only intensified the dread with which she was regarded. Her father had died before her birth; her mother did not survive it; near relatives she had none; she had lived her lonely, loveless life from youth to middle age. When a young girl came to the Court, no one knew more than that she was a poor relation. The dark woman seemed to look more kindly on this young cousin than on anyone that had hitherto crossed her sombre path, and indeed so great was the charm which Marian's goodness, beauty and innocent gaiety exercised on everyone that the servants ceased to marvel at her having gained the favour of their gloomy mistress. The girl seemed to feel a kind of wondering, pitying affection for the unhappy woman; she looked on her through an atmosphere created by her own sunny nature, and for a time all went well. When Marian had been at the Court for a year, a foreign musician appeared on the scene. He was a Spaniard, and had been engaged by Lady Draye to build for her an organ said to be of fabulous power and sweetness. Through long bright summer days he and his employer were shut up together in the music-room—he busy in the construction of the wonderful instrument, she aiding and watching his work. These days were spent by Marian in various ways—pleasant idleness and pleasant work, long canters on her chestnut pony, dreamy mornings by the brook with rod and line, or in the village near, where she found a welcome everywhere. She played with the children, nursed the babies, helped the mothers in a thousand pretty ways, gossiped with old people, brightening the day for everybody with whom she came in contact. Then in the evening she sat with Lady Draye and the Spaniard in the saloon, talking in that soft foreign tongue which they generally used. But this was but the music between the acts; the terrible drama was coming. The motive was of course the same as that of every life drama which has been played out from the old, old days when the curtain rose upon the garden scene of Paradise. Philip and Marian loved each other, and having told their happy secret to each other, they, as in duty bound, took it to their patroness. They found her in the music room. Whether the glimpses she caught of a beautiful world from which she was shut out maddened her, or whether she, too, loved the foreigner, was never certainly known; but through the closed door passionate words were heard, and very soon Philip came out alone, and left the house without a farewell to any in it. When the servants did at last venture to enter, they found Marian lifeless on the floor, Lady Draye standing over her with crutch uplifted, and blood flowing from a wound in the girl's forehead. They carried her away and nursed her tenderly; their mistress locked the door as they left, and all night long remained alone in darkness. The music which came out without pause on the still night air was weird and wicked beyond any strains which had ever before flowed even from beneath her fingers; it ceased with morning light; and as the day wore on it was found that Marian had fled during the night, and that Philip's organ had sounded its last strain—Lady Draye had shattered and silenced it forever. She never seemed to notice Marian's absence and no one dared to mention her name. Nothing was ever known certainly of her fate; it was supposed that she had joined her lover.

Years passed, and with each Lady Draye's temper grew fiercer and more malevolent. She never quitted her room unless on the anniversary of that day and night, when the tapping of her crutch and high-heeled shoes was heard for hours as she walked up and down the music-room, which was never entered save for this yearly vigil. The tenth anniversary came round, and this time the vigil was not unshared. The servants distinctly heard the sound of a man's voice mingling in earnest conversation with her shrill tones; they listened long, and at last one of the boldest ventured to look in, himself unseen. He saw a worn, travel-stained man; dusty, foot-sore, poorly dressed, he still at once recognised the handsome, gay Philip of ten years ago. He held in his arms a little sleeping girl; her long curls, so like poor Marian's, strayed over his shoulder. He seemed to be pleading in that strange musical tongue for the little one; for as he spoke he lifted, O, so tenderly, the cloak which partly concealed her, and showed the little face, which he doubtless thought might plead for itself. The woman, with a furious gesture, raised her crutch to strike the child; he stepped quickly backward, stooped to kiss the little girl, then, without a word, turned to go. Lady Draye called on him to return with an imperious gesture, spoke a few words, to which he seemed to listen gratefully, and together they left the house by the window which opened on the terrace. The servants followed them, and found she led the way to the parsonage, which was at the time unoccupied. It was said that he was in some political danger as well as in deep poverty, and that she had hidden him here until she could help him to a better asylum. It was certain that for many nights she went to the parsonage and returned before dawn, thinking herself unseen. But one morning she did not come home; her people consulted together; her relenting towards Philip had made them feel more kindly towards her than ever before; they sought her at the parsonage and found her lying across its threshold dead, a vial clasped in her rigid fingers. There was no sign of the late presence of Philip and his child; it was believed she had sped them on their way before she killed herself. They laid her in a suicide's grave. For more than fifty years after the parsonage was shut up. Though it had been again inhabited no one had ever been terrified by the spectre I had seen; probably the Cedar Closet had never before been used as a bedroom.

Robert decided on having the wing containing the haunted room pulled down and rebuilt, and in doing so the truth of my story gained a horrible confirmation. When the wainscot of the Cedar Closet was removed a recess was discovered in the massive old wall, and in this lay mouldering fragments of the skeletons of a man and child!

There could be but one conclusion drawn; the wicked woman had imprisoned them there under pretence of hiding and helping them; and once they were completely at her mercy, had come night after night with unimaginable cruelty to gloat over their agony, and when that long anguish was ended, ended her odious life by a suicide's death. We could learn nothing of the mysterious painting. Philip was an artist, and it may have been his work. We had it destroyed, so that no record of the terrible story might remain. I have no more to add, save that but for those dark days left by Lady Draye as a legacy of fear and horror, I should never have known so well the treasure I hold in the tender, unwearying, faithful love of my husband—known the blessing that every sorrow carries in its heart, that

> 'Every cloud that spreads above
> And veileth love, itself is love.'

WILL

Vincent O'Sullivan

The author of this next story is another writer whose contribution to the horror story has been seriously undervalued except among a select group of admirers. The fate of Vincent O'Sullivan to be condemned to a footnote in most histories of horror fiction may be because his life and work were overshadowed by that of his notorious friends, Oscar Wilde, Aubrey Beardsley and Frank Harris—not forgetting his undeniably minor role in the English Aesthetic movement—but perhaps more so because much of his work appeared in small circulation magazines and anthologies and has never been collected. A few of O'Sullivan's stories were also considered too strong for contemporary readers: 'The Abigail Sheriff Memorial', for example, did not see print until 1917 in an American anthology, The Grim Thirteen, *specifically devoted to such controversial material which had been rejected by editors. According to the critic Robert Hadji, however, he was 'a talented author and poet, particularly on supernatural themes, which gave free rein to his fascination with the psychology of fear, defined by an inexorable triad of sin, guilt and retribution'. O'Sullivan also deserves recognition as another Irish writer who successfully explored the vampire theme in the wake of Bram Stoker, with stories such as 'When I Was Dead', 'Verschoyle's House' and 'Will'.*

Vincent James O'Sullivan (1872–1940) was educated in Dublin and London by his well-to-do Irish parents who spent much of their time in New York. In the late Eighties and Nineties he was a familiar figure in the fashionable haunts of London with fellow Irish expatriates like Wilde, Harris and George Moore, and there began publishing the first of his weird stories. He later moved to Paris where he rapidly declined into dire poverty, surviving only on the charity of his friends and the modest fees from the publication of some of his stories in the Mercure de France *and the* Dublin Magazine.

After Irish independence, O'Sullivan returned to his native country and became a citizen of the Irish Free State. Four years before his death he published the book by which he is best remembered, Aspects of Wilde *(1936), about his personal acquaintance with the poet and dramatist.*

'Will', which was originally published in 1898, is a unique variation on the vampire theme with a particularly grisly finale. Interestingly, the story first appeared in French as 'Le Scarabée Funèbre' in the Mercure de France, *and was not printed in English until the following year when O'Sullivan included it in his now extremely rare volume,* The Green Window, *published in a limited edition by Leonard Smithers.*

*   *   *

Have the dead still power after they are laid in the earth? Do they rule us, by the power of the dead, from their awful thrones? Do their closed eyes become menacing beacons, and their paralysed hands reach out to scourge our feet into the paths which they have marked out? Ah, surely when the dead are given to the dust, their power crumbles into the dust!

Often during the long summer afternoons, as they sat together in a deep window looking out at the Park of the Sombre Fountains, he thought of these things. For it was at the hour of sundown, when the gloomy house was splashed with crimson, that he most hated his wife. They had been together for some months now; and their days were always spent in the same manner—seated in the window of a great room with dark oak furniture, heavy tapestry and rich purple hangings, in which a curious decaying scent of lavender ever lingered. For an hour at a time he would stare at her intensely as she sat before him—tall, and pale, and fragile, with her raven hair sweeping about her neck, and her languid hands turning over the leaves of an illuminated missal—and then he would look once more at the Park of the Sombre Fountains, where the river lay, like a silver dream, at the end. At sunset the river became for him turbulent and boding—a pool of blood; and the trees, clad in scarlet, brandished flaming swords. For long days they sat in that room, always silent, watching the shadows turn from steel to crimson, from crimson to grey, from grey to black.

If by rare chance they wandered abroad, and moved beyond the gates of the Park of the Sombre Fountains, he might hear one passenger say to another, 'How beautiful she is!' And then his hatred of his wife increased a hundredfold.

So he was poisoning her surely and lingeringly—with a poison more wily and subtle than that of Caesar Borgia's ring—with a poison distilled in his eyes. He was drawing out her life as he gazed at her; draining her veins, grudging the beats of her heart. He felt no need of the slow poisons which set fire to the brain; for his hate was a poison which he poured over her white body, till it would no longer have the strength to hold back the escaping soul. With exultation he watched her growing weaker and weaker as the summer glided by: not a day, not an hour passed that she did not pay toll to his eyes: and when in the autumn there came upon her two long faints which resembled catalepsy, he fortified his will to hate, for he felt that the end was at hand.

At length one evening, when the sky was grey in a winter sunset, she lay on a couch in the dark room, and he knew she was dying. The doctors had gone away with death on their lips, and they were left, for the moment, alone. Then she called him to her side from the deep window where he was seated looking out over the Park of the Sombre Fountains.

'You have your will,' she said. 'I am dying.'

'My will?' he murmured, waving his hands.

'Hush!' she moaned. 'Do you think I do not know? For days and months I have felt you drawing the life of my body into your life, that you might spill my soul on the ground. For days and months as I have sat with you, as I have walked by your side, you have seen me imploring pity. But you relented not, and you have your will; for I am going down to death. You have your will, and my body is dead; but my soul cannot die. No!' she cried, raising herself a little on the pillows: 'my soul shall not die, but live, and sway an all-touching sceptre lighted at the stars.'

'My wife!'

'You have thought to live without me, but you will never be without me. Through long nights when the moon is hid, through dreary days when the sun is dulled, I shall be at your side. In the deepest chaos illumined by lightning, on the loftiest mountain-top, do not seek to escape me. You are my bond-man; for this is the compact I have made with the Cardinals of Death.'

At the noon of night she died; and two days later they carried her to a burying-place set about a ruined abbey, and there they laid her in the grave. When he had seen her buried, he left the Park of the Sombre Fountains and travelled to distant lands. He penetrated the most unknown and difficult countries; he lived for months amid Arctic seas; he took part in tragic and barbarous scenes. He used himself to sights of cruelty and terror: to the anguish of women and children, to the agony and fear of men. And when he returned after years of adventure, he went to live in a house the windows of which overlooked the ruined abbey and the grave of his wife, even as the window where they had erewhile sat together overlooked the Park of the Sombre Fountains.

And here he spent dreaming days and sleepless nights—nights painted with monstrous and tumultuous pictures, and moved by waking dreams. Phantoms haggard and ghastly swept before him; ruined cities covered with a cold light edified themselves in his room; while in his ears resounded the trample of retreating and advancing armies, the clangor of squadrons, and noise of breaking war. He was haunted by women who prayed him to have mercy, stretching out beseeching hands—always women—and sometimes they were dead. And when the day came at last, and his tired eyes reverted to the lonely grave, he would soothe himself with some eastern drug, and let the hours slumber by as he fell into long reveries, murmuring at times to himself the rich, sonorous, lulling cadences of the poems in prose of Baudelaire, or dim meditative phrases, laden with the mysteries of the inner rooms of life and death, from the pages of Sir Thomas Browne.

On a night, which was the last of the moon, he heard a singular scraping noise at his window, and upon throwing open the casement he smelt the heavy odour which clings to vaults and catacombs where the dead are entombed. Then he saw that a beetle— a beetle, enormous and unreal—had crept up the wall of his house from the graveyard, and was now crawling across the floor of his room. With marvellous swiftness it climbed on a table placed near a couch on which he was used to lie, and as he approached, shuddering with loathing and disgust, he perceived to his horror that it had two red eyes like spots of blood. Sick with hatred of the thing as he was, those eyes fascinated him—held him like teeth. That night his other visions left him, but the beetle never let him

go—nay! compelled him, as he sat weeping and helpless, to study
its hideous conformation, to dwell upon its fangs, to ponder on
its food. All through the night that was like a century—all through
the pulsing hours—did he sit oppressed with horror gazing at that
unutterable, slimy vermin. At the first streak of dawn it glided
away, leaving in its trail the same smell of the charnel-house; but
to him the day brought no rest, for his dreams were haunted by
the abominable thing. All day in his ears a music sounded—a
music thronged with passion and wailing of defeat, funereal and
full of great alarums; all day he felt that he was engaged in a
conflict with one in armour, while he himself was unharnessed and
defenceless—all day, till the dark night came, when he observed
the abhorred monster crawling slowly from the ruined abbey, and
the calm, neglected Golgotha which lay there in his sight. Calm
outwardly; but beneath perhaps—how disturbed, how swept by
tempest! With trepidation, with a feeling of inexpiable guilt, he
awaited the worm—the messenger of the dead. And this night
and day were the type of nights and days to come. From the night
of the new moon, indeed, till the night when it began to wane,
the beetle remained in the grave; but so awful was the relief of
those hours, the transition so poignant, that he could do nothing
but shudder in a depression as of madness. And his circumstances
were not merely those of physical horror and disgust: clouds of
spiritual fear enveloped him: he felt that this abortion, this
unspeakable visitor, was really an agent that claimed his life, and
the flesh fell from his bones. So did he pass each day looking
forward with anguish to the night; and then, at length, came the
distorted night full of overwhelming anxiety and pain.

*　　*　　*

At dawn, when the dew was still heavy on the grass, he would go
forth into the graveyard and stand before the iron gates of the
vault in which his wife was laid. And as he stood there, repeating
wild litanies of supplication, he would cast into the vault things of
priceless value: skins of man-eating tigers and of leopards; skins
of beasts that drank from the Ganges, and of beasts that wallowed
in the mud of the Nile; gems that were the ornament of the
Pharaohs; tusks of elephants, and corals that men had given their
lives to obtain. Then holding up his arms, in a voice that raged

against heaven he would cry: 'Take these, O avenging soul, and leave me in quiet! Are not these enough?'

And after some weeks he came to the vault again bringing with him a consecrated chalice studded with jewels which had been used by a priest at Mass, and a ciborium of the purest gold. These he filled with the rare wine of a lost vintage, and placing them within the vault he called in a voice of storm: 'Take these, O implacable soul and spare thy bond-man! Are not these enough?'

And last he brought with him the bracelets of the woman he loved, whose heart he had broken by parting with her to propitiate the dead. He brought a long strand of her hair, and a handkerchief damp with her tears. And the vault was filled with the misery of his heart-quaking whisper: 'O my wife, are not *these* enough?'

But it became plain to those who were about him that he had come to the end of his life. His hatred of death, his fear of its unyielding caress, gave him strength; and he seemed to be resisting with his thin hands some palpable assailant. Plainer and more deeply coloured than the visions of delirium, he saw the company which advanced to combat him: in the strongest light he contemplated the scenery which surrounds the portals of dissolution. And at the supreme moment, it was with a struggle far greater than that of the miser who is forcibly parted from his gold, with an anguish far more intense than that of the lover who is torn from his mistress, that he gave up his soul.

On a shrewd, grey evening in the autumn they carried him down to bury him in the vault by the side of his wife. This he had desired; for he thought that in no other vault however dark, would the darkness be quite still; in no other resting-place would he be allowed to repose. As they carried him they intoned a majestic threnody—a chant which had the deep tramp and surge of a triumphant march, which rode on the winds, and sobbed through the boughs of ancient trees. And having come to the vault they gave him to the grave, and knelt on the ground to pray for the ease of his spirit. *Requiem æternam dona ei, Domine!*

But as they prepared to leave the precincts of the ruined abbey, a dialogue began within the vault—a dialogue so wonderful, so terrible, in its nature, its cause, that as they hearkened they gazed at one another in the twilight with wry and pallid faces.

And first a woman's voice.

'You are come.'

'Yes, I am come,' said the voice of a man. 'I yield myself to you—the conqueror.'

'Long have I awaited you,' said the woman's voice. 'For years I have lain here while the rain soaked through the stones, and snow was heavy on my breast. For years while the sun danced over the earth, and the moon smiled her mellow smile upon gardens and pleasant things. I have lain here in the company of the worm, and I have leagued with the worm. You did nothing but what I willed; you were the toy of my dead hands. Ah, you stole my body from me, but I have stolen your soul from you!'

'And is there peace for me—now—at the last?'

The woman's voice became louder, and rang through the vault like a proclaiming trumpet. 'Peace is not mine! You and I are at last together in the city of one who queens it over a mighty empire. Now shall we tremble before the queen of Death.'

The watchers flung aside the gates of the vault and struck open two coffins. In a mouldy coffin they found the body of a woman having the countenance and the warmth of one who has just died. But the body of the man was corrupt and most horrid, like a corpse that has lain for years in a place of graves.

THE BRIDE

M. P. Shiel

The pattern of eccentricity among Irish writers of horror fiction is continued in our next contributor, M. P. Shiel. He, too, wrote in a fin de siècle style for several years, published a number of influential works, but is still best remembered today for his bizarre life-style and claim to be the King of a small domain in the Leeward Islands! Shiel explained his origins and his claim to nobility in a typically colourful speech delivered in 1938. 'My parents were Irish,' he told his audience, 'and my father had the foible (Irish!) of thinking highly of people "descended from kings"—ancient kings, tamed cavemen! He had, in truth, about him some species of kingship, aloofness, was called by all "the governor", and on my fifteenth birthday had me crowned King of Redonda, a rock-island of scarcely nine square miles in the West Indies.' Although the British authorities refused to recognise this claim, Shiel referred to himself as the ruler of Redonda throughout his life and eventually made his biographer, John Gawsworth, his successor. Some less admiring of the author claimed that he used his 'kingship' as a means of obtaining credit whenever he was hard up for money!

Matthew Phipps Shiel (1865–1947) was a multi-talented man. At college he learned to speak several languages but opted to study medicine at St Bartholomew's Hospital in London. This, however, did not suit his aspirations and for a while he worked as a teacher of mathematics in Derbyshire, before finally abandoning this pro-fession to become a writer. He initially worked as a translator and ghost-writer for others until success came his way with his novel about a detective recluse, written in the style of Poe, called Prince Zaleski *(1895). This was followed by several collections of horror stories which he had been contributing to magazines and periodicals and then in 1901 by his classic novel,* The Purple Cloud, *about a gas that nearly destroys the world. Of this, the French critic Jules Claretie declared, 'The Purple Cloud should live as long as The Odyssey.' The book was later filmed by MGM in 1959 as The World, The Flesh and The Devil, starring Harry Belafonte, Mel Ferrer and Inger Stevens, and has been acknowledged by Stephen King as the inspiration for his early novel, The Stand (1978).*

Mike Ashley, in his Who's Who in Horror and Fantasy Fiction (1977) has called Shiel 'one of the overlooked masters of the horror story'. Here, in an attempt to help remedy this situation, is an example of his talent, 'The Bride', written in 1911, which I feel sure will make the reader's flesh creep with its echoes of an Irish wake— complete with a body laid out before the funeral—and what occurs during the night hours that follow . . .

*   *   *

They met at Krupp and Mason's, musical-instrument-makers, of Little Britain, E.C, where Walter had been employed two years, and then came Annie to typewrite, and be serviceable. They began to 'go out' together after six o'clock; and when Mrs Evans, Annie's mamma, lost her lodger, Annie mentioned it, and Walter went to live with them at No. 13 Culford Road, N.; by which time Annie and Walter might almost be said to have been engaged. His salary, however, was only thirty shillings a week.

He was the thorough Cockney, Walter; a well-set-up person of thirty, strong-shouldered, with a square brow, a moustache, and black acne-specks in his nose and pale face.

It was on the night of his arrival at No. 13 that he for the first time saw Rachel, Annie's younger sister. Both girls, in fact, were named 'Rachel'—after a much-mourned mother of Mrs Evans'; but Annie Rachel was called 'Annie', and Mary Rachel was called 'Rachel'. Rachel helped Walter at the handle of his box to the top-back room, and here, in the lamplight he was able to see that she was a tallish girl, with hair almost black, and with a sprinkling of freckles on her very white, thin nose, on the tip of which stood collected, usually, some little sweats. She was thin-faced, and her top teeth projected a little so that her lips only closed with effort, she not so pretty as pink-and-white little Annie, though one could guess, at a glance, that she was a person more to be respected.

'What do you think of him?' said Annie, meeting Rachel as she came down.

'He seems a nice fellow,' Rachel said: 'rather goodlooking. And strong in the back, you bet.'

Walter spent that evening with them in the area front room, smoking a foul bulldog pipe, which slushed and gurgled to his suction; and at once Mrs Evans, a dark old lady without waist, all sighs and lack of breath, decided that he was 'a gentlemanly, decent fellow'. When bed-time came he made the proposal to lead them in prayer; and to this they submitted, Annie having forewarned them that he was 'a Christian'. As he climbed to his room, the devoted girl found an excuse to slip out after him, and in the passage of the first floor there was a little kiss.

'Only one,' she said, with an uplifted finger.

'And what about his little brother, then?' he chuckled—a chuckle with which all his jokes were accompanied: a kind of guttural chuckle, which seemed to descend or stick straining in the throat, instead of rising to the lips.

'You go on,' she said playfully, tapped his cheek, and ran down. So Walter slept for the first night at Mrs Evans'.

On the whole, as time passed, he had a good deal of the society of the women: for the theatre was a thing abominable to him, and in the evenings he stayed in the underground parlour, sharing the bread-and-cheese supper, and growing familiar with the sighs of Mrs Evans over her once estate in the world. Rachel, the silent, sewed; Annie, whose relation with Walter was still unannounced, though perhaps guessed, could play hymn-tunes on the old piano, and she played. Last of all, Walter laid down the inveterate wet pipe, led them in prayer, and went to bed. Most mornings he and Annie set out together for Little Britain.

There came a day when he confided to her his intention to ask for a rise of 'screw', and when this was actually promised by His Terror, the Boss, there was joy in heaven, and radiance in futurity, and secret talks of rings, a wedding, 'a Home'. Annie felt herself not far from the kingdom of Hymen, and rejoiced. But nothing, as yet, was said at No. 13: for to Mrs Evans' past grandeurs thirty shillings a week was felt to be inappropriate.

The next Sunday, however, soon after dinner, this strangeness occurred: Rachel, the silent, disappeared. Mrs Evans called for her, Annie called, but it was found that she was not in the house, though the putting away of the dinner-things, her usual task, was only half accomplished. Not till tea-time did Rachel return. She was then cold, and somewhat sullen, and somewhat pale, her lips closing firmly over her projecting teeth. When timidly questioned—for her resentment was greatly feared—she replied that she had just been looking in upon Alice Soulsby, a few squares away, for a little chat: and this was the truth.

It was not, however, the whole truth; she had also looked in at the Church Lane Sunday School on her way: and this fact she guiltily concealed. For half an hour she had sat darkly at the end of the building in a corner, listening to the 'address'. This address was delivered by Walter. To this school every Sunday, after dinner, he put down the beloved pipe to go. He was, in fact, its 'superintendent'.

After this, the tone and temper of the little household rapidly changed, and a true element of hell was introduced into its platitude. It became, first of all, a question whether or not Rachel could be 'experiencing religion', a thing which her mother and Annie had never dreamt of expecting of her. Praying people, and the Salvationist, had always been the contempt of her strong and callous mind. But on Sunday nights she was now observed to go out alone, and 'chapel' was the explanation which she coolly gave. *Which* chapel she did not specify: but in reality it was the Newton Street Hall, at which Walter frequently exhorted and 'prayed'. In the Church Lane schoolroom there was prayer-meeting on Thursday evenings; and twice within one month Rachel sallied forth on Thursday evening—soon after Walter. The secret disease which preyed upon the poor girl could hardly now be concealed. At first she suffered bitter, solitary shame; sobbed in a hundred paroxysms; hoped to draw a veil over her infirmity. But her gash was too glaring. In the long Sabbath evenings of summer he preached at street corners, and sometimes secretly, sometimes openly, Rachel would attend these meetings, singing meekly with the rest the undivine hymns of the modern evangelist. In his presence, in the parlour, on other nights, she quietly sewed, hardly speaking. When, at 7 p.m., she heard his key in the front door her heart darted towards its master; when in the morning he flew away to business her universe was cinders.

'It's a wonder to me what's coming to our Rachel lately,' said

Annie in the train, coming home; 'you're doing her soul good, or
something, aren't you?'

He chuckled, with slushy suction-sounds about the back of the
tongue and molars.

'Oh, that be jiggered for a tale!' he said: '*she's* all right.'

'I know her better than you, you see. She's quite changed—
since you've come. Looks to me as if she's having a touch of the
blues, or something.'

'Poor thing! She wants looking after, don't she?'

Annie laughed, too: but less brutally, more uneasily.

Walter said: 'But she *oughtn't* to have the blues, if she's giving
her heart to the Lord! People seem to think a Christian must be
this and that. A Christian, if it comes to that, ought to be the
jolliest fellow going!'

This was on a Thursday, the night of the Church Lane prayer-
meeting, and Walter had only time to rush in at No. 13, wash his
face, snatch his Bible, and be off. Rachel, for her part, must verily
now have been badly bitten with the rabies of love, or she would
have felt that to follow tonight, for the third time lately, could not
fail to incur remark. But this consideration never even entered a
mind now completely blinded and entranced by the personality of
Walter. Through the day her work about the house had been
rushed forward with this very object, and at the moment when he
banged the door after him she was before her glass, dressing in
blanched, intense and trembling flurry, and casting as she bent to
give the last touches to her fringe, a look of bitterest hate at the
projection of her lip above the teeth.

This night, for the first time, she waited in the chapel till the
end of the service, and walked slowly homeward on the way which
she knew that Walter would take; and he came striding presently,
that morocco Bible in his hand, nearly every passage in which was
neatly under-ruled in black and red inks.

'What, is that you?' he said, taking into his a hand cold with
sweat.

'It is,' she answered, in a hard, formal tone.

'You don't mean to say you've been to the meeting?'

'I do.'

'Why, where were my eyes? *I* didn't see you.'

'It isn't likely that you would want to, Mr Teeger.'

'Go on—drop that! What do you take me for? I'm only too

glad! And I tell you what it is, Miss Rachel, I say to you as the Lord Jesus said to the young man: "Thou art not far from the kingdom of heaven."'

She was *in* it!—near him, alone, in a darkling square, yet suffering, too, in the flames of a passion such as perhaps consumes only the strongest natures.

She caught for support at his unoffered arm; and when he bent his steps straight homeward, she said trembling violently: 'I don't wish to go home as yet. I wish to have a little walk. Do you mind, Mr Teeger?'

'Mind, no. Come along, then,' and they went walking among an intricacy of streets and squares, he talking of 'the Work', and of common subjects. After half an hour, she was saying: 'I often wish I was a man. A man can say and do what he likes; but with a girl it's different. There's you, now, Mr Teeger, always out and about, having people listening to you, and that. I often wish I was only a man.'

'Oh, well, it all depends how you look at it,' he said. 'And, look here, you may as well call me Walter and be done.'

'Oh, I shouldn't think of *that*,' she replied. 'Not till—'

Her hand trembled on his arm.

'Well, out with it, why don't you?'

'Till—till we know something more definite about you—and Annie.'

He chuckled slushily, she now leading him fleetly round and round a square.

'Ah, you girls again!' he cried, 'been blabbing again like all the girls! It takes a bright man to hide much from them, don't it?'

'But there isn't much to hide in this case, as far as I can see—*is* there?'

Always Walter laughed, straining deep in the throat. He said: 'Oh, come—that would be telling, wouldn't it?'

After a minute's stillness, this treacherous phrase came from Rachel: 'Annie doesn't care for anyone, Mr Teeger.'

'Oh, come—that's rather a tall order, *any* one. *She's* all right.'

'But she *doesn't*. Of course, most girls are silly, and that, and like to get married—'

'Well, that's only nature, ain't it?'

This was a joke; and downward the laugh strained in his throat, like struggling phlegm.

'Yes, but they don't understand what love is,' said Rachel. 'They haven't an idea. They like to be married women, and have a husband, and that. But they don't know what love is—believe me! The men don't either.'

How she trembled!—her body, her dying voice—she pressing heavily upon him, while the moon triumphed now through cloud glaring a moment white on the lunacy of her ghostly face.

'Well, I don't know—I think *I* understand, lass, what it is,' he said.

'You don't, Mr Teeger!'

'How's that, then?'

'Because, when it takes you, it makes you—'

'Well, let's have it. You seem to know all about it.'

Now Rachel commenced to tell him what 'it' was—in frenzied definitions, and a power of expression strange for her. *It* was a lunacy, its name was Legion, it was possession by the furies; it was a spasm in the throat, and a sickness of the limbs, and a yearning of the eye-whites, and a fire in the marrow; it was catalepsy, trance, apocalypse; it was high as the galaxy, it was addicted to the gutter; it was Vesuvius, borealis, the sunset; it was the rainbow in a cesspool, St John plus Heliogabalus, Beatrice plus Messalina; it was a transfiguration, and a leprosy, and a metempsychosis, and a neurosis; it was the dance of the maenads, and the bite of the tarantula, and baptism in a sun: out poured the wild definition in simple words, but with the strife of one fighting for life. And she had not half done when he understood her fully; and he had no sooner understood her, than he was subdued, and succumbed.

'You don't mean to say—' he faltered.

'Ah, Mr Teeger,' she answered, 'there's none so blind as those who will not see.'

His arm stole round her shuddering body.

Everyone is said to have his failing; and this man, Walter, in no respect a man of strong mind, was certainly on his amatory side, most sudden, promiscuous, and infirm. And this tendency was, if anything, heightened by the quite sincere strain of his mind in the direction of 'spiritual things': for, under sudden temptation, back rushed his being, with the greater rigour, into its natural channel. On the whole, had he not been a Puritan, he would have been a Don Juan.

In an instant Rachel's weight was hanging upon his neck, he kissing her with passion.

After this she said to him: 'But you are only doing this out of pity, Walter. Tell the truth, you are in love with Annie?'

He, like Peter, tumbled at once into a fib. 'That's what *you* say!'

'You are,' she insisted, filled with the bliss of the fib.

'Bah! I'm not. Never was. *You* are the girl for me.'

When they went home, they entered the house at different times, she first, he waiting twenty minutes in the street.

The house was small, so the sisters slept together in the second-floor front room; Walter in the second-floor back; Mrs Evans in the first-floor back, the first-floor front being 'the drawing-room'. The girls, therefore, generally went to bed together: and that night, as they undressed, there was a row.

First, a long silence. Then Rachel, to say something, pointed to some new gloves of Annie's, asking: 'How much did you give for those?'

'Money and kind words,' replied Annie.

This was the beginning.

'Well, there's no need to be rude about it,' said Rachel. She was happy, in paradise, despised Annie that night.

'Still,' said Annie, after a silence of ten minutes before the glass, '*still*, I should never run after a man like that. I'd die first.'

'I haven't the least idea what you're talking about,' replied Rachel.

'You have. I should be *ashamed* of myself, if I were you.'

'Talk away. You're a little fool.'

'It's *you*. Throwing yourself at the head of a man who doesn't care for you. What *can* you call yourself?'

Rachel laughed—happily, yet dangerously.

'Don't bother yourself, my girl,' she said.

'Think of going out every night to meet a man in that way: look here, it's too disgusting of you, girl!'

'Is it?'

'You can't deny that you were with Mr Teeger tonight?'

'That I wasn't.'

'It's false! Anyone can see it by the joy in your face.'

'Well, suppose I was, what about it?'

'But a woman should be decent, I think; a woman should be

able to command her feelings, and not expose herself like that. Believe me, it gives me the creeps all over to think of.'

'Never mind, don't be jealous, my girl.'

The gentle Annie flamed!

'Jealous! of *you*!'

'There isn't any need, you know—not *yet*.'

'But I'm *not*! There never *will* be need! Do you take Mr Teeger for a raving lunatic? I should go and have some false teeth put in first if I were you!'

Thus did Annie drop to the rock-bed of vulgarity; but she knew it to be necessary in order to touch Rachel, as with a white-hot wire, on her very nerve of anguish, and, in fact, at these words Rachel's face resembled white iron, while she cried out, 'Never mind my teeth! It isn't the teeth a man looks at! A man knows a finely built woman when he sees her—not like a little dumpy podge!'

'Thank you. You are very polite,' replied Annie, browbeaten by an intensity fiercer than her own. 'But still, it's nonsense, Rachel, to talk of my being jealous of *you*. I knew Mr Teeger six months before you. And you won't know him much longer either, for I don't want to have mother disgraced here, and this is no fit place for him to lodge in. I can easily make him leave it soon—'

At this thing Rachel flew, with minatory palm over Annie's cheek, ready to strike. 'You *dare* do anything to make him go away! I'll tear your little—'

Annie winked, flinched, uttered a sob, no more fight left in her.

So for two weeks the situation lasted. Only, after that night, so intense grew the bitterness between the sisters, that Annie moved down to the first-floor back, sleeping now with Mrs Evans who dimly wondered. As for Walter, meanwhile, his heart was divided within him. He loved Annie; he was fascinated and mesmerised by Rachel. In another age and country he would have married both. Every day he came to a different resolve, not knowing what to do. One thing was evident—a wedding ring would be necessary, and he purchased one, uncertain for which of the girls.

'Look here, lass,' he said to Annie in the train, coming home, 'let us put a stop to this. The boss doesn't seem to be in a hurry about that rise of screw, so suppose we get spliced, and be done?'

'Privately?'

'Rather. Your ma and sister mustn't know—not just yet a while.'

'And you will still keep on living at the house?'

'Well, of course, for the time being.'

She looked up into his face and smiled. It was settled.

But two nights afterwards he met Rachel on his way home from prayer-meeting; at first was honest and distant; but then committed the incredible weakness of going with her for a walk among the squares, and ended by winning from her an easily granted promise of marriage, on the same terms as those arranged with Annie.

When, the next day at lunch-time, he put his foot on the threshold of the Registrar's office to give notice, he was still in a state of agonised indecision as to the name which he should couple with his own.

When the official said, 'Now the name of the other party?' Walter hesitated, shuffled with his feet, then answered:

'Rachel Evans.'

Not till he was again in the street did he remember that Rachel was the name of both the girls, and that liberty of choice between them still remained to him.

Now, from the day of 'notice' to the day of wedlock, an interval of twenty-one clear days must, by law, elapse, and Walter, though weak enough to inform both the sisters of the step he had taken, was careful to give them only a vague idea of the date fixed. His once clear conscience, meanwhile, was grievously troubled, his feet in a net; he feared to speak to God; and went drifting like flotsam on the river of chance.

And chance alone it was which at last cast him upon the land. The fifth day before the marriage was a Bank Holiday, and he had arranged with Rachel to go out with her that day to Hyde Park, she to wait for him at an arranged spot at two o'clock. At two, then, at a street-corner, stood Rachel waiting, twirling her parasol, walking a little, returning. Walter, however, did not appear, and what could have happened was beyond her divination. Had he misunderstood or missed her? Though incredible, it was the only thing to think. To Hyde Park, at any rate, she went alone, feeling desolate and *ennuyée*, in the vague hope of there meeting him.

What had happened was this: Walter had been halfway towards the rendezvous with Rachel, when he was met in the street by

Annie, who had gone to spend the day with a married friend at Stroud Green, but had returned, owing to the husband's illness. Seeing Walter, her face lit up with smiles.

'Harry's down with the influenza,' she said, 'so I couldn't stay and bore poor Ethel. Where are you going?'

For the first time since his 'conversion' twelve years before, Walter, with a high flush, now consciously lied.

'Only to the schoolroom,' he said, 'to hunt for something.'

'Well, I am open to be taken out, if any kind friend will be so kind,' she said fondly.

Now he had that morning vowed to himself to wed Rachel; and by this vow he now again vowed to be bound. All the more reason why, for the last time, he should 'take out' Annie.

'Come along, then, old girl,' he gaily said: 'where shall we go?'

'Let us go to Hyde Park,' said Annie. And to Hyde Park they went, Walter, ever and anon, stabbed by the bitter memory of waiting Rachel.

At five o'clock the two were walking along the north bank of the Serpentine westward towards a two-arched bridge, which is also pierced by a third narrow arch over the bank: to this narrow arch, since it was drizzling, they were making for shelter, when Rachel, a person of the keenest vision, sighted them from the south bank. She was frantic at once. Annie, who was supposed to be at Stroud Green! *What treachery!* This, then, was why . . . She ran panting along the bank, towards the bridge, then over it, northward, and now heard the two under the arch, who stood there talking—of the wedding. Unfortunately, just here is a block of masonry, which prevented Rachel from leaning directly over the arch to listen. Yet the necessity to hear was absolute: so she ran back clear of the masonry, and bent far over the parapet, outwards and sideways towards the arch, straining neck, body, ears, and anyone looking into those staring eyes *then* would have comprehended the doctrine of the Ferine Soul. But she was at a disadvantage, heard only murmurs, and—was that a kiss? Further and further forth she strained. And now suddenly, with a cry, she is in the water, where it is shallow near the bank. In the fall her head struck upon a stone in the mud.

For three days she screamed continuously the name of Walter, filling the street with it, calling him hers only. On the third night, in the midst of a frightful crisis of cries, she suddenly died.

'Oh, Rachel, don't say you are dead!' cried Annie over her.

The death occurred two days before the marriage-day, and on the next, Walter, well wounded, said to Annie: 'This knocks our little affair on the head, of course.'

Annie was silent. Then, with a pout, she said: 'I don't see why. After all, it was her own fault, entirely. Why should *we* suffer?'

For the feud between the sisters had become cruel as death; and it outlasted death: Annie, on the subject of Rachel and Walter, being no longer a gentle girl, but marble, without respect or pity.

And so, in spite of the trepidations and hesitancy of Walter, the marriage took place, even while Rachel lay stretched on the bed in the second-floor front of No. 13.

The ceremony did not, however transpire without hitch and omen. It was necessary, first of all, for Walter to forewarn Annie that he had given notice of her to the Registrar by her second name of 'Rachel'—a mad-looking proceeding that was almost the cause of a rupture which nothing but Walter's most ardent pleadings could steer him clear of. At any rate it was to 'Rachel', and not to 'Annie' that he was, as a matter of fact, after all married.

After the ceremony, performed in their lunch-time, they returned to business together in Little Britain.

At ten-o'clock the same night, as he was going up to bed, she ran after him, and in the passage there was a long, furtive kiss—their last on earth.

'Twelve o'clock?' he whispered intensely.

She held up her forefinger. 'One!'

'Oh, say twelve!'

She did not answer, but drew her palm playfully across his cheek, meaning consent, for Mrs Evans was an inveterately heavy sleeper. He went up. And, careful to leave his door a little ajar, he extinguished his candle, and went to bed. In the apartment nearby lay stark in the dark—with learned, eternal eyelids and drowsy brow—the dead.

Walter could not but think of this presence close at hand. 'Well, poor girl!' he sighed. 'Poor Rachel! Well, well. His way is in the sea, after all, and His path in the Great Deep, and His footsteps are not known.' Then he thought of Annie—the little wife! But instead of Annie, there was Rachel. The two women fought vehemently for his thought—and ever the dead was stronger than the living . . . Instead of Annie there was Rachel—and again Rachel.

At last he could hear twelve strike from a steeple, and sat up in bed, listening eagerly for the door to open, or a footfall on the floor.

A little American clock ticked in the room; and in the flue of the chimney was a sough and chant just audible.

Suddenly she was intensely with him, filling the chamber—from nowhere. He had heard no footstep, no opening of the door: yet certainly, she was with him *now*, all suddenly, close to him, over him, talking breathlessly to him.

His first sensation was a shuddering which strongly shook him from head to foot, like the shuddering of Russian cold. She held him down by the shoulders; was stretched at length on the bed, over him; and the room seemed full of a rustling and rushing, very strange, like starched muslins rushing out in stormy agitation. She was speaking, too, to him *in breathless haste*, whimpering a secret gibberish which whimpered like a pup for passion—about love and its definition, and about the soul, and the worm, and Eternity, and the passion of death, and the nuptials of the tomb, and the lust and hollowness of the void. And he, too, was speaking, whispering through his pattering teeth, saying: 'Sh-h-h, Rachel—Annie, I mean—sh-h-h, my girl—your ma will hear! Rachel, don't—sh-h-h, now!' But even while he kept up this 'sh-h-h, dear—sh-h-h, now,' he was conscious of the invasion of a strange rage, of such a strength as if energy was being vehemently pumped into him from some behemoth omnipotence. The form above him he could hardly discern, the room was so dark, but he felt that her garment was flowing forth from her neck in a continuous flutter, with the rustling of the starch of a thousand shrouds, like the outflow of a pennant in wind; and the quivering gauze seemed now to swell and fill the chamber, and now to sink again to the size of woman. And ever the rhapsody of love and death went on, mixed with the chattered 'Sh-h-h, Rachel—Annie, I mean,' of Walter; till, suddenly, he was involved in an embrace *so* horrible, felt himself encompassed by a might so intolerable, that his soul fainted within him. He sank back; thought span and failed in darkness beneath the spell of that lullaby; he muttered, 'Receive my spirit . . .'

After two days Walter, still unconscious, died. His disfigured body they placed in a grave not far from Rachel's.

ENCOUNTER AT NIGHT

Mary Frances McHugh

'Mary McHugh can make your flesh creep!' wrote John Gawsworth in his introduction to one of her stories which appeared in the anthology Thrills, *published in London in 1930. A prolific anthologist of the Twenties and Thirties, Gawsworth was also M. P. Sheil's biographer and 'successor' to the throne of Redonda.*

Curiously, although Dublin-born Mary Frances McHugh (1890–1955) enjoyed some celebrity in her native land where she was referred to as an 'Irish woman of letters', she was little known outside the country and few of her stories were published in England or America. Today she is perhaps best remembered for her poetry, several engaging novels—including Thalassa *(1931) and* The Bud of Spring *(1932)—and for her autobiographical writing which in Irish literary circles earned her comparison with her fellow countryman, George Moore. However, she also made a number of important contributions to the horror story genre, and 'Encounter at Night' is an outstandingly grim tale by any standards—the more so because it comes from a woman's pen. In it, she evokes Dublin after nightfall and the appalling fright that awaits one late night reveller . . .*

*   *   *

Dublin was growing deserted; only an odd car slid by in the dark, rainy night, for the second of its passing throwing a dazzle on the shiny pavements and lighting up the shuttered shops. Figures would pass, hurrying by with hunched shoulders—but less and less frequently.

Tom Donovan and his three friends scarcely felt the rain. They were hot and happy and bemused. All that each of them wanted

was somehow to continue talking and drinking and smoking in
genial company . . . But Jim, the red-haired barman at Flynn's,
had gradually edged them out into the night, and bolted the doors
against them. There was nothing for it but to go home.

'Take care of yourself, Joe!'

'Well, goodnight, boys!'

'Take care—see you tomorrow.'

The milk of human kindness flowed in them, and they patted
one another's backs affectionately again and again before each
went his separate way. Donovan, the shiftless poet, was left standing on the pavement, last and lonely. Slowly there faded from his
face its smile of convivial bliss, and into his sobering mind crept
back those thoughts which now, with the fleeting years, possessed
him more and more in his solitary moments.

Wretched, killing thoughts. No, not thoughts—not thoughts,
but feelings—or one feeling only, corroding unhappiness. A sense
that life was vain and empty, with comfort nowhere—not even in
drinking, in friendship, or in love. If even he knew friendship or
love! A certainty that never, during all his existence, even when
he had been young and gay and roistering, had he known ease:
always a shadow had been lurking at his elbow. And it whispered
to him that he was a fool to go on with the sham from day to day,
that there was only one solution to everything: a knife or a rope
for his throat.

Cruel memories came thronging. He saw a miserable, beaten
peasant child: himself. All that child had really known was suffering, though the man had made sweet lilting songs of a boy, bare-
footed, in the West, birds'-nesting or tickling for trout in a
mountain stream. The boy had been there, the sun, the stream,
the idyllic sky, the irrational light-heartedness of childhood. These
were the stuff of his verse—but not the harsh home, the pain and
puzzled grief, the cold and hunger which had been more true and
near. These things had made him!—they were with him even now.

Later, there was the man. A poet he was now, praised and
wondered at for the clear innocency of his songs, toys fashioned
for the cultured mind by a queer bohemian fellow. That he was
so different from his poetry merely gave it zest. He knew this, and
cultivated his oddity; and it was partly to curry favour with his
admirers that he drank and sang his way through Europe without
a word of any language but his own. Here, standing on a Dublin

pavement in the night, he recalled the troubadour adventure and shivered—not because the steely rain was stinging his face and sending cold arrows through his clothing. No; but because from those wanderings from which he had so triumphantly returned he could now remember only a haunting horror. He evoked without willing it a night in Russia, when he lay in a country tavern with his familiar spirit beside him. There, in a big common room, several poor travellers slept about the stove. The air was humid with their breath and the odorous damp of their clothing, and the windows were sealed to blindness by the snow outside. In the yard there suddenly arose the commotion of a sledge being unharnessed; a bulky figure stepped into the room and looked stealthily around at the sleepers and fixedly at him, Donovan, before flinging itself likewise down in a corner. Donovan through half-closed eyes saw the stranger's Mongolian face, and as though he were a child it smote him with its mystery of a locked mind, of a race other than and alien to his own. There was no reason for his sudden panic of fear, or for the anguish of loneliness which overcame him then. It was simply part of the encompassing oppression of the world to his soul, driving him whither he knew not.

He tossed his head, heedless of the rain, appealing to the sky above him to protect and save. There must be rest somewhere, a cooling of this fever: why should he, more than other men, be so tormented? Why could he not be like little Terry Shaughnessy, caring nothing for anyone, whether drunk or sober, in funds or out of them? Now, there was an idea! Why go back, in this mood and in this weather, to his cold room and unwelcoming bed, when Terry would be glad enough for him to drop in for a smoke and a talk? He'd be there, sure enough, in his attic in Eustace Street. He wouldn't be in bed. Who ever heard of little Terry being in bed? He'd have a warm fire, and maybe a taste of something— 'one for the worms,' as he called it . . . Donovan turned towards Eustace Street.

He trotted along mechanically, now thinking cheerfully of himself and Terry. They were the only bachelors among the boys— and taking it all in all, he'd swear they were as well off like that. He thought of Ned Buckley's wife, and grinned to himself. A nice exhibition she made of the poor man, running to his newspaper office or writing to the editor when she wanted money. Ned was a good sort—but what kind of man was he to put up with that?

Now, if any woman tried to manage *him*—! Or Terry: he'd swear Terry would know how to deal with her, too. Keep a firm hand. That was it.

Yet, maybe—Terry as well as himself—in their hearts they'd like to have a home, and a woman waiting for them, and children. Maybe they'd die in the workhouse, no one caring enough for them to follow them to the grave . . . At these sad thoughts Donovan's mouth turned down again behind his coat collar, and he felt nearly dismal enough to cry. But resolutely he clung to the advantages of his state. He was his own master, anyway. He could drop in on Terry like this, tonight, and Terry be welcome to drop in on him, any hour he liked.

The rain beat on his face, stood in tears on his eyelashes till the street lamps carried a halo, each of them. Then he blinked and shook his head, and the long, deserted street shone straight before him again. A clock struck twelve. Ah, here was Terry's door. God, it was good to get in out of the rain!

The door stood ajar. That saved ringing the bell. Probably someone had left it like that on purpose—goodness knew how many lived in the old rookery. Not a glimmer of light. But Donovan felt his way to the banisters, gripped them, and mounted, cautiously counting the stairs.

Terry's door was opposite the fourth turn. Two . . . three . . . The next one . . . *Mother of God, what was that?*

Someone, coming out of the darkness, had struck him softly. A blow of a doubled-up fist in the face. Like a joke, by the Lord! But where had the fellow got to?

'Who's that?' called out Donovan, his voice a little startled in the night. 'Who's there? What the blazes are you doing.?'

There was no answer. Donovan crouched a moment in the darkness, very still, then changed his walking-stick to the other hand. But he must have been flustered, for his fingers didn't catch on it, and down it went clattering against the uncarpeted stairs, stopping once, clattering again, staying finally where it was. He stopped and groped, but thought better of going back for it. He stared about him and in the blackness thought he saw a solider patch, a man facing him a couple of steps up. That was the man who had struck him. But why on earth didn't he say something?

'Who's there?' he shouted again. 'Speak up, whoever you are!'

There was no answer, so he stepped forward boldly. But again someone pushed him—pushed him so plainly, as though with a playful gentleness, that he could feel the woollen jacket of the shoulder thrust against him. As in indignant alarm he tried to grasp it, it silently eluded him, moving soundlessly, eerily, out of reach.

Donovan's blood crept in his veins, and his heart seemed to lunge downwards in his body. Suddenly he wished he felt steadier, that he hadn't had so many drinks. Then he thought instinctively how another good stiff whisky would hearten him—yes, give him fire to tell this sly fellow, whoever the hell he was, what he thought of him.

He paused and gasped, listening with all his ears. Not a sound could he catch; and swiftly changing mood, convinced that it was only some silly trick being played on him, he became wildly angry.

'Come on!' he shouted, his excited voice falling back to the cadence of his native West. 'Come on, you puppy! Come on, you coward you, if you're a man at all, and I'll wrastle you in the Connemara fashion!'

He bent down over his right knee in an attitude of defence. 'I'll fight you! I'll wrastle you!' he repeated belligerently.

For a few seconds he held up his fists, awaiting his assailant. But the latter did not move. Then, like a bull, Donovan made to rush up the stairs. *Ah!*—With a soft thud he struck his head into the stomach of the lurking enemy. The invisible man, silent and unshocked, moved stealthily away.

But Donovan followed him, and as he did so was surprised to find the other coming towards him. He flung away caution and grasped his man about the body. Something rigid but yielding, human yet cold, lay unprotestingly within his arms. He released it and stepped back, weak and shuddering.

It swung—it hung . . . Ah, God!

Donovan recoiled, as sober as at morning. For a full minute he waited where he stood, overwhelmed with a nameless dread. Then he struck a match and, peering up, saw above him the blackened face of little Terry Shaughnessy, hanging from his attic banisters . . .

ARACHNOPHOBIA

Catherine Brophy

The title hints at the theme of this story and any reader whose flesh crawls at the mention of spiders has been warned. Catherine Brophy has already proved herself highly accomplished at weaving stories built around human fears, and her novel Dark Paradise *(1991) has rightly been acclaimed as one of the best Irish fantasy novels of recent years. Her writing has embraced several genres, including historical fiction and SF, which reflect her wide range of interests, from travel (mostly alone and often hitch-hiking) to films, philosophy and humanity.*

Catherine Brophy (1941–) was born in Bray, near Dublin, and educated at University College where she obtained a BA and began her training as a teacher of the deaf. She subsequently worked as an audiologist in Dublin until being appointed a lecturer at Trinity College in 1989. The success of her first book, The Liberation of Margaret McCabe *(1985), led her to devote more time to her writing, and apart from various articles and stories she has been a regular contributor to RTE's popular soap opera,* Fair City. *Her current plans include a historical novel based on the exploits of a group of Irishmen, one of whom was her grandfather, who went to Italy in 1860 to fight for the Pope against Garibaldi, and more scripts for film and television. 'Arachnophobia' is an ingenious exercise in terror which underlines her skill in both the written and visual media.*

* * *

Arachnophobia: an inordinate fear . . . yes that was true, an inordinate fear . . . she couldn't bring herself to think the rest. Dr Bishop was right, that's what she had, arachnophobia. It was a proper disease, the doctor said so, written up in the big serious books on his shelves. He'd even taken one down to show her. She wasn't depressed or mad or anything, she was arachnophobic and he said he could cure it. The relief . . . A bus came into view and she put out her hand. It squealed to a halt and she handed the correct change to the driver.

'No drugs,' he'd said, 'there's no need for that, we'll use operant conditioning. It will take time of course . . .'

She smiled out of the window at the sliding-away shop fronts. No drugs! She definitely wasn't mad. Isn't that the first thing they do when you're mad, drugs, injections, strong-arm nurses . . . she shivered and remembered, no drugs, we can cure you. 'I suffer from arachnophobia.' she told herself over and over.

She hadn't told him about her brother . . . couldn't. The sudden jerk on the back of her collar, the threats, the choking in her throat . . . and it didn't matter what she did, he would still drop them down her neck, the . . . the things, the awful . . . She wanted to scream and scream and scream and tear her clothes but she couldn't on the bus, they'd take her away, they'd think her mad. She felt physically ill, her skin began to crawl . . . they were down her back, all black and hairy, her stomach heaved and she rushed off the bus four stops too soon.

She clung to a railing holding her breath, torn, buffeted by her crawling spine, heaving stomach and the little voice that shrieked 'Get a grip, they'll think you're mad, they'll think you're mad.'

'Breathe,' the doctor'd said, 'breathe, Ann, breathe. The brain needs oxygen and the muscles, it helps you to take control.'

She gulped in air but it wasn't till she grasped her thumbs, the right one in her left hand, the left one in her right, and repeated 'Mama's here, Mama's here' twenty-three times that she could find the strength to move.

She walked quickly and when she reached the corner of her road she ran. Running was difficult with her bag squashed under her arm and her elbows tight to her sides, but she couldn't let her thumbs go or the creepy-crawling would start again. It was hard to get the key out and twice she dropped it before she got the door open and could dash up the stairs and tear off her clothes.

Wash, she had to wash but they'd be in there. Waiting in the black plugholes. Her brother, Brian, said that was nonsense, they didn't live in plugholes, they fell from the ceiling, but she found that hard to believe. She had seen the black legs waving from the dark and the fat black heaving out of the drain . . .

'Mama's here, Mama's here . . .' she gasped and gasped and kept losing count and having to start again.

When she was absolutely sure she'd said it twenty-three times she was calm again. She looked round the bathroom warily . . . nothing, the floor, the ceiling . . . nothing. She poked a bamboo cane down the plug-hole . . . nothing, so she stuck in the plug. She could have a shower now. When she'd dried herself and put on clean clothes, every garment straight from its sealed plastic bag, she felt a whole lot better.

'I'm sure that was the beginning of your trouble,' Dr Bishop said, 'the trauma which initiated your phobia.'

She was glad now she'd told him about Brian.

'But, however interesting the cause,' he continued, 'it's the symptoms that create trouble, the fear, the sense of paralysis, that's what we're dealing with here, we're learning to control them.'

'The worst is in the kitchen.'

'The worst?'

'Yes, there's one always in the kitchen.'

'Ah, there's a spider in the kitchen is there?'

'Yes.'

'Do you think you could describe it?'

She felt the panic rising. She could see it at the table with its knees apart and its surgical stockings. The head resting in the palm, the elbow pushed amongst the dirty delft and crumbs. The tablecloth was skew-ways. She held her breath.

'Breathe, Ann, breathe.'

She held her thumbs tightly.

'Now tell me,' his voice was calm, reassuring, commanding. 'Take your time.'

'Mama's here, Mama's here . . .' she mouthed twenty-three times, and was safe.

'It's fat and black and hairy,' she said in a little girl voice.

'There now, Ann, that wasn't so bad, was it? Relax now, close your eyes. I think we're doing pretty well, don't you?'

'Yes.'

But she held her thumbs securely.

When she got home it was in the kitchen of course, as usual, so she went up to her room.

'Are you all right, Ann?' it called up the stairs.

'Yes.'

'Your dinner will be ready soon.'

'All right.'

As long as she didn't look directly at it she was all right. It thought that she was shy, introverted, depressed, mad . . . that's why it insisted that she see the doctor. Well, she was seeing the doctor and he was helping her. She'd talked about it today, not said . . . the . . . word but talked about it.

'Sp . . . sp . . . spider, now, there I've said it,' she gasped and laughed and held her thumbs close to herself.

'Wonderful . . . good girl. My, we are making progress! Do you think you could name any types of spiders?'

'The Common House sp . . . sp . . . spider . . . Tarantula . . . and the . . . the . . .' She could see it from the corner of her eye, the white podgy fingers, swollen round the ring, creeping along the kitchen table on its way to the cooker.

'I'll always look after you,' it said, 'you know I always will, as long as these poor legs can carry me.'

It grunted and bent to the oven. Ann gagged and was afraid she might vomit on Dr Bishop's lovely carpet but she couldn't get a tissue from her bag without letting go her thumbs. She swallowed back the bile and repeated to herself, 'Mama's here, Mama's here, oh Mama's here . . .'

'Just breathe, Ann, breathe . . . that's very good. Tarantula and . . . ?'

'. . . and . . . and . . . the . . . the Black Widow.'

'Good, that's very good. Now relax.'

Black Widow was what her brother called it when it first came to look after them after Mama had gone away forever. She didn't remember much of Mama, she was too young, but she remembered her cheek against a pink flowered apron and Mama rocking her and saying something lovely in her ear. The Widow never wore an apron, she wore black. She opened her eyes quickly.

'The one in the kitchen . . . the one I told you about before . . . it's a Black Widow,' she whispered.

The doctor laughed indulgently.

'Well now, Ann, that's a bit unlikely,' he said, 'they couldn't survive here, it's too cold, they only live in hot climates. It's just a common house spider.'

'But it frightens me . . . I can't get away.'

'Yes, I know it frightens you. Now take a breath, relax, and close your eyes. Imagine that the sun is shining on you, feel the warmth . . . now imagine that you are going to a safe place, a very safe place, where nothing at all can harm you . . .'

The sun was shining somewhere outside but she crouched in the dark, hiding, safe, under the stairs. Her brother was beside her, big and strong. It would never catch them there. She could hear the voice call for them out the back.

'She killed her husband,' Brian whispered in her ear.

'No!'

'Oh yes, that's what Black Widows do, they kill their husbands right after mating.'

'No!'

'Then why's she called the Black Widow? She poisoned her husband and sucked his brains through the top of his head.'

'Stop, I don't want to hear.' She tried to cover her ears but Brian grabbed her hands and wouldn't let her.

'And then she sucked out his lungs and heart and liver and all his guts and all the piss and ca-ca through the hole in his head.'

'Stop, please stop.'

'And all the insides of his legs and feet and left him like a burst balloon.'

She was crying now.

'And she'll do the same to you.'

'You too, you too,' she said, trying to hit him.

'Oh no she won't. I'm going away to school and you'll be all alone with her . . .'

'Mama's here, Mama's here, oh Mama's here . . .'

'Now I want you to imagine,' Dr Bishop's voice interrupted.

Oh yes, imagine, yes, she was safe with her brother under the stairs, the Widow couldn't suck her brains out here.

'Imagine,' the doctor continued, 'that away in the distance there is a spider, a very tiny . . .'

The Widow's step came closer, her voice louder, her hand on the door . . . she started screaming then.

'Open your eyes,' the doctor commanded. 'Ann! Open your eyes and look at me.'

She looked into his grey-blue eyes, her brother faded and the dark grew light, he had grizzled eyebrows.

'Now look around the room.'

The room was soothing, all plants and big fat books and carpets from Turkey. He was talking to her calm and quiet, she didn't really know what he was saying but his voice was soothing and he kept his distance at the other side of his shiny desk. She liked that. She hated when people touched or came too close. He put on his spectacles and took them off again, pinched his nose, rubbed his eyes and smiled. He must be what, fifty . . . fifty-five?

'Are we going a bit too fast?' he asked.

'Yes, a bit,' she replied.

As long as he covered the pictures with a piece of paper she was all right. And she could read as long as she didn't have to touch the book.

'Spiders weave complex webs of great delicacy as a safe-guard against falling, to catch prey and to nest,' she read in a rush.

'Keep breathing, Ann, keep breathing.'

That was right, that's what the Widow did. She wove her web right there in the kitchen, making savoury casserole and apple-pie and listening to the radio.

'Can you read another bit?'

'They do not hunt, they wait. And when an insect flies into the web they do not kill, they scuttle out and paralyse their victims and store them in their larder.'

'You're perfectly safe, Ann, keep breathing.'

She had been the Widow's prey a long time now, since Brian went away to school. The Widow washed and dressed and fed her. She chose her friends and kept her home from school if she thought she had a sniffle. 'She's delicate,' the Widow used to tell people on the phone, 'I have to mind her health.'

In the winter the Widow kept her indoors and when she must go out swaddled her in woolly vests, extra cardigans, mittens, thick tweed coats, knitted hat and scarves.

'Keep your throat covered,' she warned, 'or you'll catch your death of cold.'

And when she finally left school the Widow told her that she had no need to work.

'There's plenty of money, you know, besides, you're delicate, a job would kill you.'

Ann protested but it was no good.

'We can look after one another,' the Widow said. 'I'm not getting any younger.'

The Widow had her caught and wrapped in silk and paralysed . . . she held her breath so long she started to go blue in the face.

'Breathe, Ann, breathe.' Dr Bishop shook her shoulder.

She gulped the air and grasped both thumbs.

'Mama's here, Mama's here,' she told herself. 'Mama's here, Mama's here, Mama's here . . .'

There, she only had to say it ten times now. She would not stay wrapped and helpless. Dr Bishop was helping her to get out, to make her free. It was working already, his operant conditioning. He had even touched her shoulder and she didn't mind. She went home happy.

'Do you think you're ready?'

'Yes.'

Her stomach churned and she shivered but she did not flinch. She was determined now. Dr Bishop was very kind and she would not let him down. He propped the picture on his desk. She gulped and grasped the arms of the leather chair, pushing into it as though she were trying to fade backwards through the upholstery.

'If it's too close I can move it further back.' he said.

'No, no . . . it's all right . . . I'll . . . I'll just . . . just breathe.'

She closed her eyes and grasped her thumbs.

'Mama's here, Mama's here . . .' ten times, and she looked again.

'What kind is it?' she asked faintly.

'Black Widow,' he said, 'they're not nearly as dangerous as people think.'

The body was round and shiny with the red markings and the legs, oh God, the legs, all sticking out like . . . like the Widow's sticks. The black walking sticks she hobbled down to Mass on. She felt like screaming but grasped her thumbs instead.

'Mama's here, Mama's here . . .'

'Breathe, Ann, breathe.'

The legs, the hideous legs, like that photograph with the Widow sitting behind her, black arms creeping round her white Communion dress, the surgical stockings . . . Bile surged into her throat and made her cough and splutter and spit in her tissue.

'Breathe, Ann, breathe.'

The Widow had a photo taken every year in Mr McEvoy's studio and sent a copy to her only sister in England. 'Me and my little darling,' she wrote on the back or, 'Happy Christmas from my little angel and me.'

Ann was angry. I am not her darling, she thought, I'm not her angel, I'm not, I'm not. And she is not my Mama!

'I think she's dangerous,' she said aloud, nodding at the picture.

Dr Bishop chuckled.

'I know you do, but a picture couldn't harm you, now could it?'

'No.'

She did not run upstairs when she returned home. It was the first time she hadn't. Instead she went straight to the living room. They they were! Years of photographs in their silver frames. They covered every surface, the mantelpiece, piano, little tables, whatnot. She gathered them up and sat in the middle of the floor systematically tearing them out of their frames and ripping them in halves, quarters, eighths and sixteenths, every one, every single one and left them scattered on the floor.

'What on earth did you do that for?' the Widow wailed when she found them.

'I'm sorry. I was angry,' Ann said, not looking.

'You're not well, Ann, better lie down, you're not well at all.'

'I'm perfectly all right.' Ann could barely contain her anger.

'Well, we'd better clean up the mess,' the Widow said and hobbled to the bureau, sticks clattering against the furniture. 'Fortunately I have copies.'

Ann ran upstairs and screamed and screamed and screamed into her pillow.

'I think it's time to look now.'

She started breathing quickly. Out of the drawer of his desk he took a matchbox and opened it. She grasped her thumbs.

'Don't worry, it can't escape,' he said and put it on his desk. There was Cling-Film over the inside part of the box where . . .

where . . . where it was . . . It grew huge and fat . . . big round belly, red hourglass marking . . .

'She'll suck your brains and guts out,' Brian whispered in her ear.

The legs all swollen, surgical stockings . . .

'You'll kill me,' she screamed at it.

'Ann, Ann, calm yourself. Breathe. Look, I've closed the box.' Dr Bishop put it back in the drawer.

'. . . kill me, kill me.' She broke down sobbing.

'I'm trying to help you, Ann, that's all. Just breathe, relax . . .'

'No, no, not you, the, the . . .' she pointed to the drawer where the Widow had retreated.

'Ah . . . so that's what this is all about. You thought it was a Black Widow! No, no, my dear, it's just an ordinary house spider. They're harmless, you know that. In fact they help mankind by catching flies and insects. House spiders can even become pets. My grandfather had one that came down from the ceiling every time he sat down at his writing desk and kept him company. He became very fond of it. Always said it had a personality of its own . . .'

'Oh Mama's here, Mama's here, Mama's here, Mama's here . . .' She grasped her thumbs and didn't listen to his talk . . . 'Mama's here, yes, Mama's here . . .'

Eventually she calmed enough to dry her tears and look at the spider in the box. It was quite small really.

'Not bad,' he said, 'not bad at all, I think we're making progress.'

She sat in the kitchen and looked straight at the Widow. She could see what she was up to all right.

'These poor auld legs are killing me,' the Widow said. 'Ann, can you take the bread out of the oven? I don't think I can manage it, love.'

Oh, she could see what she was up to.

'Ann, I need a bit of help here, can you put the clothes out on the line?'

That's why she had kept her at home, made apple-tarts and soufflés, bought her silky nightwear and good Italian leather shoes, that's why she petted and pampered her. To make her guilty, to make her owe, to put her deep in debt. The Widow wanted to be minded while she puffed and limped and grunted and ended up in a wheelchair.

Well she wouldn't do it, she wouldn't. Spiders spin webs as

nests and safety nets, she remembered, not just to catch prey. She recalled the spider in its little prison on the doctor's desk. She could look now, she could look. The prison grew and grew, black bars and double-locked doors. The Widow sat inside, her knees apart, her legs all swollen in their surgical stockings. Her sticks beat loud against the bars, furious and helpless, demanding to get out. Ann feared the locks would not be strong enough.

'Don't worry, Ann,' her Mama whispered in her ear. 'I'll never let her harm you.'

Mama was here. Suddenly she felt exultant.

'I think we'll let it out today,' the doctor said. 'But first I want you to relax and breathe. Close your eyes . . . remember your safe place.'

Under the stairs, by herself, she was safe in the dark. A low thunk-thunk above her head. It was the Widow. Thunk-thunk, coming down the stairs, thunk-thunk, coming down the stairs. And calling.

'Ann!' Thunk-thunk. 'Ann! Where are you?'

She wanted looking after, she always wanted looking after now.

Ann grasped her thumbs close to her chest.

'Mama's here, Mama's here, Mama's here . . .'

'Take a deep breath, Ann. You're safe,' the doctor said, 'I won't let her near you.'

Thunk-thunk. Thunk-thunk. Thunk-thunk.

'She'll suck your guts out through your head,' Brian whispered from afar.

'Oh Mama's here, she's here, oh Mama's here . . .'

The Widow reached the last step, Ann could hear her grunting down the hall. A stick rattled against the door, it opened. Ann shut her eyes tight and held her breath.

'You're safe, Ann, breathe, I'm here to help you.'

She glanced sideways and there, standing at the open door, was her Mama.

'Yes, love, Mama's here, your Mama's here.'

She felt her cheek against the pink-flowered apron.

'Mama's here, love, Mama's here.'

'Take your time, Ann,' said the doctor, 'don't look until you feel ready.'

She watched the spider crawl around the doctor's hand and creep across the surface of his desk.

'Can I touch it?' she asked.

'Why certainly,' exclaimed the doctor, 'but is it not a bit too soon? Do you think that you are ready?'

'I think so, if I wear rubber gloves.'

'Of course, of course,' he said. 'I have a pair right here for just this eventuality.'

Ann crept her hand across the table, Mama's here, and stretched a finger towards the spider, Mama's here. It ignored her for a while and then climbed slowly up the tip of her glove. Her breath got caught, she couldn't breathe or grasp her thumbs. Mama's here, oh Mama's here . . .

'Take it away,' she squeaked and shook her hand violently. The spider clung and clung.

'Oh get it off, please get it off,' she sobbed, 'please, please!'

The doctor put the spider back in its little prison.

'Don't worry, I'll look after you,' he soothed.

'Oh Mama's here, yes Mama's here, she's here . . .' She could breathe again and even laugh a little at her panic.

Dr Bishop was in high good humour.

She practised every day, facing them. She bought industrial rubber gloves, a long mac with a hood and wellington boots and every day she practised. She felt invulnerable running the nozzle of the vacuum round the ceilings, into corners, nooks and crannies, sucking up the spiders and their webs. Every day.

'You really needn't do all that cleaning,' the Widow said, 'but it's nice to see you active.'

She practised in the bathroom, too, drowning them in water. Spiders could trap air, she knew, in the hairs of their body. They could go down the plughole and stay afloat and when the water stopped they'd crawl back up. She turned the showerhead to max and let it run till the water scalded. Then they'd crumple into a ball and die and flush away like so much dirt.

She was very nearly cured.

Dr Bishop was delighted.

'Do you think you need to continue coming?' he asked.

'I don't know,' she said.

'Well, how about a little break to see how you get on?'

'I don't know, yes, maybe.'

'Let's leave the next appointment for a month.'

'All right.'

There was a massive thud upstairs.

'Ann . . . come here . . . come quick,' the Widow called.

She stood paralysed in the hall. Breathe, breathe, she told herself and held her thumbs.

'Mama's here, love, Mama's here, yes Mama's here.'

There was another thump and the sound of water sloshing. She put on her mac and wellies and the industrial rubber gloves and went to the bathroom. The Widow was naked in the bath. It unnerved her. Somehow she never thought of her without black clothes.

'Mama's here, yes Mama's here.' She took a deep breath and didn't run away.

'Help me,' the Widow said faintly, 'I slipped. I think I've broken something.'

Ann stood at the edge of the bath looking down. The Widow was twisted sideways, her flesh all soft and white and wobbly. One arm was pinned under and she tried to keep her head above the water.

'Take the plug out,' she gasped.

'Mama's here, yes Mama's here . . .'

The web acts as a safety net. No longer . . . no . . . no longer.

Ann stretched to the showerhead and turned the water on full blast. The Widow screamed and struggled, slipped further down. But the plughole was too small.

'Oh Mama's here, yes Mama's here . . .'

She took deep breaths like Dr Bishop said, reached for the Widow's head and pushed.

'Mama's here, oh Mama's here, she's here, my love.'

She held her under. The legs flailed, the body heaved and flopped. Water sloshed all over her mac and wellies but she held on, jaws clenched, breathing through her nose. It struggled and it struggled but it didn't curl up tight like most spiders. It just went limp with its eyes and jaw wide open.

'Thank you, Mama,' Ann said aloud.

She removed her wellingtons, her raincoat and her gloves and put them away carefully under the stairs.

'Thank you, Mama, you can go. I'm better now, I'm cured.'

LAST RITES

Neil Jordan

Neil Jordan is currently one of the stars of the Irish literary and film worlds; his books have been praised for their imaginative skills and after the success of his three horror movies he has been labelled 'The King of Hollyweird'. If anything, his talent as a novelist and short story writer has been rather overshadowed by his successes as a film-maker, which have earned him international recognition. In 1992, for example, his low-budget film The Crying Game, *starring Stephen Rea, won him an Academy Award Oscar and an accolade as 'one of the most talented directors and screenplay writers of all time', according to a comment published in the* Irish Independent. *Overstatement or not, it still represents no mean achievement for a lad who was once a labourer and even helped finance the publication of his early work! (Interestingly, the coveted Oscar statuette which Neil received was originally designed by an Irishman in 1927—the Dublin-born Cedric Gibbons who was then regarded as one of the most influential production designers in American pictures.)*

Neil Jordan (1950—) was born in Sligo and educated at University College, Dublin. He worked for a time as a labourer and then a teacher before helping to establish the Irish Writer's Co-operative to publish novels and short stories. His love of drama encouraged him to work with a number of theatre groups in Ireland, England and America, as well as writing and directing some of his own productions. Among his plays was the critically acclaimed Miracles and Miss Langan *which appeared on Irish TV and helped bring him to public notice along with his short stories and three novels,* The Past *(1980),* The Dream of a Beast *(1983) and* Sunrise with Sea Monster *(1995).*

But it is undoubtedly his film scripts and work as a director that have earned him his greatest fame—especially his trio of horror movies, The Company of Wolves *(1984),* High Spirits *(1988) and the block-buster* Interview with the Vampire *(1994), based on a novel by Anne Rice. 'The book is one of the most original pieces of Gothic horror fiction since* Dracula,' *Jordan says, 'it's a vampire story written from the point of view of the vampire which had never been done before, and the minute I read it I had to do it.' In writing and directing the picture he remained painstakingly faithful to the original book and was later intrigued to learn that Anne Rice had come from a similar background to his own: in her case an Irish Catholic family who lived in New Orleans. Already there are plans for a sequel based on another of Rice's books,* The Vampire Lestat, *of which he will also be in charge. That Neil Jordan should have made such a success of these horror movies is arguably a natural progression from his theatrical work and the macabre stories he wrote earlier in his career. 'Last Rites' is typical of these and provides an ideal conclusion to this journey through the dark byways of Irish horror fiction. Sleep well!*

*   *   *

One white-hot Friday in June at some minutes after five o'clock a young builder's labourer crossed an iron railway overpass, just off the Harrow Road. The day was faded now and the sky was a curtain of haze, but the city still lay hard-edged and agonisingly bright in the day's undiminished heat. The labourer as he crossed the overpass took note of its regulation shade of green. He saw an old, old negro immigrant standing motionless in the shade of a red-bricked wall. Opposite the wall, in line with the overpass, he saw the Victorian façade of Kensal Rise Baths. Perhaps because of the heat, or because of a combination of the heat and his temperament, these impressions came to him with an unusual clarity; as if he had seen them in a film or in a dream and not in real, waking life. Within the hour he would take his own life. And dying, a cut-throat razor in his hand, his blood mingling with the shower-water into the colour of weak wine he would take with him to whatever vacuum lay beyond, three memories: the memory of a green-painted bridge; of an old, bowed, shadowed negro; of the sheer tiled wall of a cubicle in what had originally been the wash-houses of Kensal Rise Tontine and Workingmen's Association, in what was now Kensal Rise Baths.

The extraordinary sense of nervous anticipation the labourer experienced had long been familiar with him. And, inexplicable. He never questioned it fully. He knew he anticipated something, approaching the baths. He knew that it wasn't quite pleasure. It was something more and less than pleasurable, a feeling of ravishing, private vindication, of exposure, of secret, solipsistic victory. Over what he never asked. But he knew. He knew as he approached the baths to wash off the dust of a week's labour, that this hour would be the week's high-point. Although during the week he never thought of it, never dwelt on its pleasures—as he did, for instance on his prolonged Saturday morning's rest—when the hour came it was as if the secret thread behind his week's existence was emerging into daylight, was exposing itself to the scrutiny of daylight, his daylight. The way the fauna of the sea-bed are exposed, when the tide goes out.

And so when he crossed the marble step at the door, when he faced the lady behind the glass counter, handing her sevenpence, accepting a ticket from her, waving his hand to refuse towel and soap, gesticulating towards the towel in his duffle-bag, each action was performed with the solemnity of an elaborate ritual, each action was a ring in the circular maze that led to the hidden purpose—the purpose he never elaborated, only felt; in his arm as he waved his hand; in his foot as he crossed the threshold. And when he walked down the corridor, with its white walls, its strange hybrid air, half unemployment exchange, half hospital ward, he was silent. As he took his place on the long oak bench, last in a line of negro, Scottish and Irish navvies, his expression preserved the same immobility as theirs, his duffle-bag was kept between his feet and his rough slender hands between his knees and his eyes upon the grey cream wall in front of him. He listened to the rich, public voices of the negroes, knowing the warm colours of even their work-clothes without having to look. He listened to the odd mixture of reticence and resentment in the Irish voices. He felt the tiles beneath his feet, saw the flaking wall before him, the hard oak bench beneath him, the grey-haired cockney caretaker emerging every now and then from the shower-hall to call 'Shower!', 'Bath!' and at each call the next man in the queue rising, towel and soap under one arm. So plain, so commonplace, and underneath the secret pulsing—but his face was immobile.

As each man left the queue he shifted one space forward and each time the short, crisp call issued from the cockney he turned his head to stare. And when his turn eventually came to be first in the queue and the cockney called 'Shower!' he padded quietly through the open door. He had a slow walk that seemed a little stiff, perhaps because of the unnatural straightness of his back. He had a thin face, unremarkable but for a kind of distance in the expression; removed, glazed blue eyes; the kind of inwardness there, of immersion, that is sometimes termed stupidity.

The grey-haired cockney took his ticket from him. He nodded towards an open cubicle. The man walked slowly through the rows of white doors, under the tiled roof to the cubicle signified. It was the seventh door down.

'Espera me, Quievo!'

'Ora, deprisa, ha?'

He heard splashing water, hissing shower-jets, the smack of palms off wet thighs. Behind each door he knew was a naked man, held timeless and separate under an umbrella of darting water. The fact of the walls, of the similar but totally separate beings behind those walls never ceased to amaze him; quietly to excite him. And the shouts of those who communicated echoed strangely through the long, perfectly regular hall. And he knew that everything would be heightened thus now, raised into the aura of the green light.

He walked through the cubicle door and slid the hatch into place behind him. He took in his surroundings with a slow familiar glance. He knew it all, but he wanted to be a stranger to it, to see it again for the first time, always the first time: the wall, evenly gridded with white tiles, rising to a height of seven feet; the small gap between it and the ceiling; the steam coming through the gap from the cubicle next door; the jutting wall, with the full-length mirror affixed to it; behind it, enclosed by the plastic curtain, the shower. He went straight to the mirror and stood motionless before it. And the first throes of his removal began to come upon him. He looked at himself the way one would examine a flat-handled trowel, gauging its usefulness; or, idly, the way one would examine the cracks on a city pavement. He watched the way his nostrils, caked with cement-dust, dilated with his breathing. He watched the rise of his chest, the buttons of his soiled white work-shirt straining with each rise, each breath. He clenched his teeth and his fingers. Then he undressed, slowly and deliberately, always remaining in full view of the full-length mirror.

After he was unclothed his frail body with its thin ribs, hard biceps and angular shoulders seemed to speak to him, through its frail passive image in the mirror. He listened and watched.

Later it would speak, lying on the floor with open wrists, still retaining its goose-pimples, to the old cockney shower-attendant and the gathered bathers, every memory behind the transfixed eyes quietly intimated, almost revealed, by the body itself. If they had looked hard enough, had eyes keen enough, they would have known that the skin wouldn't have been so white but for a Dublin childhood, bread and margarine, cramped, carbonated air. The feet with the miniature half-moon scar on the right instep would have told, eloquently, of a summer spent on Laytown Strand, of barefoot walks on a hot beach, of shaded glass and poppies of blood on the summer sand. And the bulge of muscle round the right shoulder would have testified to two years' hod-carrying, just as the light, nervous lines across the forehead proclaimed the lessons of an acquisitive metropolis, the glazed eyes themselves demonstrating the failure, the lessons not learnt. All the ill-assorted group of bathers did was pull their towels more rigidly about them, noting the body's glaring pubes, imagining the hair (blonde, maybe) and the skin of the girls that first brought them to life; the first kiss and the indolent smudges of lipstick and all the subsequent kisses, never quite recovering the texture of the first. They saw the body and didn't hear the finer details—just heard that it had been born, had grown and suffered much pain and a little joy; that its dissatisfaction had been deep; and they thought of the green bridge and the red-bricked walls and understood—

He savoured his isolation for several full minutes. he allowed the cold to seep fully through him, after the heat of clothes, sunlight. He saw pale, rising goose-pimples on the mirrored flesh before him. When he was young he had been in the habit of leaving his house and walking down to a busy sea-front road and clambering down from the road to the mud-flats below. The tide would never quite reach the wall and there would be stretches of mud and stone and the long sweep of the cement wall with the five-foot high groove running through it where he could sit, and he would look at the stone, the flat mud and the dried cakes of sea-lettuce and see the tide creep over them and wonder at their impassivity, their imperviousness to feeling; their deadness. It seemed to him the ultimate blessing and he would sit so long that when he came to rise his legs, and sometimes his whole body, would be numb. He stood now till his immobility, his cold, became near-agonising. Then he walked slowly to the shower, pulled aside the plastic curtain and walked inside. The tiles had that dead wetness that he had once noticed in the beach-pebbles. He placed each foot squarely on them and saw a thin cake of soap lying in a puddle of grey water. Both were evidence of the bather here before him and he wondered vaguely what he was like; whether he had a quick, rushed shower or a slow, careful one; whether he in turn had wondered about the bather before him. And he stopped wondering, as idly as he had begun. And he turned on the water.

It came hot. He almost cried with the shock of it; a cry of pale, surprised delight. It was a pet love with him, the sudden heat and the wall of water, drumming on his crown, sealing him magically from the world outside; from the universe outside; the pleasurable biting needles of heat; the ripples of water down his hairless arms; the stalactites gathering at each fingertip; wet hair, and sounds of caught breath and thumping water. He loved the pain, the total self-absorption of it and never wondered why he loved it; as with the rest of the weekly ritual—the trudge through the muted officialdom of the bath corridors into the solitude of the boxed, sealed figure, three feet between it and its fellow; the contradictory joy of the first impact of heat, of the pleasurable pain.

An overseer in an asbestos works who had entered his cubicle black and who had emerged with a white, blotchy, greyish skin-hue divined the reason for the cut wrists. He looked at the tiny coagulation of wrinkles round each eye and knew that here was a surfeit of boredom; not a moody, arbitrary, adolescent boredom, but that boredom which is a condition of life itself. He saw the way the mouth was tight and wistful and somehow incommunicative, even in death, and the odour of his first contact with that boredom came back to him. He smelt again the incongruous fish-and-chip smells, the smells of the discarded sweet-wrappings, the metallic odour of the fun-palace, the sulphurous whiff of the dodgem wheels; the empty, musing, poignant smell of the seaside holiday town, for it was here that he had first met his boredom; here that he had wandered the green carpet of the golf-links, with the stretch of grey sky overhead, asking, what to do with the long days and hours, turning then towards the burrows and the long grasses and the strand, deciding there's nothing to do, no point in doing, the sea glimmering to

the right of him like the dull metal plate the dodgem wheels ran on.
Here he had lain in a sand-bunker for hours, his head making a
slight indentation in the sand, gazing at the mordant procession of
clouds above. Here he had first asked, what's the point, there's only
point if it's fun, it's pleasure, if there's more pleasure than pain;
then thinking of the pleasure, weighing up the pleasure in his adoles-
cent scales, the pleasure of the greased fish-and-chip bag warming
the fingers, of the sweet taken from the wrapper, the discarded
wrapper and the fading sweetness, of the white flash of a pubescent
girl's legs, the thoughts of touch and caress, the pain of the impossi-
bility of both and his head digging deeper in the sand he had seen
the scales tip in favour of pain. Ever so slightly maybe, but if it
wins then what's the point. And he had known the sheep-white
clouds scudding through the blueness and ever after thought of them
as significant of the preponderance of pain; and he looked now at
the white scar on the young man's instep and thought of the white
clouds and thought of the bobbing girls' skirts and of the fact of
pain—

The first impact had passed; his body temperature had risen and
the hot biting needles were now a running, massaging hand. And
a silence had descended on him too, after the self immersed orgy
of the driving water. He knew this shower was all things to him,
a world to him. Only here could he see this world, hold it in
balance, so he listened to what was now the quietness of rain in
the cubicle, the hushed, quiet sound of dripping rain and the green
rising mist through which things are seen in their true, unnatural
clarity. He saw the wet, flapping shower-curtain. There was a
bleak rose-pattern on it, the roses faded by years of condensation
into green: green roses. He saw the black spaces between the tiles,
the plughole with its fading, whorling rivulet of water. He saw the
exterior dirt washed off himself, the caked cement-dust, the flecks
of mud. He saw creases of black round his elbow-joints, a high-
water mark round his neck, the more permanent, ingrained dirt.
And he listened to the falling water, looked at the green roses and
wondered what it would be like to see those things, hear them,
doing nothing but see and hear them; nothing but the pure sound,
the sheer colour reaching him; to be as passive as the mud pebble
was to that tide. He took the cake of soap then from the grilled
tray affixed to the wall and began to rub himself hard. Soon he
would be totally, bleakly clean.

There was a dash of paint on his cheek. The negro painter he worked beside had slapped him playfully with his brush. It was disappearing now, under pressure from the soap. And with it went the world, that world, the world he inhabited, the world that left grit under the nails, dust under the eyelids. He scrubbed at the dirt of that world, at the coat of that world, the self that lived in that world, in the silence of the falling water. Soon he would be totally, bleakly clean.

The old cockney took another ticket from another bather he thought he recognised. Must have seen him last week. He crumpled the ticket in his hand, went inside his glass-fronted office and impaled it onto a six-inch nail jammed through a block of wood. He flipped a cigarette from its packet and lit it, wheezing heavily. Long hours spent in the office here, the windows running with condensation, had exaggerated a bronchial condition. He let his eyes scan the seventeen cubicles. He wondered again how many of them, coming every week for seventeen weeks, have visited each of the seventeen showers. None, most likely. Have to go where they're told, don't they. No way they can get into a different box other than the one that's empty, even if they should want to. But what are the chances, a man washing himself ten years here, that he'd do the full round? And the chances that he'd be stuck to the one? He wrinkled his eyes and coughed and rubbed the mist from the window to see more clearly.

White, now. Not the sheer white of the tiles, but a human, flaccid, pink skin-white. He stood upwards, let his arms dangle by his sides, his wrists limp. His short black hair was plastered to his crown like a tight skull-cap. He gazed at the walls of his own cubicle and wondered at the fact that there were sixteen other cubicles around him, identical to this one, which he couldn't see. A man in each, washed by the same water, all in various stages of cleanliness. And he wondered did the form in the next cubicle think of him, his neighbour, as he did. Did he reciprocate his wondering. He thought it somehow appropriate that there should be men naked, washing themselves in adjacent cubicles, each a foreign country to the other. Appropriate to what, he couldn't have said. He looked round his cubicle and wondered: what's it worth, what does it mean, this cubicle—wondered was any one of the other sixteen gazing at his cubicle and thinking, realising as he was: nothing. He realised that he would never know.

Nothing. Or almost nothing. He looked down at his body: thin belly, thin arms, a limp member. He knew he had arrived at the point where he would masturbate. He always came to this point in different ways, with different thoughts, by different stages. But when he had reached it, he always realised that the ways had been similar, the ways had been the same way, only the phrasing different. And he began then, taking himself with both hands, caressing himself with a familiar, bleak motion, knowing that afterwards the bleakness would only be intensified after the brief distraction of feeling—in this like everything—observing the while the motion of his belly muscles, glistening under their sheen of running water. And as he felt the mechanical surge of desire run through him he heard the splashing of an anonymous body in the cubicle adjacent. The thought came to him that somebody could be watching him. But no, he thought then, almost disappointed, who could, working at himself harder. He was standing when he felt an exultant muscular thrill run through him, arching his back, straining his calves upwards, each toe pressed passionately against the tiled floor.

The young Trinidadian in the next cubicle squeezed out a sachet of lemon soft shampoo and rubbed it to a lather between two brown palms. Flecks of sawdust—he was an apprentice carpenter— mingled with the snow-white foam. He pressed two handfuls of it under each bicep, ladled it across his chest and belly and rubbed it till the foam seethed and melted to the colour of dull whey, and the water swept him clean again, splashed his body back to its miraculous brown and he slapped each nipple laughingly in turn and thought of a clean body under a crisp shirt, of a night of love under a low red-lit roof, of the thumping symmetry of a reggae band.

There was one intense moment of silence. He was standing, spent, sagging. He heard:

'Hey, you rass, not finished yet?'

'How'd I be finished?'

'Well move that corpse, rassman. Move!'

He watched the seed that had spattered the tiles be swept by the shower-water, diluting its grey, ultimately vanishing into the fury of current round the plughole. And he remembered the curving cement wall of his childhood and the spent tide and the rocks and the dried green stretches of sea-lettuce and because the exhaustion was delicious now and bleak, because he knew there would never be anything but that exhaustion after all the fury of effort, all the expense of passion and shame, he walked through the green-rose curtain and took the cut-throat razor from his pack and went back to the shower to cut his wrists. And dying, he thought of nothing more significant than the way, the way he had come here, of the green bridge and the bowed figure under the brick wall and the façade of the Victorian bath-house, thinking: there is nothing more significant.

Of the dozen or so people who gathered to stare—as people will—none of them thought: 'Why did he do it?' All of them, pressed into a still, tight circle, staring at the shiplike body, knew intrinsically. And a middle-aged, fat and possibly simple negro phrased the thought:

'Every day the Lord send me I think I do that. And every day the Lord send me I drink bottle of wine and forget 'bout doin that.'

They took with them three memories: the memory of a thin, almost hairless body with reddened wrists; the memory of a thin, finely-wrought razor whose bright silver was mottled in places with rust; and the memory of a spurting shower-nozzle, an irregular drip of water. And when they emerged to the world of bright afternoon streets they saw the green-painted iron bridge and the red-brick wall and knew it to be in the nature of these, too, that the body should act thus—